LOVERLESS
LOVE

LOVERLESS LOVE

stories

CHRISTOPHER GUERIN

ALSO BY CHRISTOPHER GUERIN
The Story of My Universe and Other Stories (2020)
My Human Disguise, 200 Ekphrastic Sonnets (2018)

Loverless Love: Stories
© Copyright 2023, Christopher Guerin
First Edition   ISBN 13: 978-1-956872-67-5
AMIKA PRESS
466 Central AVE #23 Northfield IL 60093   847 920 8084
info@amikapress.com   Available for purchase on amikapress.com
Edited by John K. Manos. Cover art by Egon Schiele, *Sitzende Frau mit hochgezogenem Knie (Sitting woman with raised knee)*, 1917. Frontispiece, treatment by Julia Guerin of art by Egon Schiele, *Mime Van Osen,* 1910. Designed and typeset by Sarah Koz. Set in Ehrhardt, designed by Nicholas Kis in the late 1600s, digitized by Monotype in 1991. Thanks to Nathan Matteson.

*FOR
RUTH*

CONTENTS

ACKNOWLEDGEMENTS

My deepest appreciation to my wife, Ruth Diamond-Guerin, who has supported my career and writing for almost 50 years. Herself an artist, as are our two daughters Julia and Alice, she has been my constant and untiring companion and inspiration. (To satisfy the curious, I assure them that Ruth does not appear in these pages.)

Special thanks to my lifelong friend and colleague Michael Antman. His literary skill, advice, and encouragement have been invaluable to me as a writer for decades.

Thanks to John Manos and Sarah Koz of Amika Press for continuing to support my work, for their professionalism, and their patience.

The source of the erotic is mental,
As dreams remind us with fleshly chaos.
There can't be love and ideas without eros.
We decide love will be wild or gentle.
Only the lovers' minds can satisfy
Each other what is a real love, and why.

LOVERLESS LOVE

*A*s the marketing director of a top-20 symphony orchestra located in the Midwest, I had my hands full. The orchestra was running a $1 million deficit every year, steadily declining ticket sales one of the root causes.

Other than the CEO, the two individuals most responsible for income were me, Daniel Gregory, and Geraldine Hayward, the fundraising director. I had been with the orchestra for twelve years when she came aboard in 1995. We were both single, and before long our relationship became a very well-hidden affair. But this story is about Tina Hawthorne. Consider Geraldine a supernumerary who never actually has any lines in the opera.

I met Tina at the national conference of the American Orchestra League held late spring in New York City, her home. Tina was one of the two most-sought-after marketing consultants in the field. I'd heard of her work, and her successes, for years, and only because of our dire situation was I finally able to convince our CEO to let me try to engage her services. At this point, her six-figure fee was inconsequential in the face of our impending financial disaster.

Before leaving for the conference, I called her, and we made an appointment for coffee late the first day of the conference in the lobby of the Marriott on Broadway.

I arrived on time and grabbed us a table. I ordered black coffee and sat reading the conference catalogue, waiting for her to arrive.

An hour later, she called my cell and said, "It's Tina. Where are you?"

I told her, struggling to keep any irritation out of my voice.

"Is that where we were to meet?" she asked, genuinely confused.

"Yes," I said, "Where are you?"

"I'm in the Starbucks next door, like we agreed!"

I knew she was tough to engage, so I let it go. "I'm sorry. My mistake. I'll be right over."

"Hurry, please. I only have fifteen minutes."

Reluctantly, I asked, "Do you want to reschedule?"

"Not if you ever want to see me again," she said, laughing.

"I'll be right there!" I said, grabbed my satchel, thinking, is she always like this?

I saw only one young woman in the cafe. I went up to her and said, "Tina?"

"Yes, it's me. Before you sit down, please let me apologize. I only meant you might not see me again because my schedule is so full. I wasn't trying to be rude."

"I completely understand," I said and held out my hand.

We shook and she said, "I got you a latte with cinnamon. I hope that's okay."

"That's fine," I said, as I settled in. I hated lattes, and this one was cold.

"It's iced," she said, though it wasn't in a plastic cup.

Had she just fibbed, I wondered?

"Great. Thanks," I said, "I'll get the next one."

She looked at her watch and shook her head, causing her hair to fall off her shoulders.

"No time for that. How can I help? I have twelve minutes."

I started to give her the dismal history of our ticket sales for the last five years, when she stopped me.

"Let's do it my way. How big is your city?"

"Seven million."

"How many seats in your hall?"

"Twenty-one hundred."

"Good. How many masterworks performances?"

"Thirty-six."

At each answer, she nodded, but increasingly snapped her fingers soundlessly with impatience.

"How many pops performances?"

"Twenty-one?"

"Including Christmas?"

"No, twelve of those?"

"Percentage of seats sold per series?"

"Well, subscribers to Masterworks?"

"No, total seats sold. I can do the math. Percentages are fine."

"Masterworks 60 percent, Pops 80 percent, Christmas 95 percent."

"That's enough," she said, dug her card out of her wallet, squinted at it, and handed it to me. It was pale blue and pink and thoroughly wrinkled. "Come to my room tonight at eleven, and we'll talk some more. I think I can help."

In her haste to leave, she stumbled slightly stepping away from her chair and let out a whispered, "oof."

Her card read, above two email addresses and three phone numbers, "Tina Hawthorne: Marketing Consultant to the Symphony Orchestra World."

Really? I wondered. Behind the arrogance of it I sensed a child's empty boast.

Yes, Tina Hawthorne made an impression. A trim, willowy, busty woman dressed impeccably in designer dress and shoes, all in shades of gray, she wore her strawberry blonde hair in curls that cascaded down her shoulders, and which she often tossed aside or tucked behind translucent ears. Her minimal makeup was meant to reveal rather than hide flawless, pale skin, generous eyebrows and long lashes. Slightly too thick lips suggested a smile was perpetually lingering there and welcomed being brought to the surface. Calling her eyes "laughing" wouldn't be inaccurate, but I prefer the more playful "merry." Tina Hawthorne's eyes were merry.

In other words, a very attractive young woman in her upper twenties, perhaps five years my junior. People say that intelligence is attractive, but its appeal is cold. That didn't explain Tina's special allure, which was engaging, with the slightest tinge of invitation—and I don't mean flirtatiousness. She was friendly, even warm to the eye, but that only confused the issue further. Even with those starlit eyes and her lips all virtual smile, there was some hidden insistence that said "keep your distance." I would understand it soon enough.

I sat and pondered our conversation. The first question I asked myself was, is this someone I could work with? The answer was yes, of course, and her business acumen was evident, if a bit overwhelming. But what was I to make of the rest of it, the mixed-up appointment, her impatient grilling me for numbers, her blunder over the latte, and her abrupt departure, not to mention her invitation for later that night? Was there more to that than business?

At ten o'clock that night I realized I had no idea what room she was in. She hadn't said. I had to assume she was staying in the same gargantuan Marriott as I was. I went to the front desk and asked for her room number. The desk clerk said they had no one by that name registered.

I had a drink with a colleague and waited until just before 11 PM, then called the number she'd called me on earlier that day—no answer. I called one of the numbers on her card, then the other number. In both cases, I was told she wasn't available and that her voice mailbox was full. I texted all three numbers: "What room are you in?" No answer. I even took out my laptop and emailed her.

At midnight, I texted her one more time and waited, then I gave up and went barhopping with a couple of friends until 2 AM.

It was a three-day convention, and I was staying an extra day to visit the Met, MOMA, and the Guggenheim and to see a play that night.

I didn't try to contact Tina on the second day, thinking my texts were enough and I didn't want to bother her, since she'd clearly forgotten all about me. Mid-afternoon the third day, as I was walking into a plenary session about the current crisis in the orchestra field (almost every orchestra in the country was in trouble), I felt a hand on my shoulder. I turned and there was Tina.

"Where'd you go, Danny?"

"Daniel," I said rather stiffly.

"Well," she huffed, "if you're going to cop a 'tude because you stood me up, fine. See ya!" she said and started to turn away. She wore high heels and tottered slightly when she wasn't walking in a straight line.

"Stood *you* up?"

She turned back and came toward me. To my surprise she stepped out of her shoes and confronted me. I was slightly surprised that she didn't wear stockings, not that every business woman did. It seemed a statement of some kind, and taking off the shoes was just strange.

"Yes, two nights ago. You didn't show."

"You never told me where you were staying, Tina."

"Right here, stupid," she said, open arms indicating this hotel. She was really agitated now and threw her head back to look up at the enormous atrium of the Marriott.

"The front desk said you weren't staying here."

She thought about that for a second, then lowered both her arms and her head.

"Oh, right," she looked down, then up, right, left, anywhere but at me. "I register under a different name at these conferences or I get chased down every corridor by drooling, emaciated marketing directors begging for help."

Her humorous shot at my colleagues didn't help.

"I called and texted."

"What numbers?" she challenged me.

I took her card out of my wallet and showed it to her.

"Oops! That's an old card. Sorry. I haven't used those phones in months."

I glared at her in disbelief, quickly disarmed by her lovely blushing that reached to her ears.

"I also called the number you called me from before."

"Why are you grilling me?" she snapped, "I always turn off my phone after dinner."

"So all this means that I stood…"

"Look, I'll make it up to you," she broke in, smiling to stifle her embarrassment. "The conference is basically over at seven. I'll buy you dinner and we can talk."

I almost told her off for an unprofessional scatterbrain, but something told me that would be a mistake. I really did need her help.

"Where shall we meet?"

"By the front desk at nine," she said.

All of her sweet repentance disappeared as she put on her shoes and headed for the front door. I wondered if I'd ever see her again.

But at nine, there she was, dressed in the same ensemble as two days before, only in shades of dark blue. She grabbed my arm in a stiff but comradely way, and led me to an extremely expensive French restaurant right around the corner, chatting the whole time about the horror stories she'd been hearing for the last three days.

"Sometimes I wonder if I'll even have a job in another five years," she said as we settled into a large booth across from each other.

For the next three hours we ate too much, drank too much wine, and exhausted ourselves with the miseries of symphonies across the country, mine in particular. She'd agreed to take mine on by the end of desert; then, over two Drambuie's, we shared our personal stories. She'd been a New Yorker all her life, had a masters degree in arts management and an MBA in marketing from Columbia. She'd begun her career as a marketing assistant at the Boston Symphony, then became the VP of Marketing at Baltimore, working for what she described as "beaten down" marketing VPs and "insanely arrogant" CEOs. She told the story of one, from a third orchestra that was courting her, who forced an operations manager to go on a tour to Japan even though his wife would be delivering their first child at the same time. When he pleaded, the CEO said, "Tough shit. It's your job. If you want to keep it, you're going."

"Needless to say," said Tina, "I didn't take the job."

After four years, enough was enough, and she went out on her own.

"And now you're a superstar."

"Hardly," she said laughing with feigned embarrassment. "I just know how to juggle the numbers and find the right messaging."

I had noticed at our first meeting that she had a wedding band, but no engagement ring, on her constantly fidgeting fingers.

"And your husband?"

"What husband?"

"I'm sorry. I saw the ring and assumed...."

She pulled it off and put it on her right ring finger.

"One thing you'll learn about me soon enough is, don't assume."

"Got it. Sorry."

"And you?"

"I shouldn't say."

She could tell I had a secret. She cocked her head and looked under my eyebrows.

"Let me guess. You're seeing someone at work and nobody knows. Nobody is *supposed* to know."

"Yikes!" I said, leaning back. "How did you know?"

"I didn't!" she laughed. "Wild guess." She took a sip of her drink. "Sometimes I impress even myself, and that's not easy!"

The falseness, the bravura of this comment was breathtaking.

"Tina," I said, getting serious, "if we're going to work together, you can't tell a living soul. Geraldine and I are close, but there's no long-term plan. You'll meet her. She's the director of development."

"It's that big of a problem?"

"It could be. Some of the board members would object and, well, you could say I was part of the reason she got divorced last year."

"Part?"

"Just remember it's a secret. Promise?"

"Promise," she said, like a child told to eat her vegetables.

She insisted on paying the check, and as we were leaving the restaurant, she said, "Oh, shit! It's almost midnight!" Then she dropped her purse, which was large and expensive. A young man in a Yankees jacket and cap reached down for it at a speed that said he planned to run off with it. I put my foot on the purse, he backed off, then ran away. I picked it up and handed it to her.

"Thank you," she said, looking concerned.

"It's alright," I tried to console her.

Instead, she frowned rather dramatically.

"What's the problem?"

"I don't have a room."

Had she even noticed what had just happened?

"But you live here."

"Here?"

"In New York."

"Yeah, an hour away."

I didn't ask her where.

"Can you put me up?" she asked, clutching her purse to her chest, as if defending herself from a "no."

"What?"

"Oh, don't be an adolescent. I won't molest you. That's the last thing you have to worry about."

"There's only a single bed."

"So?" she said, without a trace of a smile.

Five minutes later we were in my room, and she was in the bathroom.

Between the booze and her presence, I was totally befuddled, but not so much that I didn't have a hard-on.

She came out in blue bra and almost transparent panties and immediately slipped under the blankets and turned out the lights on her side of the bed.

"Goodnight, Danny, and thanks," she said and in seconds seemed to be snoring. Was she faking?

In the bathroom, I looked at my face, which was smiling foolishly. Though I often slept in the nude, I always brought pajamas when I stayed at hotels. When I came out, I realized that there wasn't even a couch, just two armchairs. I slid under the covers and half-expected her to awaken and make some angry objection, or, I couldn't be sure, a move? She didn't stir an inch. I gave her two-thirds of the bed and kept my back to her, hoping I wouldn't roll onto her as I sometimes did with Geraldine. I was soon asleep.

I hadn't set the alarm since this was my free day. But at six o'clock I awoke with Tina's cheek against mine, her hair, which smelled of lavender, half across my face, and her right arm over my waist and perilously close to my penis, which immediately hardened. That woke her. She jumped out of bed and ran into the bathroom.

She came out calm and fully-dressed 10 minutes later.

"I need to get going," she said, her voice like dry ice. "I have one last appointment left over from the conference. I have just a half-hour to get home to change and get back here. Thanks for the place to stay. I really appreciate it."

Then she dug into her purse and brought out a yellow business card. She double-checked it, waved it at me and put it on the table by the television.

"That's the right one," she assured herself, whispering.

Fluffing her hair in the mirror next to the television, she said, "Give me a call next week, anytime, but no later than three, that's when I knock off most days. I'm a runner. We'll figure things out. I'll need you to send me a ton of information, then we can arrange a visit. I need to hear this divine orchestra of yours. Bye!"

And she was gone as if she was walking out of my office, leaving me thinking about the hour transit to her place she'd mentioned the night before. As I dressed, I decided that she'd fibbed (again), this time to keep from having to navigate New York after midnight. Not a bad reason, I concluded.

We talked on the phone later the next week. She said, in that chilled voice of hers, that she could visit anytime in the next three weeks.

"Great! When's best for you?"

"What will I hear?"

"I'm sorry?"

"The orchestra. What will I hear?" she said, with that subtle impatience that I would come to recognize as her normal speaking voice. "That will tell me when to come."

"There's the Pops on the Green series with some big names, and a Patriotic Pops show on July 3rd."

"I mean when will I hear some *music,* not a bunch of footballs (she meant 'whole notes') behind your popsters, whose names I don't even want to hear."

She was being arrogant and condescending, but I didn't think she realized it.

"The patriotic concert has a couple of Tchaikovsky...."

"If I hear the *1812 Overture* even one more time, I'm going to find an Army battery of howitzers to blow me to bits!"

"Tina, excuse me," I said and paused.

"Yes?"

"Are you always this way?"

"What way?"

I knew I was taking a big risk, but if she was going to be like this all the time, I would have to back out.

"Abrasive?"

"Abrasive? Abrasive! Honey, this is my honey voice. What, you can't take it?"

I took a big gulp of air and said, "I can take anything, Tina. It's just something I'll have to get used to."

"Yes, it is," she agreed, with considerably less of an edge in her voice. "Now, do I understand that you won't be playing real music until your fall season begins?"

"Yes, in early September."

"Let's talk in mid-August."

I thought she was going to hang up on me.

"Okay?" she asked, when I didn't respond.

I recovered and said I would.

"I hope my calling you *Honey* wasn't a problem."

That broke the ice, and I laughed.

"No, sweetheart, let's just keep it professional when you get here."

"See you then," she said and hung up.

Symphony orchestras plan almost a year ahead, so the delay didn't present a problem. The crucial time for marketing decisions was late-summer to the end of the year, for concerts beginning the following fall.

As planned, she called and we set a three-day visit; she asked me to send her all of my sales figures, ticket prices and seating charts, and marketing materials, so she could prepare.

I was very ambivalent about what I said next, but I thought why not? I was a member of a working group of major orchestra marketing directors charged with coming up with a national branding strategy for symphony orchestras. Tina knew about this because she'd mentioned it in New York, rather scoffingly. I assumed her distaste was sour grapes that she hadn't been asked to consult.

I mentioned that I would be back in New York with that meeting group the week before Labor Day and would it make any sense for us to meet?

"Sure, call me when your plans are set, and if I'm in town we'll have dinner."

We left it at that.

When I called to tell her when I was coming to New York, she said, "And you are?"

"You're kidding, right?"

"Yes?" she asked, "Who is this, please?"

Totally exasperated, I reminded her who I was, from what orchestra, etc.

"I'm sorry!" she shouted into the phone. "I'm sorry. I was just distracted when you called, working some heavy math."

Another fib?

"What can I do for you?"

"I'm coming to town on the 28th, and you said we might get together if you were in town."

"I'm in town."

"Great."

"But I can't meet, sorry. Call me next week."

Then she hung up. I was stunned. Was she crazy? She couldn't be addled, not with her credentials. She called five minutes later.

"Good, you're still there," she said, without a trace of sincerity. "Sorry, I couldn't talk. I had an angry client on the other line. I had to get you off the phone asap. But it's okay now."

"What was he angry about?" I said, knowing I was prying, and got the answer I deserved.

"Why would I tell *you?*"

"Sorry, never mind," I said, properly chided.

She thought about it a moment.

"No, look, it's a fair question, especially when you're planning to cut me some humongous checks!"

She laughed, but I didn't.

"I can't tell you who it was, but they were angry because I fired them."

"You fired them?"

"Yes, they didn't perform."

"You mean they didn't play well?"

"No, silly," she said, laughing more loudly than she ever had before. "They didn't kiss my ass!"

"What?" I asked, genuinely confused.

"Sorry, I didn't mean that literally. I mean respect. It was a guy, a marketing VP, and he treated me like the hired help assigned to do the dishes. That meant I didn't get what I needed to do my job. I won't put up with that!"

"Uh, what do you say?" I asked, wondering if it might be something I needed to be careful about myself.

"I said, I, I said…oh, hell. I'll tell you. I think I can trust you. I think. I told him he should kiss my ass not grab it."

"He did that?"

"Bet your ass. Uh, sorry to be repetitive."

"But that wasn't the reason you fired them? I mean the grabbing?"

"Nope. I'm used to it. And once they do it one of their cheeks—I mean on their face—gets very red and they know I'll get them fired if they do it again. But disrespect of me and my work is another matter. So I gave it to him good."

"Wow."

"So, tell me again why you called?"

Yes, she was going to be in town and would be available for dinner the evening of the 28th. We arranged to meet at an Italian restaurant in West Village.

"See you then," she said.

"Promise?" I said, unable to stifle a laugh.

"I always keep my promises, Danny."

"See you then," I said, quite sure I hadn't offended her and equally sure she didn't have a clue what I was referring to.

On the flight, I ran through my memories of Tina and tried to make some sense of her. She certainly seemed to have a terrible memory. I remembered what a philosophy professor had once said about memory: without it we can't live in the moment. Memories provide context for the present and without them the present wouldn't be decipherable, but merely unprocessed experience or perception, immediately lost.

But, I wondered, if she had even a partially damaged memory, how could she be so brilliant? She had no trouble at all recalling past events. Was it just short-term memory dysfunction?

I didn't know, but I was to learn that she had other issues as well.

I arrived at the restaurant. She was only 15 minutes late. I rose to greet her with a hug, but she stepped back and held out her hand and explained, "Sorry, I'm not a hugger."

Slightly embarrassed, I mumbled an apology and shook her hand.

We settled into a plush red booth and took up our menus. Tina seemed subdued and distracted. She was again dressed in her shades-of-gray ensemble, but had virtually no make-up, not that her high color required it. I had expected a business-like discussion, extending my previous download of all that was going well or poorly at my orchestra. She seemed to have forgotten everything I'd told her.

Early on, she interrupted me and said, "I thought this was supposed to be a social thing, a chance to get to know each other since we have a lot of work to do and we'll be shoulder to shoulder once I get to (my city)."

Having actually slept in the same bed with her, this seemed absurd, if not laughable, but I stifled myself.

"I don't have an agenda, Tina. We can talk about anything you like."

"Seems to me we've covered my past and yours. Let's talk about theater. I like theater. Do you like theater?"

"Yes, I do. In fact, I'm seeing *Hamilton* tomorrow night."

"Gad! Really? It's horrible. Save your money."

The disgust on her face caused her chin to move her lips almost up to her nose. I held back a giggle.

"You're kidding."

"It's rap. I can't believe I let a friend con me into seeing it. Of course, I hate musicals anyway."

"Actually, I do too. I just thought that *Hamilton* was so big I'd go see what all the hoohah was about."

"Hooohamilton rather!"

It was the first time she'd ever tried to say something funny. I chuckled, even though it wasn't.

"You should know," she continued, "I also hate country, bluegrass, disco, pop, rock, and most contemporary music written since 1950."

"That sure narrows it down! Reggae?"

She laughed and clapped her hands twice. "Bingo! Very clever of you! I have a soft spot for Bob Marley. He was very sweet."

"What if I told you that Philip Glass was one of my favorite composers?" I said with a straight face.

"I'd say you were not very good at making jokes."

"No, really," I insisted, "I think minimalism is like listening to clouds."

"Go fuck yourself,"

We both laughed. It was spooky how good she was at reading people.

"I met Philip once," she revealed with another grimace. "His 'Thousand Airplanes on the Roof' was playing at Avery and he was doing a Q and A beforehand. Some idiot actually called him 'Our Wagner,' which just about made me puke. So, I put up my hand and asked him, 'Can you tell us about the music?'"

At this point, she was almost in a rage. She pounded the table rhythmically and her eyes were as cold as her voice could be.

"He said…this great and famous composer said, 'Well, I've been toying with some triplets.' I laughed in his face."

The disgust in her voice was almost frightening, far beyond anything I'd heard from her before. It was like killing a dog for pooping on the rug.

"Toying with triplets! Our Wagner! And he's what passes for a popular contemporary composer! The musical world is in a co-dependent relationship with these fakes, enabling them with lame, boring, repetitious performances. Repetition of repetition. And people wonder why people are staying home to watch movies in their new home theaters!"

"I couldn't agree more," I said, and left it at that.

She steamed silently for a few minutes, then seemed to calm down.

"I dislike at least half of the genres you mentioned," I said just to set the record straight.

"Then you have half the good taste that I have."

Her lovely eyes, turned hard as diamonds, told me she was serious.

"Thanks for pointing that out."

She didn't seem at all curious what music I did like, so we ate in silence for the next few minutes before she dropped her fork noisily on her plate and confessed, "Something's bugging me."

"What's that?" I asked, afraid our musical tastes actually did make a difference to her.

"How come you have to keep your affair a secret? It's going to be very awkward. You know that."

I realized we were into our second bottle of Chianti.

"Some of the board members are very religious. Everyone knows she got divorced because she was having an affair. It so happens her husband was too," I added, chuckling, "But no one knows that I was her, ah,…"

"Lover."

"Yes."

"They find out and you'd both lose your jobs? Something like that in Manhattan wouldn't rise to the level of not covering your mouth to cough."

"It is a drag," I agreed.

"You'd really be fired?"

"Yes, we could. At least I might be. When it comes down to the numbers, they might keep the better earner. Geraldine's a great fund-raiser. Besides, I'd be branded a home-wrecker."

"And you're a shitty marketing director. Then why am I sitting here?"

She said it with no inflection whatever.

"Do you enjoy doing that?"

"What?" she said, defensively.

"Insulting people?"

"Man, do you have a thin skin!" she said and actually reached across the table and slapped my cheek, ever so softly, almost a caress. "I was projecting the stupid opinions of your stupid board. If I thought you were shitty at what you do, I *certainly* wouldn't be sitting here," she concluded and sat back.

It was that exact moment—when she smiled so gently and her merry eyes glistened—that I realized I was just a tiny bit in love with her.

"So, I'll stop worrying about Gail or whatever her name is."

"Geraldine."

"If I couldn't keep a secret, I'd be a dead dachshund in this business. And just remember," she added, wagging her finger at me, "you have to keep my secrets too."

"Not to worry."

She absolutely refused to let me buy dinner, but when she looked into her purse she said, "Shit! My wallet!"

She became very agitated and started to shake.

"God help me if I lost it!"

"Could you have left it at home?"

"Never! I never have before."

"And you didn't stop anywhere between your home and here tonight?"

"Nowhere. No. Where."

Her trembling got worse as she kept digging through her tiny purse.

"Then it must be there. You run along home. I'm sure it's there. I'll take care of the check and call you later."

"No, no, no, you have to go with me. If it's not there I'll go fucking berserk!"

I agreed to go with her, paid the check, and as we stepped into the street—struck by that New York smell, like every kind of trash you can imagine boiled in pitch and rising as steam from every manhole cover and drain—she took off her high heels and handed them to me, then took my other hand and said, "I live only three blocks from here."

We ran the whole way. I wasn't drunk, but not entirely in control either.

She lived in a corner studio on the fourth floor of a brownstone. I was surprised how small it was until I remembered that this was

New York. It probably cost a fortune, not that she couldn't afford it.

She unlocked the door and charged in, looking in every direction. I saw the wallet immediately, but by then she was almost shrieking and for some reason couldn't see it, in plain sight, on her coffee table.

I handed it to her.

She looked at it, then into my eyes, and started crying hysterically. She could sense I was going to hug her and took a step away from me. It was the shortest bout of hysteria I ever saw, less than ten seconds.

Immediately calm, wiping her eyes and gesturing toward the couch, she said, "What can I get you? More wine?"

She ran into her little kitchen alcove and opened the refrigerator.

"How about some champagne? It's Mumms, a gift from a happy client. I've been waiting for someone to share it with."

I said sure, and she had the top unwrapped and uncorked in moments. Our glasses filled, she sat at the other end of the couch.

"Here's to 'all's well,'" I said, raising my glass.

"Never!" she said emphatically.

"Okay?"

"I have never done that in my entire life!"

"You were pretty upset."

"You were great," she said, a bit perfunctorily. This was not a person comfortable saying "thank you."

"You're welcome."

She hadn't returned my toast, so I took a long pull. It was lovely.

"I shouldn't say never. I once lost my passport."

"Yikes!"

"Actually, everything went wrong. I needed my Social Security card, driver's license, and a credit card for cash to pay for the passport. I left the Social Security card, license and credit card on top of an ATM. Running back to get them from half a block away, I dropped the cash, three hundred dollars' worth, which water in the gutter sent down a sewer grating. When I eventually got the passport a month later, I left it on the subway."

Strictly speaking, I thought, she may never have left her wallet on her coffee table, but only strictly speaking.

The subject somehow turned to movies, what it was like to live in our respective cities, and a dozen other things. We also learned we both had minor degrees in philosophy.

"It's been very valuable to me," I said. "It taught me how to think."

A rather obvious statement.

"Me too," she said, and, though I believed her, her thought processes and mine bore little resemblance to each other.

It was two when I said I should be heading back to my hotel. I was sharing a room with a colleague at the Empire across from Avery Fisher Hall.

"I had no idea!" she said, "You don't want to go all that way at this hour. Stay here?"

"Oh, I couldn't."

"Hey, I owe you one."

I decided I had no intention of arguing with her, not about this.

"But there's no couch. Do you have a daybed?"

"What's a daybed?"

"Never mind."

"We'll do it like we did last time."

"I don't have pajamas."

She paused, considering. Then, with a broad smile, she asked, "Boxers or briefs?"

I knew immediately what she meant.

"Boxers."

"Works for me."

And so we shared a bed for a second time. It was like a replay of our night two months before, up to a point. She was out of the bathroom in a few minutes in gray bra and panties and instantly under the covers of her bed. The main difference was that her bed was a single, not a queen-size bed. I hadn't noticed that when I agreed to stay. Then I remembered that when she slept in my hotel room, she wouldn't have come with pajamas. Why wasn't she wearing them now? The answer, of course, was that she didn't have any.

After my own ablutions, I came out in black boxers and a t-shirt and slid under the covers, practically hanging off the edge of the bed to avoid our bodies' touching.

We'd been laying there for a few minutes, when she said, "You're probably wondering something."

"Yes."

"Let me guess."

"Guess away."

"You're wondering if we're going to have sex or not."

"If I was, you've already disabused me of that idea."

"How is that?"

"Can I be candid?"

"Please."

"It wasn't much of a seduction, was it, the way we got to where we are? Not this time. Not last time."

"No, and that's the point."

"The point?"

"Yes," she said, sighing, turning onto her back drawing her hair behind her, "You see, I don't do sex."

"We'll, I'm not every girl's type."

"I mean, not at all."

I couldn't believe what I said next.

"Girls, then?"

"Nope."

I turned to her and asked, "Let me understand. You don't like sex."

"That's not what I said. I said I don't do sex. It doesn't interest me. Like or not like isn't the point. It has nothing to do with you, or men, or women. Nothing that touches me physically affects me. Nothing human, I mean. Don't misunderstand. I'm not recovering from some traumatic experience. I wasn't abused as a child. In fact, I've had a pretty great life. I've had so many friends, people I've liked, people I've loved. But I've never been interested in having sex with a single one of them. Not one. This is about me, understand? It's who I am."

"And yet you sleep with people."

"Yes, you're not the first. I find it enjoyable."

I almost said, just like having a big warm teddy bear. Instead, I pretended to take her seriously.

"And as for the people you've slept with but haven't slept with? How about them?"

"As I said, this is about me."

"Hmmm."

"I know what you're really asking. What about their sexual desires? Their frustration perhaps?"

I couldn't believe the total lack of inflection in her voice.

"Yes. That."

"I'll tell you this. It's never hurt a single one of those relationships. If anything, it's made them better."

"It's made who better?"

"The relationships. It's made the relationships better."

I paused, wanting to say the right thing. It took a minute. Finally, I couldn't help myself and said, "So you're a virgin."

"Technically, yes."

Hurrying on, I said, "Thanks for telling me."

"You're welcome."

"Goodnight, Tina."

"Goodnight, Danny."

I almost said "Daniel," but the moment was too perfect and I didn't want it to end. What she'd said? I didn't believe a word. Honestly. Wouldn't it be stranger if I had believed her? In my brief three decades-plus on this over-sexed planet, I'd never even heard of someone saying so directly and dispassionately that sex was out of the question.

Tina had clearly explained there wasn't some terrible secret, some horrific experience, behind it. She wanted me to believe it as though it was in her DNA—it was just the way she was. She was different and it didn't seem to bother her at all. As simple as that. She'd confessed all this to me as calmly as describing a visit to the pet store.

Again, honestly? I found it endearing. Her ditzy behavior with losing and forgetting things was a different matter—in a way, more serious and something to be on the lookout for as it might affect our professional relationship. Could I really trust her never to mention Geraldine? Would she somehow confuse all of my orchestra's metrics with those of another orchestra and create financial havoc I might not discover until it was too late? Would she blurt out that we'd had a sleepover, like two teenage girls? Not once, but twice?

The famous Japanese novelist Yasunari Kawabata wrote a novella called "The House of the Sleeping Beauties," about an establishment where older men sleep beside the naked bodies of narcotized young virgins, which produces extraordinary dreams. As with Tina, there was no physical contact. I read the book in college, and Tina mirrored its chaste eroticism, even its dreamlike unreality.

I fell asleep with this warm woman beside me, scantily clothed, more attractive every time I saw her, feeling as innocent as a drowsy five-year-old in the back of the family car driving home late at night.

When I awoke at nine, she was gone, which was a trick; I'm a light sleeper. I had told her that I didn't need to set an alarm if she didn't, my meeting being scheduled for late morning. She said she never set an alarm and always woke up when she needed to.

She left a note: "Danny, I have to be on a plane by ten and didn't want to wake you. I enjoyed last night and look forward to seeing you in (my city). Tina."

On the side table, two feet from where the note lay, was her plane ticket. I dressed and left the room as fast as I could, afraid she'd come charging in shrieking.

Instead, she called me while I was in a cab headed to Lincoln Center.

"Hi, it's me. Did you see my plane ticket?"

"Yes, I did."

"Why didn't you call me?"

She seemed confused rather than angry.

I knew it was only plausible, but I answered, "I saw it too late, and figured they had your reservation and would board you without the actual ticket."

Silence.

"Did they?"

"Yes, I'm waiting to board. The flight was delayed."

"I'm sorry if I upset you somehow. I just assumed you'd figure it out."

"I am *not* upset," she insisted. "Thanks for your confidence. Gotta go," she said and hung up. By her acid tone, she wasn't thankful for anything.

Though it isn't necessary to bring Geraldine onstage, as I mentioned earlier, I should explain our relationship. She had been married for six years when we met. She described it as a loveless marriage from the beginning and a terrible mistake. She'd cried the entire day before the nuptials. She couldn't explain why she went through with it or why she let it go on so long, except that they never fought and they lived comfortable though very busy professional lives. She once described it as two figurines trapped in Lucite. And there was never a word of children.

Once we became lovers, she asked for a divorce, which her husband agreed to almost with relief. For appearance's sake, we agreed that living together was too dangerous, and as her apartment was closer to the office than mine, at first most of our intimacies took place at hers. Later, she expressed some distaste for my apartment, which was sparsely furnished, definitely a bachelor's pad, and required an extra 20 minutes to get to work.

Consequently, we made two decisions. When we slept together it would always be at her apartment. And, to be careful, it would be wise if I stayed over no more than two or three nights a week, and, never on concert nights. We soon fell into this pattern of nocturnal behavior and it suited us well.

One more thing. Crucial. We had an understanding. As long as we never spoke about it, neither of us wanting to know, and because we gave no consideration to the possibility of marriage anytime in the future, if ever, each of us was free to have the occasional fling. But with the understanding that they must never take precedence over Daniel and Geraldine. We loved each other and there was nothing wanting in our sexual relations, a subject I'll come back to.

It was two weeks after my second night with Tina that she and I talked to finalize arrangements for her first visit. This would include meetings with the CEO, the Music Director, and members of my marketing staff, and, of course, two performances of the orchestra in our acoustically exceptional but architecturally mundane concert hall. The program, the season opener, which would be repeated twice, was to her liking, so she wanted to hear it twice—Beethoven's *Consecration of the House Overture,* Wagner's *Siegfried Idyll,* and, on the second half, Beethoven's *Seventh Symphony.*

As we were discussing her flight plans and car arrangements (she planned to rent her own, which was not in my budget, rather than relying on me for transportation), she asked about hotels and I said, "What about my place?"

I expected to get a laugh, because in truth I wasn't sure I was being serious or not.

"And Geraldine?" she asked, in that dry-ice voice of hers.

"She never stays at my place. I stay at hers a few times a week."

"That doesn't sound like much of a liaison," she said, a bit of snark in her tone. "But why not? I know the score and if you say it's safe...."

"Very safe."

"Geraldine's that dumb?"

"Geraldine's that *understanding,* if you take my meaning."

"I do."

"We just can't poke her in the eye with it."

"Ah, discretion, discretion," she sang. "What would we do without discretion?" She thought for a moment and said, "Deal."

Our first meeting was lunch with the CEO, Jason Hackamore, a sleek bald man in his early 50s with a small gold ring in his right earlobe—his way of saying, "Don't fuck with me." He liked my work more than he liked me. Tina was dressed in her usual ensemble, light purple this time. We met at Jason's "club," one of his perks. I could tell he'd taken to Tina immediately. From the way she leaned away from him, so unlike the way she always leaned toward me, I knew she despised him.

His first offense was to order for the three of us: shrimp in milk sauce with sliced carrots, garlic mashed potatoes, and a Caesar salad.

"Does that sound okay?" he asked Tina and through metaphorically gritted teeth she said, "Oh, that sounds lovely."

The days of the drinking lunch having long disappeared in the hinterlands, if not New York, we drank water with lime.

Jason proceeded to grill Tina not on her thoughts about his orchestra's woes—he would never get around to that—but about the different major orchestras she'd consulted with. He wanted to know what she thought of the CEOs of the largest orchestras in particular, their relationship with their boards of directors and the players union, their demeanor and leadership style, and peccadilloes of any kind whatsoever (always with a hint, never quite voiced, of the sexual). I'd seen him in this mode before, during meals with famous guest artists who'd played with all of the majors. Tina answered honestly and openly, and managed—quite a feat—not to tell him a goddamned thing he didn't know already.

Finally, to get back at him just a little, she asked, "How long have you been here?"

"Twelve years," he said with some hesitancy.

"Are you thinking of moving on?" she asked, right thumb up.

"Biding some time," he said awkwardly, then taking some water,

"Biding *my* time." As though he could have his choice of the plum jobs.

I could tell Tina was struggling not to laugh. Jason wasn't going anywhere. He knew it, we knew it. There was no Boston or Cleveland in his future.

"Where are you staying?" he asked out of nowhere, quickly changing the subject.

"The Hilton," she said, without inflection. I thought she was taking a risk.

Later, as I drove her to our offices, she told me she actually had taken a room there, just in case this very question was asked.

"Clever girl," I said.

She laughed and gently clawed my arm.

"You know that's what the hunter in Jurassic Park says to the velociraptor that's about to tear him apart."

"I better be careful then."

The rest of the day was what I'd expected. A presentation to staff of her analysis of the orchestra's pricing strategies and marketing materials. She was gentle, diplomatic, complimentary, but very clear that there were deficiencies in everything we did. If I'd seen her more than once in less than perfect control of her life, when it came to marketing she was, by a parsec, the smartest person in the room. No one but me seemed to notice she didn't make eye contact with a single one of us, as if hiding the real truth.

I took them all to an early dinner and then it was time to go to the concert hall. I normally worked the room at the pre-concert cocktail party, but I spent the time with Tina instead. When she told me the conclusions she'd drawn so far, it wasn't pretty.

We sipped champagne on concrete benches outside, overlooking the river and, without making me feel totally inept, she managed to convey a simple concept that was at the root of all our problems.

"You think strategy when you should think tactics; you think tactics when you should think strategy."

Not even sure what she meant, I was too tired to go into it right then. We decided to take our seats for the concert.

A few minutes before the downbeat, hands clasped in her lap, she leaned over and said, "You need to understand, I'm a terrible perfectionist. You're incredible. You've got a great staff. Everything's in place. On a scale of five, I'd give you a four and a half. I intend to get you to five."

Still feeling slightly hurt, I asked, "Can I say 'clever girl' again?"

"Not if you want to give me a back rub tonight," she said, her hands still clasped in her lap.

Okay, okay. On how many levels was she making fun of me, making a fool of me? At that moment in our friendship, which was to last for a long time, I felt like a mouse with a very long tail. Tina had both paws on it, and she wouldn't let me go.

I use that comparison because she said, just before the concert started, "I've always called this piece 'The Consecration of the Mouse.'" I'd heard this jape before, but from Tina it was a form of apology.

"Thank you," I whispered.

"For what?"

I said nothing. As usual, when it was just between us, we often talked right past each other.

The concert over, I introduced Tina to the Music Director at the after-concert reception; we were quickly interrupted by a wealthy donor. It was easy to convince Jason that Tina had had a long day and there was no need for her to stay any longer. I didn't give him a chance to say, "Tell her she can go," before we both left together. Twenty-five minutes later I was opening the door to my apartment. Driving separately, Tina arrived seconds later.

Here, it's necessary to explain the nature of my sexual relationship with Geraldine. Without going into detail, let me say that she was multi-orgasmic, which more often than not led to more than one orgasm on my part as well. She wasn't in the least perverted, yet if the definition of that word includes the ability to move ever so slightly beyond the norm, then she was some variation of the word. I was reasonably fit, even athletic, playing squash three times a week, but physically she was my match in every way. After each encounter I felt sated and sedated. My point is that, in terms of sex, I didn't *need* Tina. No, it was in a very different sense of the word that I *wanted* Tina.

As I showed her around my apartment, repeating the words "back rub" in my thoughts, over and over, she suddenly turned to me and took me by the shoulders. Astonishingly, she pressed her lips to mine for a good five seconds, then stepped back and shook her head.

"I apologize for that," she said, "I'm sure it was confusing if not actually inappropriate. But I needed to make sure, you see? You see that, don't you?"

I did, and nodded.

"I like you a lot, Daniel," she said with a wink. "Daniel. Daniel. Daniel. Can you get me something to drink?"

We settled into opposite ends of the couch with wineglasses in hand.

"You see. I don't completely trust myself."

She looked away and laughed, then looked me with those merry eyes.

"Hell, I can't afford to trust myself with just about anything, as you've probably figured out by now. In your case, though, the last thing I wanted was to be surprised by physical contact with you. Maybe it's something in your voice, or your eyes. You're very appealing to me as a person. I really like you. So, I had to find out if that changed anything about me at all."

"And of course it didn't," I said without the least disappointment or accusation. "No matter, Tina. I like you too."

"Most men would think me a fantastic tease."

"Maybe. But it's never occurred to me. I mean, we've slept in the same bed twice. That kiss was like checking the padlock on the gate was still locked."

"Oh, don't say that," she said and started to tear up.

"No, no!" I rushed in, reaching toward her, then pulling back. "I didn't mean it that way. What a stupid way to put it. I just meant to suggest a sense of finality, in case there was any question. I've already concluded there is no question, why shouldn't you be allowed to do the same?"

She wiped her eyes, smearing what little mascara she wore.

"You *do* understand!"

"Yes."

We paused and looked away from each other. It was like a ten-count.

"Do I still get that back rub?"

"Only if I get one too."

"Deal."

I don't need to describe a friendly back rub, do I? As before, she came to bed in bra and panties. I wore pajamas. She took some rose lotion from her purse and lay on her stomach. I asked if I could unhook her bra and she said, sure. Straddling her upper thighs, I couldn't help my own unavoidable condition, and she could not have been oblivious of it. We simply chose to ignore it. Then I took off my pajama top and she really worked me over, saying, "This, Daniel, is how to do a proper massage."

She wasn't kidding. My shoulders the next day were spaghetti.

Then with hardly a word more, we got under the covers and, back-to-back, went to sleep.

There are only two more events worth mentioning of her first visit to my city: our lunch with the Music Director and our second night at my apartment.

We ate again at the club. Tina, having first gone back to her hotel to change, wore a white blouse buttoned at the throat and a black ankle-length skirt that that seemed an almost extreme change toward the prim and chaste from her usual attire, which was very feminine without exuding sexuality. As we settled in, the Music Director, a handsome and slightly English-challenged Spaniard by the name of Eluardo Confligrante, said to Tina, "I'm sorry we had no time yesterday. You know how concert night go."

"Of course, maestro. I completely understood."

To my surprise she briefly covered his hand with her own.

Not every conductor likes the pretension of "maestro," but I'd told Tina that he loved it.

"I tried finding you, later," he continued. "I even called your hotel at 11:30. You weren't there."

He'd done his homework. Hackamore must have told him what hotel.

"I'm sure they didn't tell you that."

"Yes. I think."

"No, maestro, I went to bed at eleven and left a message at the front desk that I was not to be disturbed."

"I'm sorry," he said, "I misunderstand."

Later, she told me she had in fact told him the complete truth. His lack of facility with English took care of the rest. He had also, she said, left her a message: "Sorry I miss you. Look forward to see you again."

We ordered, separately, Eluardo having a bottle of red wine for himself. Tina took control of the conversation. She complimented the previous evening's performance as if Toscanini himself had been on the podium. She even dropped the great conductor's name in comparison. She asked him about his repertoire likes and dislikes and agreed with him on every composer, and tossed in a few of her own, including the Austrian Hans Rott.

"You know him?" she asked.

"I do not," Eluardo admitted. "I appreciate. I will explore this music."

He didn't take his eyes off her face for a second.

While waiting for the meal to come, I excused myself only to return to what seemed a strained joviality.

"The maestro's really very humorous, Daniel," she said, a little too loudly. "He tells wonderful stories. Maestro, tell him what you just told me about Isaac Stern."

"No, my dear," he said, clearly embarrassed. "He's heard the cigar story many times."

Then we turned to business.

"Maestro," she began, sitting bolt upright, "how do you feel about how the orchestra *uses* you?"

I detected the slightest venom in the question.

"Excuse, please?"

"I mean in advertising you. How they *use* you."

He seemed almost distressed.

"How they present you to the community," she persisted. "How they use your face?"

"Fine. Oh, fine," he said with relief.

"I agree, Maestro. Such a handsome face sells tickets."

"It does?" he asked, clearly defeated.

"But I think you should smile more to show the real you."

He responded with a frown and a vivid blush.

"I don't smile?"

"Some. Just smile more."

The tension at the table was growing as Eluardo emptied his wine-glass and poured another. If I had to guess, he was scared to death of her.

Tina leaned forward and turned to me.

"I can tell you this," and she said it sincerely, "any ticket sales problems don't have anything to do with the orchestra. They're great, how do you say, Maestro? *Gran banda!*"

With that, Eluardo drained his glass, looked at his watch, pushed back his chair and stood up.

"You must excuse. I have appointments with musicians. Performance issues."

He made a point of coming around to shake my hand and merely waved at Tina as he left without another word.

Tina followed him into the foyer, put her hand on his forearm, and spoke a few words to him, then returned.

"What did you say to him?"

Seated, sighing deeply, then pouring her water glass into his wine-glass, then filling her own half full of wine, Tina turned to me and said, "Want some?"

I flagged down a waiter and asked for a glass.

"I told him 'If you ever touch my tits again, I'll tell John Ward.'"

John Ward was the chairman of the board.

The glass came and she poured the rest of the bottle in and we touched glasses.

"Didn't you know?" she asked with a cynical smile that crinkled her nose.

I felt like a fool.

"Honestly, Tina, I had no idea."

"None?"

"Maybe a negative vibe now and then from female guest artists? General distaste. But I assumed they didn't like his arrogance."

"They want to be invited back."

"I suppose."

"I'll guarantee you Jason knows."

"He doesn't like Eluardo at all!"

"Of course, because he's in a difficult position. The bastard's popular, right?"

"Very."

"Well, I forgive you."

"You forgive me?"

"For being such a dunce."

"But what should I do?"

"Nothing. It will come out someday. As for me, I don't give a shit. If other women are willing to be treated that way, that's on them."

She drained her glass and laughed.

"That Hans Rott rot? That was my second clue he was working

on me. No conductor on earth doesn't know of Hans Rott's first symphony."

"And calling you late was the first," I offered.

"Yep!" she said and poured the last drops of wine into my glass. I think if she could, she'd have thrown the bottle across the room.

(As an aside, Eluardo's contract wasn't renewed the following spring.)

There was no post-concert reception that night, but we were forced to dine late with John Ward and his wife. Pleasant enough, but a bit too long. The Wards were wine-lovers, and we'd all downed close to a bottle each of a very fine Bordeaux. We reached my apartment at midnight and promptly had our first argument.

It had been my impression that Tina held her liquor as well as I did, so I was caught by surprise.

As soon as the door was closed, she said, "I want to be asleep in ten minutes."

Being exhausted myself, I was joking when I said, "No back rub tonight?"

She didn't answer and was in and out of the bathroom and under the covers, like always, in just a few minutes.

When I came out of the bathroom, she said, her face turned toward the wall, "I think in the future we might want to do this only one night at a time."

I sat on the bed and almost reached out to her, pulling back just in time.

"What's wrong?"

She rolled over and looked at me angrily. Then she punched my arm hard.

"Ouch!" I cried.

"You're presumptuous. And very possibly sly and manipulative. What, you think a back rub is prelude to something more just because the bed's still, metaphorically, warm."

"What?"

"And why is that always in the way?" she said, pointing at my slightly tented crotch.

"Now wait a minute. You expect…."

"I expect nothing. That's the point. I thought we had that all ironed out."

"You're mad because I mentioned a back rub? I was joking!"

"No, you were not. I could hear the disappointment in your voice. Your Johnnie of Arc schtick."

She drew a deep breath and really blew up, her face as red as her hair.

"How can I make it any clearer? I will not, now, or ever, fuck you. Not ever! I could rub your back. I could stick my tongue in your ear. I could suck your toes one by one. I could give you a hickey on your forearm. As meaningless as all such contact would be. But! But! But! I will never let you fuck me. Understand, Danny?"

"Tina!"

As if every word I uttered attempting a defense only made her angrier, she jumped out of bed and ran into the bathroom.

"I'm going back to my hotel," she shouted through the door.

"No, you aren't, Tina. You're drunk. I shouldn't have let you drive out here as it is, now that I can see it so clearly."

I found her purse and took out her keys.

She came out fully dressed. I handed her the purse, and said, "I hid the keys. Feel free to walk."

"Bastard!" she cried and crumpled on the couch, drawing up her knees. She cried and cried.

After only a few minutes, she jumped up and ran back to the bathroom, her feet flapping on the linoleum. She didn't come out for almost half an hour.

She was in bra and panties again and crawled under the covers.

Already under the covers, I said, "I'm sorry."

"For what?"

"I'm not sure."

"I'm sorry too."

"It's okay," I said.

"You're supposed to say, 'for what?'" she said drowsily.

"Goodnight, sweetheart," I whispered, but she was already asleep.

We never spoke of that night again.

The way Tina did business, one visit to her client's city was usually enough. She was on a two-year contract, expected to provide pricing, marketing, and other advice for the next two seasons, all of which she could do by phone and computer. Because the second year would end up involving a search for a new Music Director, she would be contracted for additional work to help create excitement about the guest conductors brought in as candidates.

Happily, with my various Symphony Orchestra League activities, including spring and winter conferences and my work on the national branding committee, I had to visit New York every month on average.

Still smarting from our argument, I casually let it drop in an email that I would be in New York for two days in late October. To my surprise, she answered, "Great, what would you like to do when you're free?"

"Dinner?"

"There's also a concert at Jazz at Lincoln Center I'd love to see."

"Great!"

"Where are you staying?"

"The Empire, as usual."

She didn't even pause to consider.

"And I can stay there?"

"Of course," I said.

Over dinner, she told me about a situation that eventually led to her being fired by an orchestra. I recount it here as an example of her over-earnest desire to be liked and appreciated, and her total obliviousness to consequences. Said orchestra's marketing director, Joe Hander, was incompetent, which is why the CEO had hired Tina—

the only time that had ever happened. She was always interviewed and hired by the marketing director. She told me that she had prepared, in essence, a performance review of Joe after working with him for more than half a season. It was very critical and might result in his being let go.

I strongly urged her to bury her report.

"It's not your job to evaluate the staff you work with as a consultant, Tina."

"But they need to know," she said, pounding the table so hard people turned to stare. "This person is not only incompetent, but abuses his staff and says terrible things about the CEO, even to me, behind his back."

"That doesn't matter. It's none of your business."

"Then why am I there?"

"Not for that, Tina."

"But they'll appreciate it," she said, softening, almost pathetic. "They'll thank me. Maybe they'll extend my contract. Who cares what happens to this idiot?"

"Listen. You have no way of knowing who might protect him. And just because the CEO may have some concerns about him, that's no guarantee he'd even consider firing him."

"Then maybe he'll just want me to make him do a better job."

"That's the best thing that could happen, and the unlikeliest. Ultimately, it will be your word against Joe's. Why should they believe you? Don't do this. They might fire you!"

"No way."

"And then what happens to you? Do you want to become known as the consultant who gets her clients fired?"

"Don't be absurd. I'd require total confidentiality, with a nondisclosure agreement if I have to."

Now she was full of bravado and conviction.

"Right. You honestly believe that's the way things work?"

"Of course. I'd sue them if they broke my confidence."

"And Joe could sue you for libel!"

There was no talking her out of it. She submitted her evaluation later that week and was given her 30-day notice the next day and asked to sever all communications immediately.

She never told me. At a conference a few months later, I was told by Joe Hander. I'd asked him how things were going with Tina, and he said, guardedly, that their contract with her had run out. I asked her about it over the phone.

"Yeah, you were right. They fired me. It really sucks. They bounced me, and I'll bet they didn't even take a word I said seriously."

"It sounds like they're keeping it quiet.

"They'd better."

"Can I say one thing?"

"I'd rather you didn't."

"Just this. You can't make some people love you by making other people hate you."

"Got it," she said and hung up.

Here's how things went for the next eleven months. If I came to New York, and she was in town, it was assumed she would stay at my hotel or I would stay at her apartment. We always slept in the same bed, even when there was more than one.

As strange as this sounds, it brought to my life a delicious sense of anticipation in between visits, and, in bed, a tremendous sense of comfort. We might have philosophized about it once or twice, or tried to; once we got into the notion of just accepting it for what it was and removing it entirely from the universe into our own simple two-ness (or one-ness that wasn't one-ness), which nonsense led to our giggling ourselves goofy. A few times, usually when we'd had a few, we played around like two eight-year-olds. Once, we kissed for ten minutes or so, which she seemed to enjoy, though it didn't move her in the least. Once, we took a bubble bath together, which she stepped into nude with all the hesitancy of someone complete-ly alone. The unavoidable contact only made her smile and squirm.

It wasn't unusual for her to parade naked in our hotel room, from the bathroom to her suitcase. Who was I to complain? Once, pointing at my erection as I climbed into bed, she said, "It certainly is dependable."

"No comment," I said.

"Doesn't it hurt?"

"Never had blue balls, if that's what you mean."

"Blue balls?"

She kept looking at it, dispassionately curious. I didn't cover up.

"Some guys when, uh, unrequited, get an aching. And their testicles actually turn blue."

"Will you show me if it ever happens?"

"Nope."

"Since we're on the topic...."

"Yes?" I said with a sigh. I really didn't want to talk about it.

"It wouldn't bother me if you took care of it yourself."

Now she looked up, into my eyes, as though making a generous offer.

"No chance."

"You can't tell me you haven't thought about it."

"What, you want me to go into the bathroom?"

"I'm not that stupid."

"What then."

"Here," she said, patting the bed. "I wouldn't look, of course."

"You obviously have no idea what you're suggesting."

The humorless directness with which I spoke stunned her into silence.

"Look. It's not your fault, because you don't understand, but it would be the most humiliating and embarrassing thing I've ever done in my life."

Now she was crying.

"It's okay," I said, as gently as I could. "Go to sleep."

And that was the extent of our explorations.

As for her work, things were not as I would have liked. She always got it done, when it came to meeting a deadline, providing a work product, or coming up with creative ideas. And her work was brilliant. But I've never known anyone more infuriating when it came to communicating. By her own admission, she had two cell phones and a land line, a Mac Mini, a MacBook, and an iPad. But how many emails does one have to write to get a single response, how many calls and messages or texts left, to hear back? And, most frustrating, I couldn't yell and scream as I would at one of my own staff members or a media buyer when I felt I was being ignored.

I repeatedly, yes, rather meekly, complained, but it was like telling a bunny to stop being cute. She thought I was exaggerating and that I didn't comprehend how busy she was. I believe she actually thought that what was a lack of professionalism was just an endearing quirk.

Admittedly, I was compromised in our business relationship by our sleeping arrangement—too much to make a big issue of it. And, in truth, it all amounted to a series of minor irritations, and had no effect on what I really felt about Tina. I won't pretend that I knew her feelings about me to a certainty, so the best I can do is suggest our feelings were reciprocal. I loved her in a way I had never experienced. I can't compare it to familial love, or a boyish crush on an attractive woman, or unrequited love with all of its frustrated intensity. It wasn't passionate, and if it was strong, it was equally tentative, almost fragile. And there was nothing cerebral about it—this was all heart.

She was always there, a physical presence more real, at times, than when I lay beside her. She brought a calm, a clarity, and a warmth to my often-turbulent day, just with my thinking or whispering her name. On particularly bad days I'd call just to hear her voice.

And, somehow, none of this detracted from my love of Geraldine, which had sex at its core, but without it limiting or distorting the other aspects of our relationship. We never argued, as Tina and

I did now and then, and we had a great number of mutual interests, books and music especially. (Tina read voraciously, but only mysteries and science fiction, which didn't interest me.) Geraldine and I working for the same organization was another factor, and while we didn't talk shop much, the fact that we were both trying our best to nurture and grow a symphony orchestra further enriched our mutual attraction.

Neither woman was the quote love of my life unquote, but there was nothing casual or vague, or fading in my emotions toward either one. I was, I am, convinced that it's entirely possible to love two people simultaneously, one as much as the other, though in totally different ways. But that excludes a "love of one's life," doesn't it?

The next year passed, from month to month, much as I've described. Geraldine and I fucked each other crazy on a regular basis. The orchestra's fortunes, due to Tina, began to look promising. I flew to New York and "slept" with Tina and watched with dismay, sometimes first hand, the clueless mistakes she made in her life.

For example, I came out of the bathroom one morning to hear her reading some numbers off a card. It was her Social Security number, and in less than an hour several thousands had been withdrawn from her savings account. Only her bank's automatic monitoring system stopped the scammer from getting more. She cried all day about that.

My biggest fear was her walking around New York. She had absolutely no sense of direction or distance and, if I hadn't quickly schooled myself, we'd have been lost half the time. I warned her again and again about not wandering around by herself ("Take a cab," I'd say, "you can afford it!") and thankfully she was never mugged, or worse. I worried about her all the time, particularly about her jogging, though she kept to a strict route every day that seemed safe enough. She thought I was nuts.

The worst was the night I had to get her out of jail. She'd been arrested for indecent exposure, fleeing an officer, and suspicion of prostitution. Late on a Saturday night she'd decided to run out to buy some wine. The liquor store was only half a block away; instead of dressing like a normal person, she threw on a robe over nothing but her panties and stepped out of her apartment in sandals. A policeman blocked her path and grabbed her sash. Tina screamed and ran, leaving the policeman holding the sash, with Tina bearing all her forefront to the world. It didn't help, I later learned, that there had been more than the usual trouble with hookers and the policeman was there to keep his eye out for them. She led him a wild chase around her block, tripping now and then on her sandals, and back to her apartment where he grabbed and wrapped her up, and dragged her three blocks to the nearest precinct building. Thank goodness she didn't resist, and instead went almost limp. By the time they reached the precinct building, she was in hysterics and didn't understand what she'd done wrong. She thought she'd been attacked. Finally, they agreed to let her call me. It took her five minutes of spluttering and outcries to tell me what happened. I spent half an hour trying to convince the arresting officer not to press charges. I told him that she wasn't exactly crazy, but just different, etc., etc. He asked what my relationship was to her, and I said the wrong thing: "Just a friend." Then his antennae really went up. "Really? I know a lot of hookers with *friends*. You a john? Or maybe her pimp?"

"Her boyfriend, officer. Please, she isn't a hooker," I pleaded. "She just does dumb things sometimes."

Eventually, he let her go and even escorted her back home at my request. His last words to me were, "Okay, she's not a hooker, but she sure is a looker. Keep her dressed, will ya?"

Yes, it sounds funny now, but I wasn't amused and after my bawling her out, all she could say was, "It was the cop's fault."

Things went on as before. Our sleeping together in New York continued with a rare and innocent foray into the erotic, which I'm sure she forgot the minute we were done. We never touched each other, except one time; out of sheer curiosity, she agreed to our taking off our underthings in perfect darkness and touching intimately. The entire experience lasted less than ten minutes and left her giggling, as if I'd been tickling her. My reaction was more natural, but I won't go into that.

On several occasions, Tina asked me about the national branding committee. She was extremely curious about it and had dozens of questions. One day she asked if she could be invited to one of our meetings.

"Totally unpaid. Just tell them I'd like to offer advice or answer questions."

"Tina, they'll see it as a bid for business."

"Nonsense," she scoffed. I thought she was going to slap me again. "They know I don't need to promote myself. As it is, half of them call me every week begging me to take them on."

"And what if they don't like what you have to say?"

"Don't worry. That's not an option. Most of them are too clueless to know good advice when they hear it."

"It's that attitude that could piss them off."

"Oh, come on! I'd be on my best behavior. All sweetness. You know me."

"I know what you did to Joe Hander, or tried to."

"That was different, and totally confidential."

"Exactly. And this won't be. There are twelve of them, beside myself, so if it doesn't go well...."

"Tell you what. Just say I'd like to see what they've come up with so far."

"I could give you that," I said.

"That accomplishes nothing," she said impatiently. "Just say I'd like to see it and if I feel I can be helpful I'm offering to meet with them for free. How could anyone object to that?"

I said "no" a dozen times, but she wouldn't let it go. Finally, I relented and received the group's permission to show our work to

Tina in confidence. Most of them were excited about it; a few, I could tell, resented it. Pure jealousy.

That evening, as I watched a tennis match, Tina spent two hours, in a fever of page turning and grumbling, pouring over the mission and vision statements we'd drafted, a timetable, the results of our research so far (funded by a national foundation), and a few trial images and slogans we were kicking around.

When she was done, she dropped the note book on the coffee table, stood up and point at me accusingly, "*You* have to get me in to see these idiots!"

"Hey, I'm one of those idiots," I answered, refusing to get upset.

Her anger was shocking, as if I'd let her read a bungled police report of a rape.

"It's all nonsense!"

She was actually spitting.

"Look, I know it's very raw. What do you expect from a committee?"

"Raw? Listen to this. 'Orchestras need to reimagine themselves as an industry the way the NBA did in the '90s!' What utter bullshit!"

"That's just conjectural positioning, Tina."

"And this," she said, ignoring me. " 'Recordings need to be minimized as a primary listening experience, since their popularity reduces concert attendance."

"It's just a researcher's suggestion. What's wrong with that?"

"Doesn't he know that the union turned recording over to the Europeans fifteen years ago by pricing American orchestras out of the market?"

She was right, of course, but the vehemence was almost personal. She went on and on.

Again, she demanded that I get her invited to one of our meetings.

"They all need a lesson in marketing 101!"

"You yell at me and think I'm going to trust you to be gentle with my colleagues? Forget it."

She continued to badger me for another week, but finally let it drop. I told the committee she'd said nice work so far and forge ahead. She had nothing to offer at this time. I lied, but for once I was able to save her from herself.

The incidents of forgetfulness and cluelessness continued, sometimes in quick succession, sometimes months apart. And, with her contract with my orchestra coming to an end, I began to feel taken for granted in a way I hadn't been since the first day I met her. When I'd come to town, she would sometimes make some lame excuse and refuse to get together. She became virtually impossible to get on the phone. And, falling short on a final major project, she made a casual, entirely insincere apology and gave 30 days notice to cancel her contract.

I didn't make a lot of all this, because in fact we'd gotten far more than we paid for and there wasn't much more she could teach us.

"You won't tell on me, will you?" she asked when it was all over.

"What do you mean?"

"That I bailed on you."

"No, of course not."

Her question pissed me off, but I let it go. I thought her sudden departure might be personal, when she confessed that she was considering a full-time job offer. It would be the biggest mistake of her career, taking a senior position with the New York Philharmonic. She said this was her dream job and that they'd thrown an astronomical salary on the table.

"Why give up your independence?" I asked her.

From what I could tell she was making as much on her own as what the Philharmonic was offering, and she had the freedom to do whatever she wanted, take whatever work, or work with anyone, she wanted.

It led to an argument in which she switched from accusing me of trying to hold her back, without explaining why I would even think of doing that, to arrogantly yelling that it would make her the biggest marketing name in the arts in a couple of years.

"You really want to work 80 hours a week?"

"Don't be absurd. That's just a rumor."

There was no reasoning with her. She took the job.

Almost immediately the calls began, all regret, complaint, and incomprehension. She understood going in that, unlike consulting, where there was always an exit, she'd be under the thumbs of the Music Director (a total narcissist and a mediocrity as well), the Senior VP of Marketing, and the imperious CEO.

"My boss has insomnia and calls me at two in the morning!" she'd complain. "They have so damn many meetings I have to work all weekend just to keep up."

I tried to encourage her, assure her that she'd get used to it. It just got worse and worse.

The CEO pinched her bottom in the elevator and she couldn't do a thing about it. ("One word and I'll fire your ass!") Her only defense was to stay as far from him as possible, which thwarted her desire to be part of the inner circle and make a real difference.

Her work was criticized to the point that it was unrecognizable after all the changes demanded. The Chairmen of the Boards of both the Philharmonic and Lincoln Center, seeing a potential ally in a young woman in a male-dominated world, confided incredible secrets that would have made front page news if they were ever revealed. I refused to let her tell me what they were.

The Music Director complained she made him look ugly and stupid.

"You've heard of putting lipstick on a pig?" she said, "This is like trying to sew Van Gogh's ear back on after he's dead."

"At least you're keeping your sense of humor."

"That wasn't humor. That was bitterness."

"Then just quit, Tina!"

"What, and be known as that pussy who couldn't hack it at the Phil?"

She was right about that, at least.

She didn't last three months. At a senior staff meeting, after being shouted at for missing a deadline on something she'd delegated to staff, she told the CEO to go fuck himself and, as she walked out, she thrust out her bottom, pinched it, and said, "Remember this— in the elevator? It still stings!"

With her combination of cerebral strength and emotional vulnerability, she just wasn't built to work in a corporate environment. The orchestra world being like frat brats yammering over beers at three in the morning, her career was somewhat compromised. Only respect for her parting jab at the CEO, which became almost legendary, saved her from becoming a total pariah.

I didn't hear from her for two months, and I had to learn all this from a colleague. She wouldn't return any form of communication, except the last one, an email into which I put all the anger, frustration, and complaint I could throw at her, to which she responded: "I think we need to take a break. Bye."

At the next meeting of the branding group, I asked if anyone had worked with her recently. No one knew where she'd gone.

I was now sincerely worried and went that evening to her apartment. It was midnight and the lights were out. I didn't ring, not really wanting to know whether she was there or not, alone or not.

Though it hurt a lot at first, the longer we were apart the more my love turned to fury. I should have known better. As she always said, "This is about me."

Then came the total breach. Why she chose the most direct, reliable, and stilted form of communication available—the registered letter—I would never figure out. It simply told me to call her, provided a phone number, and three times, any one of which would be fine and she'd pick up. I chose the last one, to let her sweat.

If what I'm about to relate seems totally unsupported by everything that's gone before, such inconsistency is essential to Tina's psyche.

"Hello."

No inflection.

"Tina, it's me."

"Good."

"What's going on? I haven't...."

Her interruption was actually rude, which was rare for her.

"I have three things to say. One, I'm pregnant. Two, I'm married. And, three, this is the last time we'll need to talk."

I knew that I'd never get an answer to any question I asked, so I waited silently. After a few seconds, she started to cry.

"I'm very happy, Danny. I wanted a baby and this was the price. I could have asked you, but I knew you wouldn't marry me, and I had to be married. I could never have asked you to do that. My husband understands everything. He even knows about you. He doesn't care. I don't think he loves me, but he wanted children too. He's wealthy...."

Here she began wailing.

"He's very wealthy and we have sex even though...he doesn't like me that way. It's the price, don't you see?"

"It's okay, sweetheart," I said.

What I thought I wanted to do was say something final and hang up on her, but I couldn't.

"I'm happy for you," I continued. "I understand. Please stop crying. It's okay."

I gave her a moment to calm down. Now I was about to cry.

"Tina, you're right. This is the last time we should talk. I want you to be happy. I wish you and your baby every happiness. I will always remember you and love you."

"I love you, too."

"Can we say goodbye now?" I asked.

"Yes, goodbye, Daniel."

"Goodbye, Tina."

Geraldine and I were married a year ago. We don't have children because we're just too busy. You could say our orchestra is our child.

I know too many people in the orchestra business with screwed up kids not to know that the inability to be there for your kid because of the constant concerts, receptions, rehearsals, dinners, meetings, or fundraisers, is as bad as being a divorced parent with scant visitation rights.

Six months ago, I was staying at the Empire for a special conference on internet marketing. It was almost midnight. I was finishing a beer and watching an old movie when a knock came at the door.

I looked through the keyhole. It was Tina. I opened and she fell into my arms, crying so hard that her convulsions almost knocked me down. I led her to the couch and she said, "Can I stay here tonight?"

"Tina?"

"He divorced me! He's gone! He took my Candace! The courts gave her to him. He's so rich! The big lawyers. The golf-partner judges. He didn't wait even a year, saying I was an unfit mother! He said I was unhinged. Careless. Unloving. A danger to my daughter! He said that! They left yesterday. I don't even know if I get to see her. Candy, Candy! I think I'm dying!"

We "made love" (not the same as "having sex") for the one and only time, ever, at her tearful insistence.

"Are you sure, Tina? Are you sure you want to do this?"

She took my face in her hands and said, "Yes. Please! It will help me to forget the disgust I feel that I ever let that monster inside me."

When we were locked (the only word I can use to describe it) together, it was like she was trying to tear herself apart the way she threw her body back and forth. She seemed to gain some emotional comfort from it in the end, nothing more.

What could I do? We started all over again. Same story. Variations on the theme. Same Tina. Same me.

Nothing changed with Geraldine, as our marriage hadn't altered our "understanding." At least not yet.

Tina and I talked almost every day as she tried desperately to fight the custody decision.

One day, she called me from LaGuardia Airport.

"I have Candy. He let me take her for the weekend. I'm leaving."

She started to babble on and I shouted at her.

"Go home right now! Right now, Tina! It's illegal. They'll put you in jail!"

She continued to babble, though in a more pathetic register.

"It's kidnapping, Tina. Take Candy back home and don't even think of doing it again."

She hung up on me but did what I said.

During my next visit to New York, in bed for the second night, she took my hand in both of hers, which was very unusual. Again in tears, she said: "You have no idea."

"No idea what?"

"About how I am."

I almost laughed, thinking "who better?" but I could sense something was coming.

"What it means to be a freak."

The longer she spoke, the more jagged the words came as she cried harder and harder.

"Come on, now."

"I want a normal life."

I found it overwhelming. I had no response. I tried to hold her but she pulled away, turned away.

"You know what it means, don't you?"

"No, Tina."

"It means I'm alone, on the verge of disappearing entirely. And as much as you mean to me, sometimes you make me feel even more lonely, especially on the phone."

"The phone?" I said to her trembling back.

"It reminds me that it makes no difference whether you're here beside me or five hundred miles away. Either way, I'm alone."

I refused to cry, but it took everything I had not to.

"Hush, Tina," I said, "Go to sleep."

Eventually, she was awarded a huge sum, a bribe to accept seeing her daughter no more than four days a month. She didn't have the money to fight for equal custody.

There was nothing I could do.

Soon after, the ex-husband called me and said four words, "Take care of her," and hung up before I could speak.

I've told Tina to find more people like me close to home. Friends.

She just says, "I have friends. I need someone to love me. Someone to be with every day."

I had no answer to that and never expect to.

There's no knowing how it will end this time, but it can't go on forever.

MR.
GRADE A

*T*HIS is the story of people fated to.... No, let's take them one at a time.

EDGAR SAGE

After seven years as an adjunct professor of English at three different schools simultaneously—a community college, a state university branch, and a small private college—Edgar Sage decided he had the right to sleep with any student he wanted. What did he have to lose?

Teaching freshman composition for as many as 18 credit hours per semester (earning a total of less than $40,000 a year, with no benefits) brought him into close contact with 100-odd students each semester.

He hated teaching. He had loved his wife, but lost her to teaching. She earned a PhD (in Elizabethan drama), which he couldn't, and went off to Wellesley and a tenure-track position to earn twice as much as he did for working three times as hard. She said he was a loser. He told her, "Shove your PhD up your quim."

He spent his days in classrooms and meeting with students in his offices (typically shared with three or four other adjuncts), and his nights grading papers. He was teaching from the same textbook the same lessons he'd written his first year, and he hadn't changed a word. Who knew the difference?

His seductions were the only thing he found of interest in an etiolated and pointless existence. He targeted roughly a dozen students per semester, usually popular, pretty girls with good figures, whose ability to write a complete sentence was tenuous at best.

His batting average was roughly .300. Every three he approached, he ended up seducing one. He never let an affair last more than a week or two, since his conquests usually considered two or three sessions in his bed more than enough to deserve the compensatory A.

He wasn't handsome in any normal way—a flattened, rubbery nose, pale gray eyes, scant eyelashes and eyebrows, biggish ears, and not the straightest mouthful of teeth, so a crooked smile. The assets he did have were a narrow, muscular, six-foot-three body that allowed him literally to look down on everyone, and a full head of bright yellow hair. He had a movie star's body and hair, if not a movie star's face.

Over time, he judged that the private school, with all of its politically correct coeds, represented too much of a risk, so he confined his predations to the other two schools.

He was very careful. You could have photocopied his approach from girl to girl. First, he gave the young lady a D and told her she could do better. Then, even with improvement, he repeated the D. Then he handed out an F, and warned the student she had a good chance of failing. This never failed to create panic.

"But that will follow me around forever!" the cute little thing would complain.

He'd shrug his shoulders and offer to walk with her out of the building. Then he'd say, "Do you have some time Wednesday night?"

He always chose Wednesday nights because the risk of anyone seeing the student arrive at his little home just off campus seemed to be less than on any other night.

Before the student could even respond, he'd say, "I could use some help. If you can't make it, I'll understand."

Then he'd scribble his address on a scrap torn from one of his students' papers, hand it over and walk away.

This approach provided all the plausible deniability he needed should the student complain instead of showing up. He could say he was planning to let her earn extra credit by helping him grade papers, which would also give her writing skills a workout. He'd never once had to use this excuse.

Not once in three years did a student let him down if they actually showed up. He attributed this to a native intelligence about sex in certain young women and the fact that he had a pretty canny sense —he knew it when he saw it.

If the young lady didn't show up, he considered her a lost cause and gave her a better grade than she deserved, never less than a B.

The ones who did show up already knew what to expect. He got them a little drunk and then, every time, he asked, "Can I ask you a favor?" They always said "Yes." "Would you come here and kiss me?" That's all it took.

Yes, there were a couple of exceptions. These said, "No, I think I better be going."

He never pushed it.

"I've enjoyed our little chat," he'd say and show her out, adding, "Let's keep this visit a secret shall we? You won't regret it." These too always got a B or better.

None ever asked about the "help" he'd mentioned. He understood that sometimes a young woman will not make up her mind until confronted with the question. And, at least so far, no one had ever complained after the fact, simply because they would have had no other excuse for being in his house to begin with. He bedded eighteen coeds in three years using this technique.

Of course, he'd always known there was a risk, as well-planned as his seductions were, that someone would tell other students and that it would get around. But, short of someone coming forward and confessing that she'd fallen into his clutches, it could hardly rise above the level of a rumor. And it never did.

AIMEE CORBETT

Aimee Corbett was four years older than the 18-year-olds he normally taught. She was a single mother of twins and worked as a waitress in order to make ends meet. She was also the most attractive student Edgar had ever had. She too had bright blonde hair and was just shy of six feet tall, yet lithe and graceful, and her beauty was the kind in which none of the individual parts, lips, eyes, nose, cheekbones, chin, etc. were by themselves exceptional. What drew all these components together, at times overwhelmingly, was the presence of sexual suggestion, if not actual invitation, in every square inch of her.

Edgar had never met a blonde bombshell before. In his eyes, Aimee Corbett was a blonde neutron bomb.

The reader will agree that this account so far is not of a particularly nice person. Edgar was a pathetic womanizer (he had other conquests outside of the classroom) and seducer of young women for whom sex provided the only real satisfaction in life. In other words, a creep. And as with most creeps, he was more than slightly deluded.

Aimee, in fact, was sexy, the way she smiled so boldly and swung her hips down the hallways—but most men saw a rather typically exhausted and forgettable single mother, and hardly the goddess of Edgar's dreams.

Aimee Corbett was a force, if not of nature, at least of feminine will. That hadn't always been the case. Until she got pregnant by her high school sweetheart, Rod, during her sophomore year of college, she was a typical young woman with the dream of becoming a grade-school art teacher. Rod refused to marry her, no matter how much she threatened, screamed or cried. His old man, a corporate lawyer, agreed to pay for the abortion. Discovering she was carrying twins, she decided to keep them.

But she wasn't going to let Rod off so easily.

They had been going together for so long, he'd made a copy of his car key for her, which he'd apparently long since forgotten because once she went away to college (and he stayed home), she didn't need to use it.

Over Christmas break that year, she found a long nail and a small piece of wood in her father's garage, which was so cluttered with junk no one would ever miss it. She hammered the nail through the wood and slipped it into the center of the driver's seat of Rod's car. She wore latex gloves for this entire operation, which were quickly and thoroughly disposed of, along with the car key. Her feeling was that one of two things would happen. Rod would see it before it was too late and be scared to death, which would have been revenge enough. He didn't. So the second possibility occurred. Rod was in a hurry and didn't see the nail, which penetrated his right testicle and entered the flesh around his hip. It just missed his femoral artery; had it been pierced, he might have bled out in minutes. He lost the testicle, and the nail tore up a significant amount of tissue and nicked his pelvis near his hip bone, all which had to be reconstructed.

Aimee had been clever enough to do her work when Rod was out of town with friends for three days. She went to visit her college roommate during the same time, ensuring an ironclad alibi, since there was no way to determine the time the "weapon" was placed in Rod's car, which was discovered with both front doors unlocked.

Yes, she was questioned, reluctantly, by the police, since the whole thing looked like a crude teenager's prank. The father suspected the worst, but knew that if he prosecuted, his son's embarrassing injury would become public, along with his paternity. And there wasn't an atom's worth of evidence.

A month later, doubling down, Aimee demanded child support of $2,000 a month in order to leave town. She chose not to ask for more, afraid she might push Rod and his father over the edge of caution.

She took an apartment in her college town. While the money was enough to live on and take care of the twins, she couldn't afford school, and for the next two years she took to waitressing. Finally, she'd saved enough to begin taking courses again and still afford child care.

Which brings Edgar Sage and Aimee Corbett together in the same classroom. I trust the reader will have noticed a similarity between the two. Both were capable of detailed and dedicated calculation. They were blessed with a genius for method and execution, and seemingly incapable of remorse, either in the pursuit of their aims or in consideration of past actions. They seem made for each other, don't they?

EDGAR VS. AIMEE

Aimee and Edgar woke in each other's arms on a Saturday morning, hung over and physically exhausted after making love all night. This had been their twelfth night together, and neither felt it was time to call it quits. The sex was beyond conceiving (so to speak). Edgar found himself capable of energy, imagination, and tenderness he never though he possessed. Aimee, quite unaware that her attractions, in his eyes at least (never Rod's), excited him to heights of erotic pleasure she'd never experienced before, but was totally capable of enjoying and reciprocating in equal measure.

It started when Edgar gave Aimee's first paper a D-minus. He was so desperate to get her home that he almost failed her. During the conference, when he failed to explain precisely what was wrong with Aimee's (actually quite accomplished) writing, she smiled her deliciously downward-curling smile and said, "So, you want to fuck."

It was not a question. He almost swallowed his uvula.

There were two more conferences going on in the same room, separated only by cubicle walls. She hadn't raised her voice, but she hadn't whispered either.

"You make a good point, Miss Corbett," he said, loud enough to be heard throughout the room. "Let me reconsider and I'll get back to you."

"Thank you, professor," Aimee said, stooped and whispered. "And make it an A plus, thank you very much."

Had she deliberately exaggerated the swishing of her hips as she turned and walked away? He had been mildly tumescent through their brief meeting and now had a thumping erection. He quickly grabbed a marker and obliterated the D-minus. He wasn't happy with it and actually tore it off the paper. Talk about exhibit A! What was he thinking?!

Let's give Aimee the credit to assume that no one had warned her about Edgar. She knew a bald lie when she saw it, and the intent behind it. What Edgar didn't know was that in her five semesters of college so far she'd received straight As.

The result of this confrontation was the immediate cessation of Edgar's predatory moves on even the most attractive of students. It wasn't a burden because not one of them held the least erotic charge for him compared to Aimee. They could have all been his sisters. And, as a result, he began to treat them all with the respect he would as if they were.

When Aimee was in his classroom, he turned into a paragon—a combination of adviser, counselor, friend, and gentle instructor to every person in the room, even the boys. He called everyone Mr. this and Miss that, and apologized for the slightest misstatement or misunderstanding. He made every effort not to call on Aimee too much or too little, just enough to make her feel valued without sensing solicitude, which others might see as faked.

Most strange of all, he became a real teacher. He actually worked hard to help students become better at writing the English language.

A comment from Aimee during a conference gave him an idea. He started spending hours devising defective sentences and putting them up on the blackboard. Much of class time was then spent fixing them as a group. He told them—what Aimee had said—that they all typically spoke in complete sentences, which meant they knew how to write without actually knowing it, so why couldn't they translate that to paper? And it worked. He didn't give even a single D to anyone that semester.

He was on probation with Aimee and he knew it. In his secret subterranean heart he knew that no woman (and she was old enough to be referred to as a woman) would have said, "So, you want to fuck" if she wasn't, somewhere in her secret subterranean heart, flattered by his lack of disingenuousness in approaching her the way he had, and adult enough about sex not to use such a phrase without intending, however vaguely, a form of invitation.

He wasn't wrong about any of this, as far as it went, but she had greater ambitions than either publicly humiliating or privately bedding the dear professor, as she came to think of him.

Aimee was on the hunt. She was lonely, bored, and though she loved her daughters beyond any emotion she ever imagined herself capable of feeling—day after day after day, never diminishing for a moment, but only growing stronger—she wanted love, she wanted a lover, security, a suitable home, a garden, pets; in short, a life. She wanted a husband.

Yes, of course, the obvious questions is, "Why Edgar?" We know, though she doesn't really know, what a creep he's been. But from Aimee's viewpoint, he was employed, not unattractive, tall, as she was tall for a woman (which had always been an issue with boys, even Rod), capable of being sympathetic toward others, and, as she'd noticed at the end of their first conference, not exactly un-endowed between his pants pockets. She turned him on, which was a turn-on.

Roughly two months after the infamous student/teacher conference that started all this, Aimee got impatient and asked him over for dinner. Just like that. She had her babysitter take the twins overnight and cooked Edgar pot roast and noodles because of something he'd said in class about liking stew. She asked him to bring "plenty of red wine." And that was it. She had to turn down the meal so it wouldn't burn while they jumped into bed. Then they ate dinner in the nude and were back at it, two bottles of red wine gone, before the plates were cold.

Their pillow talk wasn't of much interest, and though they never talked of love, let alone marriage, both were happy, happier than they'd ever been with anyone of the opposite sex. They had plenty to talk about, between their past and present trials, and they didn't skimp on the gory details of their failed romances, or at least Edgar didn't. Aimee revealed all about Rod Genter except the nail in the board. As for their upbringings, they had nothing much of interest to relate; both had nice, supportive and not-at-all-well-off parents. But they had both enjoyed their parents' love. The only interesting, mutual and sad discovery was that all four parents died when Edgar and Aimee were both 17 years old—all in four separate car accidents. The moment of this revelation left them sobbing in each other's arms.

The morning of their twelfth tryst was interrupted by a phone call from none other than Rod Genter.

EDGAR AND AIMEE VS. ROD GENTER

Rodney Genter was perhaps the smartest student in his high school class of 400, though his IQ was never tested. He told the high school principal he didn't want to know, and he didn't want anyone else to know, either, and firmly refused to take the test. His father backed him up, not without a threat of a lawsuit for invasion of privacy.

The argument for the test was that he was also the most underachieving of bright students. He earned a consistent C in every class, as though he could calculate exactly what to do and what not to do to force his teachers to give him that grade.

Rod's mother was the most sought-after volunteer in town. The boards of the largest non-profits, the symphony, the art museum, etc., begged her to join them. She was the president of the country club board for 15 years, and the first woman ever to be elected. The hatred between Rod and his socialite mother was founded in her virtual ignorance of him as a human being since the moment she could hand him off to day-care. He loved his father because, like many young men, he wanted to follow in his footsteps, if not as a lawyer, at least as a rich man of business. His father, too, barely acknowledged his existence until he was twelve, when they could play golf together. Immediately, they had a bond, mostly in sports—golf, tennis, sailing, and as sports spectators.

Upon graduation, with grades insufficient to enroll him into any institution above a community college, he lived at home and did precisely that, majoring in business. His father, a man of considerable perception, realized that Rod's distaste for school didn't matter—he would eventually succeed in whatever he attempted as a career.

Rod and Aimee started dating as high school juniors, with Rod's father laying down the law about sex, a law which they broke in their sophomore year in college, with the results we've seen. They had unprotected sex numerous times, Aimee naively believing they would marry, so what difference did it make?

The result of Rod's injury had the effect of actually increasing his sexual prowess and stamina, though he would have a slight limp for the rest of his life. Like water forced through a funnel, his sexual energy in bed was a subconscious compression of his libido, as opposed to an actual physical enhancement. Young women sensed this intensity, and for the next two years, Rod bedded a total of 26 women, most of them no more than two or three times. The want of any lasting relationships was due to the simple fact that Rod had nothing but contempt for women, and each one quickly came to understand that fact, especially the ones he yelled at, laughed at, or treated violently or vulgarly.

Edgar and Aimee were in her bed when Rod called.

"It's me," was all he said by way of hello.

"Yes?"

"We need to talk, Aimee."

His voice was cool, too cool to Aimee's ears.

"No way," she said, refusing to use his name.

"We have to. It's important," he insisted.

"I have someone else, so there's absolutely no point."

"I know all about your professor. Is he there right now?"

"Goodbye," was her answer. She hung up.

He called right back in a tone she well remembered, of suppressed fury.

"You will meet with me or I will beat the living shit out of your professor."

"He's eight inches taller than you," she said, unconvincingly.

"I've felled taller trees. Ha! And when I'm done with him, I'll slap you, I'll pull your hair, and punch you in the stomach, just like I did that one time."

It had been after a homecoming dance. Aimee said something complimentary to a guy on the football team, and when they got to the parking lot, he pummeled her.

"Give me the phone," interrupted Edgar, who could hear every word.

"I understand your dad is a pretty big gun back home, is that right?"

"Buddy, you just said the last thing you should have said, the very last," Rod shouted, "Later!"

He hung up.

Edgar and Aimee were understandably put on edge, but they didn't hear from Rod for two weeks. In the mail came an obituary of Rod's father, who had died of a heart attack three weeks before. On a sticky note was written: "See you soon."

A month later, Aimee received a letter on legal stationary informing her that Arnold Harten had left in his will a trust in her name providing $2,000 a month for the rest of her life, on one condition: she must provide Rodney Harten visitation rights of two days per month, which access was up to Rodney to avail himself of or not, and always with her not unreasonable agreement as to the time and place. This proviso would be in effect until the twins were 16 years of age. Failure to comply could result in the trust reverting to Rodney.

On a Saturday, ten days later, Edgar and Aimee were married in a civil ceremony attended only by the twins, beautiful girls now almost five, and two witnesses provided by the judge that married them. They moved into Edgar's house the following week.

Though neither could afford it, they made an appointment with a lawyer to find out what could be done. At the very least, they wanted an injunction filed against Rod, prohibiting him from approaching them within 1,000 yards on any day when he was not seeing his daughters. The lawyer said it wasn't possible, that no judge would accept anything but "all or nothing," and nothing wasn't possible because of visitation rights. He also pointed out that Rod had done nothing so far but make some threats over the phone, which was hardly legally sufficient.

"We'll give up the money," said Edgar on the drive home.

"You don't mean that," Aimee said, "You told me what you make and I've seen how hard you work just to make that."

Here began the first of many relatively mild arguments about what to do.

Two days later, they'd had enough. They were sitting exhausted at the kitchen table with a daughter in each lap.

"Maybe it's a bluff."

"What is?"

So new to fatherhood, Edgar was already obsessed with the twins. They had already agreed that he should adopt them at the earliest opportunity, and the attorney had been set to work on the legal work.

"Maybe if we don't agree to let him see the girls, he won't do anything. He doesn't need the money."

"You think he cares about the money? This is about revenge."

"Revenge for what?"

Aimee recoiled, realizing she'd never told him.

"I cut off one of his balls," she said without any emotion or gesture.

Then she told him the whole story.

"And you got away with it?"

"I was very thorough. He had no proof, and the police wouldn't prosecute me because his father wanted it dropped. I actually think he sided with me over it, because Rod had knocked me up. I can imagine the arguments he and Arnold must have had before and after I did it."

Edgar laughed.

"Stop it. It's not funny."

He stifled himself.

"Well, it is, actually. So that's what's behind all this," he said shaking his head as the truth of it all hit him. He looked at Aimee reassuringly. No, it didn't change anything between them.

"But I think you're right," Aimee said finally. "We should give up the money, and get the injunction. I'll just have to quit school and work full-time."

They looked at each other, just beginning to understand what this meant for their future.

"You don't suppose the mother would help, do you?"

Now it was Aimee laughing.

"You won't believe this, but I dated Rod for four years and I never met her. She wouldn't know me from you."

"But maybe she's as mad at him as your father was."

"It's possible. But I doubt she cares."

"We could write to her."

And so they did. A simple letter, offering to give up the trust to Rod if she would set one up herself for Aimee, without the visitation requirement.

A week later they received a remarkable letter: "Dear Aimee, I don't know you. We have never met even though you dated my son for several years. I'm sorry now that I didn't take time to make your acquaintance. I feel some real guilt and regret over that, and I ask you to accept my apology.

"I'm sure you've known from the beginning of your relationship with Rodney that he and I were never close. I will admit to you now that I just don't like him, not as a son, or as a person. He is brilliant, and a terrible waste of brilliance. He doesn't have an ounce of compassion or love in him. There is rot where his heart should be and brains ten times larger than he deserves. I never understood how he could have any girlfriend for as long as you two were involved. But, honestly, we never talked about it.

"Rodney left the house when his father died. The will left almost everything to Rodney, except the small trust set up in your name. I got the house, but Rodney even got the contents, which he's busy selling off. The house is in the process of being sold and I should be able to live comfortably on the proceeds, in much reduced circumstances. I have some small savings as well. As for your request, I have hardly the means now to support myself, let alone provide for you.

"Why my husband did this to me, I do not know. We weren't close, either, but it all came as a surprise. My husband tended to take sides. I guess that comes with being a lawyer. He sided with you over the pregnancy (yes, I knew about that, but only later), and he sided with Rodney against me. I was not a good mother, but I had a no-good son. That didn't seem to matter. What did matter was that my husband and I were estranged for the last 15 years of our lives, living the lie of a happy socialite couple when we didn't even sleep on the same floor of the house. (I'm sorry to be so blunt.)

"My advice to you is give up the money. It's not a fortune. My hope is you can cope without it. Nobody should have to cope with Rodney. I know I can't.

"I wish you and your new husband all the best."

Edgar and Aimee moped for another couple of days, waiting for Rod to call for his first visit.

Then Edgar had an idea.

"What if we assign the trust to Mrs. Hetner on the condition she assigns half of it back to us in a new trust?"

It seemed worth a try, but the Hetner estate's executor responded that the will stipulated that the trust could not be assigned, liquidated or otherwise transferred to anyone but Rodney himself.

Then came the call, except it wasn't at all what they expected.

"I'll make this short," Rodney growled. "Is hubby listening?"

She waved him over.

"Yes, he's listening."

"Good girl," said sarcastically. "That's a good one. Aimee as the good girl."

"Rodney, please? When?"

"Rodney? Rodney!" he laughed. "You never once called me that."

"Please, Rod. When?"

"No time soon, little bitch. You know, the worse thing about losing one of your balls is it itches all the time. Would you like to come over and scratch my remaining ball? Give you a chance to grab that one too."

"I didn't do that to you and you know it," Aimee said firmly.

"Yeah, you're right, this call is being recorded. Smart cookie."

"When, Rod?"

"Here's the deal," he said, calming down, all business. "I have no interest in dealing with the twins. Babies bore me. Besides, I'm going to Europe this month and I'll likely be gone a long time, maybe years."

After a pause, he said, "I heard that sigh. Don't be too relieved, dear lover of mine and mother of my children. I don't know how long I'll be gone. I don't know when I'll decide to exercise my visitation rights. It might be a month from now. It might be five years. It might be never. 'Why?' I'm not giving you time to ask? Because I want you to sweat. Sweat and suffer. You see I figure your fear of me is worse than my actually showing up, but be very, very sure, dear lover, that I shall."

"You prick," Aimee whispered.

"Yes, no thanks to you. I might have lost that too."

"What the hell are you talking about?"

"That's right, stick with the story. Oh, and by-the-way, my lawyer says the will wasn't all that iron-clad and given the, shall we call it, the otherwise long-term consequences to me of your preggies, I might have a good chance of getting my hands on your trust even if you follow its rules to the letter. Who knows, I might even get a prosecutor to re-open the case. My dear Daddy can't fuck with me on that anymore. I know it's a long shot, but rest assured—actually I hope you don't rest at all—I have the means to go after the trust and you, if the mood strikes me."

Edgar and Aimee were silent.

"So long for now," he said, "Oh, and for the record, this is no *Fatal Attraction* or *Pacific Heights* movie. I have no intention of hurting either you, your hubby, or my two daughters. Yes, I know you explored having an injunction filed against me. You can't imagine how much I know about you and your little Eddie and his fucking of little girls. You probably saved his career. At least for now. Let's hope you can keep him in line. Bye."

As she hung up, Aimee gave Edgar a sour look, but only because she didn't need a reminder of his sexual history—he'd divulged all that before they were married, making a particular point of stressing how it was she, Aimee, who had brought about the change in his behavior. She knew he was never going back.

KATERINA TUVOSKY

Rod soon revealed what he meant by "At least for now." After dinner six weeks later, the twins in bed, the Sages just beginning to relax, feeling that Rod wasn't going to bother them for a good long time, Katerina Tuvosky knocked on their door. She had been the last student he'd slept with before he'd met Aimee.

Katerina Tuvosky was almost as tall as Aimee, with black hair, blonde eyebrows, and a wicked shape-shifter of a smile. A theater major, she had played a credible Miss Julie, which Aimee and Edgar had admired. Now, they realized that she was clearly in the third trimester of a pregnancy.

"Can I come in?" she asked Edgar.

Quick calculations told him that it couldn't be his. He looked at Aimee and shook his head.

"Please, Kat, come in," he said.

"Katerina, please, professor," she corrected him curtly.

"Yes, of course," he responded softly, abashed.

He led her to the living room sofa and asked if he could get her anything. She immediately began crying, loudly and abjectly.

"I don't know what to do," she wailed. "I should have come to you when it wasn't too late. Now I have to go through with it. At the very least, you have to help me to live, professor. I can't go to my parents for money. They threw me out!"

"But, Katerina, it can't be mine," he explained. "That was a year ago!"

"Sorry, professor, but your math isn't so good. I have witnesses from my dormitory about when I told them."

"But it's not mine I tell you!"

Now he was crying and Aimee was clinging to his arm.

"I stopped doing that. You were the last, Katerina, and I'm so sorry."

"The last?

"There were no girls after you."

"What are you talking about?" she shouted.

It was Aimee who caught on first. She stood up and said, "Quiet, Edgar," then grabbed the young lady's tummy.

"Just as I thought."

She turned to Edgar and said, "Rod."

Katerina began laughing, then beat her tummy like a gorilla his chest.

"Damn, I almost got it," she said. "Rod wanted more. But I got close didn't I?"

She stood up and pulled a bulbous rubber "pregnancy" from under her blouse.

She held up the prosthesis and waggled it.

"I borrowed this from costume storage."

"Where's the tape machine?" Aimee demanded.

Katerina pulled a tiny cassette recorder from her purse.

"Give me the tape or I'll call the police."

"You wouldn't dare," she answered, but pulled the tape out and handed it over.

"Either way, I get the money," she said as Aimee ripped the ribbon out of the cassette. "It would have been more if I got asshole here to admit to trading grades for sex."

"I never did any such thing," Edgar shouted.

"Don't worry, darling, there's no second recorder. You can stop pretending."

"Get the hell out of here," shouted Aimee.

"Oh, Rod wanted me to tell you he is paying me $4,000 just to get this far," she said, adding, regretfully, "It would have been five if I'd gotten more of the goods. He just wanted you to get the idea. He's got plenty of dough, more than enough to pull gags like this any time he wants. And who knows what other chicks as stupid as I was with you, professor, he's been talking to."

"You fucked him too, I suppose," said Aimee.

"Yes, actually. And probably will again. He was great."

"You're lying."

Katarina just turned and sauntered out of the apartment, swinging the prosthesis, and laughing the whole way.

HOW IT ENDED

That would not be the last time they heard from Katarina. Almost six months later, Edgar got a call as he was leaving for home.

"It's me, Kat," she said, using her nickname with an edge of spite.

"Yes," said Edgar, feeling a vague nausea.

"You're going to receive a rather thick packet of papers in the mail tomorrow. You and Aimee need to do exactly as instructed, or else. Bye."

It's perhaps understandable that Edgar might choose not to say anything to Aimee until he knew what was going on. That made for a difficult night. The twins were cranky, as though they could tell something was wrong. Edgar went to bed early.

The package arrived as promised at the community college English department office.

He had just finished his class there for the day and ran out to the car to open it. The envelope, which was indeed thick, contained eighteen depositions and a letter. As he quickly flipped through them, he could tell they were not the work of a lawyer. There was no return address. Each "testimony" contained a third-person account of his, Edgar Sage's, seduction of a young woman, identified by initials only. In every case the young woman had received a good grade for services rendered. He had no trouble figuring out the actual names, and his technique having been nearly the same every time, he was assured of their authenticity simply by the small discrepancies from one to the next.

The letter said: "If you want to keep your shitty jobs, you'll convince your wife to assign the trust to me no later than 60 days from today. Otherwise, these documents will go where you don't want them to go."

A postscript explained that though the documents couldn't be traced, Rod also had signed, witnessed, and notarized versions ready to go.

Aimee arrived home from class at five while he was feeding the twins. The babysitter arrived at six to Aimee's surprise.

"I thought we deserved a break," he explained. "Let's go out for dinner."

"Sounds lovely," Aimee said with a sigh of exhaustion.

Once they were settled in at Ruby Tuesday's (the upper limit of what they could afford), and had ordered dinner, Edgar began by saying, "We have him."

"Rod?" Aimee said, knowing there could be no other "him" in their lives right now."

He nodded, smiling widely, almost beside himself with excitement. "What?"

"I didn't bring it with me, because it would just upset you, but he's got written documents from 18 of my former students. He says if we don't reassign your trust to him in two months, he'll turn the documents over to the schools."

"But that's terrible!"

"No, Aimee, it's great! He's blackmailing us. He's breaking the law."

"Are the documents real?"

"Yeah, real enough," he admitted, collapsing in his chair. Then he rallied and sat up straight.

"But blackmail is blackmail!"

They made an appointment with their lawyer for late that week, but it was canceled, so it was another ten sleepless and anxious days before, in his office, the lawyer said, "Not so fast."

"What do you mean? It *is* blackmail, isn't it?"

"Yes, but this stack of paper doesn't prove anything. He's very cagey, this one," said the lawyer. "Yes, he could probably cause you a lot of trouble with these, but it's all untraceable, and these initials mean nothing."

The lawyer let this sink in.

"To call his bluff by going to the police, we'd have to assume that we can accurately decipher the initials and that each young woman would fess up that it's her 'testimony.'"

Edgar stood up and started pacing the room, clenching his hands high, low, behind his back.

"Don't count out that he's probably bought these girls."

At that moment, Edgar looked to Aimee so vulnerable and weak that she wondered, not for the first time, if she really did love him.

Edgar sat down and stared off into space, trembling.

"My advice?" said the lawyer.

"Yes?" said Aimee.

"Give him the money. Let me handle it. I'll get him to turn over the original documents and sign a release. Then you can get your injunction against him if he bothers you anymore."

"And would that end it?" asked Aimee.

"Well, who knows? You can sue anyone for anything. If he thinks he's got anything else on you, he could bring that up any time down the road. One thing's certain, you need to take perfect care of those kids and make sure you can trust the babysitter."

"He wouldn't dare. You really think he might…?"

In her terror, she was trying her best not to look at Edgar, because she didn't expect to find any comfort there.

"I have no idea. He's clearly not doing this for the money."

"No, probably not," Aimee said, totally defeated.

As they drove home, Edgar pulled into a library parking lot.

"This has to stop now, Aimee."

"But how?" she cried out.

"We get a divorce, as soon as possible. I'm done."

"No!"

Edgar started to get out of the car.

"I didn't sleep with all those girls!" she cried.

"And I didn't cut off his testicle," he replied and started to walk home, which was only a mile away.

When he saw that she had passed him, he stopped and looked around. He saw the black Mercedes parked around the corner. He got in.

"It's done."

"Are you sure?"

"Yes, I think so. She's already softened up. When I threaten to go to the police about the nail—oh, because I can't stand the guilt any longer," and he wiped away a crocodile tear, "she'll cave."

They both laughed.

"Perfect."

"I'll lay low until the divorce comes through, which the lawyer told me that, under the circumstances, shouldn't take but a month or two."

"Sounds like he played his role well too."

"Perfect."

Rod handed him an envelope. Edgar peeked inside at the stack of hundred-dollar bills.

"You'll get the third and last installment after the divorce is final."

"And the trust?"

"You'll have to trust me on that, so to speak," Rod said, chuckling, "but you'll get it. She has to cooperate first."

"I don't think she'll fight it."

"I think I'll send her $100 now and then, just for fun. Let her know she's not rid of me completely."

They sat silently for a moment.

"You drove a hard bargain the other day," said Rod.

"Sympathy for revenge has its limits."

"What now?'

"With a hundred K? I haven't a clue."

"Teaching?"

Edgar laughed. "I don't think so."

"Yeah, there're a lot easier ways to get laid."

Another long pause.

"How many?" asked Edgar.

"I thought you'd ask. Twelve of 'em. You have good taste."

"Not bad. But then again they all got paid, right?"

"True. But some of them come back for more."

"You're a real nice person, you know that?"

"You too, man. You too."

And they shook on it.

BRACES

I FIRST saw Joanne "Jo" Villery in a lunch line the first day of class in fourth grade at Broadmeadow Elementary School in Champagne-Urbana. I noticed that someone a few kids ahead of me was wearing a leg brace. I was too.

Once I had my tray filled, I left the kitchen and found her sitting by herself beneath a huge mosaic that boasted images of 20th Century scientific accomplishments. Dead center was a huge $E = mc^2$.

I approached her and didn't ask if I could join her because she was so intently staring at the mosaic. I put my tray down across from her and said, "Hi."

"I'm busy," she said, curtly.

"That's okay. I'm hungry."

Somehow this got a laugh out of her. She had a bright, trilling giggle, which went well with her blue eyes and tiny, straight teeth. She was cute; her features were regular, but animated, a little pale. She wore a simple blue dress, but she had an unfortunate haircut, as though someone went at her locks with a knife. "I'll leave if you want me to."

"I'm sorry. I was rude. Stay where you are. Just don't take it personally if I don't pay much attention to you. I'm just fascinated by that," she said, pointing at the mosaic.

"Are you interested in science?"

Ignoring my question, she said, "You have a brace too. Polio?"

"No, *legge perthes.*"

She smiled for a moment and said, "I almost said, 'Really! Me too!' as though it was the funniest coincidence. I can be a real dope sometimes."

"It would have seemed normal enough to me," I said, squirming to get comfortable.

"It's a new one, isn't it?"

"How did you guess?"

"You're not used to it yet. But being able to bend your knee when you sit now is such a relief."

"How much longer do you have?" I asked, meaning how long until the brace comes off.

"At least another year. How about you?"

"My dad's a doctor, and he says maybe six months."

"Well, we both have something great to look forward to."

Though I had hardly taken a bite, she stood up and picked up her tray. She told me her name and I told her mine, Arnold Davidson. She reacted with slight surprise hearing the name, but she didn't say anything at the time.

"It was nice meeting you."

"It was nice meeting you."

"There must be an echo in here," she said, laughing, as she limped away.

Because *legge perthes,* or at least the brace that helped to cure it back in the '60s, plays a significant role in this story, I should explain. The disease, which was confined to children who were breech births (hence its rarity today, breech births being now a rarity), causes a loss of blood to the hip bone, which makes it soften. There's no actual cure, except time. It tends to strike when children are between four and six, and can last for two or three years, and can even switch from one leg to the other, as it did to me. The leg brace was designed to take weight off the hip, to give the bone a chance to heal without being misshapen. Thirteen pounds of steel and leather, it transferred the body's weight above the hip. This was accomplished by a boot with two sliding tubes around two steel rods welded into a "heel" two inches below the foot. Metal armatures connected to the rods went up the leg to a leather-encased ring above the hip. On the other foot was the same boot, built up with two inches of rubber.

If the idea of wearing such a contraption for four years, as I did, sounds extremely unpleasant, and painful, you're right. The only improvement they ever made to the brace was a "joint" at the knee guarded by a metal ring. When seated, I could pull up the ring and free the joint so my leg would bend. The trick to the design was that the minute I stood up the ring automatically fell into place again, locking the brace straight. This joint was what Jo was referring to as "new."

We didn't see a lot of each other that year, being in different classes. At recess, the girls kept to themselves. No boys allowed. Which left me in the familiar position of either being by myself or joining the other boys and taking the risk of being bullied, as I often was.

One day in early October, a game of kick ball was underway, and one of the worst of the bullies, Albert Furnett, asked me if I'd like to play catcher behind home plate. He said, "Since you can't kick or run fast enough for the outfield." He seemed genuinely happy when I accepted. What a dope I was. As a catcher, there was little to do because few let a ball go by unkicked. First time up, Albert hit a long line drive that bounced and bounced deep into the out-field, and he was coming into home plate when the ball reached me. I caught it and reached out with it to touch him. Being a head taller, he ran right over me, and I dropped the ball. He was called safe. Before I could get up, he stood over me and said, "I know why you wear that thing. It's because your father beats you. Beats you every day, doesn't he?"

I struggled to my feet and, knowing better, I slugged him in the stomach as hard as I could. He stumbled backwards but kept his footing. I'm sure he hardly felt it. Then he charged forward with his fists raised only to find Jo standing in his way. As he came up short, she swung her braced leg and caught him just below the kneecap with her rubber-elevated boot. Lucky for Albert, his weight was on the other leg, so his struck leg only slid out from beneath him and he went down on his side instead of on his knees.

Please don't think of this violence as something out of a martial arts movie. No, she didn't pivot and hit him in the groin or the head. In fact, what she'd done terrified her and she ran away—just like ole Chester in *Gunsmoke*—with two hops for each step.

Albert was so shocked, he just stood up and walked away, nothing hurt but his dignity.

Then a funny thing happened. Albert stopped bullying me, and the others, who hadn't been that bad, toned it down as well. I tried to figure this out. Were they impressed because I had stood up to Albert and punched him? Did they have some new-found respect for me for having a friend, even a girl, stand up for me? Or did they, finally, just take some pity on me and decide to leave me alone?

No, it was all a ruse. I shouldn't have been thinking just about myself.

Jo wouldn't come near me and turned and walked away when I tried to thank her. I decided it was best to leave her alone.

It was a week later that Albert trapped her behind a long silver climbing wedge in the playground after recess was over. I saw only their feet under the wedge, but I'd seen Albert tugging on Jo.

I felt totally helpless, and I knew that Albert wouldn't let her surprise him with a kick. I didn't have a chance against Albert, but, nonetheless, I hid around the corner of the gym and quickly took off my brace. I was so used to doing it that it only took a moment to undo the laces on the brace boot and the leather padding around my thigh.

Just because I wore a brace, I was not crippled. I could walk and run as well as anyone—the brace being a matter of a long-term cure. Not having time to take off the other boot, I picked up the brace by the ring and ran behind the wedge, where Albert had Jo pinned by both arms and was whispering and chuckling and shaking her. To this day I don't believe he meant to hurt her. He was clearly trying to frighten her, though, so I didn't pause. I held the brace up high by the ring; the joint lock came down and the brace bent so that when I swung it the leverage of the boot swinging on the joint increased its speed, and it hit Albert just below his right ear and knocked him down. In fact, it knocked him out.

I said to Jo, "Go back to class. Act like nothing happened."

She looked at me in horror and then, without a smile or otherwise touching me, she kissed my cheek and left as fast as she could go.

I went back around the gym and quickly put the brace back on. I realized that one thing I had in my favor was that Albert hadn't seen me coming. He couldn't know for sure what hit him.

That night a terrible thing happened, something that I had never experienced before. The parents of a fifth-grade student in another class—someone I knew pretty well and liked—were killed in a blazing car crash with a freight train. We were all so shaken that nobody said a word the entire day, not even whispers. The next morning our teachers told us the boy was taken away to live with his grandparents, and we shouldn't expect to see him again. Slowly over the next few days, things returned to normal. Later, we'd learn the father was drunk. There was even a rumor that he'd been beheaded.

Partly because of the diversion of this tragedy, what happened to Albert was never mentioned. He had a large red welt below his right ear for a few days, but I didn't appear to have seriously hurt him, let alone permanently. When he passed me in the halls or on the playground he frowned with his usual disdain, but gave no indication he knew that I had felled him.

My surprise at having gotten away with hitting Albert was equal to my disappointment with Jo. She wouldn't talk to me, would turn away if I tried to sit down next to her at lunch, and wouldn't even look at me when we passed each other.

That November, as we were sitting in class, the principal made an intercom announcement that President Kennedy had been shot and was believed dead. As I stared off into space trying to absorb those words, many of my classmates began to cry. My teacher tried to comfort us with the usual words, and the principal came back on and said that school was being let out early, that we were to wait in the halls or outside for the buses to arrive.

I found Jo close to the front door crying uncontrollably. I whispered, "Jo? Are you okay?"

She hugged me and I hugged her back until her body stopped shaking. Then she let go and turned away, leaving me there without a word.

I wish I could show you the difference between her class yearbook photos for fourth grade and sixth grade. As I've described, when I first met her, her hair was chopped short. In the yearbook, she looks plain, though hardly homely. Not a photo you'd stop to ponder. A different person altogether appears in the sixth-grade yearbook. She'd become a twelve-year-old beauty, with pronounced high cheekbones, an impish smile, and lovely long dark curls that she tucked behind her little ears. I fell in love with that picture, even though we had hardly spoken in two-and-a-half years.

To be honest, for those years I virtually forgot about her. My brace came off the summer before fifth grade, and my life was transformed. I was no long the "little cripple" whose father beat him. I lost all shyness and reserve and without being obnoxious became something of a cut-up, a firecracker. I discovered I had a sense of humor, and boys and girls alike liked me. I was invited to parties and made the softball team. Teachers called on me when no one else put up their hand, and more often than not I knew the answer. We had a talent contest, and my improvised imitation of a drunken Red Skelton won the top prize. I got straight As, and our chorus teacher auditioned and selected me and my friend Tom as Angels, as sopranos for the Christmas pageant.

The only time Jo and I spoke was when I noticed her brace was gone. I went out of my way to congratulate her. This was a few days after the pageant. She congratulated me, as well, then said, before turning away, "You were great in the pageant. You sing like an angel."

At that moment, I wanted so much to talk to her, but I realized her distant behavior toward me hadn't changed.

The opportunity didn't arrive until the last day of our sixth-grade year. The yearbook provided the opportunity. I searched her out and asked her to sign mine. She blushed. I handed her a pen, which made it harder for her to say no.

She wrote: "I'll never forget what you did for me, even if I'm still scared of you."

I looked at her and for the first time noticed that her blue eyes had silver highlights. I asked for her yearbook. I wrote: "You can't be scared of someone who likes you so much." I handed it back and walked away quickly, blushing, before she had a chance to say a word.

One of the prescribed therapies for former *legge perthes* patients is swimming—and as much as possible—to strengthen the legs and the muscles around the hip joint without putting weight on it.

My father wanted me to take a swimming class and signed me up for almost the entire summer. Jo too was signed up by her parents.

Please remember that Jo and I were only twelve years old, and the notion of sexual interest in each other was nonexistent. That didn't mean that we couldn't look at each other in our swimsuits for the first time with curiosity and appreciation, however platonic. In her one-piece yellow and purple striped suit, her body was no longer boyish yet hardly womanly. Certain curves above and below were beginning to show. The only regret I had was the yellow bathing cap she had to wear over her lovely curls. She was every bit as pretty as her picture.

She was also a good two inches taller than I, which initially made me feel a little sheepish. But I had good upper body strength, and I wasn't ugly, though my teeth were a bit crooked and my dad made the barber cut my hair too short.

Another difference between us was that I had a slight limp that I would have all my life. Jo had no limp at all. Medical personnel had discovered too late that the disease had switched to my left hip, so that when the brace came off the ball in my hip joint was slightly misshapen.

For the first week of the class, we didn't actually avoid each other, though we didn't talk either. I would catch her looking at me and vice versa. She was a strong swimmer. The instructor put us in the same race, and she beat me, but it made her suspicious; the first time we spoke, she said, "You let me win, didn't you?"

"No, honestly. You beat me fair and square."

Instead of walking off, as usual, she invited me to bring my blanket over and sit down next to her. She started a discussion about our braces and what it was like to have them off. Our experiences of liberation and the changes it made in everything made for a lively conversation; hers were not that different from mine, as I have described them.

"Can I ask you a question?" she asked hesitantly.

"Sure?"

"I understand your limp. I was lucky that way. But I wondered about how tall you are. The doctor said my brace probably cost me at least an inch in height, which I'll never get back, even though I'll continue to grow."

"My doctor said almost the same thing. He thinks it could have been at least two inches. And I won't get them back either."

She laughed to throw off the slight sadness she might have heard in my voice.

"Well, you're still likely to be a lot taller than me. Your father must be over six feet tall!"

"When did you see my father?"

"He was my doctor on another matter."

"When was that?"

She stood up, clearly regretting she'd mentioned it.

"Oh, it was a while ago. We don't need to talk about it."

She started to walk away, then changed her mind and sat down again. We didn't speak for a while. She broke the awkward silence and said, "Please don't tell him we talked about him. Okay?"

"Sure."

Though he never talked about it at home, my dad was a cancer specialist.

That night I went against Jo's wishes and told my Dad I'd made a new friend. I said her name.

"You've mentioned her before, son," he said without looking up from the book he was reading. "She wore a brace just like you."

"That's her."

I waited for him to say something else. He frowned, seeming to concentrate even more on his book, though I was still standing there. He was a smart man. He put the book down and said, "She told you I was her doctor."

"Yes, just today."

"And?"

"Does she have cancer?"

"I can't tell you anything. It's private."

"Just tell me she's okay."

"Do you remember a few years ago when you mentioned that she had rather scraggly hair?"

"Yes, she did. It's beautiful now."

"Well, back then it was a wig. Okay? That's all I can say, and you can never tell her I told you."

"I understand," I said, hardly relieved.

"I'm glad you're friends," he said. "I like her very much. She has a lot of courage."

"Thanks, Dad," I said and started for the TV room. Then I turned around and said, "You're right about her courage. She once knocked down a bigger guy who was bullying me."

"How the heck did she do that?" he asked.

"She kicked him."

He chuckled slightly, genuinely pleased. I think he felt he'd already said too much, so he kept on silently with his book. I wanted to tell him how I'd saved her from the same bully, but he would not have been pleased to know I'd taken may brace off to use as a weapon.

My friendship with Jo strengthened through the summer, and we began to invite each other to our homes, with our mothers (never my father) driving us back and forth. We'd sit on my front steps and play Crazy Eights or checkers for hours. She had a small pool table in her basement, and we played eight ball and drank lemonade.

In one regard, it was an odd friendship. We didn't talk much. It didn't feel like we needed to. The usual subjects never came up. We didn't gossip, and movies and TV shows were only lightly touched upon, though we had similar tastes. The Beatles, though, who had been around for almost two years, was one mutual enthusiasm we talked about a lot, and we played their records all the time, often just sitting on the floor and listening without saying a word until the record needed to be flipped over. When *Beatles '65* came out, we tossed a coin to see who would buy it, since there was no need for both of us to own it. She was disappointed when I won, so I let her buy it anyway. I think we both saw the implications of this joint ownership. Going to see the movie *Help* was probably the closest thing we had to a first date, with her father taking us to and from the theater.

When September came and it was time to return to school, my father refused to let me go to the public junior high school. He was adamant that I attend a lab school on the university campus where he taught oncology, in addition to his regular practice. Nothing I could say would convince him otherwise. He felt that getting a free lab school education would set me up for life and open many doors in the future. When I mentioned Jo, he simply said, "That's not a good enough reason. For heaven's sake, you're only twelve years old!"

When I told Jo, she said, "That's okay. Don't worry about it."

But it soon became apparent that things had changed. When I'd call to see if she wanted to get together that Saturday, she often had some reason why she couldn't. And our moms were much less willing to drive us around, to the point that I suspected they had talked to each other and were deliberately keeping us apart.

I had a birthday party at a bowling alley in October, and it was the first time I'd seen Jo in six weeks. She gave me a new copy of *Beatles '65* and left before the party was over. When I got home I left the album unopened in my record rack.

We lost touch after that.

It was Thanksgiving vacation of my sophomore year at the same university where my father taught. I was majoring in English after a half-hearted attempt at pursuing a pre-med degree. I wasn't only daunted at the prospect of up to ten years of classwork and residency, but the coursework itself was intimidating and simply over my head. I've got a reasonable IQ, but my memory for certain things is sorely inadequate, especially when it comes to mastering complicated minutiae. I couldn't memorize poems either, but it wasn't really required in English Lit. I was a good scholar and writer, and I loved reading. When I declared for English at the beginning of my sophomore year, my father wasn't pleased, but he let the matter drop when, during an argument after Thanksgiving dinner, I told him I'd sooner quit college altogether than be a doctor.

In the middle of the argument, as an aside, he said, "Did you know that your childhood friend Jo is studying medicine here? If she can handle it with her, well...."

He interrupted himself and went on with his harangue.

The next day, after tempers had cooled, I asked him about Jo. I hadn't thought of her in quite a while and I wondered how she was doing.

"I shouldn't have mentioned it," he said and tried to change the subject to the football game we were watching.

"Why not, Dad? I didn't even know she was enrolled here." He didn't answer for awhile, then, when a commercial came on, he said, "On second thought, you should see her. It would be good for her. I think she's pretty lonely."

"What do you mean?"

"I'll let her tell you."

"Are you one of her teachers?"

"No," he said emphatically, "I just know…like I said, I'll let her tell you."

"How do I reach her?"

He told me she had a class (I can't remember what) that was over at three on Tuesdays and Thursdays. I knew the building.

"How come I never ran into her last year?"

He started to get irritated again.

"How would I know?" he grumbled.

I almost asked him about her cancer, but I knew I was pushing my luck. I let it go.

The next Tuesday I waited outside Faegre Hall for almost 15 minutes after the class would have been over and was about to leave when she walked through the door. She smiled, but the way she looked frightened me.

"I thought you might be here today," she said. "Your Dad mentioned it."

The beautiful sixth grader I knew had vanished. Jo was hardly any taller than she had been then, no more than five feet tall. Her hair was darker and uncombed. My first thought was that it was a wig, but I dismissed that immediately. Her entire person was uncared-for, as though she never looked in a mirror. She wore no makeup, which gave her a light-brown pallor and accentuated mild acne around her snub nose. Her jeans were frayed at the bottom and held up with a white leather strip and a plastic buckle. She wore a long-sleeve university t-shirt and hoodie that were clean but stained. But none of this was as shocking as how she walked. She grabbed the steel rail on the stairs and took one step at a time.

"Let's talk over there," she said, pointing at a wooden bench a few yards away.

I wanted to grab her arm and help her, but I hesitated. She was certainly capable of walking, but it was as if she had a double limp. Each step forward was halting and unsteady and caused each hip to dip more than normal. She was so unsteady, I wondered why she wasn't using crutches. But we reached the bench safely and she sat and patted the wood right next to her.

"Sit here," she said, "I want a good look at you."

She looked me over and smiled and, I felt, had the graciousness not to be complimentary, because that might force me to respond to how she looked. And the more I looked, I could see vestiges of the pretty girl I'd known—she was simply buried under a lack of attention to appearances of any kind. In other words, with a minor makeover, she'd be quite attractive.

Her body was another matter. She was very thin, entirely boyish in shape, as though the nascent curves I'd peeked at during swim class had been flattened out somehow.

She seemed to be waiting for me to speak first, so I said, "It's wonderful to see you again, Jo. I didn't even know you were here until my father mentioned it."

"Yes, he told me he had."

"How come we never crossed paths?"

"I dunno," she said, "I keep to myself."

Then she looked at me as if something troubled her.

"I did see *you* a couple of times."

"Oh."

"Sorry."

"No need," I said and changed the subject.

"Can we get this out of the way, Jo? I mean, about my Dad?"

"How much has he told you?"

"Hardly anything. The only thing he said, years ago, was that you were wearing a wig back in elementary school. He refused to say any more. And you'll remember you told me he was your doctor."

"Yes, and he still is."

"But, he's an oncologist. You're not...."

She put her hand on my knee by way of interruption.

"No. I'm not. But he keeps a close eye on me."

"Can you tell me now?"

"I don't see why not."

She looked away, and squinted as if reassuring herself that it was okay. Her expression said there was nothing to lose if she did.

"In third grade I had internal cancer. They had to remove my, uh, my lady parts."

I took her hand.

"But it worked. That and the chemo."

"And that's it, right?" I said, urging her on with my own hopes.

"It was until seventh grade. Your Dad and my orthopedic doctor discovered that the cancer, or more likely the chemo, had affected my bad hip. Remember how I didn't limp. Well, I started to, and when they looked at it, they realized that my hip joint was deformed after all. In fact, it had weakened so much the bone was in danger of breaking."

She had been looking ahead up to now, when she looked me in the eyes.

"That's why we didn't see each other after you went to junior high here. I didn't want you to know. I don't want to go into all of it, but let's just say that what they had to do to save both of my hips caused me to stop growing and left my legs weak. And that hasn't changed, even after five years of therapy."

"You get around just fine," I lied.

"Right. I'm the only person on campus who can run the one-hour mile!"

She genuinely wanted me to laugh, and I obliged.

"What's my dad afraid of?"

"What isn't he afraid of? You need to understand that I'm very fond of your dad. I feel like he's mine too. He genuinely cares for me, even to the point of pulling strings to get me into pre-med. They didn't want a 'cripple,' but he convinced them I was fine. Which, as you can see, is a bit of an exaggeration."

To this day, I regret what I next said, even though she hadn't seemed to be hurt by it.

"Dad said you were lonely," I blurted out.

She frowned, and I could see she was about to cry.

"I'm sorry," I said quickly, "I shouldn't...."

She took a deep breath to keep from actually crying.

"Do you remember what it was like when we had our braces off? We talked about what that was like when we both were free of the damned things. How it changed everything?"

"Yes."

"But, before that, it was very isolating. Well, I'm back in that same place. Nobody bullies me like they used to, of course. But I've discovered two things about what I've been through. First, people are scared of people who had cancer. They never say it, but then they never say anything. And they're even more scared of people who, like me, can't hide it."

"But how would they know?"

"Because I tell them. I don't want false sympathy. I'll take being lonely now and then over that."

"Well, it doesn't scare me and I'd like to see you as often as I can."

She leaned and kissed me on the cheek; then she stood up. I stood up too.

"No, you wait here. I think I need to be alone right now. I need to think."

"Can I call you?"

She wouldn't give me the name of her dorm, but I told her mine and told her to call me any time. Then I watched her double-limp away, and it was hard for me not to cry as well.

That weekend I decided to call my dad and ask him to tell Jo I would genuinely like to be her friend again. I didn't have to. She called me late that morning and we arranged to meet at the library lounge that afternoon.

She was already there when I arrived. I was greatly relieved, mostly for her sake, to see that she'd spruced herself up. Her hair was combed and pulled back in a ponytail, which suited her. She had touched up her cheeks and her lips were slightly glossy. Most remarkably, she wore a pretty white blouse, a blue cardigan, and a knee-length blue skirt that matched her eyes. I had seen enough in our first meeting to know she hadn't "dressed up" for me as much as to prove that she was what she was. There was little for her blouse to hide, and her legs were almost fleshless. She was saying, "Here I am. This is me at my best. Now you know."

As I sat on the couch beside her, which faced a large window looking out on the campus arboretum, I said, "You look great, Jo."

"That's nice of you to say. I'm sure the contrast with the other day is a bit of a surprise. When I'm in a mood I don't care what I look like."

"That's sort of what I figured. And, after all, you must be buried in class work."

"It's grueling, but I love it."

"Do you know what you want to do?"

"Ha! My teachers tell me not to even think about it. I've far too much to learn to know what kind of doctor I want to be, but I know it will have to do with children, somehow."

"That makes sense to me."

The reader can imagine what we talked about by way of catching up, but there's no reason not to leap to what Jo really wanted that day. That I must make a short narrative of it is simply a matter of delicacy, and not because what we did was in any way strange. I still had a crush on Jo, even though I had dated my share during high school and college, and sometimes had intimate relations. Apparently, she felt the same about me. It was natural then that, after we'd chatted for more than an hour, she asked me back to her dorm room.

"Funny," I said, "I was going to ask you the same thing."

"Please tell me you really mean that."

"Don't be silly, Jo. Of course, I do," I said, taking her hand and helping her up. "I might have waited until our second date," I added, "just to be sure you would say yes."

She giggled and said, "When we're alone, I'll explain why I didn't want to wait."

When we were both naked under her covers holding each other close she explained that she was a virgin, not because she hadn't been asked, but because she didn't feel anything for the boys that asked. Any vague apprehension that I was acting improperly immediately vanished.

Making love with Jo wasn't much different than with any other girl I'd known. Understandably, she preferred having me under her. She was astonishingly light, which I found arousing; her kisses even more so. The only awkwardness occurred when I mentioned protection.

"Nothing to worry about there," she whispered and buried her face in my neck.

"Yes. Oh!" I said. "I'm such an idiot."

"It was a very courteous question. Don't give it another thought."

The kissing continued.

She might have been a virgin, but she didn't betray a second's hesitancy and she came at least twice before I did. When it was over, and she had rolled off me and snuggled under my arm, I asked,

"Was that okay?"

"Oh, my."

Her flat tummy contracted as though squelching a laugh.

Then, as if startled, she raised herself on her elbow and looked me in the eyes.

"For you?" she said, as if alarmed it might not have been.

I hugged her and said, truthfully, "I wasn't a virgin, as you might have guessed, but that was the loveliest…."

She snuggled again and was asleep in moments. I fell asleep soon after. She was gone when I awoke. I chuckled, thinking it slightly absurd; this was her bed, not mine. Where could she be?

As I've suggested, Jo was disposed to be surprising, not to thwart expectations, but almost like a writer cuts a scene short to allow for conjecture before moving on to the next scene.

But I didn't believe she was being deliberately mysterious or even less that she was trying to send me a message. I dressed and went home and called her the next afternoon.

"I can't tell you how much studying I had to do last night. I didn't want to wake you, so I slipped off to the library. I closed the place down!"

That became the pattern of our behavior for the next six months. We'd meet at either her dorm room or mine and make love, always in the afternoon. Once in a while, we'd grab a quick bite, but by six o'clock she was studying, either in her dorm or at the library.

I had my own work to do of course. I was almost as buried as she was. That second semester, my teachers loaded me up with American fiction, Shakespeare, the poetry of the Romantics, and Homer; if I didn't read 100 pages a day I'd be hopelessly behind in a week; and that didn't count 20-page papers and prep for tests.

Every other Saturday or so we'd grant ourselves the luxury of a dinner in town and sleeping over. In the morning we'd take a walk after breakfast, before returning to our studies. During those walks, for the first time, I noticed the couples wandering about the campus and realized, from their expressions and the way they held hands, and in particular the aimlessness of the paths they took, that they too had spent the night before in bed.

I once said, pointing, "Look at them, Jo. Do you think they are as much in love as we are?"

When she didn't answer, I said, "Jo?"

She turned, seeming confused, as though she hadn't heard me, and said, "I'm sorry, I was thinking about my...."

"What?"

"Sorry, I'm a dope. With as little time as we have together, I shouldn't be worrying about my studies."

We stopped and kissed with ardor, smiling as we kissed.

This happened about three weeks before the end of the semester, summer being something we didn't need to worry about, since we'd both decided to stay on campus and take classes year-round. Or, more accurately, though I hadn't originally planned it, I chose to because I didn't want to be across town from Jo, stuck in my parents' home.

This decision led to a conversation with my Dad that changed everything. He knew we were in a "relationship" and, until now, he had more than once offered his approval, for both our sakes.

Before the end of the semester, he took, for him, the elaborate step of taking me to a pizza joint for dinner. He even managed to slip me a glass of wine, though I was under age.

When we were done with the main course, he asked me a few perfunctory questions about how things were going. Then he got very serious.

"Son, it's time I talked to you about Jo. You need to know things that she only suspects and that you must never tell her yourself."

Already petrified, I didn't say anything; he continued uninterrupted.

"I know you know that she can never have children, so let's get that out of the way. That's not what I need to tell you. Jo will never be a doctor. As much as she wants to be, as hard as she studies, and no matter how good her grades are, it isn't physically possible for her to be a doctor. I know you're thinking, then why did I help her get into pre-med? The answer is I had no choice. As tough as she is, this is her greatest weakness, her inability to imagine what it would actually take, physically, to go through a residency, let alone be able to practice day after day. I had to help her with that dream, while it still seems remotely possible. The likeliest scenario for Jo is that she'll be in a wheelchair in another five years. You may have wondered why she hasn't had her hips replaced. The answer is very technical, but let's just say you can't mend a bent wheel. Replacements might actually kill her, which leads me to my main point. Her life expectancy, even if she remains cancer free forever—and that's a big question—is maybe 40."

"Dad," I said, finally, "None of this matters. We'll get through it."

"Let me finish. The problem isn't you. I know you. I know what you've been through. You're a tough guy, and I mean that as one of the nicest compliments I ever gave anyone. In fact, I absolutely admire you—the way you coped with those damned braces. Do you remember what you said—you were only six—when I had to tell you that you'd need a brace on your other leg?"

I couldn't and said nothing.

"You said, 'Dad, please get it built as soon as you can.'"

"Yes, I guess I do remember that."

"The problem will eventually be Jo. I know her, probably better than you do. At least as well. I think she's already beginning to feel like you are sacrificing yourself for her."

"She said that?"

"Not in so many words. You know that I see her several times a year and we talk. She hasn't said anything about you that you wouldn't love hearing. She's so *grateful*," he added with an intensity I hadn't often seen. "But I'm not blind. Maybe not this year, or the next, but certainly something will happen once she learns—and this is what you can never tell her—that her chances of getting into med school are little to none. She may even get into med school, but she won't survive it. She's simply not strong enough."

I leaned forward as if to speak, but he went on.

"Yes, she could do something else, especially if she takes care of herself, which she's only barely doing now. She's probably told you that her therapy hasn't accomplished much." I only nodded.

"It's not because she hasn't really worked at it. The best I can say about her therapy is that it keeps her from getting worse, and that's all."

"This is all stuff we can get through, Dad. I don't get your point."

"You need to prepare yourself for the moment when she tells you she doesn't love you anymore. It's going to happen, son. She's not going to let you tie your fortunes, your considerable future, to hers. She loves you too much to do that."

"Has she said anything like that? I can't believe she has."

"No. As I said, I understand her. The minute that she believes you are no longer equals, physically and emotionally, she will break it off. For your sake. For your sake, she'll sacrifice herself so that you won't have to sacrifice yourself for her."

"But I'm not sacrificing anything!"

The last thing he said was, "If that proves to be true, if you both come to believe it, it will be a miracle."

It all happened much sooner than my father predicted. When the semester was over, with all our school work done, and summer classes not starting for two weeks, we were lying in bed. Her face was buried in my neck, one of her favorite things.

"Sweetheart, I have some good news, only you're not going to like it."

I sat up, but she held on to me, refusing to look at me.

"I've decided not to stay for the summer. I'm going to stay with my parents in Chicago." (They had moved there two years before, her father following a promotion.) "I need a rest. I can read and get ahead of my studies this fall. And there's a therapy group there that uses a special technique called *myofacial release* that your father thinks might be good for me."

"My Dad told you to go?"

"What a question! He didn't know a thing about it until I told him. Then he recommended this therapy."

What could I say, except, "But I won't see you."

"I'm afraid not," she said, stroking my arm, "I mean you can come to Chicago, but we won't be able to do this. *Obviously.*"

I didn't like the way she said the word—it was too pointed, too unsympathetic.

"Are you sure, Jo? I could make things easier for you here. I could get things for you, help you get around."

"What do you mean?" she said, slightly angry.

"I could go…or if you wanted not to walk, I could…."

"Stop right there, Arnold. I'm just fine. Understand? I want to go home for the summer, that's all. I want to see my parents. I want to relax. I want to study. Get ready for the fall. I can't do all those things here, now can I?"

Again, that slightly unsympathetic tone. Her body had grown tense, unyielding.

"When did you decide all this? I mean, I wish I'd known. I might not have stayed here for the summer either."

"It's not too late to cancel your classes. I canceled mine a week ago."

"A week?"

"See? This is why I didn't mention it till now. I knew you'd get upset."

Remembering my father's warning, I didn't dare risk giving her a reason to hurt me. I told her that maybe it was a good idea, and that I would cancel my classes. I didn't want to graduate ahead of her, and I could earn some extra money over the summer. When I told her this, she palpably relaxed, but I could tell she was upset, though not with me.

Though it wasn't in the same words, that was how Jo told me that she didn't love me anymore.

I would offer to drive up a couple of times, but she always had some excuse against it. We talked on the phone, especially when she didn't come back that fall, but I haven't seen her since. At first, she told me that she'd met someone, which I didn't believe. After a little probing, she confessed that it wasn't true. With little enthusiasm, she said she'd decided to transfer to Loyola's nursing program.

I asked my dad if he knew anything; he said that the doctor he'd sent her to in Chicago had said she was okay, but not as strong as he would like.

I won't record our final conversations. They were just what my dad predicted. And the last one was sweet, tearful, and final.

That was five years ago. I'm now enrolled in the PhD program at the University of Chicago. I've checked with Loyola and, as I suspected, no Joanne Villery ever enrolled there.

Maybe someday she'll call me, reaching me through my dad (as she always had before, in a way).

I could try to find her through her parents, and call her, but she'd pleaded with me not to.

The thing I regret most is there was nothing I could say or do to make her feel better about breaking my heart.

PEACHES

O F course, no one names their child Peaches any more, if they ever did. But a nickname is a different matter. Cynthia "Peaches" Comus earned her nickname in high school when, during a performance on the pommel horse, her shorts and her undershorts split wide open in the back, revealing her lovely bottom to half the gymnasium.

Having a playful and forgiving nature, she accepted the nickname with good grace and never complained. It was a lot better than some of the other nicknames in her class, like "Butter Flake," "Brick," or "Baby Girl," being only some of the nicer examples.

When she graduated from high school and walked up to the dais to receive her diploma her classmates shouted, "We love your peaches, Peaches!" Her parents were not amused.

Going to college at a state university halfway across the country might have been the opportunity to lose her nickname, but it lasted only a year. A student one year behind her showed up and her nickname was soon current once again.

When she took her first introduction to poetry course, she was horrified to learn that, according to T.S. Eliot, "peach" was not what she, and everyone else, had thought it was. (Or they were all very clever not to reveal it.) Consequently, any potential boyfriend was firmly instructed never to call her by that name. To little avail. When she was faced in her junior year with holding to her demands or giving up the first boy she'd ever really liked, she let it go.

It didn't hurt that he was the first boy to perform quite revelatory oral sex on her, so she determined that the nickname had its uses. She ceased to be defensive about it, and very soon she was again generally known as Peaches. I didn't learn her real name until we'd known each other for years.

But this is not the story of a nickname. Peaches Comus graduated cum laude from her university with a degree in political science. She went on to Harvard on a full scholarship and received an MA in Abnormal Psychology. At Georgetown University she finished her PhD in a breathless two years. Her dissertation was a national security secret.

It wasn't until much later that I came to realize that our relationship was both a matter of love and a cover for Peaches' role as a consultant with a shadowy government agency.

My name is Aron Noane. Peaches and I were introduced by a mutual friend, Jeremy Ivey. I graduated from Columbia with an MBA in advertising and was hired by a powerful New York agency. After five years, I was promoted, and Jeremy was my boss.

Peaches' role with the agency was to consult on sex in advertising. This might appear to be an exhausted advertising topic, but its permutations had grown tremendously since the naughty sixties, becoming more subtle and, as I came to learn, more solidly based on research and development rather than what had seemed obvious assumptions all along.

Jeremy invited me to dinner at his apartment on 5th Avenue to meet his wife. I didn't know that he'd invited Peaches as well. We hadn't met, though I'd heard rumors of a gorgeous young woman with peach-colored hair meeting regularly with upper management.

Yes, Peaches, already a redhead, had embraced her nickname by dying her hair the same rosy yellow with orange tints. She stood up when I entered the room and took my hand, then kissed me on the cheek. It was a sweet gesture, genuinely friendly, which I took as similar to the French form of greeting. She had contacts that tinted her eyes to match her hair. Her lipstick, the same. This might sound a bit bizarre, but somehow, for Peaches, it worked. She was tall, my height at 5'11", with generous breasts pressed into a purple sheath dress that stopped just above her knees. Her legs were perfect in peach-tinted stockings, and when she turned to return to her seat, I gulped at the perfection of her waist and hips.

(I'm slightly embarrassed to be so exact in my description of a woman that I was destined…. Let's just say that it's important to understand that, in addition to being beautiful, she was formidably sexy, and that attribute cannot be separated from her intellect or her professional success, which we'll come to shortly.)

As we sat waiting for drinks, I realized she bore a very strong resemblance to one of my Spanish teachers in college. She had been— true story—with Castro in the hills during the revolution. When Castro achieved power, she became his Minister of Education. But, after a while, when she and some of her colleagues realized that Castro had broken most of his promises to the people and was intent on dictatorship, Castro discovered their disaffection and only out of gratitude for their past support, gave them two options: go to jail or get on a boat for Miami never to return. In the classroom, all we had to do was ask a question about Castro or Cuba and she would spend the rest of the period talking about nothing else. I got a C in the class because she didn't teach me anything. But I adored her. She was lovely and a great storyteller. And, but for the peach-tinted contacts, she bore a remarkable resemblance to Peaches.

I told Peaches all this. She liked it so much, she said, "I'd die to have been her student!"

"What do you mean?"

"She was a woman, and a warrior! Can you imagine what she must have gone through? I'm sure there's plenty I could have learned from *her!*"

That night, for the most part, we made small-talk. Jeremy's wife, Jennifer, barely 25 to his 35, was beautiful in the way that young women who are already losing their freshness are beautiful. Your heart rises and sinks just looking at them. Jeremy was dapper and homely, but his toothy smile made up for his big ears. He'd married for love; she for money, was my guess.

It was the only time the four of us ever spent together. Jennifer cooked a spicy Mexican dinner and we all got a bit drunk on tequila.

There was only one interaction worth mentioning. As we retired from the dinner table and settled into couches in their living room, Peaches sitting a bit closer to me than she had to for appearances sake, Jeremy asked an odd question:

"Aron and I want to know what part of the male anatomy is most attractive to promiscuous women."

Of course, Jeremy and I had never discussed any such thing.

"So we're talking shop?" said Peaches.

"Why not?"

"Why promiscuous?" said Peaches.

Jennifer looked at Peaches for concurrence and said, "And how would we know?"

"I don't follow," said Jeremy.

"We're not promiscuous."

"Of course, you aren't, or at least I have no reason to believe that you are. What I'm seeking is conjecture. What do you both *think* is the biggest turn-on for loose women?"

When no one spoke up, he said, "Okay, I'll start. I think it's the smile."

"Sure, mister gorgeous smiley-pants," scoffed Jennifer.

"She's right, you know," said Peaches. "You have a killer smile. Which means you're not playing fair."

"Caught me," he said, beaming. "Okay. Honestly, I think the answer is their waists."

Everyone laughed.

"Look, the last thing I can boast is a narrow waist, but I think women look at a narrow waist and they think about...."

"All right, spit it out," said Jennifer.

"Let me put this delicately as I can. They see where their legs can comfortably go."

"Jeremy, I'm impressed," said Peaches. "That's actually a fascinating conjecture. It's total bullshit, of course, but it certainly has a kind of logic."

"My turn," I said.

"No," countered Peaches. "Girls next."

She thought a moment and said, almost with vehemence, "Loose women want loose men, not monogamous men, married or not. Nothing physical matters, at least not as much. They want what they are themselves."

"Don't you think that's rather banal?" asked Jeremy.

"Let me finish. Yes, it seems obvious that a woman who is promiscuous, and therefore doesn't want entanglement, would look for men who feel the same way. But I would add this: loose women hate one-night-stands. Players, as we called them in college, love them."

"That's also banal, or obvious. You're simply saying that both want to be the ones to call it off."

"I said let me finish," she insisted, getting slightly testy. "What the woman wants is love."

"Now you're being contradictory."

"No. Just a *little* love. Loose women require revenge, which is what promiscuity is all about. I'm not talking the big 'L,'—just enough love so that she can walk away knowing the poor dope has been hurt, if just a little bit."

I looked at Jeremy and said, "Seems pretty sophisticated conjecture to me, Aron. No banality in that last bit."

"Thank you," said Peaches, and leaned over and kissed me again on the cheek.

Jennifer declined to answer, perhaps feeling she had nothing that could match Peaches' answer.

I said only, "I think promiscuous women want to kill their fathers and bonk their mothers."

And with that, and the laughs I was gunning for, the topic was exhausted. The party broke up soon after.

＊

I emailed Peaches the next day and asked her to lunch. She readily agreed, I hoped because she was interested, but I had to assume her role with the agency was possibly her only reason. I would pay for lunch and the hours, for her, were billable.

We met in the lobby of the Seagram Building, three floors of which were occupied by my company.

We had reservations my secretary had made at an Italian restaurant five blocks away. I wanted a good walk. You can learn a lot about a woman when you walk with her.

As we left the lobby, Peaches said, "I'm glad the restaurant's not too close. You can learn a lot about people when you walk with them."

"How did you know?" I let slip.

"Know what?"

"That I did this on purpose for that very reason."

"Aron, darling, I know more about you than your mother does."

By the time we'd reached the restaurant, we had exhausted the high points of our various upbringings and education, which, it turned out, were rather boring—at least, what each of us was prepared to reveal on this first outing was boring.

Unfortunately, that left only business to talk about, which appeared to be exactly what Peaches wanted.

"So, how can I help you?" she asked, after we'd settled into a corner booth.

"Shall we order first?"

"You go ahead. I don't eat lunch. I'll have a dry martini," she said, and winked, "Just one."

When her martini came, she took out the olive and set it on her plate.

"Do you know what a virgin olive is?" she asked, straight-faced,
"No idea."

"One that's never been pimento-ed!"

I laughed louder than she did, but she was pleased at my reaction.

"I'm sorry to throw a rude joke at you like that, and such a bad
one," she said, taking a sip of her drink. "Occupational hazard."

Lunch ordered, I began to explain my job. She interrupted me
almost immediately and said, "You oversee the work of four account
executives, all with accounts related to women's products."

"You've done your homework."

"I've talked to all four of them."

That caught me by surprise and I felt slightly angry, not so much
at Peaches, but at Jeremy and my four AEs for keeping me out of
the loop.

"Don't worry. I wasn't spying. It's my job. I've talked to every
mid- to upper- level manager in the entire company. The only one
I haven't talked to yet is you."

"Why is that?"

"Jeremy asked me to wait."

"And why?"

"For the same reason, I think, that he brought us together last
night. I think he has some notion that we'll hit it off and that will
make me even more committed to your company. He'd hire me for
an obscene salary tomorrow, if he could."

Now I was slightly offended. I leaned back, my hands flanking
my plate, and said, "So you've been one step ahead of me since we
left for our *long walk?*"

She covered both my hands with hers and said, "It only seems
that way, Aron. I have that effect on people, men *and* women. Call
it intuition. I just see things other people don't."

I looked away from those peach-tinted eyes and wondered if we
should just leave. The manipulation was bad enough, but my being
attracted to her had grown to the level of embarrassment, since I
clearly couldn't hide it.

"I don't know what you're thinking, Aron, but I can guess. I think we should try dating. I'm an old-fashioned girl. I'm no virgin, but it takes some time before I even look at a man with anything more than intellectual interest. I liked you very much last night, what you said."

"I liked you."

"Thank you."

She held out her hand, with her long peach nails. I took it and we shook.

She opened her purse and gave me her card.

"Call me tomorrow at the second number."

The card read only: "Peaches Research" and listed her email address and two phone numbers.

As I put it in my wallet, she said, "Do you want to talk work now or later?"

I could tell she was finished for now with the personal, so I suggested she tell me about my staff. As I ate my lunch and she sipped her martini, she told me what I had not thoroughly surmised about the one man and three women who reported to me. She ranked them according to creativity, integrity, professionalism, tendencies toward secrecy and backstabbing, intellectual capacity and grasp of the business, and, most importantly, what she called their "emotional aptitude for meeting their client's needs." We spent two hours. I asked a great many questions, and she convinced me that, out of five stars, I had one female five-star world-beater, one four-star woman with great potential, a two-star mediocrity, also a woman, and a half-star disaster who should be let go quickly, a man. I didn't tell her, but the only thing she said that *wasn't* a surprise to me was, now, Mr. Gone.

When we were done, and getting up to leave, I asked her, "Was that my interview too?"

She laughed and said, "I don't put lipstick on my ears."

Somehow this made sense. A lot of sense.

*

There's not much to say about the first two months of our "romance," simply because it was so conventional. We went to movies and art galleries and to very nice restaurants (where she ate copiously to make up for her missed lunches). Afterwards, we spent hours on her couch or mine, necking and petting, but never more than that. Mostly, we talked. Peaches had a way of always talking away from herself. She seemed incurious about me and assumed, wrongly, that I felt the same about her.

I don't believe she was a genius, not in the IQ sense of the term, but she was a genuine polymath with an incredible ability to draw conclusions, fascinating conclusions, from entirely unrelated topics, which she understood at the deepest level. There didn't seem to be anything she didn't know about western and eastern history and philosophy, psychology, biology, physics, world literature and poetry, and a dozen other fields. She felt that most of what she'd been taught in college had been embarrassing nonsense, from women's studies to historicism. She understood every word written by Derrida or Foucault (and dozens of their ilk) and felt they didn't contribute a single coherent or useful idea to the sum of human knowledge. She hated "political correctness," not because she disagreed with its goals, but with its methods.

She knew of my interest in literature, the one area, besides advertising, I could talk about on an almost equal footing with her. One night over dinner she asked, "What's the single most obvious similarity between Anna Karenina, Tess of the D'Urbervilles, and Madame Bovary?"

"They're all tragic love stories."

"That's a bit too obvious, don't you think?"

"Okay. In all three the heroine dies."

"Better. Try again?"

"They were all written by men."

"Well, you're getting closer."

"You go."

"In all three cases, the women are either emotionally or physically tortured, or both, by their male authors, and they all die horrible deaths."

"Now *you're* being a bit obvious."

"I suppose. The question, though, is why? We're talking about three of the greatest novelists of all time, and in all three cases perhaps their greatest books."

"I can't argue with that."

"So, the question, again, is why?"

"Listen," I said, catching on, "I've heard you talk enough privately and at work to know where this is going."

"Yes?"

"Because in each book the root of the tragedy is sex."

"And?"

"And women must be punished for their sexual desires and transgressions."

"Bravo! Why?"

I considered it for a minute and chickened out.

"Your turn."

"You were so close," she said. "Okay, I won't torture you any further. The answer is because men *like* to read about the suffering of sexy women. They enjoy it. They want more of it. It sells books. Tolstoy, Hardy, and Flaubert were trying to sell more books!" she concluded triumphantly.

I thought about this a moment.

"Okay, smarty-pants...."

"Smarty-panties," she interrupted me.

We laughed.

"If you're right," I forged ahead, "then why do we spend so much effort to sell products with sexy, beautiful, idealized women, instead of sad, suffering adulteresses?"

"You want to talk shop?"

"Sorry, you brought us here."

"Okay, who says they're idealized? And notice how you said that. You put sexy first, beautiful second and idealized last."

"You're saying they are none of these things?"

"Of course, they're sexy and beautiful, but since when does a man, or woman, for that matter, idealize an attractive woman they've never met? I would think they do just the opposite."

"You're saying, I think, that because we're using sexy, beautiful women in advertising in order to sell things, the reason we're successful is that we're implicitly degrading them."

"Oh, my. Now that's a feminist talking."

"No?"

"Of course not, though I must admit your conclusion could easily be drawn from what I'd just said before."

"I'm lost."

"As you should be. What I'm talking about exists in the basement of male/female perceptions. It's not that we are degrading them, though sometimes advertisers do. The one I hated most was the beautiful broad puffing on a Virginia Slim. Disgusting."

"I agree."

"No, it's the customer. It's his or her imagination. That's what we traffic in. Not the physical beauty of the man or woman in the advertisement. We're manipulating the imagination of the viewer, and I believe—and this is all a matter of my own research—that physical beauty and sexual attraction brings out the very worst in the human imagination."

"Don't tell me you're saying that we're all a bunch of de Sades deep inside and to sell stuff you only have to light that fire."

"Don't be silly. I'm saying that buying shit is disgusting, but necessary. Marx had no concept. And what advertising does is tap into the shameless imaginations of men and women and releases them from that shame in the form of going out to buy shit, as an apology, an atonement, if you will, to the sexy, beautiful creature they've just, deep, deep down, imagined in any one of a billion less than holy scenarios."

All I could say was, "Wow!"

"Now you know why you and I, having gotten this far with this relationship, which I'm really enjoying, have such a long way to go before we fuck."

"I don't understand."

"Believe it or not, neither do I. That's why it will take time."

✳

You would think that the first time I saw Peaches in the nude (almost) would be when we were about to have sex. Not even close. As improbable as it seems, what I'm about to relate about Peaches and nudity is the reason why our agency paid Peaches so much money.

Everyone knows that online pornography is pervasive—a multi-billion-dollar industry. Yet no company with a national profile has ever been known to advertise on a porn site. It just isn't done.

One day, the CEO of a company that sold women's products took me aside and asked my opinion. He wouldn't accept any argument I presented and swore me to secrecy. If my company wanted to keep his business, we'd have to figure it out. Or, I should say, Peaches and I would.

The easy part was to convince our client, Reginald Owen, the CEO of one of the largest privately owned companies in the U.S., that his company's name or logo could not be used. Nor could the product or product line being advertised already be successful or have any name recognition. Even further, a "front" company would have to be created to sell the product so that no one could trace it back to Reginald's company. Owen was so bent on his idea, all this was easy to convince him was necessary.

This led to renaming a line of rather garish lipsticks the "Pretty

Puss" line. There were excellent reasons why the line had been a relative failure from the beginning. It had been poorly branded to begin with, and it made most women look whorish.

"That's precisely my point," Reginald Owen would rant. "That's what we're trying to appeal to!"

"But our research shows that the number of women who watch internet porn is minuscule," I explained.

"I don't want to market to women, you dolt," said Reginald, "I want to market to men." Then he turned and pointed at Peaches, "And for this little experiment I'm willing to pay her, and your firm, $1 million dollars each."

It took some doing, but once the old line had been re-packaged and re-branded, it took only the greasing of palms before Pretty Puss lipstick was available at Amazon and other online retailers.

The legalities were formidable: how to ensure a "model" wouldn't talk, no matter how much we paid her? Also, it became clear that, however convincing Peaches could be with "research subjects," getting them to appear in the nude on internet porn sites wasn't going to happen. And then there was the issue of sexual abuse; no one wanted to hear back later from some starlet that we had forced her to do something against her will. Oh, there were more than enough porn stars, even porn amateurs, who might be willing to sign up for a big check, but none of them had what Peaches called "the thing."

"Who does?" asked Reginald.

"I can't tell you," said Peaches.

Reginald almost swallowed his eternal prop, the un-lit cigar.

"You're going to have to wait and see," she continued. "This 'experiment' is going to be very controlled, as in secret. Until and after it goes online, the only people who will know the real story are Aron here, my videographer, myself, our 'actress,' and an editor who'll never see her face."

"Why, that's unheard of. No advertiser signs off on something he can't see first."

"Sorry, that's the deal."

He thought about it and smiled. He stood up, put one thumb up, and left the room.

That evening, Peaches and I had our first argument. I don't need to recount the whole disagreement. It will be obvious from what started it.

"Have you ever read any of Anais Nin's erotica?"

"Who hasn't?" I said, a bit too sarcastically.

Peaches wasn't fazed.

"Remember the scene with the lipstick?"

"You mean when the woman puts it on her, her…."

"Her labia. How's that?"

"Fine. I guess."

"I'm going to be the naked woman in front of the video camera …."

"You're what?" I interrupted.

"I'll be fully clothed. Then I'm going to pull up my dress and pull down my panties. And then I'm going to smear lipstick down below for about 15 seconds. Then, fade to black."

"The hell you are!"

"My face won't be in the frame; you'll make sure of that. No one will know it's me."

"I'll know."

"Only you."

"What if Reginald guesses?"

"So? He's paying enough for it."

"You'd whore yourself that way?"

The word didn't bother her in the least.

"Listen. This is what's called the willing suspension of disbelief. I'm not a whore, and no one who watches this will think I'm really a whore. They'll think I'm a model or at worst a porn actress."

She paused, considering, then added: "We'll have her say something like. 'I'm not a whore, sweetheart. I'm just acting this way because it turns you on. And it will turn on that special lady in *your* life.' Then, the motto: Pretty Puss, gloss for your lover's every lip!"

"And how's this going to get women to buy lipstick?"

"It's not intended to! Remember what Reginald said? It's going to drive men crazy until they buy Pretty Puss and use it on their wives or girlfriends—or watch them use it on themselves! At least that's the theory."

Of course, I was adamantly opposed and offered a hundred objections, but Peaches was equally adamant. In the future, I would win my share of arguments, but never ones about her work.

✳

For the shoot, I did wrench a few concessions out of her. I refused to do it if she didn't paint her nails purple and dye her pubic hair anything but what I assumed was her natural color: peachy red.

"What makes you think I have any?" she said, and winked.

I said it again and again: "There can be no hints." The voiceover would be someone else's. During the shoot, she chose orange lipstick and I nixed that too. We went with fire-engine red.

How do I discretely describe the first and only shoot ever made for Pretty Puss? It was brief. It took two takes and might have taken only one, but she thought she'd overdone it, so after a thorough washing off, we started over. It was my idea, not hers, that she should direct herself via mirror. I refused to look. Once the camera was positioned to frame her belly to her knees (she was seated, still in her dress and panties), I walked away. She leaned forward and hit the record button, and 15 seconds later it was over.

"You really are a gentleman, Aron," she said afterward and leaned in to give me a kiss, accommodating my palpable erection.

"Let's just say I'm saving myself for you," I replied.

The reason why there was only one Pretty Puss advertisement ever made is that it was unnecessary to make another. Sales went up with almost no end in sight from the day it premiered. Reginald spent a million on ad placements and saw a ten-fold return. Over time, sales leveled out to roughly $5 million a month with ad buys totaling $1 million per month.

Anonymous surveys, conducted by a dummy consulting group, proved that no one wanted a second version, because no one could imagine improving on the first one.

More and more, sites ran the ad for free just to draw customers.

One interesting twist, somewhat unexpected, was that a majority of Pretty Puss was actually purchased by women.

"I anticipated this, believe it or not," Peaches explained. "Women like to please their men."

The ad ran for almost five years, when Reginald Owen passed away, taking the secret to his grave. For the previous three years, we'd been gradually pulling ads until there was nothing purchased after Reginald's death. The new CEO was briefed on a line of lipstick that was sold by a subsidiary and was doing quite well because someone had posted a video about it on porn sites years ago. By then Pretty Puss was an established brand—still appearing on thousands of sites, for free. The market had been saturated and we'd been richly rewarded. Time to move on.

*

I mentioned earlier that Peaches' dissertation was classified for national security purposes. Obviously, she could never talk about it, though it was a matter of record that her PhD was in Information-based Psychological Warfare and Military Media Relations. It was never published, and all copies were handed over to the Pentagon (in return she had no expenses at Georgetown), along with her computer and back-ups. Otherwise, the contents of her dissertation resided only in Peaches' prodigious memory.

I estimate that Peaches consulted with the government only a few weeks per year. She spent a lot of her time with my company, and by contractual agreement was prohibited from working for other ad agencies. How she spent the rest of her time was also something she didn't talk about, I believed more out of a sense of professional loyalty to those non-agency companies paying her outrageous fees than for any need for secrecy.

✽

I mentioned that our relationship was in part a cover for her government consulting, as was everything else in her professional life. Then I was brought into the game.

I can write this because it's not anything the government worries about keeping secret, and because I have permission from a certain colonel at the Pentagon. He said, "Sometimes, there are things we want out there. This is one of those times."

It began when Jeremy Ivey took Peaches and me to lunch.

"I got a call today from a colonel at the Pentagon."

"Yes, I know," said Peaches.

"They want us to move ahead with Peaches' plan."

I knew enough not to ask "what plan?"

"This is the last thing they want us to do for them. Or Peaches, for that matter."

"My decision," she said, looking at me. I'd never seen such a serious expression—it made her lovely face look hard. I couldn't tell why.

"I'm not really sure why they asked me to deliver this message, except that you, Aron, are going to be involved, and you're my responsibility. I'll let Peaches explain it all."

Then he stood up.

"The less I know about the details, the better, for my own peace of mind and not because of any security issues. Lunch is on me," he said and walked away.

Peaches immediately relaxed.

"I've never known him to do that," I said. "He's the most controlling guy I've ever met."

"He knows what he's doing."

I moved to the other side of the table and said, "Okay? We can talk here?"

"Yes. This place is secure."

"Wow! I never thought I'd hear those words outside of a movie."

"Yeah, well don't get all excited. This isn't about something you'd find in an action movie. Most of it's pretty boring."

Nonetheless, I was pretty uncomfortable.

"I've never asked or even wanted to know about that side of your life."

"I know, and I've always appreciated it."

"I never felt it would be good for us."

"Don't worry. I wouldn't have agreed if I thought it would be a problem."

The waitress came with my lunch and a martini, and Peaches began to talk.

"You know what psychological warfare is, right?"

"Only the obvious stuff. Tokyo Rose and Radio Free Europe. Dropping pamphlets on troops. Propaganda. Infiltrating publications in order to plant stories."

"In my case, we don't have a word for it. I invented it and even I haven't given it a name. We've never even tried it. Now they want to see if it works."

I knew enough by now to shut up when I had nothing to add.

"It has to do with fake sex."

I dug into my lunch.

"Or virtual sex. Or, more accurately virtual subliminal sex. We all know what some foreign governments are subsidizing in the form of hackers. You have no idea how many foreign governments do it. Do you know how many countries there are?"

"Around 200."

"You get an A. There are 195, including Palestine and the Holy See.

"Virtually every one, including the Holy See, is engaged at some level in hacking somebody's database, and for more reasons than there are countries. Thousands more. But of course we don't care why the Holy See wants to hack into the Hague.

"Now, and this is the only thing that is classified that I am allowed to tell you. Understand?"

"Yes."

"We know how, better than anyone else, to detect when we're being probed, let alone hacked. We know it the second it happens and we can stop it the minute we think the hacker is getting close. You might have read about actual hacks, but that's all disinformation. We have a 99.99 percent interception rate. Usually we just cut them off at the knees. But almost as often, however, we steer them to what they think they're looking for, and not to what they are actually looking for."

She took a sip of her martini and leaned forward.

"As you can imagine, it takes enormous resources to monitor and act upon every conceivable breach. And we're not just talking about the government, but anything that might impact national security, including the economy.

"Much of it is mischievous. Little enemies trying to screw with us. But more often than I can reveal, someone gets wind of something and we have to up our vigilance.

"Now I'm not talking about the big guys. And by that I mean both our enemies and our friends. Though they all deny it, of course, everyone wants to know what we know. England just as much as Russia. Let's say it's the cost of being the richest country with the biggest army and the most secrets in the world.

"This is where we come in. The last thing we want is for the big boys to stop doing what they're doing. We've got them covered.

"It's the little guys, in their tens of thousands of little basements, trying to either toss us a virus, or cause a database to crash, or dig up dirt on some pathetic lieutenant colonel at Camp Lonelyhearts whose mistress is blackmailing him, so they can blackmail him instead.

"To better cope with all this, we need something to cause a lot of them to stop, to stop because they believe—*believe* is the operative word—that they have, for want of a better word, 'come.' I mean as in C-U-M."

I put down my fork.

"Peaches, this is so nuts I actually believe you. I wouldn't believe it from another person on this planet. But I believe *you*."

"Believe what?"

"Let me guess. You mentioned subliminal sex. You want to create a subliminal sex virus that will be triggered in any computer that is being probed."

"I'm impressed," she smiled and touched her martini to my glass of red wine.

"I was talking out of my butt. I have no idea what you really mean."

"Yes, I'm taking about a virus. And, if we design it properly (and a lot of the platform work is completed, minus the content), when a hacker sees it or experiences it, he or she will have a kind of mental orgasm so fulfilling that he or she will feel that their goal as a hacker has been achieved."

"So they'll stop.

"We don't want them to stop. That's the last thing we want. Rather, we want them to chase the tail. Sorry, I'm being cute. Chase the fake data we've already created, or, to be more precise, which is self-creating, and never return to the firewall hiding the real data.

"Think of it as a kind of porn site. Long ago they figured out what the viewer wants and continually feeds him that. What we're planning works the same way, at least in terms of automatically generating the false data. We've had that capability for years. Only, too often, the hacker sooner or later, usually sooner, realizes they've been misdirected, like a magician's hands, and leaves off to pursue the original goal or target. We want to create the equivalent of a mental orgasm that will convince the hacker to keep coming back, to the wrong place, for more.

"Now, be patient. I'm almost finished. Your first question, I'm sure, is what form does this orgasm take. Is it a voice, an image or images, appearing so quickly that the senses don't consciously take notice? Like the old cigarette ads that used to bury the words "smoke Lucky Strike" so low in the audio mix of a TV comedy that no one ever noticed.

"But, no. Nothing that crude. Here's where I come in. I've invented a sex algorithm attached to password protection. Hackers spend forever trying to break through passwords. When a hacker spends any time at all with my algorithm, he or she experiences a virtual euphoria based on the promise of success through feedback that appeals to certain areas of the brain that process sexual desire.

"All of this is in place. What I've created? Call it immensely pleasurable foreplay. What we need now, what's missing, is the message. What pornographers call 'the money shot.' That's where you come in. I need you and your creative folks to come up with a dozen or so images, sentences, even number sequences (I can help there) that we can place at the end of my algorithms."

I shook my head and said, "What the fuck?"

Without hesitating, Peaches said, "No, we thought of that. Doesn't work."

"Very funny. You really think it will work?"

"I've done a lot of testing and the results are promising. But the subjects are too preconditioned to react as I want them to. There's been no 'control' in the experiment. You understand what kind of 'control' I mean, right?"

"Yes."

"Well, I've been working with nothing but 'control.' I need to try this out on the real bad guys."

"And what if it doesn't work?"

"That's the beauty of it. It can't fail because there are actually two ways in which it works. The best result will be as I've described it. But, worst case, they don't 'orgasm.' Sorry, I hate using words like that, but the options aren't any better. Let's just say they don't, you know…. My algorithm has a trigger to tell when it *hasn't* worked. Then the computer will throw up an actual image or a few words —nasty, insulting, sexually offensive—which will basically tell the hacker he's been had and to fuck off. Who knows, we might even use that. Either way, they'll get the message, and what they do after that, if it's more hacking, will start all over again. Or maybe, we hope, they'll give up. But, and here's the real goal, if we can automate this misdirection to reduce repeated attempts at the hacker's real target by even ten percent, it will be a huge benefit to national security."

She let it sink in for a minute as she finished her martini.

"What do you think, Aron? You in?"

"What do you think, Peaches? It's nuts. I love it."

At this point, I can't go into much of what happened next, but what we created is still in place, though there were dozens of permutations before we had a working model. And, ever since we successfully launched, there have been ongoing modifications, which is why nobody cares that people know the program exists (though the sex component is still a closely held secret). The military is happy to have created a sense of futility for potential hackers. Of course, there are just as many out there who relish the challenge. No matter. The results are always the same. And we ended up reducing serious attempts by almost 20 percent, for which the agency and Peaches were well remunerated.

One thing I've never felt comfortable with, but which the government doesn't worry about at all (in fact they're thrilled), is the fact that an extremely small segment of those who experience the "experience" become crazed and virtually suicidal. We're not aware that anyone has actually died, and we believe the effects are temporary. Nonetheless, it's there, and it's known that screwing with the U.S. can cause mental illness, one form of which is an obsession with breaking the password that can last for days, even weeks. At least that's how far the rumors have gone, as far as I know.

✳

This leads me, finally, to our sex life, Peaches' and mine. For reasons related to everything I've revealed so far, I can't be specific about dates, but, we'd been together between one and two years and had still not slept together. I hope that I've described Peaches in enough detail to make this understandable. As for me, all I can say is that the last thing I wanted was to rush her. Marriage was something we talked of now and then, but agreed that it was not going to happen anytime soon.

It was after our involvement in the project just described came to an end, that we were watching a DVD in my apartment after an expensive French meal. We could afford it. The movie was *A Clockwork Orange,* which, early on, has a particularly violent rape scene. Before the arrival of little Alex's droogs, Peaches got off the couch and turned it off.

"I can't take that."

"I'm sorry.

"You said you saw that before?"

"Yes," I admitted. "It's Kubrick."

"It's ugly."

"Yes, there are some pretty harsh sex scenes in it. That's not the only one. Overall, it's a great movie."

"You consider rape great?"

"Of course not."

Was she trying to pick a fight?

"I'll show you what's great, Aron," she said and held out her hand.

She pulled me to my feet and practically ran me into the bedroom.

"Please sit down," she said, motioning to the bed. "Now, watch."

She turned her back on me and began to undress. That night

she was wearing a black dress and shimmering pearl stockings. She pulled the dress over her head and threw it into the closet. She had on a garter belt, which she unhooked, and peach panties. Those, too, went into the closet.

She bent over and rolled down her stockings.

"Did I ever tell you why they call me Peaches?"

"No."

"And you never thought to ask?"

"A million times. But I assumed it was your real name."

"No, you didn't," she said, rather hotly, looking over her shoulder.

"Okay. Probably not. Am I supposed to ask now?"

"I'll tell you why."

She told me the story about her high school embarrassment.

"And no one did anything about it?"

"What? You were never sixteen? If I'd complained it would have been immeasurably worse."

"But later? Even after college?"

"By then I was stuck with it. I mean I owned it. It was mine. I liked it. I decided to use it, as you've seen. It's been very helpful at times."

"And never a problem?"

"Do you think any man or woman would dare mess with me about my nickname?"

"No," I laughed. "I do not."

"Well, what do you think?"

I didn't know what to say. I certainly couldn't say anything about her "peaches."

"About what?"

"My peaches."

I got slightly upset.

"I don't know what to say. The ground is shifting. You're a beautiful woman and I love you."

She turned and came to the bed, put her arms around my shoulders and kissed me deeply.

"I knew I could count on you," she whispered and smiled. "My name is Cynthia. Call me Cynthia."

In other words, discretion and the truth, the truth that mattered, won the day. And that's all I have to say about our sex life, other than this: the Kubrick scene didn't turn her on; she meant sex that night to drive that scene right out of our minds.

✳

A year later, Cynthia and I would marry and have two girls. She would give up consulting after a few more jobs that bored her. She became a mother and housewife and, when the kids were old enough for pre-school, a high school social studies teacher. She could have had a tenure track professorship at any of a dozen colleges and universities, but she said she wanted to have a real impact on young women, and, if she had learned anything in life, that meant high school. I would continue on with the agency until I too got bored. Money would never be an issue, so I retired and became a novelist of moderate critical and financial success. Cynthia was my "first reader." She was particularly helpful with sex scenes.

X-RAY

XAVIER Raymond Jacobi, known as "X-ray" to his friends, though his wife and children called him "Zavy," entered the bookstore at two in the afternoon feeling like a brigand on the run. There was nowhere else he was supposed to be, and nowhere to go. That he had deliberately started an argument with his wife and stormed out of the house was not the point. It happened; a pressure valve they were both used to him turning on whenever he grew restless.

"Then go back to work!" his wife had complained.

"I don't need to work! I don't want to work! Ever again!" he'd yelled over his shoulder.

But, a bookstore? It was like cheating on your television set! He'd been true to electronic media ever since college. He didn't read newspapers. The stacks of *TIME*, two years' worth and counting, a subscription purchased from his niece's fund-raising for her God-awful marching band, grew in a single monolithic stack beside the fireplace. He didn't even look at the pictures. Nonetheless, the book-store, the first new one in this small college town in more than 20 years, seemed inviting. If nothing else, he'd buy a cup of coffee.

At 36, now joyfully independent, having inherited his father's for-tune, in turn inherited from his grandfather, the owner of a casket hardware company, X-ray had returned from Chicago to his home town to live in his father's house. A dropout from Normal University, he'd worked first as a lowly legal assistant and eventually became the law firm's business manager. He hated every moment. He married his high school sweetheart after not seeing her for almost ten years. He thought it was coincidence, her showing up at a party thrown by a former girlfriend, Rita. What he would never know is that Rita, having heard X-ray go on and on about her, in bed no less, had tracked her down and called her. X-ray and Amy were married the next year.

They had two boys, five and seven, who kept Amy busy and for whom X-ray had little patience, thus little time.

After spending a small fortune completely renovating the house and filling it full of expensive furniture and every other modern convenience, he was bored. He had nothing to do. But, he told himself, boredom's not so bad. Beats working.

But sometimes what he felt was worse than boredom. "Aimless, estranged," were two words he had for what he felt. What was he doing living in the town he'd practically run from 16 years before, and in the house he grew up in, no less? Yes, he'd knocked down half the walls in the place, put on a metal roof, painted its gray bricks dark green, and added two porches, but he was still sleeping in his old bedroom, though now three times the size it had been.

Most disorienting was that X-ray had expected to encounter an old flame or two and never did. The few old male friends he'd see coming, he avoided. They hadn't been great friends anyway, and if they were still living in this town, they were probably losers, so why bother? But when it came to women—and he had dated his share— he felt that some exodus had taken place. What were the odds that not once in almost a year would he meet even a vaguely familiar face?

So it stirred his blood, as he browsed the media section, when his eye stopped upon the upturned chin and beveled nape of a woman on earphones at a listening station.

The impression was considerable. Could this be Jeanine, his partner in mutual virginity-loss (in college, a year after breaking up with Amy), not seen or talked to in 16 years?

He tapped the presence on her shoulder and said, "Hi."

What turned to confront him was a lovely simulacrum.

"Do I know you?" she asked.

"Um, I thought so. Please forgive me. I thought you were some-one else."

Such a smile! Long black hair in a pony tail, dark grey eyes, a slightly snubbed nose and a small black mole by her right ear. But she was easily ten years too young.

"Really, I'm sorry," he pleaded, "I didn't mean…it's such an…."

"It's okay."

"I'm sorry. I thought…."

"Really, it's okay. *Should* I know you?"

"No, no reason."

"Hey, don't worry."

"Such a screw up."

"I can see, though. You really meant it."

"Well, yes."

"You're *emotional*. You thought…."

"But that's my fault. You're very kind."

He started to walk away.

"I've made mistakes too. Please?"

"The last thing I want…."

He took another step away, pivoted, put his hands out wide and, again, turned away.

"No. Really. Would you like to talk? I'm headed toward the café."

"Would you like something?"

She pointed at her cup.

"No, thanks. Get yourself something and join me," she said.

He followed her.

"I'll be with you in a moment."

As he ordered, he watched as the young woman sat down by the front window, sipping her drink. He bought a latte he knew he would not drink.

The first time he'd met Jeannine, she betrayed him. The bar was across the state line, where the legal drinking age was 18. Every Saturday, he crossed over sober and often returned with a drink in his lap. Twice he'd left the road and he and his friends had all laughed. A fourth beer in hand, he'd introduced himself to the slender thing in a tight purple dress standing alone, smoking, staring out the only window in the room.

"I'm with someone," she said, preemptively. With charming inquisition, he learned her date's name—blond, bland, Solly Mortimer, his former high school classmate and negligible friend, home for vacation from U of I, who was across the room playing pool, running the table for beers, winning game after game, the prick. She was from Rockford, twelve miles from his hometown. X-ray bought her a drink, then another. She grew impatient, but not with him. He poured it on, probing, illuminating their mutual loves, Stanley Kubrick, the current President of the United States, and the dishonest clincher (thank you, English teacher!), Willa Cather. She even leaned forward to shout her agreement in the din, scalding his ear. "Have you ever read anything like that wolf attack!" Sensing the danger, too drunk to think twice, he asked her to leave with him. She said she'd think about it. He persisted. She turned her back to the room and kissed him on the cheek.

"Why the fuck not," she said, almost angrily, and took his hand. Solly arrived one second prior to inevitability and hustled her away. A few minutes later, as he sat at the bar, X-ray's nose struck the rim of his cocktail from a punch in the neck. He wheeled to confront a scarlet Solly swearing in his face. The crowd ushered them into the street. His former friend didn't hit him, just shouted and pushed. X-ray's new leather-bottomed platform shoes skidded on the pavement. He considered striking back, but that would have been like striking the girl, his true enemy. Solly shouted and pushed and pushed and X-ray's shoes slipped out behind him until he dropped to his knees. Solly swore one last time, slapped the top of X-ray's head, and stomped back into the bar, back to Jeannine.

"This is a bit ridiculous," he said, sitting down across from her. "You *could* just tell me to go away."

"No, this is interesting to me. You really *reacted!*"

"I did, didn't I?"

"I'm a psychologist. Or, rather, I'm working on my doctorate."

"I understand."

"Reactions. How people connect."

"Well, one thing is obvious."

"What?

"You had to think I was just coming on to you."

"But I didn't and you weren't."

"No."

"It's my theory. Well, mine and my professor's."

"Theory?"

"Yeah. That men, I mean people, need that."

"What?"

"A connection to their past. People without a link to what they know, what they've experienced in the past, get lost in their present selves, all input and no connection, no context, sometimes with disastrous consequences."

She looked down at the small round table and drew her finger through the residue of moisture from her cup.

"I'm not sure I understand."

"They lose themselves in themselves, which are just not sufficient nourishment."

"Well, maybe some of the time."

"Most of the time. There's no mystery. No surprises. It's all just new, all day every day. We become, well, I don't have a clinical term for it, though this is clinical work, absolutely!"

"I'm listening."

"We begin to die inside. It's like being trapped in a house with room after endless room of gray wallpaper. The same *new* thing. A kind of reverse sensory deprivation. New things, new experiences, one after another, and because it's all so strange and new, it provides no nourishment. There's no way to process it. Its very newness is what chokes us."

"Can you give me an example?" he asked, genuinely interested.

"Take abused children. The last thing they want is to remember or confront their past, even the good moments, which is why they remain so lost and confused, sometimes their entire lives. Sometimes it's why they *end* their lives! But if they could both confront the bad things and embrace and cherish the good things, they would find much greater balance in their lives."

"I see."

"In other words, it's not what we experience, what comes at us every day, that makes us what we are. It only confuses, or dopes us up. Do you know what comfort food is?"

"Only too well."

"Well, believe it or not, comfort food makes us grow. The intake of what we know and rely upon for its flavor and texture allows us to judge new subtleties, new richness in the familiar, and by contrast allows us to cope, to absorb the new and strange in a healthier fashion."

"I think I understand."

"We all become smaller and less interesting with each new experience unless that's balanced by a healthy memory and a willingness to retrieve and embrace past experiences."

He nodded and smiled, but he couldn't think of anything to say.

"Even better when we actually get reacquainted with those things we once experienced."

She paused, as if to gauge his interest. He was careful to keep his eyes on hers.

"What would you rather do? Go see a new movie or watch reruns on television?"

"I'm not sure."

"That's my point! Are you married?"

"What?"

"I'm sorry," she said, pulling back from the table. "I'm too direct."

"It's fine."

"Well, I mean, don't you discover more about sex every time you make love with your wife than you would if you made love with a different woman every night?"

There were two ways he could approach an answer. He chose the cautious route.

"You worry about such things?" he said.

"Well, yes, but worry," she said, hurrying on, "isn't the point. I'm a *researcher.*"

"Tell me again."

"Let me be silly," she forged ahead in the face of his seeming incomprehension. "When you hear a Beatles song for the umpteenth time, do you like it more or less?"

"It depends on the song."

"Right. I understand. But what means more to you, seeing the same great movie, let's say, *The Godfather,* for the tenth time, or seeing a brand-new gangster movie?"

"It depends."

"I'm still not getting through."

"I'm trying," he said, trying not to lose her interest in himself.

"Okay. Okay. Let me put it this way. What's the reason why you reacted so strongly to me, so emotionally?"

"I did. I can't explain it."

"Good. The reason is because I reminded you of a woman you knew long ago."

"I didn't try to hide it."

"Don't you think it would have been a far greater moment in your life if I had been that woman, instead of being just me? This person you never met once before in your entire life?"

"I'm not sure."

"Why?"

"Well?"

"Be truthful."

"Because I've never met anyone like you. You're fascinating."

"Now you're not listening. You've already begun to rationalize what's happened since you had that reaction. Think! What did you feel when you first saw me?"

The way she said this, her blue eyes demanding mirrored intensity from his own, plucked at memories hard-wired to those of Jeannine.

"I was excited."

"See? That's what I'm talking about. Whoever it was…."

"I'm sorry," he interrupted, "I'm excited now."

"That because of what I'm saying, because I look like the person you remember. Use your imagination. What if I'd been that person?"

"I might have been disappointed."

"Might have?"

"She might not have looked like you…," he paused, "like *she* did."

"What?"

"And talked like you do."

Of course, he thought. Ann Baxter in *All About Eve.* The same sweet maniacal intensity. The same perfect chin.

"Now you're weaseling," she accused him, her brow so crinkled he feared he may have breached her limit of patience.

"I'm sorry. I'm confused. You're quite lovely, you know."

"So, what's that? A line?"

"It's a little too late to accuse me of that."

She blushed and drew her finger across her chin.

"The perils of honest research," she admitted. "I deserved that, but don't give up on this. You're half again my age and I'm not so stupid that I can't see the difference between intellectual conversation with someone who has an intellect and the effect of my own physical attractions."

He stood up.

"You're not leaving."

"I really should. I'm afraid I've embarrassed myself."

"Sit down," she said, her lips turned—neither up nor down, he thought. She added, sweetly, "Won't you?"

The next time they'd met, same place, same hour of the night, Jeanine, in the company of girlfriends, put her full glass down and took his hand before he'd said a word and led him to the door. It was dark and cool outside. They stood in the parking lot and talked for almost an hour. "Solly?"

"History."

"Sorry."

"I'm not."

He took her in his arms, their tongues barely touched. Then, in his car, they found a cemetery through mutually enthusiastic investigation of a little town that didn't take them long to know. They got out and walked beneath a pale elastic moon. He kidded her with a scary story of Indians buried in grass-covered graves.

"There could be one right beneath our feet."

Her laughter gave him an immense sense of pride, and he felt perfectly alone with her in the universe. In the back seat of his car, she took the initiative, disassembling her dress. "Promises to keep?" she said, and sighed at his pat, literary response. When he paused and accused her with a look, she said, "Forget it, won't you! What else could I have done?"

"Something else," he said.

"I knew I'd see you again," she said.

"I don't follow."

"Follow this?" she answered, swinging her leg over his.

No fool, he quickly and unequivocally absolved her. The logistics weren't that simple. She squirmed beneath him. Entry was problematic. She whimpered, but without discouraging him.

"That hurt a little," she said, squirming in her seat, as he drove them back to the bar.

"I'm sorry. It was my first time."

"Really?" she asked, laughing.

"Please don't make fun."

"I'm not," she said, "believe me."

"I *am* sorry."

"Don't be. I enjoyed it," she said, leaning over and kissing him on the side of the lips.

Not wanting to face the wide eyes of her girlfriends, he embraced and kissed her deeply, but didn't escort her back into the bar.

The next morning, he discovered blood on the back seat. Thank God he'd thought to look before his father might have seen it. An application of diluted bleach erased everything. So that was why she wasn't upset with him for hurting her. He couldn't believe that she had chosen *him* for her deflowering. But, as he was soon to discover, she would never be willing to see or talk to him again. His calls went unanswered and eventually her father threatened him over the phone. He never did learn why she cut him off so cruelly.

He sat back down and almost held out his hand.

"I'm curious," he said, choosing a tack most likely to please. "How does one research such a thing, what? The antidote of recurrence?"

"What a lovely phrase!" she exclaimed, with sincerity. "Do you mind if I quote you?"

"I am your creature," he said with a slight laugh.

She frowned.

"Do you watch old *Dick Van Dyke* reruns?"

"I do, as a matter of fact."

"A British comic said on one of his shows, 'I'm not here to be tittered at.'"

"I remember! It was very funny."

"Well, I am not either."

He looked over her shoulder, toward the front entrance, unable to hide a smile of recognition. He waited a moment then, again, stood up to leave.

"Please don't go."

He assessed the possibilities, and sat down again. His indecision made him feel cold under his t-shirt.

"Who was that?" she asked.

Once again, he hadn't hidden a thing.

"Someone I…might know."

She started to turn.

"No, don't look. It's too embarrassing."

"Someone you *do* know."

"I'm not sure," he said and drained his cup.

"Is this a joke?"

"Absolutely not," he said.

"Well, who then?" she asked, testily. "The woman you thought I was? I mean, that's a bit too perfect, don't you think? Or was there some pre-arranged…."

"Shut up, will you?" he interrupted.

"Sorry."

He felt uncomfortable; they were no longer entirely alone.

"Would it help if I held your hand?" she asked, her fingers inching toward his.

"What?"

"Teach her a lesson."

"What?"

"Okay. Fine. Tell me about her."

"No thank you."

She was enjoying herself. She'd quickly, again, put him on the defensive.

"You've known her for quite a long time, haven't you?"

"You're being cute."

"Don't be insulting."

"You might be right, okay?" Strategically, he let a slight irritation into his response.

"Look," she continued, apologetically, "You *have* to confront your own attitudes and feelings. The situation couldn't be more perfect. It's what precisely what I've been saying."

"If you must know, I've known her since I was ten years old," he lied.

"Ah."

"Please," he pleaded.

"I'm only trying to help," she said, and reached to cover his hand with her own. "Listen. This could be my next paper. The annals of research are full of such *personal developments*. I'll keep it *entirely anonymous*."

"Stop it," he hissed. Her fingers came even closer.

"My hypothesis?" she continued. "You were adolescent friends. Later, you discovered a certain feeling. You *expressed* that feeling. She reciprocated. You engaged in modest physical contact. A kiss perhaps. Perhaps nothing more than holding hands. Am I right?"

He assented with an ambiguous down but lateral nod.

"Later, perhaps even four or five years later, you engaged in the rites of courtship."

"Please."

"You went on a date."

"Yes."

"Many dates."

"Only one."

"But there was intimacy. All, of course, within the appropriate boundaries."

"Of course!"

"It was quite lovely."

"Lovely," he responded dreamily.

"Then? Then?" She looked into his eyes. He betrayed no objection. "Then you told her off."

"How did you know?" he asked, with his eyes, to encourage her understanding of the game. Her inaccuracy was unimportant.

"Unimportant," she said, challenging him with her stare.

"Right," he said, slightly stunned by the confluence of their respective thoughts.

She paused. Smiled, as if she had the upper hand.

"Big mistake," she proposed.

"And as it turned out, I was unfair," he started to explain.

"Of course," she interrupted. "But that's beside the point. It always is."

He crushed the paper cup he was holding.

"How old are you?"

"Don't pull that shit. Really! Hear me out."

He raised the cup up over his head in frustration and made as if he would throw it across the room. She ignored the gesture.

"Now, after all these years—how many? —*obsessing* about it, you're full of...?" She took a big breath before going on, "You have just in the last few minutes discovered in the most personal way what I have been, as a researcher, trying to prove as a fact of human experience."

She took another breath, then raised her hand, refusing to let him interrupt.

"You *know* that what will fulfill your life is what your life offered and you refused."

She paused for effect. He sat before her composed and docile, a ready victim, though he kept his eye on the woman across the room.

"My dear," she ventured, "Those lost, sweet, remembered kisses and caresses are your way home to the core of your emotional life. You might be married, with children, happy in every possible way. You don't need anything else! But!" she added, triumphant, "Nothing! Nothing will ever be as real, as sweet, as life-affirming as what you remember. I could be twice as attractive, three times as intelligent, infinitely caring and connected to the essence of your soul, and still, not I, not any other woman, could measure up to what just passed behind my back and wandered away."

She stopped, breathless. X-ray thought, if I had said what this young woman has just said, it could be chalked up as the single most concerted effort at seduction I have ever expended.

"Who *are* you?" he said, looking at her in a totally new way.

This young beauty smiled as if she had, just that moment, triumphed in the most difficult sexual contest imaginable.

"I think the question is 'Who are you?'"

"I just don't understand."

"Oh, I think you do. We *are* onto something, don't you think?"

"Do you have any sisters?"

"What?"

"I'm serious."

"About what I'm saying?"

"Yes. Sure. But. A simple question."

"I'm confused. What are you asking?"

"How many sisters?"

A pause.

"Two. I'm the youngest. The oldest is about your age."

"I see," he said, softly, in due reverence of the wince that had accompanied her response. "What is her name?"

"Margaret, why?" she replied, boldly and sadly.

X-ray shook his head. He stood up to leave, for the last time, but couldn't help asking, though he knew he would regret it, "And your other sister's name?"

"Jane. Now answer *my* question," she added, angrily.

"Anything," he said, feeling himself blush even as he looked down at her flushed, upturned face.

"Why do you think I'm such a little twit *not* to deserve a few more precious moments of your life?"

"The answer to your question is across the room," he said. He reached down and touched her cheek with his fingers, and walked away, into the center of the store, drawing, he knew, her insolent, perfectly lovely eyes, toward the tall, blonde, buxom female holding a dictionary, who, on further inspection, disappointed him completely, as he predicted she would have to—the laws of coincidence being that unforgiving. And he wasn't even thinking of Jeanine. Any former girlfriend would have been a pleasant surprise. Then, careful not to give the game away with anything like indecision, he actually touched her shoulder as he asked her a question calculated to cause a shake of her head—"Do you work here?" Satisfied that the response had been sufficiently demonstrative, X-ray turned and stepped toward the front door. He was not in the least surprised when his young prey approached him as he reached the door. He offered her his hand. They stepped out into the sunlight.

"Mistaken identity."

He disengaged his hand and put his arm around her shoulders.

"Your car or mine?"

"You drive."

"Where are we going?"

"You choose."

"Your place?"

"Yes, please."

As he drove the few miles to her apartment, they didn't speak. She let him put her hand on her bare knee, and she put her hand on his.

In her bedroom, they fucked twice before separating, both head-in-palm, face-to-face with each other.

"I have a confession to make," she said finally.

"I really am married," he said quickly.

"Surprise, surprise! You leaked that even before I asked you just by the way you tried to walk out on me."

"It was a pretty half-hearted attempt."

"So was that little play acting with the bimbo."

"Smart girl," he said, impressed. "So, what's your secret?"

"I fucked you about eight years ago."

He pulled away from her and sat up.

She smiled, having received the reaction she desired.

"I was fucking my way through college."

He looked at her and thought, what a jokester!

"You're a cute one."

"I'll prove it to you. You've bought it before, haven't you?"

He didn't want to answer.

"Come on. I'm the last person who would object."

"Go on."

"How many have you paid an extra $200 to…." She leaned forward and whispered in his ear. "Fuck their tits?"

"Holy cats!"

She continued to whisper.

"I held them together and you came on my neck and chin. I wiped it off and licked my fingers."

She couldn't seem to get enough of his astonishment.

"And I liked it so much I gave you a freebie. Remember that?"

"Yes, I do."

"As I recall, you were visiting your father and you weren't married yet. We met at the bar at the bowling alley."

"That's right."

"I had blonde hair then, cut real short."

Now she sat up and put her hand on his prick, which wasn't yet ready to stir.

"You didn't recognize some old flame when you saw me. You recognized me."

He laughed, thinking he knew where this was going.

She laughed in return.

"No, you don't owe me anything, you asshole."

She wasn't offended, he realized. Then he thought maybe he understood.

"This was research?"

"Well, mostly," she said, blushing. "But I'll tell you this. Everything I was telling you at the bookstore?"

"Yes?"

"I wanted you again the minute I saw you, for all the reasons I explained."

She gave his prick a squeeze and said, "And I won't be happy until I've again become familiar with every cell of your body."

AVANT-
GARDE

*H*E had nice eyes and though he looked at her a little too boldly in the beginning, Irma gave him the benefit of the doubt;
then he asked her to join him in a work of performance art.
She boxed his ears.

She met Ernst Marcel in the spring of 1991 at a bulgogi restaurant
in the Village. The room was tiny, and a Korean woman with large
arms squeezed them together like a priest hugging newlyweds and
sat them down at the same table. Unshaven face buried in the paper
menu, he didn't talk to her at first. His unwashed, uncombed straw-
blond hair told Irma that he didn't care how he looked. He made
quick glances over the top of the menu. He was sizing her up. No,
it wasn't quite that. He was studying her, categorizing her, but not
with the transparent calculation that says "what are my chances?"
Yet, there was that in it too. Irma wondered if he weren't a sociolo-
gist or something similar. Then he started to stare. The menu had
gone beneath the table. His eyes shifted, focusing on one and then
another portion of her anatomy. She was about to get up and leave
when he spoke.

"Tell me your name and where you grew up?"

She'd put him in his place.

"I am a lady, sir, and I don't make conversation with impertinent
strangers."

He straightened in his seat, not unpleasantly shocked. He grinned sympathetically. He held out his hands, palms up, as though to prove that he carried no concealed weapons.

"I'm sorry," he said, "I think we misunderstand each other. It's tough being alone in the big city. Am I right?"

She had to smile too. He did have kindly big brown eyes.

"Yes, I suppose it is."

"Here, faces are like pictures and without the thousand words to go along with them, what are they worth?"

"My name is Irma."

"How do you do? Mine's Ernst."

"Ernest?"

"Ernst. No second 'e.' "

Naturally, they chatted.

She worked as a secretary for an insurance company, loathing it. The work didn't begin to satisfy her, but she wasn't qualified to do anything else. She'd grown up in a small town in Wisconsin and had always wanted to be a model. Irma was a golden tiger lily, all lovely stalks of arms and legs, with bursting-bud breasts and dark green-flecked eyes and bobbed hair, more red than blonde.

"That's a totally justified ambition," he said.

"Thank you."

What else was there to say? She wasn't dating anyone, but she could hardly tell him that.

He was an artist, but he didn't appear to want to talk about it.

Irma didn't care much for art. There were only three paintings she'd ever liked, she told him. The *Mona Lisa. Whistler's Mother. American Gothic.* The rest was nonsense. She couldn't understand it, so it meant nothing to her. She supposed there were other paintings out there that she might like, but three was plenty. She had posters of them in her apartment.

Then he said it:

"I wonder, Irma, if you would be interested in joining me in a work of performance art?"

Slowly, smiling, she leaned over and held out her hands, palms up. He leaned forward too and she boxed his ears smartly.

"Ouch!" he yelped, recoiling, almost tipping his chair back and over.

"You pig!" Irma whispered vehemently.

"I am a serious artist."

"I'm sure you are. The question is what kind?"

Then dawn appeared in the artist's eyes, or that's what it seemed like to Irma.

"What a minute. You think that I...?" He chuckled. "No, no, Irma. I'm talking about art. Real art. I'm a performance artist. I create mixed media modules wherein living persons, sometimes myself, sometimes others, become integrated components of the experience field. I deal with the ID's perspective, the death of metaphor, local color, the inhuman experience. I have a show next month at the Clock Gallery!"

"And you'd like to show me your drawings, right?"

"No, no, no! Irma! I want you to become a performer in perhaps my greatest work. I call it "Secretariat!"

"Why," Irma countered, "would I possibly be interested in doing that?"

"Well," said the artist, laughing again, "it would be nice if after seeing my work you thought it original and important. It would be even nicer if you thought me a great artist and wanted to learn more about me. And about art."

"Strike two."

"And then, of course, there's the money."

"Why *you!*" She raised her arms again, threatening him.

He didn't flinch.

"Again, you misunderstand me. I propose nothing that would shame you."

"Well, you better not. I'm no cookie," she said, curtly.

"I'm talking about paying you for performing in a work of art in an art gallery."

"I'm listening."

"I have a grant, sizable actually," he said, thumbing natty lapels that she hadn't notice before now. "The National Endowment for the Arts has given me thirty thousand dollars based on an exhaustive grant proposal. I get half of that for myself and expenses and the performer in my "Secretariat" gets the other half.

"Fifteen thousand!" Irma exclaimed. "That's half a year's salary!"

"Interested?"

"But why me?"

"Because I think you're perfect for it."

"But why?"

"Why not?"

"What's the catch?"

There had to be a catch! He seemed so sincere, businesslike, but passionate. Nothing added up.

"Well, there're two catches. One, you'd have to get at least a month off of work, because that's how long the show will be up."

"Why, I'd have to quit my job!"

"You said it was half a year's salary. You said you don't like your job. This will give you five months of breathing space to find a better one."

"And what's the other catch?"

"You have to perform in the nude."

"I thought so," she said, standing up.

"But your, shall we say, private lower physiognomy, will not be visible."

"But the rest of me will be?" she asked, crossing her arms on her chest.

"Yes."

"My boobs."

"Yes."

"Is that absolutely necessary?"

"Yes, Irma. But look at it this way. Nudity is everywhere. In the movies, on the stage, everywhere. This is no different."

She sat down.

"I want the money up front."

"Of course."

"One last question."

"Yes."

"What do I *do?*"

Ernst leaned halfway across the table and whispered:

"Irma, you type."

Irma turned out to be the perfect subject. She was prompt, courteous, patient, and uncomplaining, except for one detail. She was required to sit at all times. Ernst had made provision that her privates be obscured from view, but Irma found the surface she was meant to sit upon quite irritating, until Ernst found a velvety material, which could be changed every day or two, for her comfort. The rest of her was boldly and gloriously on view.

The opening of Ernst Marcel's one-man show at the Clock Gallery caused little more than the usual voyeuristic snickers until "Secretariat"—what the show catalog called "a daring statement on sex and sports in the workplace"—was purchased by the Whitney Museum for one point one million dollars.

The Times critic said, "Imagine, if you will, a black and white spotted pinto, stuffed. Out of the back of its neck, like a reverse goiter, grows an IBM Selectric typewriter. Astride the pony sits a well-endowed and pretty young woman with straight red hair. She's as nude as Godiva, only her hair doesn't reach below her shoulders. Only a small saddle, strategically arranged, hides her backside and —there's no other word, so be prepared—her genitalia. Otherwise, 'Secretariat' leaves nothing to the imagination. And what is she doing? What the hell is she doing? Ladies and gentlemen, she's typing, hunt and peck. This is 'Secretariat.' This is worth more than a million bucks according to the Whitney Museum. This is great art! This a cruel joke."

The critic turned out to be not far from wrong, but *The Observer* got the scoop. Pat Lock, owner of the Clock Gallery, was quoted as saying, "We put the price tag on there for a giggle. It was part of the work of art!" Ernst Marcel said, "Admittedly, I had at first no intention of selling her, but when I heard that the Whitney was serious, I said to myself, 'What a way to make a statement in the art world *and* at the bank.'"

An aside: yes, around this time Senators Jesse Helms and Dan Coats and others in congress were making a stink about the National Endowment for the Arts, proposing to put it out of business. Fortunately for Ernst and the Whitney, compared to what infuriated the righteous legislators the most—and we won't rehash all that here —a partially nude woman didn't even rise to the level of the irritating, let alone the objectionable, let alone the outrageously obscene.

Nonetheless, for the sake of the Whitney's reputation as a serious institution, its board of directors voted to fire half the curatorial staff, threatened to jettison the board member chairing the acquisitions committee if he didn't personally write a check for $1.5 million (the balanced to be used for undefined maintenance fees), which he was happy to do, and hired Mary Cunninghimm, a former vice president in charge of special operations at AT&T. Her first day on the job she came up with the way out.

"This is very easy to sort out," she told the board at a special meeting. "You bought a work of art, and a work of art is a totality, is it not? It is not a work of art if it is not whole. Am I correct?"

This being the board of a museum of contemporary art, not all of its members were certain that this notion wasn't a bit reactionary. But, there being other things at stake here, every member nodded enthusiastically.

"Good. Now, in any court of law in the country, it would be confirmed that unless you've received every bit, every portion, every aspect, every element, every soupçon of the M&M&M—I mean the mixed media module—then, without question, you have been cheated and are entitled to consider the purchase null and void. And, most importantly, your sterling reputation restored."

She looked triumphantly around the room and concluded: "Bribe the babe to stay home."

His check having been deposited, the chairman of the acquisition committee was the only person to vote against this plan.

Unfortunately for Cunninghimm—who was fired a week later (and the orphaned curatorial staff members returned to their former positions)—this was anticipated by Marcel and Lock. They'd already given Irma $250,000 in return for signing an iron-clad document (which they slipped into the purchase agreement with the Whitney) in which she committed to making her performance in "Secretariat" permanent, as long as she was in good health, thus making the Whitney Museum her *de facto* place of work.

Initially, "Secretariat" was installed—"in cowardly fashion" as *The Times* critic put it (trying to redeem himself after trailing *The Observer)*—in a dark and remote corner of the lowest floor. Irma didn't mind; the fewer people to see her the better. No sum of money, however large, could convince her that she wasn't being made to look a fool. But it soon became apparent that, whatever the show upstairs—soft kitchen appliances, painted paintbrushes and shovels, or rose-colored Lolita sunglasses for pets—the museum crowd had found a new darling.

At first all these people were simply an unwelcome and embarrassing distraction. The curatorial staff, determined—ordered by the board chair—to make things as unpleasant as possible for Irma, demanded that she type, audience or not; there'd be no reading, no doing of nails; they'd paid for a work of art; Irma doing anything else but typing with only two fingers, no more, no less, was not a work of art. If she hadn't threatened to march herself down to the ACLU, they wouldn't have allowed her to relieve herself or to eat lunch either.

Soon the crowds began to work a change in Irma she would never have anticipated. Sure, some jokes were cracked, and occasionally somebody would toss a marshmallow or a piece of cracker, seemingly all in good fun. But more often than not the people stood still, politely silent, as she tapped and tapped and tapped. One day, thirty or forty people squeezed themselves into her little room. They moved as one, inching closer, watching very, very intently, then moving back a bit so as not to get too close. (The staff had told Irma that roping her off was a non-starter.) All Irma could hear was their breathing. She began to wonder. These people were here to watch her perform. (Yes, she was nude, but a more sympathetic staff member had turned her away from her audience by 260 degrees, so that only a side view of her right breast was visible.) They believed—even if she didn't—that she was indeed a work of art. Who was she to say they were wrong? Nothing jarred the silence as she tapped away (the typewriter was not turned on), holding her tummy in as Ernst had demanded, and concentrating very hard on not losing her concentration—what Ernst said was "the focus of the locus of 'Secretariat'": her brain. Thus, she tapped and tapped for the entire afternoon and nobody left.

Then a stern voice said, "Closing time." The spell was broken. The crowd wandered out, whispering, "Wow!" and "Who'd have thought?" and "Virtuoso performance!" and "I finally got it there at the end," as Irma collapsed in confused, but happy, exhaustion. The judgment of the public! She said to herself, "Like it or not, Irma, 'Secretariat' is art!" She liked it.

After two weeks of this, "Secretariat" was moved to a special gallery on the second floor and an admission fee of $10 was charged to see her. They even put up a rope and stanchions and assigned a guard just for Irma.

*

Within a year, Irma had become a celebrity. "DESK JOCKEY LEADS

THE FIELD!" read one headline. During the day, she was New York's most famous artist, of the gallery, the stage, or the television set. At night she went out with Ernst Marcel and lived a thrilling life. Though she hardly ever said a word, they were invited to all the best parties. George Plimpton offered them a standing invitation, where they met the Mailer's and Onassis' of the *beau monde*. Talk shows begged her to appear, but she always turned them down. Ernst was fascinated by her response: it wasn't that she was shy, she'd say, or that she had nothing to talk about. She was a work of art and works of art don't speak, at least not to the public for which they were created.

In two years' time, Irma had become a public institution. The mayoress presented her with a key to the city for the boost she'd given to tourism and the local economy. The museum was building a separate gallery, exclusively for "Secretariat" and other works of performance art, including several by Ernst Marcel (almost hidden in the background). Irma had her own contract now; they paid her a bundle. The Met invited her onto its board of directors, but, of course, she politely refused. "Ernst Marcel" had been eclipsed by "Irma" in the public eye, though she honestly tried to set the record straight. When "Who actually created 'Secretariat'" had become a popular trivia question, Irma finally went public. On the Donahue show (where she appeared in a diaphanous blue robe), when asked if "Secretariat" was her own creation, she shook her head and pronounced her immediately famous dictum, "I am Art. Watch me be!"

None of this hurt the love that had slowly grown between Irma and Ernst. He'd made his fortune, and though he still created, he was frankly more interested in Irma. She told him that he was the first man she had ever loved and that he would be the last. The night he asked her, over dinner, to marry him, he also begged her to quit her job.

"How can you ask that?" she exclaimed. "This isn't a job. It's my life! And yours too!"

"I know, I know, Irma," Ernst said softly, "but what about the future? I want to have children. I want a normal life. We've had our fun. We don't need the money. Let someone else take over!"

The thought had never once occurred to her. Irma quickly realized why—because it was unthinkable! If she understood anything at all about art by now it was that you couldn't change a thing about it. Not without destroying it. Wood's old farmer and his daughter could not be holding a shotgun between them. The Gioconda could not be leering. Whistler's Mother couldn't be whistling. She was "Secretariat" and no other woman could be!

She told him so.

"That's ridiculous! Any good-looking broad with a nice body could do the job."

"How dare you!" Irma shouted angrily. "Manipulating your own aesthetic just to get a ring on my finger. You chose me out of all the women in New York City! That was an artistic decision, wasn't it? Or was it?" she added softly, growing suspicious. "Or was it a seducer's ploy after all?"

"Well, if it was, it sure hasn't paid off yet," he shouted sarcastically.

"Very funny."

"Okay, you've got me. Of course it wasn't, but...."

"So, art is absolute or isn't it?"

"Yes, of course it is, if it's art. But be reasonable. Using your logic, what happens when we have children? I want to have children with you, Irma!"

Irma hesitated. She knew where he was heading. She wanted them too, she supposed.

"Well?"

"I'll have to think about it.

"That's right. Think. You can't be a pregnant lady and still be 'Secretariat'. Not *my* 'Secretariat'! And what about your age? You're twenty-seven now, sure. You don't look any different than when we began. What happens in five, ten, twenty years? What happens when you are no longer the woman I chose?"

"You tell me? Is that when you'll want a divorce?"

"Don't play games, Irma. I meant when you no longer look like the woman that I, the artist, chose as his material?"

"Art doesn't conquer time!" she said defiantly. "Yes, you do have a point about pregnancy. No question. But just as paint ages on the canvas, so I will age. Let's hope that I do so gracefully. But the aging of what an artist chooses as his materials is nothing he can do anything about. I will still make a statement as 'Secretariat' when I'm eighty."

"Now you're out of your depth. Performance art is not a painting. It isn't meant to last forever. No performance does."

"Then why did you sell me to a museum?"

She had him there. They both took deep breaths.

"Okay. I'm sorry. You're right. It's dangerous business, what we're talking about. So let's drop it, okay? But there still remains the question of children, and...."

"What?"

"Well, sex. I love you."

"And I love you, but...."

"Maybe if we finally have sex, it will decide everything."

She looked at him as if for the first time. Did her feelings for him run that deep? What was a marriage without a compatible sex partner and children. At least that's what her mother told her years ago. She let herself daydream for a moment. All the cliches of married life passed before her eyes. She stood up and said, "Let's go to my place."

In her bedroom, they were both very nervous. Ernst was not a particularly handsome man, though his body was firm and fit. Irma's body was no secret at all to Ernst—he knew its every curve and crevice—which is perhaps the main reason why their one night of love was such a disappointment.

The next morning, they woke on opposite sides of the bed, their backs to each other.

Finally, she said, in a tone she realized later had been unfairly sweet, "You're right. I can't continue my performance and have children."

He turned and reached for her.

"My darling!"

She held him away.

"I'm sorry. Really, I am."

Two years later, Irma made art history when "Secretariat" was purchased by the Museum of Modern Art for $20 million, $5 million of which went into her bank account. There was always controversy when a museum sold one of its holdings, especially a famous one, but in this case, the price shut up the critics, one of whom wrote, "'Secretariat' is literally a wasting asset. Who can blame the Whitney for cashing in for such a huge reward when they still could?"

She was installed in the new addition, in the gallery next to Picasso's "Les Demoiselles d'Avignon". The admission price went up, with a five-minute viewing limit. In an eight-hour day, with 20 people spending five minutes at $25 per viewing, and factoring in another five minutes to get each group in and out, that meant total capacity brought in $24,000 a day. Capacity was often total.

For the next fifteen years, Irma aged, but not as gracefully as she, or MOMA, would have liked. She developed a little paunch from lack of exercise, and cellulite deposits pocked her thighs. Her hair faded from its bright orange hue, and she refused on artistic grounds to have it dyed.

With the waning of her physical beauty, it became apparent that "Secretariat"'s attraction for the general public had not been without its element of tee and ay. Attendance and revenue inexorably declined. By the time Irma was fifty, she'd become little more than a curiosity. The museum finally stopped a lot of jokes by making admission to her gallery free, after gradually reducing it down to a dollar. No one more than peeked in for a moment.

Finally, they removed her to the basement. They kept her in the catalog as a courtesy, and an historical oddity.

At night, Irma limped (arthritis in her hips) home to her little apartment in the building that towered over (and was owned by) MOMA. She had asked to be allowed to live in the empty storage room at the end of the corridor in the basement. She even offered to pay to have it built out as an apartment. One curator suggested, "It might make the news." Another countered, "Yes. We could look like jailers." Her request was denied.

The apartment was the next best thing. It was small, clean (she had a housemaid), and sparsely furnished. Since Ernst Marcel's death from a brain hemorrhage five years before, she had no visitors. No one ever knew how she spent her nights on a kitchen chair stacked with roll-ed up newspapers, practicing her technique, trying to hold in her stomach, tapping her fingers on the kitchen table.

In the middle of her sixty-seventh year, "Secretariat" attained a certain vogue when *The New Yorker* "rediscovered" it. In a 30,000-word profile of both Ernst and Irma, the writer confessed to being intensely intrigued by what she saw as "the time bomb effect that had been built into 'Secretariat' from its creation; the exciting statement made by an aging, wrinkled, naked crone astride a stuffed pony. The artist was, *is* commenting on time in art, and not life in art, after all!"

This led one ambitious young curator to conceive of a Marcel retrospective to prove out the artist's theories in his other works, only to discover that not a single piece had survived the artist's death. "Secretariat" spent a month on the third floor near the minimalists, generating more articles and a carefully shot and edited spot on CBS news. Then the world moved on.

Back in the basement, Irma died of a coronary two years later. A *Village Voice* wag pronounced, "She died in the saddle." People laughed in spite of themselves.

MOMA was at a loss. Internal controversy raged over what to do with "Secretariat." One faction said to let it alone, that the work had entered a "new stage of expression." Others felt that a look-alike contest be conducted to find a youthful replacement. Finally, against the recommendation of its own curatorial staff that the work be destroyed altogether, the board of directors voted to commission a wax body to be constructed from pictures of Irma in her heyday. To appease the National Endowment for the Arts, the wax was clothed in a teeny pink bikini. MOMA justified its actions with the simple formula: "Twenty million bucks is twenty million bucks." No one, however, suggested that the new "Secretariat" be appraised by Sotheby's or anyone else.

"Secretariat" took its place in the permanent collection, installed—hermetically sealed in a plexiglass cube—in a sun-and rain-shielded corner of the Rockefeller sculpture garden directly behind the museum. The wax didn't move, certainly, but the expression of total concentration on its face was a perfect imitation of Irma's technique. With the return of the sexual element to "Secretariat" (the waxworker achieved admirably in this regard, employing poetic license with the physical proportions of what the bikini only partially hid), the work enjoyed a resurgence of popularity. The board of directors was vindicated. "An unqualified triumph," crooned *The New Criterion*'s art critic.

As stipulated in Irma's will, her ashes had displaced an equal amount of sawdust from the equine brain of "Secretariat." Irma had no heirs. She left a pension to the janitor who used to brush the dust off the pinto and put clean velvet on the saddle every day. Her millions went to MOMA.

THE NECK

The neck, or water nixie, is a shapeshifting water spirit.

I MET her while walking along a stream that runs through the heart of the campus. For the most part, this narrow watercourse is quite open to view, with few trees or shrubs on its banks. Every few hundred yards, arched walking bridges look like they came from paintings by Monet. Only two bridges allow for motor traffic, and they are at opposite ends of the "old campus" half a mile apart. Beyond them are all the newer buildings, dormitories and sports facilities mostly. In the heart of the old campus, though, it feels like another world, nothing but limestone and red maple trees, and gardens of perennials everywhere.

I found the neck sitting on the bank of the stream between two bushes, one nestled up against one of the bridges, the other a couple of yards further downstream. I saw at once that she was lovely, with golden hair and a yellow flower tucked behind one ear. She wore a luminescent blue-green dress that stretched from her throat to below her feet; in other words, as long as a wedding dress with a train. I stopped and she turned to look at me, pulling her dress up slightly to reveal lovely bare feet.

"Hello," she said, surprising me. Most women on campus, students or faculty, would have simply turned away from a stranger who stopped to look at them.

"Hello," I said.

"Would you like to sit down?"

"I would, if you don't mind," I answered. I was carrying a load of books and papers and the idea of a short rest was appealing, not to mention the company.

She pulled her dress across her knees and made room for me between the bushes.

"I know what I remind you of," she said, as I settled down.

"That would certainly impress me if you did."

"A neck, or nixie."

"You're right! How could you know?"

"Because that's what I look like!" she said and laughed.

"Yes, but only a professor of northern mythologies, among other things, would even know what a 'neck' is. And most people can't tell a nixie from a pixie, and you're no pixie."

She laughed again and put her hand on my knee for just a moment. "You're funny."

I began to feel a bit ridiculous and suspected some kind of game was going on. I looked around, expecting to see a camera phone peeking out from behind a tree. I almost got up and walked away, but, even if it was a game, I thought, it seemed harmless enough.

"Thank you, I guess," I said and patted her knee slightly, which caused her to just slightly pull away.

"I'm sorry. I'm harmless enough," I said, echoing my thoughts.

"Sorry for what? What do you mean harmless? Of course, you're harmless. Why else do you think I asked you to join me?"

"Good point," I said, a bit confused. "Can I ask why you're wearing such a beautiful gown?"

"Why, don't you like it?"

"I do like it. It's charming. It's just a little unusual given the circumstances."

"I don't understand," she said and frowned, almost on the verge of being upset.

"I only meant that most women on campus don't wear such lovely clothes, except at parties or other events in the evening."

I paused, but received no reaction.

"You don't dress like that all the time, do you?"

Now I was really off track. A tear fell from her eye, which she touched with her forefinger. I thought she was about to stand up and leave. Instead, she laughed and touched the tear to my cheek.

"There, now you're mine, not that you deserve it," she said, her smile half human, half flower.

"In what sense?" I asked, playing along.

"You know exactly in what sense."

"I'm sorry. I don't think I do."

"Forever," she said.

Again, I looked behind me, even under the bush on our left.

"Why do you keep looking away? You like looking at me, don't you?"

"Yes."

I thought, from this moment on, the less I said the better, and wondered if even saying "yes" might have been inappropriate.

"Good. I like looking at you," she said, but quickly continued. "Can we talk about something else?"

"Or maybe just sit here and enjoy the Marigold."

"The what?" she asked. Now she was looking around in every direction. "I don't see any marigolds."

"The stream. It's called the Marigold. Didn't you know?"

"Of course not. And that's not its name."

I wasn't about to argue, but curiosity couldn't prevent me from asking, "What do you call it?"

"It's not what I call it. It's its name."

"And what is that?"

"I can't tell you. I'm not supposed to tell you. Besides, you wouldn't understand anyway."

She was smoothing the dress along her thighs, not in the least suggestively, but in simple admiration of its stunning fabric.

"I'd tell you if I could," she whispered.

"That's okay," I said quickly, since she seemed on the verge of upset once again.

"Why do you call it Marigold?"

"I'm not sure," I said, trying to remember, but nothing occurred to me. "Perhaps before they built the campus the area was full of marigolds?"

"I think it was named after Mary Gold. A young woman like me, with hair like mine."

"That would make sense," I agreed. "In fact, I like your explanation far better than mine."

"I would like to meet Mary Gold."

I thought, just look into the river, which at that moment was still as a mirror. But I didn't say anything, afraid again of saying something inappropriate.

Here I must explain that I was, at that moment, 47 years old, a tenured professor, and a married father of a daughter attending Harvard on a full scholarship. I was homely as a shard of broken concrete, but people liked me because I was a nice, honest, hard-working fellow always ready to help out or listen to a friend. My wife of almost 30 years was no raving beauty either, but she was liked for many of the same reasons I was. I adored every bone in her slightly plump little body.

Thus, it came as a huge surprise when a student, I was later to learn a graduate student in biology and a former member of the football team, came up from behind and said, "Is this guy bothering you, young lady?"

She turned and looked at him and said, "No. He's my friend."

"I saw him put his hand on your knee."

"I did nothing of the sort," I insisted. "I barely touched her knee in an innocent gesture of agreement."

"That's not how I see it, buddy," he persisted. "I see a man sitting in the grass talking to a young lady half his age and I'm pretty sure you made her cry."

He turned to the young woman and smiled sympathetically.

"Did he make you cry?"

"Indeed. He made me shed a tear. Now he's mine forever."

"Okay, that's enough. Get to your feet, professor, and be on your way."

"How do you know I'm a professor?"

"Who cares? I could throw a rock across the quad and have a 50-50 chance of hitting a professor."

I started to get up to have a private word with this young asshole, but the young lady grabbed my arm, holding me back, then stood up. She leaned down and said, "Remember, you are mine forever. That's when we'll meet again."

Then she kissed me, lingeringly, just for a moment, on the lips.

She turned to the young man and slapped his face so hard he fell backward on the ground, his head just missing the sidewalk.

"What did you do that for? I was trying to help!" he cried.

"You wanted me for yourself. I am no one but his, and he knows when we shall meet again."

Then she turned back toward the Marigold and dove in, her body as straight and strong as a young willow.

The young man stood and came forward.

"Yowza!" he cried.

Shoulder to shoulder we stood waiting, but she didn't surface.

"Hurry!" I shouted and took off my shoes and jacket. We entered the water at the same time. It was a stone bottom stream, so the water was very clear. There was no sign of the young lady.

After diving numerous times both up- and downstream, we gave up any hope of finding her. The campus police had been called and arrived almost immediately. They too shed their heavier clothing and dove in repeatedly. The water was only four feet deep, so there was no need to drag the bottom.

Just as the sun was beginning to set behind the campus library, I noticed something fluttering under one of the foot bridges. I called everyone to that point and went in after it. I came out of the water with the young woman's garment, which was all that was ever found.

There was an investigation, of course, by the police and by the college administration. Both the young man and I were accused of vaguely inappropriate behavior, but nothing could be done with no witnesses and no more evidence than a shimmering dress.

There was never a report of a missing young woman. Every young woman on campus and from the town nearby was accounted for.

I never could convince myself that it was all a hoax to demonstrate inherent male issues of disrespect toward women, and that the woman, having stripped off, was met by someone with a robe and hurried away from the stream. But it was the likeliest explanation.

The dress would eventually be donated to the theater department to be worn by young actresses, perhaps in the part of *Hamlet*'s Ophelia or *The Tempest*'s Miranda.

Why me? I often asked myself. Why put in an aging professor's head the idea, which never faded, that someday he would again meet such a creature, and be hers forever. Forever.

THE MEANING
OF THE WORD

"*B*UT *do* you know what it means?" she repeated.

Maybe the silliest question he'd ever heard.

The sun seemed to be frying the hairs on his chest, which he rubbed to moisten in the sweat on his flesh.

"Do you?"

"Is this a test?"

"Do you?" she persisted.

He turned on his side, facing her, his elbow biting into the coarse plastic weave of the deckchair. In the midst of this maneuver, she'd managed to cover with a pink towel what she'd been only too happy to display not five minutes before.

"Don't smile like that," she said.

"Sorry."

"I'm serious."

He turned on his back and sighed, staring up at two thick clouds flanking the sun.

"You're sure you want an answer?"

"I'm sure."

"It means two things. To engage in sex is one."

"Go on."

"It also means to hurt someone."

"Wrong on both counts!" she cried, triumphantly.

He turned again to look at her. What a smile, he thought. Such a fine profile, from the hairline to the hips—the rest, since the towel, as bound and monolithic as the bottom half of a mummy.

"Okay, I give up."

"No way. You used the word. You didn't even apologize."

This was what you got for not letting the taunts from a car full of nasty teenagers go unanswered.

"What do you want from me?"

"The *definition*."

"Do you know what *that* reminds me of?" he asked, pointing toward the sky.

"What?"

"The sun, with those two long clouds coming up to it."

"Let me think."

He turned to look at her. *Such* a smile.

"The clouds? Or the sun?"

"The sun," he said.

Her lips formed a word, then a big frown.

"I didn't think a girl like you could blush like that."

"I'm not a girl. And don't change the subject."

"Okay. Sorry. You tell me."

"It *means* to do whatever it takes to make ah…. You understand that I *will* have to be explicit?"

"I do."

She paused and looked at him questioningly, as if he really did know.

"It means to do whatever it takes to make your lover come," she said, grabbed her towel and tossed it in his face.

✳

His friends called him Jeroboam. Gerald Bowman lay beside the motel pool on an August afternoon, most of a six-pack of beer in a cooler beside him.

He had worked hard to create these gaps in his travel plans so he could play golf at the local public course or bask in the sun and not even think about returning to the road for two or three days at a time. Each new gap of luxury and endeavor he'd learned to maximize. It was, after all, a demanding job.

That this small, firm body—graced with provocative and insolent lips, not 90 inches away from his—had appeared at the pool and lay down nearby before two in the afternoon, was merely a vindication of the lifestyle—high earning, full of opportunity—he'd always admired.

"I never thought of it quite that way."

Jerry laughed and made a show of folding the towel again and again into a small cube.

"Who the hell *are* you?"

"Today?"

He nodded.

She sat up and planted her feet on the deck. She was not, he had to admit, quite pretty. Her face was dark-toned, with flat cheekbones. Her sweet smile marred by slightly protruding incisors. Her bright blonde hair fell in damp folds on her sloping shoulders. But she smiled with the confidence of women with provocative bodies; her plain, unpainted face fronted an energetic and precocious mind. The definition, he thought, of the word "babe."

"No man will ever know," she said and laughed at the absurdity.

He lay back, shading his eyes with his hand.

"Can I tell you a story?"

"I'm listening."

"Last night, I sat in the very nice bar in a town 100 miles away, until almost midnight. Finally, a pair of faintly rusted roses sat down beside me. I bought drinks. The conversation didn't seem to have anything to do with me. Bored, I looked back and forth between them, their looks going back and forth between them. Finally, I got the gist. 'Get the fuck lost,' I told them."

The woman sat forward, hugged herself and smiled, accepting the challenge.

"You wouldn't be surprised to know that I was once married for three years. One day it was over. I signed the papers and it *was* over. That's all it took. Today, I am eminently fuckable by every standard any man might judge me."

"I couldn't agree more."

"So here's the deal. I promise to provide you with *no less than eight* demonstrations of the *meaning* of the word we've just been discussing, between now and four o'clock tomorrow afternoon, if you will promise to return the favor."

Her words, he thought, might have been just as angry as seductive. "Why four o'clock?"

"It's a goal. You need a goal in life."

He laughed in spite of her seriousness.

"Eight."

"Eight."

Exhaling, he said, "Fine. I could do that with my finger."

"You're not *with* me. My math."

"What?"

"You're the eight."

"And you?"

"I'm more."

"More?"

"I know what I'm capable of. You, I believe, do not. At least I don't believe you've been tested."

"Eight?"

"I figure if I'm attentive and allow your natural excitement to take care of things early, you can manage it."

He frowned, not meaning to, but she ignored it.

"There's a ratio, you know? Between friction and coming? I figure, with what I have in mind, you can make it to five between now and bedtime. After that, only three to go tomorrow!"

"Eight."

"You don't find me sufficiently sexy?"

"Right," he said sarcastically.

She stood up and held out her hand. He stood up and took it. He couldn't think of a single word to say.

She dragged him toward the water. He looked around to make sure they were alone.

In the deepest part of the shallow end, she pulled down his swimsuit. He was already hard and had been for the past twenty minutes, which she must have known. With a quick look toward the passing cars and the motel office, she pulled down her bottom. He put his hand on her left breast.

"That's for later," she said, swatting him.

He laughed softly.

"Look out below!" she whispered in his ear.

He stopped laughing.

With an athletic lunge and plunge, wrapping her legs around him, she took him inside her. A few moments later, he came. They parted and quickly pulled up their suits. Bringing her knees up out of the water, she pushed off the side of the pool and backstroked away.

"Damn!"

"You still owe me eight!" she cried, laughing at the sun.

He couldn't help himself. "Wasn't that one?"

"Not for me," she said sweetly, swimming back to him. "Don't worry. That wasn't the idea."

He climbed out of the pool and plopped into his chair. As he toweled off, she performed a handstand in the water, came up laughing, then dove again and swam both lengths of the pool underwater. He closed his eyes and waited until she'd settled into her chair beside him.

Vigorously toweling her hair, she asked, "So, what's your record?"

"What?"

"In twenty-four hours? With anyone?"

"I never kept score."

"Hell you didn't."

"Did you?"

"'Did' is a bit nasty, considering."

"Well?"

"Women don't need to."

"So," he said with conviction, "I don't either."

"Lame, very lame."

"Truth is by definition lame."

"Women don't because it's meaningless," she said, ignoring him. "Do you think we're the same, men and women?"

"No."

"Then what's the problem?"

"No problem at all."

"I'm thrilled. So, what's the answer? How many?"

"Does this answer your question?"

He was already hard again.

"Lovely." She stood and took his hand and led him behind a privacy wall by a shower.

She pulled down her bottom and bent over.

"Remember, no friction. Just come for me."

He did as asked; she was so wet he came after only a few thrusts.

As they pulled on their clothes, he asked, "And you?"

"Oh, yes," she said, and kissed him, he realized, for the first time.

They returned to their deckchairs and stretched out.

"I'm going to nap for a bit," she said and turned away.

"Good idea."

When he woke, she was with him, her left leg thrown over his, a towel draped over them. The afternoon sun was about to drop below the trees.

She was stroking him, very gently.

Without looking, he said, "Sure we're alone?"

"I'm sure," she said, adding, "You know what this is?"

"Some kind of lotion."

She left off long enough to hand him the tube.

"You too."

Well concealed, they proceeded to rub each other.

"Gently. Gently," she whispered, between kisses.

Again, he came quickly. She bucked under his finger.

"Now, into the pool with you!"

They bobbed around in the cool water, cleaning up.

"Twice, right?" he whispered in her ear.

"Yes, sir."

"Five left."

"Are you ready?"

"What do you think?"

"I know I am," she said, climbing out of the pool, drying off, and throwing her towel over her shoulders.

He did the same.

Their things gathered, he took her hand. She resisted, grabbed his arm and steered him toward the street.

They waited for the traffic, heralded by a few wolf-whistles and shouting from passing cars. They crossed. She smiled serenely. He understood that she felt her own near-nakedness as nothing. They could have been invisible. They walked through the parking lot of a burger joint, through a mangled gap in a link fence and into a park full of trees and playground equipment. A few heads turned as they walked through it and onto a street lined with small, neat houses. They walked two blocks, past house after house after house. She led him up a driveway toward the left side of a duplex, unlocked the door, and ushered him into a kitchen, all red-and-white checkers and shining surfaces.

"Welcome home, darling," she said.

PHILIP ROTH'S LAST STAND

BY

PHILIP ROTH

*I*KNOW, a snarky title for this "story." But you'll see it makes sense in the end. I knew Philip personally, for a brief time, long before he'd quit writing altogether.

First, an anecdote. In the early '90s, the artistic director of our university theatre department had convinced Claire Bloom to visit and do a reading and some Q & A with the audience. He didn't have much of a budget, but she agreed, even to his driving down to pick her up three hours away and bringing her to town. As they were leaving the city where she had just performed, she looked behind her and waved, "Goodbye, Columbus."

As we would learn later, Ms. Bloom wasn't always so charming.

I recount this not only because it is charming, and true, but to assure the reader that I was and am interested in anything Roth.

I've read, sometimes multiple times, nearly every work of Roth's fiction I could find, including some very obscure stories never published in book form. After myself writing a story about the nuclear tests at Bikini Atoll (my uncle had captained one of the target ships), I discovered he beat me to the punch decades earlier in *Esquire*. The others I photocopied at the library from crumbling copies of magazines like *Cosmopolitan* and *The Atlantic Monthly*. I have small-press hardback treasures like "Novotny's Pain," first published in *The New Yorker,* and "His Mistress's Voice," first published in *Partisan Review.* Why he never published these half-dozen stories is beyond me. The writing is on a par with anything in the book *Goodbye, Columbus.* Maybe he just forgot them.

Full disclosure—I just can't get through his baseball novel, *The Great American Novel.* I've tried five times. I keep jumping to later chapters hoping things will pick up. I think he thought it was all very funny, but for me the words are dead on the page. No Great American Novel for Mr. Roth. (It doesn't help that I haven't watched ten seconds of baseball since Pete Rose turned out to be such an asshole.)

Still, that's the only exception. I even love the universally derided, all-dialogue *Deception.* Sue me.

My short relationship with Philip, which consisted of two letters and (possibly) two phone calls, began when I finished reading *The Dying Animal.* I'm not a fan-boy (hate that word), and had never written to a writer before, but I decided to write to Philip.

I'm a public relations consultant who just happens to like reading and writing fiction, though my list of publications is embarrassingly slim. Why would any writer bother to respond to me? But something told me he just might if I pushed the right buttons. It was a long letter, so I'll quote only the highlights.

Dear Mr. Roth,

Portnoy's Complaint *was my first time.* (Pretty cute, huh? He never said so, but I know he liked it.) *I read it at the age of 15. I bought it for the dirty parts, of course, but I was still able to give my older brother, a junior at IU, an only slightly sophomoric exegesis of the book's themes. You made me a literary critic without my knowing it!*

Then I went on to tell him how I'd read almost all his books, plus the obscure stories, and told him about my uncle and Bikini Atoll. Then I really laid it on:

This doesn't need to be said, but I'll say it anyway. No one writes a better sentence. Not Bellow, not Mailer, not Updike. I know what I'm talking about. (Love the chutzpah of that.) *And, taken as a whole, there is no body of work comparable to yours written in the last fifty years.*

In hindsight, it's surprising he read another word, after such a sucking up. But, maybe he liked that sort of thing, maybe a lot. Then I got personal:

Before I get to the point of this letter, I'll say only, as a bookend to the account I began with, that I've never seen my Dad angrier than when he finished reading (and he did finish) The New Yorker *excerpts from* Sabbath's Theater, *especially the scene when Sabbath spills his seed on the flowers on his lover's grave. He's a staunch Catholic and promptly cancelled his subscription (which I'd bought him a year before as a Christmas present). I love my Dad, but I've issues with the man; without going into details, let's just say I mentally thanked you that day.*

I never learned differently, but I've always felt Philip got a special glow from reading of my Dad's anger, at least if his depictions of his own father provide any hint. Finally, I cut to the chase:

Here's my question. I recently finished The Dying Animal. *I've read several attempts to identify the narrator's interlocutor. A friend of mine says he thinks it's another woman. I plump for Death. I'd like to think we're both right. Who is it?*

Looking forward to your next book, I am,

Sincerely,
Phil Roth

Okay, so what? If you Google "Phil Roth" you'll get 38,000,000 results. My last name is actually Guerin, but I'd already taken a chance bringing up Catholicism, so I went for Roth. Having read all the Zukerman books, *Operation Shylock* and *The Facts*, I figured he'd know it was either a jape or a distant cousin of the kind of coincidence—some confrontation with a seeming doppelgänger—that (I theorized) launched the very idea of Zukerman and "Philip Roth."

I also included my phone number, plus an email exchange between my friend and me.

I sent the letter in early April of 2001. I received Philip's response in mid-May. I don't have permission to quote from the letter, so I'll have to paraphrase.

First, and most disappointing, he sided with my friend, though he refused to say who the interlocutor was. My friend had suggested that the narrator, David Kepesh, was impotent, and the interlocutor was a young woman he'd tried and failed with. I still think she was Death. I mean *The Dying Animal*? Come on.

The other interesting bit was my friend had suggested that Roth, then Kawabata, then Updike, were his list of the most breast-obsessed novelists, and that the book weirdly reminded him of *Valley of the Dolls*. Philip said he'd never read *Valley*, had read and admired Kawabata (didn't mention Updike), but declined to agree to being "breast-obsessed." Most men admired breasts, he said (a bit obviously), especially beautiful ones like Consuela's (the heroine of the novel under discussion), but women did too, he maintained, and not just lesbians.

He concluded his page-long letter with a statement on the lines of it being a pleasure to know that there were still readers in the world like me and my friend.

Needless to say, I was thrilled with such a lengthy response and immediately had the letter enshrined in a gilded frame.

It so happened that I was taking an extension course in Contemporary Fiction and had decided on this title for an essay assignment: "Who Should Win the Nobel Prize for Literature?"

Pressing my luck, I wrote Philip again, this time to the return address on his envelope to me (my initial letter having been sent via his publisher). It was a couple of months later, so I reminded him of our earlier correspondence and asked him a single, two-part question: "How do you feel about having been so unfairly passed over for the Nobel, and do you think you will ever be so honored?"

Again, I included my phone number.

A week later I got a call.

"Hello, this is Philip Roth, is this *Mr. Roth?*" he said with sarcastic emphasis on repeating his own last name.

"Yes," I answered, voice atremble. I was so excited! "It's so nice to talk to you, Philip."

My first mistake.

"Please do not call me Philip. We are total strangers, which I'd have preferred remained that way, but Philip asked me to call you."

"Philip? What Philip?"

"Why, Philip Roth, of course. The novelist?"

"And you, I suppose are his doppelgänger," I said and chuckled.

"What the hell are you talking about?"

"Oh, come on, Mr. Roth. I read *Operation Shylock.*"

"I haven't read a single word of my friend's work. He forbids it, if we are to remain friends."

"This is all very amusing, Philip...."

"I said don't call me that!" he shouted.

"I'm sorry, Mr. Roth. But, as I was saying, this is amusing, if a little weird, if you don't mind my saying so."

I shut up, remembering the old adage that you'll learn a lot more if you keep our mouth closed.

No response. The silence went on for more than a minute, so, fearing he'd hang up, I continued.

"You, I mean, Mr. Roth, got my latest letter?"

"That's why I'm calling."

Of course, given the amazing nature of this phone call, I couldn't give a fuck about my paper or the Nobel prize.

"I'm listening," I said.

Again, an extended silence. I couldn't even hear breathing.

"It would mean a great deal to me if I could quote Mr. Roth in the essay I wrote to him about. You can't imagine!"

"Out of the question."

"Well, if you could just give me a sense of his feelings about the Nobel, which must be a matter of some distress for Mr...."

"Why do you keep talking such nonsense? I know nothing about his feelings about the Nobel. That's not why I'm calling."

"But you said you were calling about my letter. My letter's about the Nobel."

"Beside the point, bub," he said, deliberately, I thought, coarsening both his language and his voice. "I'm calling about this 'Phil Roth' shit."

I decided the best approach at this juncture was to show some aggression myself.

"Are you calling my name shit?"

"I'm calling you a shit for using Mr. Roth's name, you wee dollop of schmutz, *Mr. Guerin!*"

Oh, crap! I thought.

"What are you talking about?"

"Don't give me shite, sonny. Vee av ar vays."

"I can call myself anything I choose to. Mr. Roth does."

"What does that mean?"

"You wouldn't know, would you, if you haven't read his books."

"No, I wouldn't."

"And yet you feel free to use his name, don't you?"

"Philip Roth *is* my name!" he shouted.

"Phil Roth *is* my name!" I shouted back.

That got an uproarious laugh, which tricked me into thinking I'd broken through to the real Philip Roth, who this most certainly had to be.

"Enough of this," he said, abruptly, "Here's what I called to say. Stop writing Mr. Roth. You got that, you tit? You homunculus! You bog of butts! You...."

I'd had enough.

"You know what, PHILIP!" I screamed, "Fuck you! Go fuck yourself! Stick your tiny prick between your own fat cheeks and squeeze!"

Then I hung up on him, thinking, *Ha! Beat you to it!*

The next day I received another phone call.

"Hello, is this Mr. Roth?"

The voice was not unlike the earlier Roth's, but it was pitched lower and possessed an almost cooing mellifluousness.

"Yes," I said.

"This is Philip Roth."

"Now, wait a minute...."

"The *real* Philip Roth."

"It's very nice to speak to you," I said, as politely as I could.

"It's nice to speak to you."

"How can I help you?"

"I'm calling to apologize."

"Oh? For what?" I asked warily.

"You did receive a call from a Philip Roth not long ago, correct?"

"Yes. Yes, I did. Yesterday. A rather unpleasant call, I'm afraid."

"That's what I understand." He said nothing for a few seconds, then took a deep breath. "Listen, you need to believe me. The person who called was not me."

"He said he was your friend."

"Oh, he's no friend of mine. He's a monster."

"That's a pretty good word for him."

"He's been the plague of my life for years, and I just can't shake him."

"How did he find out my real name?"

"What are you talking about?"

"Never mind, Mr. Roth," I said, and hurried on, "He spouted a lot of nonsense."

"I'm sure he did. That's his MO." Again, a pause. Deep breath. "Can you tell me a little of what he said?"

"You have no idea?"

"Virtually none. Only that he called and wasn't polite, and proud of it."

"Well, he knew about my letter to you. The second one, about the Nobel."

"And what did he say about that?"

"He had nothing to say. Didn't even know about its content. He only wanted to make a big deal about my name."

"Yeah, he does that. Not the first time. He's badgered several Roth's—Kepesh's, and Zukerman's too."

"Yet you told him about the letter. Why?"

"But I didn't. He's a stalker, you see. He gets into my mail somehow, and I don't know about it until I get a call, usually after he's accosted someone like yourself. I'm very sorry. I've asked the police for help, even hired a private dick once, but nobody can find the guy. I try to just ignore him and do my work. Work. Work. Work. That's my life. Then he calls me and tells me he's done this or that in my name. It's very upsetting.

"I've even met him. I thought he was a mugger when he grabbed my arm just outside the Plaza Hotel where I was having dinner with a lovely…I'm sorry." He paused. "Got sidetracked there. After I was leaving the hotel, he grabbed my arm and stuck his tongue in my ear and then into my friend's ear. It was disgusting. She almost threw up. Then he ran across the street into the park. We even went to a doctor the next day to make sure he hadn't given me some disease.

"What did he look like?"

He ignored this.

"My best guess is he's read *Operation Shylock*…."

I interrupted him.

"He said he'd never read any of your books."

"He always says that. He thinks it makes people think that's the reason we're such intimate friends, as he would have it. But he's read everything, even the obscure stuff from old magazines."

"I have too."

"But to continue," he said, ignoring this. "My PI thinks he might have a military background, perhaps special ops or intelligence. But that's just tea-leaf reading. He never got any closer to him than you did today.

"Now, let me tell you something very secret, but it's necessary because I want to make sure you believe me."

He paused, seeking my assent.

"Yes?"

"He's taken pictures of me in, how should I put it? You know what 'in flagrante' means?"

I should pause here to say that I was beginning to smell a rat. Just a sniff, a wisp. I decided to fake it.

"No. Sorry. I don't."

"It means in the act of kissing a woman."

"Ha!" I shouted. "What is this, Philip?"

"Please, can we keep this on a last name basis?"

"What kind of a fool do you take me for? Of course, I know what it means. It means being caught in the act. You know what I mean? THE ACT!"

"You're getting excited about nothing, Mr. Roth," he said, calmly, "It was simply out of a sense of delicacy that I didn't say what else was going on during the kissing."

"You weren't so damn delicate when you wrote how Mickey Sabbath showered Drenka's grave flowers with his spume."

"Delicately put, Mr. Roth. You've just made my point for me."

He had me there.

"I apologize then, okay? Please continue. This weirdo's camera found its way to your bedroom?"

"Yes, and elsewhere, on several occasions. And some of them with women that made it rather, ah, inconvenient for me."

"I'll bet."

"Let's pass over that, shall we? I mention it only, as I said, to convince you of the truth of all this, but also to make it clear how invasive his stalking has been into my private life."

"And now mine."

"Oh, there's nothing to that call of his. Just his way of having fun. He won't harm you unless you do something to harm him."

"What did you do to harm him?"

"Good question. I'm not completely sure. I suspect that I ignored him, didn't take him seriously, didn't answer his letters, hung up on his phone calls...."

"I hung up on him."

"You did? Hmm. Probably not a good move, but I wouldn't worry about it. It's me he's got a hard-on about."

"So to speak. Do you think he's gay?"

"No, of course not. Why would you think that?" he said, his voice rising a pitch with irritation.

Again, I felt as though a veil was slipping ever so slightly.

"Men don't usually stalk men, do they? Unless...."

"No, no, no. You're way off course. There's never been a hint of that. In fact, it's my virility that turns him on. It's what he wants for himself. Instead, he's some nobody living vicariously through a famous writer who happens to do rather well with the ladies."

For the third time, I found myself doubting what I was hearing.

"I'm sorry. I have to ask this, Mr. Roth. So please don't be upset."

"Go ahead."

"Are you the real Philip Roth or the joker I spoke with yesterday?"

"What an asinine question!"

"Okay, probably. Your 'doppelganger'..."

"Please don't call him that. It's too dignifying."

"Your stalker, then."

"Better."

"He called about the second letter I wrote to you."

"Yes."

"I'm not sure he knew about the first one. Can you tell me what my first letter was about?"

"The Nobel?"

"No, that was the second one. What did I write in the first letter, the one you answered?"

Slight intake of breath, then a long pause.

"Uh, I'm sorry. I don't really remember. You can't imagine how much fan mail I get."

"But how could you forget a letter signed 'Phil Roth'?"

"I get letters signed by virtually every name in my books. I think they do it, among other odd reasons, to make fun of my always using aliases in my books."

"You mean like Nathan Zuckerman?"

"Exactly."

"I still find it hard to believe you wouldn't remember my first letter. It was only a month or so ago and included an email exchange between a friend and myself. Just tell me what novel I was asking you about."

"Oh, that's easy. *The Dying Animal.* Now, can I continue?"

"Not so fast. You said that with no conviction at all. *The Dying Animal* is your most recent novel, so of course the odds are that I would have written about that."

"What do you want from me, bub."

"Your stalker called me 'bub' too."

"He got it from me. I call everyone 'bub.'"

"Fair enough. So you still can't remember what I wrote about?"

"No, sorry."

"Let's try multiple choice."

"Please," he said, losing patience.

"Bear with me. A central point of my letter had to do with one of these three things. A: masturbation, B: breasts, and C: John Updike. Which one was it?"

"Hmm. I'm beginning to remember. It wouldn't be Updike, because ever since he trashed me in *The New Yorker*, I've torn up any letter that included his fucking name."

"Actually, I did mention Updike in passing, but he wasn't the central point of the letter. Try again."

"What were the other options?"

I gave them, and added "C: The Nobel Prize."

"Oh, of course! The Nobel!"

"Sorry, that was in the second letter."

"Nice little trick, bub."

"One last try."

"I'm sorry, friend. I just don't remember. Obviously, your letter didn't have much impact on me if I don't remember it."

"Yet you wrote me a full-page letter in reply."

"I dictate a couple dozen of those a day."

"Fine. Let's agree not only that you don't remember—the correct answer was 'breasts' by the way—and that I'm still not 100 percent sure you're the real Philip Roth.

"Look, I'm...."

"No. My skepticism is my problem, not yours. Now what else did you call to tell me?"

"Man, you are one difficult person. You ought to be a critic."

"In my first letter I told you about my first exercise in literary criticism. Does that ring a bell?"

"Nope."

"Let's move on."

He sighed and took another deep breath. Miraculously, I hadn't managed yet to perturb the great man. "You go by the name Phil, right? Not Philip?"

"Yes."

"And Philip is your real name?"

"Yes."

"Why Phil?"

"It's my nickname."

"Fair enough. And your last name is actually Guerin, correct?"

"Now wait a minute, Mr. Doppelganger...."

And the earpiece filled with loud, cackling, raucous laughter.

"I told you ve av ar vays!"

He hung up.

A week later I received this letter. For obvious reasons, I feel at liberty to quote it in its entirety.

Dear Mr. Guerin,

Thank you for your letter asking about the Nobel Prize for Literature. I have no comment or opinion on the matter, at least none that I would share publicly. Thanks for asking.

Sincerely,
The "Real" Philip Roth

I compared the envelope, the return address, and the signature with Philip Roth's first letter. Identical.

IT'S PREFERRED IF
YOU FALL IN LOVE

As the garage door closed behind him, Audie climbed out of his car and tried not to leer at the surprisingly good-looking young woman who held out her hand.

"I'm Eliot," she said, not smiling. She held his hand weakly, only for a moment, and turned away. He followed her into a large, bright kitchen; she pointed toward a chair at a table with a plastic cover printed with strawberries. The cover, the floor, the sideboards, everything in the room, spotless.

"Unusual name for a woman," he said, sitting down and crossing his legs in a feint at comfort.

Without response, the young woman sat down across the table from him. She wore blue jeans and a short Kelly-green t-shirt that didn't cover her bellybutton, and had pale green eyes and dark ginger hair in a shoulder-length ponytail. She looked at him appraisingly. Finally, when she smiled, she pierced him like an icy finger in his heart. She was thrilling.

She flipped open the cover on her phone and typed several words before looking up again. She stared at him without expression, for perhaps five seconds, then looked away toward the late afternoon sunlight that filled the window above the sink. She appeared to be making up her mind.

"I think this will work," she said, and smiled at him even more invitingly. "Any questions?"

"I don't think so," he replied, looking at his hands pressed flat on the table cover. "It seemed pretty clear on the phone."

"You seem uncertain."

"No. It's just…."

"I understand. But I hate confusion. Remember, no more often than twice a month, but no less than once. That's absolute."

"Right."

"And nothing else. Ever."

"But what if you…?"

"I won't, because it's…," she interrupted herself. "Just accept it."

"Okay," he said, not liking the way she said it.

Her frown verified this feeling.

"There's one thing I didn't mention," she said.

"Yes."

"Something happens. It's okay. In fact, it's *preferred* if you fall in love. Everything works better. The thing is, don't worry. Don't think about it."

She let that sink in, then added, "And don't make it into more than it is, because I won't."

He didn't know what to say but worried that he needed to say something.

"Got it. No problem."

"That's good. I like your attitude."

"Thank you for telling me," was all he could say.

"Well, then," she said with a sigh, standing up. "Let's go into the next room."

For the first time, following her, he allowed himself to look at her body. She was maybe five-foot-five with long thin legs that didn't quite meet at her bottom, thin hips and waist, and a long graceful neck. The skin he could see was pale with a sheen of sweat. It was spring, and she hadn't turned on the A/C yet.

She had him pull down his pants and underwear and sit in a wooden chair. She knelt in front of him and put her hands on his knees. He'd been erect since they'd left the kitchen.

"Nice."

"Thank you."

"Oh, I almost forgot," she said, pulling off her t-shirt to reveal smallish breasts with brown, peaked nipples. "Visual aids."

He smiled and closed his eyes as she took him between her lips. This being the first time, he came almost immediately in his excitement. He tried to pull away but she grabbed his knees and swallowed.

When she leaned back, she smiled and said, "See? No mess."

During the next week, Audie hung up the phone ten times before dialing, remembering the rationing stipulation. Succumb and he'd have to wait that much longer until the next time. His friend, the co-worker who'd given him her phone number, hadn't warned him about that.

They never once talked about it. At first, Audie was puzzled at his friend's determination not to, his near-anger the one time he'd tried to thank him. Then, it occurred to him. They were sharing her, and with who else? Something better not dwelt upon.

He called again exactly fourteen days later, and she agreed to see him late that afternoon. Almost everything was the same as before, even the brief interview in the kitchen, which served to reiterate the basic rules of their arrangement. She was pleased that he had waited to call.

"I just want to be sure you remember," she concluded, almost apologetically.

In the living room, after she pulled off her t-shirt, sky-blue this time, she put her arms around him and kissed him deeply, for at least a minute. He tentatively brushed her nipples with his fingers, which she didn't seem to mind.

After that, the procedure took slightly longer than the first time, leaving him shaken, gasping.

As she escorted him to the garage, he put his hand on her arm and smiled.

"I see now what you were trying to tell me."

"Hmm."

"About what's preferred? That kiss really got me."

"Yes, well, maybe that was a mistake," she said, removing his hand. "Sometimes what I do is also for me, but don't talk about it. *That* does not help. Remember what I said."

In his car, he realized that he was angry. It passed, as he sorted it out. Of course, she's right, he thought. After all, that crisp hundred wasn't a Valentine he'd placed in her palm after fastening his belt.

The next week in the office was not the finest of his career. Twice, his superior handed work back to him scrawled with red marker. Not a word was spoken, but he understood that he was now on probation. He knew, of course, what the problem was, and he was sleeping only a few hours every night. That Saturday he got himself good and drunk in front of the TV. Sunday morning, remorsefully hung over, he reprimanded himself and made two resolutions. Work hard and forget her until next Sunday.

Seven days later, congratulating himself for being rested and having received a warm compliment from his supervisor on Friday, he made his call. Oddly, all this reminded him of freshman high school basketball. He'd been small, weak, and unskilled. The coaches had driven him to his limit, trying to force him to quit. After a month, they'd reluctantly awarded him his jersey, and though his muscles ached and his shins were split, he knew he'd make it through the season. Now he felt the same joyous feeling.

She seemed quite pleased to see him the next day, taking him by the hand and leading him directly to the wooden chair. Instead of blue jeans, she wore a lovely yellow summer dress, tight around her breasts. Her legs were perfect. She pulled the dress over her head, which left her in tiny yellow panties. She again put her arms around him and kissed him, opening her mouth and letting his tongue touch hers. His hands fell to her hips. She pulled away, carefully, as though she did not want to imply criticism.

"Can I see you naked?"

She set her light blue eyes to his.

"Ask me again in two months."

"Okay."

"Do you understand?"

"No."

"That's why."

"Okay."

"Case in point?" she said, getting down on her knees. "You'll find today nowhere near as nice as last time."

She was right, though she did everything exactly as before.

✳

As he drove home, Audie found himself angry, this time with himself. Why had he asked that question? From an erotic impulse merely, or was it some yearning of adoration? And what had it got him? So, it was okay to fall in love with her. Just don't let the idea escape that hothouse behind the eyes. Well. So. Be. It.

His next resolution was more complicated. Not only would he not let thoughts of her obsess or distract him from week to week, he determined to keep his affection, which was likely to grow stronger with each visit, focused exactly where it belonged, on his pleasure. If such was her advice, he'd hone his "love" down to a fine point of oblivious self-interest. He'd keep his love to himself. He'd starve her of it. He'd suck from her lips whatever it was that fueled his passion and force it down to his throbbing cock. Simultaneously, he would remind himself, as often as possible, of the deception, the manipulation she had attempted. Yes, he'd love her, even when she held out her tiny, dry hand for her emolument, but he would prove to her, to himself, that her being loved was nothing, a zero love. And to that end, he began again, what he hadn't in over a year, to date other women.

Dating had never been difficult. There were women in his apartment building, at the office, at the bars he frequented, who were delighted to accept his invitations. Several quick successes in the next two weeks reaffirmed this. One resulted in frenzied sex with hardly any effort, not even dinner.

As he dialed for his next appointment, he congratulated himself on the sophistication of what he'd come to think of as an exquisite and rare luxury, justified entirely on its own merits, but which was hardly integral to the deeper emotional and sexual existence of a man with the means to afford it.

That visit, and the next, proceeding as planned, proved to be experiences more complimentary to his ego than any he could remember since—a memory dear to him—a girl in high school, a pretty senior, had asked *him,* an awkward sophomore, to the prom. By proving himself in command, he elicited a submissiveness and compliance, still strictly within their agreement and previous practice, which leveraged his growing attraction to her into extremes of ecstasy he had never known before. He found it supremely gratifying that she seemed more than delighted with this development. In her own words, things were as easy as easy could be.

Yet, something began to gnaw at him. He pushed it away at every turn, when it slipped into his thoughts during a meeting, when he found his eyes wide open an hour after falling asleep. Drinking made it go away. Throwing himself into his work made him laugh at its inconsequentiality. When it betrayed him in the midst of Eliot's ministrations, he ground his teeth. Soon he felt slightly depressed and hollow, a feeling not unlike guilt, when he was with another woman.

After weeks of this, of repeatedly reassuring himself that what-ever it was had been reduced to simple background buzz, mental white noise, like a mild headache on a busy day, he found himself, after straying absent-mindedly from his normal route home, parked in front of her house. He remained there, watching. He saw her lights flick on and off, from lower floor to upper, until all the lights were off.

He called in sick the next day, and, in daylight, parked a block away from her house. No one came or went all that day, or night, or the next, or the next, a Friday. He spent all but ten hours over the weekend parked in the same place. Twice, she left alone and returned alone. On Sunday night, at dusk, the garage door opened, and a red Miata pulled in, leaving 20 minutes later.

He called her with his cell phone. She said she was busy.

"It's been 19 days," he said.

He forced himself not to make it sound like pleading.

"Well," she paused. Twenty seconds passed. "Give me an hour."

Greeting him, her body spitefully obliterated in gray sweatshirt and pants, she grabbed his arm and said, "We need to come to an understanding."

He looked away. She let go and took a deep breath.

"Don't do this again. My life is ordered. When has to be *my* call."

"Right."

"Are we in agreement?" Her voice dropped. "Because…."

"We are."

He still didn't look at her.

"Are you okay?"

"Yes."

He expected another interrogation, but she patted his back, al-most a push, betraying her impatience, and followed him into the next room. He turned around by the wooden chair and looked into her eyes.

"You said I could ask after two months."

"Ask what?"

Damn you, he thought. Damned, if I will ask.

"I want to see you naked."

"Sit down," she said, then took several steps back. In a moment, she had complied. After ten seconds, her sweatpants were back on. He saw only a few curls of red trimmed pubic hair. But the whole picture finally revealed, he was close to hyperventilating, which he'd been prone to as a teenager.

"I want to."

"I know."

Finally, some sensitivity, he thought.

"But that isn't possible."

"I know, but I could…."

"What."

"Reciprocate?"

"It's not allowed."

"Even for me?"

He almost wept saying it.

She took a step forward, paused, then, with a sweet smile, she backed away and said, "Sit down."

"Should I take off…?"

"No."

He sat. She stepped up, pulled down her pants, and put her right foot on his knee.

"Give me your hand."

She put his fingers into her mouth, then placed them on herself, moving his fingers with her own.

It didn't take three minutes. When she came (he was sure she did), she gasped softly, dropped her leg and pulled up her pants.

"And me?"

"That was it."

Again, pushing him, she hurried him out of the house.

"Don't ever ask again," she said, closing the door on him.

✻

Sitting in his driveway ten minutes later, he called her.

"Hi, it's me."

"Yes." Her voice entirely neutral.

"Tomorrow?"

"You know what that means."

"Yes."

"I don't recommend it."

"What time?"

She said nothing for a moment.

"Come back right now."

"What?"

"You heard me."

"Okay, forget it."

"No, you're committed."

She met him at the kitchen door in a pink wrapper, fresh from a shower.

"Sit down, please," she said.

"Here?"

"Yes."

"Sure. Whatever."

He pulled a chair away from the bare white Formica table and sat with its back against his chest.

"You're pretty pleased with yourself," she said, pulling up a chair beside him.

"This was your idea."

"It was not."

"I couldn't help myself."

"Are you becoming a problem?"

Don't take the bait, he said to himself. "I'm only following your instructions."

She looked away, as she had once before, staring out at the night sky through the kitchen window.

Audie noticed, for the first time, that there was almost no color to her eyebrows. He began to regret his insistence.

"Do you know how many men there are?"

"Not many."

She thought about this, still not looking at him. "You seem so sure."

"I'm pretty sure."

She turned to him, clearly angry. "One of them watches out for me."

"He's your…?"

"Insult me," she interrupted sharply, "and you'll never see me again."

"I'm sorry."

"You've been hanging around."

"A little."

"*Stalking* me."

"Don't try to intimidate me."

"I'm trying to reason with you." She smiled. Was she enjoying this? After a brief pause, she said, "What is it you want from me?"

"I want you to let me tell you how I feel."

"Do you know," she said, exasperated, "how many men have said that to me?"

"I don't care."

She stood up, walked to the door to the garage and opened it.

"Call me in a month."

"That's not our deal," he said.

"Fine. Take off your pants."

"Here?"

"Right now."

He obeyed. She knelt in front of him.

"No 'visual aid'?"

"You won't need it," she said and showed that she could make a man come almost immediately if she chose to.

Minutes later, when he pulled out his wallet, she said, "For earlier, too."

"But that was for you!"

"Like hell it was," she said dismissively, poking her left forefinger into her right palm.

✳

Somehow he kept to his resolutions for all of the next thirty days. He put her from his mind. His devotion to this regimen contributed to a re-acquaintance with a past lover—someone he had once considered a potential wife—which occupied many of his evenings. He even took the initiative with his supervisor to suggest his preparedness for greater responsibilities, careful to avoid any mention of increased compensation. Receiving encouragement, not the least bit begrudging, he began, for the first time in his career, to see himself as an effective professional man. Not so long ago, he'd thought of himself as a working stiff, with a well-paying job he didn't care about, which afforded him the freedom to pursue, outside of work, the things that made life worth living. Now, he saw himself as that staple of American business, the ambitious man. His co-workers, such as his friend, the one with her phone number, seemed to him poor drudges, in comparison.

The day he could call her again, he did not. Three days later, after a particularly satisfying night with his newfound old lover, he decided not to call her again, ever.

The next day she called him.

"Where've you been?"

"I thought you'd had enough of me."

"I can hardly afford that," she said, laughing.

Though she was trying to make it all light and funny, he hung up on her, thinking, "Enough."

He was proud of himself.

She called back a moment later.

"I have a present for you," she said, undaunted.

"Yes?"

"It will make a difference."

"Why are you calling me?"

"You."

It was Sunday afternoon.

"When?"

"Now?"

He pulled into the open garage twenty minutes later. The door to the kitchen was not locked, so he opened it. Audie saw no one waiting there for him.

In the next room he found her standing, with her hand on the back of the wooden chair, in nothing but a gray t-shirt that fell to her knees. She gestured toward the chair.

"Take your seat," she said.

He sat down without adjusting his clothing. He looked up at her.

"The surprise?"

"That's me." The voice came from behind him.

Startled, Audie looked around and found a petite black-haired young woman sitting on a couch, swathed in purple cloth. How had he not noticed her before?

"My apprentice," said Eliot. He tried to stand up. She put her hands on his shoulder and steadied him.

"Relax," she said, "You're going to love this."

Audie smiled.

As in the past, she directed him to strip down. Then, she took off her own covering, leaving only a gray film of panty. She embraced and kissed him, allowing him to fondle her above the waist. Then the other woman stepped up and replaced her. She made quite a production of removing all of her own scant clothing, enveloped him with her arms, and kissed him deeply. Then she quickly produced a condom and sheathed him. She sat in his lap, facing him.

Eliot leaned in and whispered, "She has her own ideas."

The new woman sighed deeply and whispered to Eliot, "You were right."

As he entered this stranger, he looked up at his love and said, "Is this what you want?"

She leaned in and kissed him and said, "Yes, this is for me, too."

Both women exchanged kisses when they weren't kissing him. Soon, his tears wet their faces, and then he came. It was the single most intense orgasm of his life; then, like a recoil from a powerful rifle, he pushed the other woman away with such violence that she fell to her knees and skidded across the hardwood floor.

"Bastard!" she screamed.

Audie grabbed his pants and stood up.

As he stumbled toward the kitchen, the women clutched each other protectively on the floor, screaming. Reaching the door to the garage, he remembered himself and took out his wallet. He returned to the living room and threw all the cash he had at the naked flesh huddled there. Their screams rose a pitch as he left the house.

✳

Three days later, he called to apologize. No answer. That evening he drove by her house. No lights. The next evening, he parked on the street and rang the doorbell. Nobody home. He looked in the window. No furniture. Two weeks later, he asked his friend at work about her. He had no knowledge and seemed to resent the question. A month later he asked the lover he had once thought to marry to marry him. She said no.

✳

The following year, Audie died from injuries incurred in an automobile accident, his blood alcohol level three times the legal limit.

He lingered for almost a week, in and out of consciousness. Though he hadn't been to church or confession in more than a decade, he asked for a priest and made a full confession. The priest, absolving him of his sins, told Audie he should be grateful that the only other victim had been a tree by the side of the highway. Audie nodded, then asked, "What 'other?' Me?"

"No, my son," was all the priest said.

Audie slipped into a coma, his question unanswered.

SUCCUBUS TANGO

*I*T was unclear exactly when a woman started "raping" or "molesting" young men in their sleep in their dorm rooms. The words are in quotes because, for obvious reasons, the sex wasn't consensual, not because the young men felt that they had been violated. Just the opposite. But it's important to be precise under such mysterious circumstances.

Nonetheless, for the purpose of this chronicle, let's settle for variants of "ravished."

Rumors began to circulate when two counselors were overheard mentioning two different students' confessions, which they considered laughable. The reason for the students' (both already in counseling for emotional problems) mentioning their nocturnal emissions was simple embarrassment caused by having cried out at what seemed a bizarre dream, waking their roommates; that, and the state of their bed clothes.

This took place at a midwestern state university where the dorms were same sex, alternating male and female floor by floor. The notion that a young woman was repeatedly finding her way secretly into male dorm rooms (in most cases with two occupants) defied explanation, and the counselors took the matter no further. But, as stated above, their conversation had been overheard, and by several students, in the student union.

Within a week, the number of students sharing their own similar experiences with other students had proliferated. At first the phenomenon seemed to be nothing more than a rash of wet dreams. If a female was actually involved, then she was apparently manually manipulating penises. Then it was revealed that she had refined her technique and that young men were waking up to find themselves wearing condoms with a full bulb. In all cases, these were gentlemen who slept in the nude. As word got around, sleeping in the nude became *de rigueur* for all but the shyest and most prudish of students.

Embellishment became almost expected of those who chose to reveal their figurative (and often literal) deflowering. Some swore that they were aware of the young woman the entire time, but feigned sleep to prevent her making a quick exit. Some swore they woke only at the moment of climax, which invariably was the moment of the creature's disappearance. Others, dejectedly, had to admit that they had slept through the whole thing.

Many of these accounts were considered "bullshit," regardless of protestations to the contrary. Some felt compelled to conjure up the evidence, to general disgust. Several fistfights broke out, started by those who resented being called liars, sometimes by their best friends.

The rumors were briefly sidetracked to the point of being almost thoroughly disbelieved. When asked to describe the young woman, those who professed having actually seen her provided conflicting accounts. She was a big-breasted blonde; she was a virtually weightless, lithe nymph with tiny breasts and raven hair; she was a redhead with pale skin and long fingernails, or a black goddess with corn rows and cone-shaped nipples. Not surprising, once the disparities were discovered, the subsequently ravished chose to assert that the young woman's face and body could not be seen in the dark. No one, the victims in particular, wanted to believe that there were multiple ladies of darkness roaming their dorm floors unseen and unheard.

The second diversion, which might have hushed up the entire affair, was the suggestion that it wasn't a woman at all, but a gay man.

The idea conveniently provided some plausibility for the repeated and apparently effortless entrance to men's dorm rooms. But this angle was quickly discredited when a number of openly gay men made it clear, with resentment they couldn't well conceal, that not one of them had received a nocturnal visit. The idea that a gay man was making the rounds of heterosexual men was universally thus refuted, to the great relief of both the gay and the straight.

It didn't take long before the succubus was the talk of the entire campus. The jealous asserted that the chosen ones were pathetic losers who couldn't otherwise get laid. The campus jocks and studs claimed the "horny bitch" as their own and that it was only a matter of time before she got around to each and every one of them.

Most female students saw things differently. They refused to believe any of it and proclaimed it a sophomoric hoax. They went so far one night, by way of ridicule, to conduct their own form of "panty raid," with hundreds of chastely pajama'd young women marching from dorm to dorm shouting, "Rubbers! Rubbers! Throw down your rubbers!" (For almost a decade the "Rubber Raid" at this particular campus became an annual rite.)

One thing everyone agreed upon—they all refused to believe that the succubus was a witch or evil, supernatural or devil-sent. If she did exist, she was a flesh-and-blood sexual predator with uncanny physical and intellectual powers—a combination of cat burglar and nymphomaniac.

Before long, the Chancellor convened a meeting of the two counselors, the head of campus police, and two members of the university's medical staff. It was brief. The Chancellor demanded that a full report be on his desk in one week, including blood tests of recent "victims" to determine if drugs were involved; interviews with male RAs on the floors where the abuses took place, in particular to determine the potential means of dorm-floor and dorm-room access by the perpetrator; interviews with female RAs focused on any unusual sexual behavior of their charges, including stalking, nymphomania, or unusual secretiveness; thorough searches, and dusting for finger-prints, of violated dorm rooms; DNA test results for at least a dozen condoms, inside and out; and thorough psychological evaluations of at least a dozen "victims."

That night, a fact he shared with the head of police in order not to be caught in a lie at a later date, the Chancellor, a bachelor in his early 40s, was visited in his bedroom by a young woman who woke him to say, "You're wasting your time." She was nude and disap-peared the minute he turned on the light. She hadn't touched him (whether to the Chancellor's disappointment or not must be left to conjecture).

Fourteen ravishments took place in the time it took for the report to be compiled. Two each night. All were almost immediately con-fessed to friends because the students, one, didn't know about the investigation, and, two, because it had become a badge of distinction to be one of the "chosen." News of some reached RAs, who were all informed of the investigation and sworn to secrecy, and required on pain of losing their positions to report what they'd learned to the head of police. Five of these most-recent incidents were added to the work product of the Chancellor's report.

There were two new developments during the time of the report's development. Most of the latest victims were discovered to be hum-ming a tango, often at the most inappropriate times, during lectures, or while taking tests. The humming was almost inaudible, but in-sistent and vaguely recognizable. Eventually it was determined to be the famous tango "La Cumparsita" ("The Little Parade"). The young men, when confronted with their behavior by teachers, con-fessed that they had only vaguely been aware of their humming. Word soon got around that it was obviously a form of ear-worm, by definition a tune that gets into one's head and is difficult to shake. Eventually, many would realize that the melody had originated with their involuntary sexual experience. The tango became a constant feature during the crisis, and very few young men were able to fend off its infection. And it was not lost on some that the old phrase "it takes two to tango" was implied, though ironically, by the musical miscreant.

The second occurrence was the behavior of a junior, Marjorie (not her real name), majoring in physical education, of average looks but powerful build, who had managed to have intercourse with an entire dorm floor of freshmen in a single night. Receiving an insult to her feminine endowments from a "virgin jerk," as she later described him, she challenged him to bring to her, in his room, every floor resident who was willing, on a single night between midnight and three in the morning. They were all forced to wear condoms and she dispatched each one (like the famous royal Roman slut Messalina) in less than a few minutes apiece until all 18 were drained dry and somewhat abashed that one of their own fellows (who was denied her favors) had so mistakenly insulted such a sexual prodigy. She had hummed "La Cumparsita" the entire time. The rumors that grew from this orgy, at least early on, transformed Marjorie into the suc-cubus to everyone's satisfaction. She was confronted by the head of police and ordered to leave the campus for the rest of the semester, which, there being only two weeks remaining until the holiday break, she was only too happy to do. Though her parents were told that their daughter was suffering from exhaustion and was sent home for bed rest, they were called every day by one of the campus doctors seemingly to hear an update on her progress, but really to confirm that she had not snuck back on campus. Alas, in Marjorie's absence, the ravishments continued unabated.

Two days before the report was delivered, a faculty musicologist sent the Chancellor a confidential email providing his analysis of the use of the specific tango creating ear-worms in students. He de-termined that its initial melody, comprised of four descending notes, then a return to the top note, followed by another series of descend-ing notes, could have been chosen as the musical equivalent of a fe-male during intercourse, sitting astride her partner, gradually pushing down, then up, then down on an erect penis. The musicologist went on to note that the tango dance as currently performed is characterized by a highly sexualized charge between male and female dancers, including repeated pelvic contact, and a significant amount of bared female flesh. Finally, he pointed out that it was probably not accidental that the word "cumparsita" began with the vulgar slang word for semen or orgasm.

When this email was shared with the two counselors, both agreed that the female under investigation possessed not only a supercharged libido but a wicked sense of humor as well. The Chancellor was not amused, though the musicologist's analysis was included in the final report.

The conclusions of the report were as follows:

Blood tests: traces of amphetamines and marijuana were found in numerous blood samples; however, nothing was found that could be said to induce passivity or somnolence. No evidence was found of the "date-rape drugs" currently in use.

Interviews with RAs produced, as the police chief explained, virtually no evidence or conclusions; his opinion was that RAs were so involved with affairs of their own, both academic and sexual, that they were virtually unaware of what was going on with their charges.

Searches of dorm rooms, including fingerprinting, produced no evidence pointing to a single individual, since virtually every room, doors knobs in particular, were covered with fingerprints, many of them presumably female, no two identical. Panties were also found, usually under mattresses. DNA tests found no matches among them.

DNA tests of used condoms found in all instances that exterior DNA had either been wiped clean or dissolved by spermicides.

Finally, the psychological evaluations of 17 "victims" found no sexual proclivity that might invite female rape, other than one unsurprising thing that all subjects interviewed possessed: raging hormones. As for what they experienced, the differences could be reduced to three categories: 1: Excessive fantasizing about the experience to the point of obscuring any reliable memory of what had happened; 2: Reasonably obvious lying that the experience had been more akin to standard, consensual intercourse; and 3: Total obliviousness to what had occurred other than the physical evidence.

In 1841, an Englishman, Charles MacKay, published *Extraordinary Popular Delusions and the Madness of Crowds.* Among many other phenomena of mass hysteria, he wrote about the Crusades, witch trials, economic "bubbles," (predicting the tech bubble of the late 1990s), and popular admiration of great thieves and criminal politicians.

A psychology professor requested a meeting with the chancellor once the report was shared with members of a special committee, formed by the Chancellor, charged with trying to get to the bottom of what had come to be called "The Succubus Tango."

The professor (a member of the committee) brought along a copy of MacKay's book for the Chancellor to read. He chose to meet privately with the Chancellor, rather than to share his theories with the entire committee, because the nature of his conclusions, might, if prematurely rumored abroad and not carefully handled, lead to behavior dangerous to the health and reputation of the students who professed to having been ravished.

The professor began by stating the obvious—that the report was useless and provided not even a hint as to the identity of the young woman under investigation. Then he read aloud the following from the introduction of MacKay's book: "In reading the history of nations, we find that, like individuals, they have their whims and peculiarities; their seasons of excitement and recklessness, when they care not what they do. We find that whole communities suddenly fix their minds upon one object and go mad in its pursuit; that millions of people become simultaneously impressed with one delusion, and run after it, till their attention is caught by some new folly more captivating than the first."

The Chancellor considered this for a moment and then asked the professor if what he was suggesting was that the entire succubus affair was a delusion, the madness of a crowd. The professor replied that, of course, he couldn't prove anything. In fact, the source of mass delusions, by their very nature, were extremely difficult to identify. The same applied to the beginning of most rumors that enjoy a wider currency over time. But, he asserted, if entire countries can go temporarily mad, why not a bunch of young men living in the same building with young women?

The Chancellor then challenged the professor on a crucial point. It was not, he suggested, the fact that the "victims" were all sexually frustrated or introverted misfits when it came to women. In fact, if the report proved anything, it was that there was "a damn lot of sex going on all the time."

Admitting that he'd anticipated this very question, the professor said that having occasional and casual sex with one or multiple partners was not the same as being ravished in one's sleep. He proposed several illustrations: 1: It was common knowledge that in most cases the male was required to pursue the female and that assent was often not forthcoming, leading to disappointment and embarrassment; 2: Alternatively, most women who were aggressive in initiating sex were often branded with negative descriptors like "slut" or "whore"—and this stigma then attached to the act, tarnishing the experience for the male; 3: Sexual relations are complex, often leading to emotional ambivalence and confusion, even guilt, not to mention the complications of "love," which often lead to fighting and hurt feelings on one or both sides. The advantage of a succubus (even an imaginary one) was that the male could enjoy either the experience or the reputation derived from it, from an entirely passive and submissive posture, with none of the difficulties just described. No form of sexual congress could be purer.

The Chancellor conceded that the professor made a compelling case, then asked two essential questions: Was there not even a single incident that launched the delusion, and how could it all be stopped?

The professor insisted that he couldn't answer the first question and that the source of the delusion wasn't even an issue anymore. Nothing could be stopped by going back to the beginning unless there was a plausible case to be made against one or more young women actually ravishing several young men, and, as the report clearly demonstrated, this could not be proved.

As to the second question, the professor proposed that the report be made public, in an easily digestible and relatively brief format, along with a statement from the Chancellor that the entire affair was without foundation in fact and was therefore discredited and, in other words, "over and done with." Finally, any young man from this point forward making claims to the contrary would face disciplinary action and possible expulsion.

The Chancellor then told the professor about the nude visitor in his bedroom. How did he explain that? Without hesitation, the professor explained that it was the nature of such delusions that no one is necessarily immune from its effects. Not even chancellors of universities.

The professor's strategy, once fully executed by the Chancellor the following Monday, appeared to work, if not immediately, then gradually. One could argue that the phenomenon simply went underground, in the sense that it became a closely held secret among friends, for obvious reasons.

Eventually the ravishments ceased altogether. My friend and I, who compiled this chronicle, simply got bored. We would have quit the game sooner or later anyway. We'll leave it to the reader's imagination whether we are two women or a man and a woman. We are definitely not two men.

For the most curious who wish to know how it was done, we can only offer this hint. The Chancellor should have hired an accomplished professional magician. Someone of David Copperfield's or Dorothy Dietrich's sophistication could easily have determine how it was done, though certainly not by whom. We are magicians too, after all.

And the sex was real.

ACTION

*T*wo things kept me out of Vietnam. Scarlet fever as a child left me with a weakened heart and rendered me 4-F on paper. A high lottery number meant I didn't even have to take the physical. My dad, a surgeon and retired Air Force colonel, had been reassuring me of my 4-F status since I was twelve, the year the war began.

A former lieutenant colonel and flight surgeon in the Army Air Corps stationed in New Guinea during WWII, he had killed his man, an assassin he shot with his service .45 when he caught the man slitting throats in his hospital tent. He also helped to develop the first Mobile Army Field Hospital, the precursor of the Mobile Army Surgical Hospital or MASH unit. He performed surgery— I've seen the 16mm films—under primitive conditions: an open tent, stretcher, folding table laden with instruments, water dripping from a canvas bucket. John Wayne, on a tour of military facilities, visited my father's unit; you can see him in one faded fuzzy gray film watching the amputation of a soldier's leg. He looks like everyone else, tired, his face a blank. The film ends with the severed leg shown, knee bent over the side of a wooden box.

But this story, which will offer little atonement, given my father's sacrifice, is about my senior year in high school. I spent it with Margaret, whose boyfriend was in Vietnam. In our small school, friendships changed like the planets. Everyone knew everyone's name, but depending on the season, the sporting event, or the dance, the shifting circles of dating and breakup moved us toward or away from the people we saw over and over every day. Each of us had a reputation and a group. Some straddled. I, for instance, being a doctor's son, was afforded some respect in more "aristocratic circles," (read: kids whose fathers were doctors, lawyers, or successful businessmen), but I played at being a hippie, read "Ramparts" and Eldridge Cleaver, smoked pot, and even had my one bad acid trip. Margaret, a year younger, had no cache but her body.

Margaret was smart, perhaps third or fourth in her class, but no one ever noticed. Her mother worked in a drug store to make payments on a tiny ranch house behind the gray iron foundry. Her father had died in a motorcycle accident when she was sixteen—left a country road at sixty miles an hour. It was speculated famously in the papers that, having slipped backwards off the vehicle, he actually ran more than a tenth of a mile—only three or four strides at a mile a minute—before he hit a phone pole. I tried to imagine what he felt—wonder, terror, hope—as his feet made those heroic strides, inertia making it impossible to steer.

Margaret's status didn't derive from her family, or the girls she hung out with—plain, nice kids who never went out for anything and commandeered a corner of the library during home room. She was tall, buxom, cute, freckled, and rumored to have spent a summer in the downtown apartment of a nineteen-year-old drop-out before he was drafted and sent to boot camp. Somehow, this made her a subject of fear and admiration, as though she had given her body to an older boy, not for love, but for solace and protection. It seemed like such an adult thing for a junior to do. The guys I knew called her "easy," but none of us ever thought of talking to her, much less asking her out. Yet, I can remember seeing her in the halls and stopping to watch her body, always, it seems, sheathed in a short summery dress, which made me think of nothing but her naked on an old bed, shouting "No!" as the draft officers banged on the door.

We drew nearer to each other the night of a dance. The dance was over. Most everyone was gone. My friend Alex had gone on with Martin, the class pusher, to smoke dope, but I had to be up early for a golf tournament. (Enterprising Martin sold double dome acid and orange sunshine mescaline in the hallways, and made a great friend of the social psychologist the local police planted in the school, filling her full of nonsense about his beautiful dead aunt's having molested him to the point of ecstasy when he was ten years old.)

I was starting my father's yellow Duster when Margaret tapped on the glass. I rolled down the window.

"Hi," she said. I couldn't see who it was. "It's Margaret Keeler. I need a ride home."

She sounded upset.

"Are you okay?"

"I need a ride."

"Sure, get in!"

I was enormously pleased as she settled into the passenger seat, drawing in her legs, long and bare beneath a yellow summer dress. In the dome light, she seemed to be fine. A rather indecipherable smile winked into the darkness as she closed the door.

As I steered us out of the parking lot she gave me directions to her home, then asked for a cigarette.

"In the glove compartment."

"Do your parents mind?" she asked, pushing in the lighter.

"My parents don't know."

"My mother buys them for me," she said and lit hers. She took a deep drag and put her hand on my hand, which was on the wheel. I took the cigarette, fully conscious that the contact had been a bit more than was required by the transaction. When I handed it back, I passed my fingers over hers. She didn't pull away.

We did this hand dance as we talked.

"I'm glad I saw you," she said, "My girlfriends got mad and left without me."

To say that I was glad too didn't seem too smart, so I asked her what had happened.

"They said I was talking too much. They always say that. They're such twits, sometimes. If I don't keep things lively, we'd sit around in silence all night. I guess I overdid it."

"What about?"

"Sex."

"I thought girls *liked* to talk about that," I ventured and chuckled cautiously.

"Only when it's imaginary," she said, a bit angrily, "You can talk about how you'd like to ball the quarterback all you want, but throw out a few facts, a few experiences into the conversation, and they turn into a bunch of nuns!"

What could I say? This wasn't a normal conversation, either, and Margaret didn't seem to understand that. We sat in silence for the short distance left to her house. I pulled up to her driveway.

"Thanks," she said, stubbing the cigarette into the ashtray.

As she opened the door, I asked her what she was doing Friday.

"I've got a boyfriend, you know," she said.

I wished I could see her eyes when she said it.

"I know. This wouldn't be a date, really. Every Friday I work until eight, then I go spend half my paycheck on records, then I go to Dodge. I just thought I might see you there."

"Just friends?" she asked.

"We can just talk."

"This'll be interesting," she giggled, and got out, "A boy who likes to just talk. Bye."

She waved her hand over her head backwards as she sauntered up the driveway.

Dodge Lanes: the center of the high school universe in our little Midwestern town. Flanked on three sides by huge expanses of asphalt, it was the roundhouse for generations of kids who cruised State Street every Friday night. None of us bowled, opting instead for the nine-foot Brunswick pool tables and the jukebox in the back room. We gambled, of course, or thought ourselves good enough to, won cokes or dollars when we kept to ourselves; every now and then, some out-of-town ace waltzed in and hustled somebody like me for his part-time earnings.

Having completed my weekly pilgrimage to the record store (I bought *Layla* and *Ummagumma*—the latter with a title I couldn't resist: "Several Species of Small Furry Animals Gathered in a Cave and Grooving with a Pict"), I arrived at Dodge Lanes around nine, but Margaret wasn't there. I checked out a table and shot a few racks, having punched "Ride, Captain, Ride", "Whole Lotta Love", and "He Ain't Heavy, He's My Brother" into the jukebox. I decided that Margaret wasn't coming, and of course she walked in. She wore another thin dress, this one patterned with slate blue flowers. Her thick, auburn hair fell in large curls upon her shoulders. Her face, more made-up than usual, though smiling, suggested a specific anxiety.

"You want to go for a drive?" I asked without even saying hello, her expression being that imperative.

"I sure don't want to stay here," she said, putting her hand on my arm and scanning the room with impatience. "I'll meet you outside."

I watched her saucy, firm stride as she left, and saw the hungry looks of the other guys in the room. Nobody looked at me since no one would believe that anything was going on between us.

Outside, I found her standing by my car, arms crossed, staring off toward the procession of cars in the street.

"Look," she said, putting her hand on my arm again. "I'm not sure why I'm here. It was a pain in the ass just getting my mother to drop me off. You're a nice guy, and I wouldn't mind sitting and talking somewhere. I get tired of being with girls, nothing but girls and my mother, all the time. It's like having somebody in prison, only I can't go visit him. And I'm not even sure he loves me that much. It's just all so fucking scary!"—gripping my arm tightly now, almost

shouting—"But it's up to you. Deal with it or not. There's no reason you should even try. There's nothing in it for you! But if you
can live with that, then okay. We can go."

It's said that men mature sexually more slowly than women. At
seventeen I didn't have the perspective to know that the difference
was even a possibility; at that moment I felt as though Margaret had
just reached down from some high steamy cloud and hauled me up
to stand beside her, absolutely naked and on fire. To put it another
way, I became aware, for the first time, how erotic plain speaking
could be. She knew she didn't have to explain about her boyfriend
with any specificity. She trusted that I understood! I was, of course,
entirely confused. Was she saying I was wasting my time in order to
entice me? Was she revealing her turmoil and passion to drive me
away? But that hand gripping my arm!

I turned away. For just a moment. No word or gesture else would
have left my excitement unrevealed. Then I looked back. Neither of
us could see each other's face clearly in the dusk. I stepped toward
the car and, with my arm tingling, motioned her to get in.

We cruised once through town. I bought her a strawberry sundae,
then we pulled into the parking lot next to the small dam that turned
the town's creek into a river. She sat on the bench seat of the Duster,
her shoulders pressed against the door, her legs crossed at the ankles.
As her fingers repeatedly smoothed her dress, which didn't quite
cover her knees, we talked of school, music, drugs, friends. Margaret
seemed to know her own mind, clearly, as though her sense of wonder, about men in particular, had long since evaporated. We talked
of people with the superior detachment of two psychologists discussing patients; we found it convenient to agree in our diagnoses,
wowing with that fake wonder people express at the discovery of the
banal similarity of shared tastes and feelings.

Jim, her boyfriend, was what we did not talk about.

"I thought you liked Holly," Margaret said, not quite out of the
blue. "You went out a lot, didn't you?"

"Yeah, for a while. We both lost interest, I think. She was rather stupid. I think she just wanted someone to take her to homecoming."

"No! No one would do that!" she said, laughing.

"Don't rub it in."

"Sorry. But Holly Wigstaff! She gets Ds in remedial reading, for Chrissake! I know she's pretty, but...?"

I chuckled with embarrassment.

"I admit it was a low point in my career. But what about you? What's this guy like?"

"What guy? You mean the guy sitting in this car with me? He's nice enough, but he hasn't the foggiest idea about girls, especially girls that are almost as smart as he is."

"Come on!" I complained, not quite hurt. "I'm serious. I told you."

"That was a tactical error. You don't make too many of them in the infantry, or you're dead!"

"This is forbidden territory, I take it."

Her smile was incredible, pursed but flat, as if offering to shut me up with a kiss.

"I hardly know a thing about you except you can be duped by dumb chicks."

I decided to ignore this.

"I thought that was why we were sitting here. To talk."

"That's why I'm sitting here."

I knew what she was saying.

"Do you want me to take you home?"

"Did I say that?"

"No. So I understand. We can talk about anything except...."

"You like to talk even more than I do!" she exclaimed, touching her lips with her fingers. "Let's talk about something else."

After another hour, I took her home. Not wanting to wake her mother, she asked me to drop her off at the curb. We said goodnight, friends, I thought. Meg—I can now call her Meg—pulled the door handle, paused, then said, "You know, I think you may be an ass. I'm not sure. But I enjoyed myself. Thanks for that."

Then, to my amazement she leaned over and kissed me. It was the kind of kiss—a reward, not an intimacy—usually given on the cheek. It was not just its kind, but its place, its full-lipped pressure on my lips, not hurried nor lingering (unlike the fleet, sweet smile that followed), remembered and relished a thousand times, which was to guide my actions from then on.

An incident that took place a week or so later drew us inseparably together for the rest of the year. It was plain to me that Holly and I had had a mutual parting, but I kept hearing that she'd dumped me for a certain Frank—a goon half a head taller (I was five-ten and 135 pounds) and twice as wide as me. Frank was a real swell guy. One Sunday afternoon, as I was cruising downtown, Frank and Holly pulled up next to me. Frank gave me the finger and sped ahead. I thought, foolishly, "Do unto others, brother," pulled up and returned the favor. So Frank followed me home, honking the whole way, riding my bumper, and while Holly sat quietly in her car, he got out and punched me out, rather repeatedly. I couldn't extract even one righteous jab from my flailing defense against the windmill fury of his well-trained rights and lefts. I managed to rip his shirt pocket as I crumpled to the grass. My father, when he found me, and Frank had run away, wanted the "hoodlum" jailed. When I wouldn't say the name, he concluded I was a pansy and launched into a tirade! To my astonishment, the story was later broadcast that while I stood up to the big bastard like a man, the bully was rewarded with Holly's everlasting disfavor.

That Monday afternoon, Meg found me in the library reading the *New American Bible* (the whole thing, for a term paper, the sheer bulk of it to mitigate the planned brevity of my book report). She slid into a chair across the table. Her thick hair tangled as from the wind, she began to draw her ten fingers through it like two combs. Her eyes suggested a re-thinking in progress.

"You don't look bloodied," she said.

I said nothing, closing the book on my index finger, returning her smile.

"Ah, the silent warrior. Okay. I know the type. Jim doesn't put one damn thing about it in his letters. Everything is questions. What am I doing on weekends? How is my mother? Am I keeping the boys at arm's length? I think his last letter said, 'Let them all cream in their jeans.' It seems like I'm about all he can think about. Like I'm the war. But I don't like it," she said, letting the arch tone drop, "I want to know what's going on! So don't be like that."

"He beat the shit out of me."

"Really? But you look fine."

"I've felt better. It was pretty humiliating, if you want the truth. I ripped his shirt pocket. That was the glory of my self-defense."

She didn't say anything. She was getting the message.

"The stupid thing was even bothering to return…to give him the finger," I continued, now a little excited. "What was that all about anyway? It wasn't like I was defending anything."

"Here," said Meg, holding out her hand.

"You see? I realized that if he wanted to, he could have done anything! He could have broken my neck! He was already on my chest. If my father hadn't come out…and for what?"

"Hush, Peter," she said, putting her hands together, having failed to attract mine, "sshhhhh."

She stood up to leave, looked around the room and then at me and smiled. She came around the table and leaned over. Her fingers squeezed my shoulder, her hair brushed my forehead.

"I could kiss you right here," she whispered. Her breath smelled of lavender candy. "Come over tonight. At seven."

I arrived fifteen minutes early at the little ranch-style house with the great smokestacks and streaked corrugated steel walls of the foundry looming behind, making a sound like the distant, muffled scraping of an immense shovel on a concrete floor.

Meg opened the front door, only after I'd rung three or four times. Dressed in tight, faded blue jeans and a work shirt embroidered with little flowers, she looked mildly upset, but reached for my hand and pulled me inside.

"Someone's here," she whispered.

What I saw struck me with the incongruity of a dream. Some previous owner had reconstructed the tiny living room to reproduce the masculine ruggedness of a hunting lodge. Large, dark-stained pine poles stretched across the ceiling and down the corners between walnut paneling. A fireplace of jagged gneiss blocks filled half of one wall, flanked by a half-a-dozen stuffed deer, big cats, and a moose. From the ceiling hung a wagon wheel chandelier. On a shiny blue satin couch, set against the wall opposite the fireplace, sat Meg's mother, a ravaged, once-pretty woman in her late forties, flame red hair and great legs in a pink and white striped dress. Beside her sat her beau, small, stocky, dignified, balding, with a pocked nose and a crooked but perfectly sincere and affable grin. They were holding hands. On the phonograph turned some ancient big-band number I didn't recognize, but reminded me of old movies—jitterbugging and the USO.

Meg introduced me; both remained seated as they shook my hand, suggesting that only the briefest interruption to their courting could be tolerated. Neither anger nor frustration with my presence expressed itself; rather, the nervous, blushing smiles on their faces said, "You are young. You have nothing but time. But we haven't many opportunities like this left to us. Surely you can understand."

Meg and I quickly retreated to her bedroom.

"She met him last night at the league," Meg said, as she closed the door.

Then she was in my arms. Or rather, I was in hers, which wrapped around my neck; her fingers cradled my head firmly. Leaning, she pressed her lips gently in, her body angled away from mine. That kiss, for me a shock and a wonder, seemed to be for her a meditation, slow, searching, intense, her thoughts ranging through the variations in pressure and moisture, seeking some resolution to the enigma of the fact of the kiss itself. And she must have found something, since, finally, her lips parted, her tongue searched out mine, and she smiled right through her kissing of me.

When she broke the kiss, she said:

"I have decided to go out with you."

I kissed her once more.

"What about Jim?"

"I'm writing to him about you. That you are my friend, my protector. You're keeping me company. He'll appreciate that, actually."

"That's not what I meant," I said, holding her away, "I mean I want you too!"

"I'm not stupid, Peter," she said, looking me right in the eyes, "I know what you want. But that is the arrangement. There's you and there's Jim. I couldn't break up with him, I couldn't do that to him even if I wanted to. And I don't want to. It's not even a matter of choosing yet!"

So, it would be a trial, and the merits of my suit were not in arguing about the distant Jim, but in asserting the fact of my physical presence. She'd put no emphasis on that final "yet," but she'd pronounced it, and that was enough for now. Without the slightest qualm, I shut up and drew her to me. We stood there kissing until her mother knocked on the door.

"Come join us," she said, "we're having dessert."

It took us a minute or two to respond to the summons, each of us more than once reversing the breaking of our embrace to kiss again. When we entered the living room, everything was laid out on a coffee table—colas and strawberry shortcake.

The two were still on the couch, both smiling happily now, no longer jealous of the interruption. An understanding had been reached between them as well. Meg and I sat in armchairs that flanked the coffee table as Meg's mother sat forward and began to serve. I recognized a Glen Miller tune on the record player and said I remembered the Jimmy Stewart movie. The boyfriend—his name was Frederick —began to tell us about his experiences at the end of World War II. He had enlisted in the Navy in 1945, but the war ended two weeks before his ship was due to sail from San Francisco.

"Do you know how the bikini got its name, young man?"

I had no idea what this had to do with anything and looked at Meg, who squinted and shrugged. I had a fleeting vision of her perfect body bursting from a two-piece swimsuit.

"From the atomic bomb, that's where," Frederick said. "Bikini Atoll. That's where they sent me. For the first atomic testing after Hiroshima. Through black glasses thick as those pop bottles, I stood and watched the mushroom rise...then those beautiful little islands just got covered with fallout."

At the age of seventeen, I had no politics, other than a rock and roll-inspired dislike of the war on the principle that killing people was wrong, period. Peace, man. Had no religion either: if God existed, I couldn't know Him. He pulled the strings, and I dangled.

In short, I had no morals recognizable as such; a qualm here, a relativistic posturing there—no system, no belief, a temporary void that existed between the missal-clutching fervency of my pre-adolescence and the responsible agnosticism of my twenties, which is why, an hour later, I could park my father's car in an abandoned subdivision known to my classmates as Heaven, and steam up the windows with the girlfriend of a man risking his life for his country in the jungles of Vietnam.

But what of Meg? Was she falling in love with me, slowly working her way through that unemphatic "yet"? We sat in the dark, kissing and hugging; we didn't talk, words seemed a wasteful interruption of purer forms of communication,

Perhaps a month later, in the same clutch, my hands now expert surveyors of her slender back, I asked if I might touch her breasts.

"If you have to ask, the answer is no," she said, and she meant it.

I did touch—a fleeting pass at her tight blouse—and she grew angry, cut the evening short with a lame excuse. The next Friday —we went out only on Fridays—I began with both hands; she responded with an "it's about time" shudder.

Perhaps it shouldn't take six months to progress from fevered kissing to frantic sex. Yet, in taking an entire night to savor the revelation of each new intimacy, we showed a certain restraint and decorum. Our bodies held back at every stage, in deference to the ambiguity of the situation: if she had helped Jim, in desperate urgency, to build a wall against death and time, what lay between Meg and me was to be peeled away in layers. Sex was the least part of it; we probed each other every day at school, every night on the phone, in countless, endless conversations about everything from Thoreau to our parents to Maria's pizza; we wanted into each other, so that surrendering one more bit of flesh or stitch of clothing, hers or mine, only softened the next layer, making it split.

She wore sweaters and let me beneath them. Hiding the fact from her mother with a jacket, she left her bra at home. The night we first bared our chests—an unseasonably hot October night—we swam in and licked each other's sweat. A police car rolled up beside us mere seconds after we'd put on our clothes.

"What's wrong, officer?" I asked, Meg giggling breathlessly, clutching my arm.

"Let's just move along," said the cop.

"Do you have a light?" I asked, holding up a cigarette.

He frowned at me, pulled out some matches and tossed them in, shook his head and grinned, letting it pass.

"Just you be careful," he warned, and drove away.

It would be another month before I felt bold enough to reach beneath her skirt, and weeks after that, beneath her cotton panties. And though Meg reciprocated, an actual orgasm seemed to be the furthest thing from our minds. We explored further and deeper, with our fingers and with our mouths, not to reach a destination, but to intensify the process of the exploration itself. Until the night Meg had me lie between her legs.

My father had lent me the keys to his new station wagon, a massive flatboat of a Chrysler with a rear deck nine feet long when the back seat lay flat. It was dead winter now, and with ten inches of snow on Heaven's pavement, the car running, heater on, we lay fully clothed on that hard deck necking side by side, until Meg pulled me on top of her. I soon saw what she wanted, and though it gave me more pain than pleasure in purely genital terms, this was it: the position, the motion, the rhythm, and it was having a profound effect on Meg. She called out to me twice that night. Then there was the morning after the Prom, six AM, lying on her mother's couch, Meg in her white satin dress with its plunging neckline and heaped clouds of petticoats, and me between her slippery, white stockinged thighs, making her call out to me in whispers again and again and again.

Sitting in the school library the last week of the semester, her bright blue eyes laughing, Meg whispered, "It's time, my friend. This Friday."

"What time?"

"It's time we clinched the deal."

I hadn't a notion.

"Vatican roulette. This Friday."

She saw that I didn't believe her. She stood from across the table and came around, her yellow sun dress singing on her stockinged legs. Her awareness that the moment, her leaning over (though she was oblivious to her own lavender breath), was a perfect replay, glinted in her eyes.

"Time to separate the men from the boys. It's now or never."

Her voice a husky whisper.

We made love three times. The first, fearfully, fumblingly, satisfactorily, near-fully clothed on the couch in my dad's basement. The second, languorously, deliciously, stark naked, parked for three hours in the deepest little back alley of Heaven. The third, in her bedroom

—her mom out on a date with Frederick—panting, tearing at each other's jeans, crying out together, a week before her soldier's safe return.

As I said at the beginning, I couldn't have gone to Vietnam if I'd wanted to. Well, probably. I could have enlisted and maybe found a way to hide my heart condition, which was really not that serious. And maybe they wouldn't have read too deeply into my medical records, knowing they had a live one, an actual enlistee.

If I could have swung it, would I have gone? I have tried to imagine all this countless times, to no conclusion. But the fact is I didn't.

The week of Jim's return is blurred by the death of my friend Alex. Alex loved to swim. He loved to drink beer and to smoke marijuana. Alex had just received *the letter* from Uncle Sam. At two that Sunday morning, drunk and stoned, he hiked a mile out of town to a quarry he and I used to fish. I can still see him diving off that rock face into the deep darkness. They said he tried to climb out at the wrong end, where nothing but three stone walls jutted from the water. I've always wondered how they knew that.

They held an assembly at the high school. Alex's girlfriend said a few words, then burst into tears. Everyone was crying. I spent a day in my bedroom, staring at the patterns of flowers and medallions on the wallpaper behind my headboard. Meg didn't even try to call.

It was now almost a month since Jim's return. I hadn't tried to talk to Meg; she'd glide past me in the halls like some figurine on the prow of a ship, head up, eyes into the wind. Perhaps, I wondered, it's my fault, a great mistake. She wants a competition, a fight for her hand!

But she hadn't even called about Alex!

Finally, I wrote her a letter: "Dear Meg, How are you? I still want to see you. What do you want me to do? Love, Peter."

Two days later, eyes averted, she stuffed a piece of paper in my hand as we passed in the hall. It said, "Stay away from us." Had she meant it for my sake, or for hers?

I think the heart is like something organic boiling; a new core asserts itself every now and then; the heat not anything within, nor brought by any other living soul, but the constant rubbing of simple human time. By midsummer, my ache for Meg was gone, something sloughed off. Gone, not consciously, not with regret, but from necessity sensed like a property of physics, understood, if not in its complex mechanics, then in its outline of cause and effect, the remaining residue of each succeeding day.

Then I got this in the mail:

"Peter, At first, I wanted to go to your home, tell your father, your mother, your whole family. Then I'd find you hiding in some closet, haul you outside, and kick the living shit out of you. I've decided not to do that. Instead, I put that case of beer on your front porch. Good old Budweiser, a headache in every can. Because I want to thank you for saving my girl for me. A beautiful girl like Meg could have got tired of waiting and fallen for someone else, someone better than me. Thanks for keeping her occupied. Stay away, fucker. I know everything. James."

Two years later I had a summer job working night maintenance at the Chrysler factory. When I wasn't mopping spilled coffee or swabbing ventilator shafts with mineral spirits, I sat in the john reading, everything from *The Fountainhead* to the *Tao Te Ching*. There's a corner of my library where all the dog-eared paperbacks have the same curve, that of my left, twenty-year-old buttock.

I knew, of course, that Meg worked the line, the second shift, two to ten, but with five thousand employees spread over ninety acres, I didn't know where. I glimpsed her once, in a great crowd heading toward the parking lot, but I didn't think she saw me.

Finally, she found me, the last week before I returned to college. The line was down, just; I was kneeling in front of a large metal frame covered with clamps that held body parts together for welding. With a putty knife, I was scraping yellow gobs of sealer off the clamps and smearing them on a piece of oily cardboard.

"I always knew you'd go far, Peter." The voice familiar at my ear.

I jumped up, wiping my hands on my jeans.

Meg stood leaning against an iron pillar, her hand on one hip, gorgeous even in stained denim jumpsuit and work boots. Her hair was tied with a yellow scarf. Her blue eyes smiled.

"How are you?" she asked.

"I'm fine. How are you?" I responded with genuine interest.

"I'm good, Peter," she replied, with false pointedness neutralizing mine. "I knew you were here. I've been avoiding you, if you want the truth. But I heard you were leaving soon. So. Back to school?"

She said it with the academic curiosity of a doctor speaking to a former patient.

I told her about it. I exaggerated the importance of a young English major I'd dated twice.

"And how's Jim?"

"Oh, he's gone," she said with bored nonchalance. "He re-enlisted. He's somewhere in the Carolinas. I think he's a sergeant at some boot camp."

"Gone gone?"

"Yes, Peter," she said, like a bemused big sister, "But I have a new boyfriend. Someone you've never met. He works here, actually. He came from the South."

"I wish I'd known."

"It wouldn't have made any difference," she said flatly.

"You were pretty horrible to me."

"It was for your own good."

"I liked you a lot," I said, feeling it all sink away.

"It was just a bit o' fun, as the English say."

"Not for me."

"Especially for you!" she said and laughed.

Then I reached and took her hand. She didn't resist, smiled as if to say, "What are you going to do now, Peter?"

"I mean, you really did something for me."

"Peter, I liked you, okay? I liked you enough to ball you a couple of times."

"That's not…."

"Don't make more of it than…."

"I'm not…."

"Look, I like you now, not that it means anything! We could go into the cushion room this minute. There's a little nook Bob and I found. I'll ball you right now, just to show you."

"Okay," I said, trembling, tugging her, "Let's go!"

Her laughter was loud enough to drown out the nearly spent throbbing of the factory.

When it was over, I understood exactly what she meant.

TALKING TO A NUDE FOR SEVEN DAYS

*I*N Jack Kerouac's novel *The Dharma Bums* the narrator spends a summer as a fire lookout on a mountain in Washington state. I took a similar job twenty-five years ago and had an extraordinary experience there. I met a woman and talked with her for an hour or so each day for seven straight days. She was sunbathing and entirely nude. I kept notes on that experience and have finally gotten around to typing them up in narrative form. Why didn't I do this many years ago? The simple answer is that for a long time the experience was too precious to me, and I didn't want to share it with anyone. Sometimes, years later, when I thought maybe I should write about it, I delayed, thinking that my skills weren't up to doing the experience justice. Now, after having published two novels, I'm ready. I confess that though my notes would suggest seven consecutive days, there was more likely at least one day in which storms might have prevented an encounter, though it was definitely in the driest part of the summer. I'm just not sure. To avoid needless repetition, I should explain that each encounter took place after I had made my required fire lookout observations and had reported in. On the first day, which was my fifth day after being left, well-provisioned, on the mountain alone, I decided to walk down to what, from above, looked like an inviting mountain meadow. That's where I met the nude woman. I never learned her name, though she knows mine, and I've never seen her since. Let me assure the reader that as strange, even dreamlike, as this account may seem—and it seemed that way to me at times as well—every word of it is true.

DAY ONE

From atop the mountain that it was my job (that summer of 1985) to keep safe from fires, I saw only forest and more forest, an endless sea of trees, mostly evergreens of some kind (I am not a botanist), except for a mountain meadow directly below me to the west. I chose a particularly sunny day (though every day there was little cloud cover) to walk down to explore that meadow. The walk took less than an hour, and when I stepped out of the woods, I saw that the meadow was a lush field of grasses and small flowers rolling downhill to more woods perhaps a quarter of a mile away. While the woods smelled, sometimes stiflingly, of fresh pine and nothing else, the meadow exhaled dozens of odors with every gust of wind that rose from below. Some were delicious, sweet, or sweetly sour scents, and some were astringent, almost like alcohol, but tempered with grapes, like wine. The varieties of flowers were numberless, and their colors seemed equally limitless. This was a rolling meadow that didn't reveal itself entirely from any angle. As I walked toward its center, new mounds and declivities opened, so that the meadow seemed to renew itself at every step.

Almost like that scene in the *Wizard of Oz* when Dorothy and her friends are approaching the Emerald City, I began to feel drowsy and decided to take a nap. I found a flattish area that was mostly grasses and lay on my side with my backpack, which contained nothing but a water bottle and some cookies, under my head. As I was dozing off, I heard a kind of singing sound. At first, I thought it was insects chorusing. Then I realized it was a human voice. I stood up, grabbed my backpack, and marched toward the sound. I say "marched" to indicate that I wasn't trying to sneak up on what was causing the sound; rather, I was intent on satisfying my curiosity. Thus it was that I walked right up to within three feet of a young woman, lying on a blue blanket, totally nude.

"I'm sorry," I cried and turned away. But I didn't walk away.

"It's okay," she said, laughing, "if I'm going to lounge around naked out in the open, I can't blame someone for walking up unannounced. Come and sit down."

I turned slightly and saw that she was still naked.

"Don't you want to cover up?"

"Not unless you want me to."

Without approaching her any farther I sat down with my back to her.

"You can look. I don't mind. I'm sure you've seen women before."

"It's a little awkward."

"Not for me. Turn around. I want to see you too."

This didn't seem a moment for half-measures, so I turned around completely and sat with my legs crossed. She was perhaps no more than 22 or 23. She was on her side, facing me, with her right leg over her left, hiding all but a wisp of dark pubic hair. She had modest breasts, thin shoulders, and her legs and arms were strong but slim. Every inch of her glistened with suntan lotion. A freckled redhead, she had blue-green eyes that seemed to pierce my own with an intensity that was not shameless, but unashamed. They were marvels of curiosity. Her nose was just slightly flat at the tip, and her lips naturally pursed. She smiled, but cautiously. Maybe, it occurred to me, she was actually shy. She was not stunningly beautiful, nor, on the opposite spectrum of good looks, simply cute. She was a lovely creature to look at.

"You're probably wondering where I came from?"

"Well, that and a dozen other things."

"I've been camping in this area for two weeks now."

I looked around.

"You won't find my site and I certainly won't tell you. With that uniform on I can't be sure you won't tell on me."

"I won't," I said, "but you don't need to tell me anyway."

"I don't build fires, in case you're worried about that."

"Fires are exactly what I'm here to worry about, so I'm glad to hear it."

All this time, she was plucking at different small flowers and tasting the stems, though she hardly looked away for a moment.

She was covered, head to toe, with freckles, in some places dark and dense, in some lighter and spaced apart.

To break the ensuing silence, I said, "I came to see who was singing."

"What singing?"

"You weren't singing?"

"I hum a lot, if that's what you mean?"

"If that wasn't singing, you're a great hummer."

"Ha!" she laughed, "that's a good one."

I blushed and buried my head in my hands. My off-color remark had been totally unintentional.

"I'm so sorry. I didn't mean to…."

"Forget it. A great hummer! That's a good one. I've been humming all my life and no one's ever made that joke."

"Probably no one dared. Really, I apologize."

"I know you didn't mean it, or at least you didn't *consciously* mean it. After all, look at the two of us."

It took her only two seconds to stand and wrap the towel around her body. I saw a flash of nether red.

"I'm going to stand here and watch you go away if you don't mind. I don't want you to follow me."

"I won't. I promise," I assured her.

"Promises. They are stupid things, but I take you at your word."

Then she smiled, a bright sweet smile, revealing glorious teeth.

"I'll be here tomorrow, so maybe I'll see you again. It won't be the same place. You'll have to find me."

"I'll be going then," I said, taking a last, slightly lingering look.

"Go on. Show's over," she said and giggled, for the first time revealing a small pang of embarrassment.

What else could I do? I walked away.

DAY TWO

The next day around the same time, two in the afternoon, I returned to the meadow and, following a hunch, went straight to where I saw the nude woman the day before. She was on her stomach, as if it was only polite to let me see the rest of her.

"Aren't you clever?" she said. "You didn't have to look around for me at all."

I sat down and gave her a sly grin.

"Just a hunch," I said, shrugging. "I think you're the clever one."

She laughed and threw a flower at me.

"Tell me about yourself."

"You first," I said.

"Oh, you'll never get much out of me, not when it comes to my past. My being here like this is revealing enough."

"So to speak."

She laughed again and said, "I know why I'm here. Why are you?"

I felt almost obligated, considering her—how to put it—visual generosity, to tell her about myself.

"I've just finished pre-med at Stanford and I'm about to go into the real grinder to become a doctor. I can only hope I'm prepared to endure another eight years or more. So, I decided I needed to get completely away and make damn sure being a doctor was what I really wanted."

"You wanted to be alone with your thoughts."

"I guess."

"And I'm in the way, then," she said, her eyebrows coming together with an insistent sincerity.

I didn't say anything.

"This is where you say something about studying anatomy," she said and we both laughed.

"No, you're not in the way. The first thing I learned after five days here was that if I wasn't careful, I'd go nuts with all this solitude."

"Maybe you are."

"Are what?"

"Nuts."

"Oh, you mean delusional," I said and laughed again. "I thought about it last night and concluded that you were absolutely real. Which, of course, you are."

"Are you sure?"

"Tell me you aren't."

"Delusions don't deny themselves."

"That's a good one. You have a nice way with words."

"Thank you. So, keep going. Girlfriend?"

"Yes, and no."

"Not sufficient, your honor. The witness is avoiding the question."

Then she held up her hand.

"Could you turn away for a second?"

I did as she asked.

"Okay. Go on," she said. She'd returned to the posture I found her in the day before, on her side.

"It's complicated. We've known each other since we were twelve, but we never actually dated until this past year."

"You don't live together? Sleep together?"

"Nope, especially to your second, *impertinent* question."

I made sure to smile to show I didn't resent it.

"She's rich, isn't she?"

"How did you know?"

"And you aren't. My guess is you got a full ride at Stanford because you were top of your class in high school."

"Close. Can we stop talking about this?"

She took this slightly amiss and turned on her back and stretched out her legs. Every mystery was revealed.

"Sorry. Does this make up for my impertinence?"

I turned and laid on my back as well, in such a way that she knew I couldn't see all she'd just shown me.

"I'm not trying to tease you."

"I didn't say you were."

Things had gotten a little tense, so I said nothing for a while.

"Can I ask you a question?" she said after a few minutes of silence. It seemed like she'd come to a decision.

"Please."

"Do you like me? As a person I mean?"

"Yes, I do."

"Do you think you could love me?"

"You overestimate my ability for conjecture."

"Now you're talking fancy."

"I wasn't being flip," I said and turned on my side toward her. "I just don't know. It took me ten years to think I *might* be in love with Jean. I've known you for less than two hours."

Again, in seconds, she was on her feet with the towel wrapped around her.

"Will I see you tomorrow?" she asked, as though anyone in my position might say "no."

"If you want to."

"I do. Sorry to have you rush off, but I have something I have to do."

"Here, tomorrow?"

"Yes. We don't need to play that game again."

"See you then," I said and left her there.

CONTEXT NO. 1

It's important to understand that though what you're reading is largely dialogue, we weren't just rattling off questions and answers, quips and comments. Imagine it all as though it were in slow motion. It seemed that way to me. There were a lot of long pauses, either because neither of us knew what to say next to restart the conversation, or because we took a while to decide how to answer a question. She let me look at her, at every inch of her, without inhibition or impatience. She knew that she was gorgeous and that I was visually scintillated, like a pulsing filament in a lightbulb, yet neither took the other for granted, on the one hand, or over-reacted, however unusual the situation might be. We simply enjoyed each other, what we were doing and saying, and where and how we were. I said "slow motion." Maybe "as though time had stopped" is a better description.

DAY THREE

I found her as I did the first day, in the same flattened area of grass, on her side, facing me, though she'd changed from her left side to her right. She smiled as I walked up to her and sat down with my legs crossed as before.

"I was getting over-cooked on the other side," she said with a slightly sarcastic, quite fetching grin.

For the first time, she stretched out her hand and took my fingers. She rubbed them, her fingers greasy with lotion. Then those blue-green eyes, like cornflowers surrounded by the tiny green leaves, took me in, totally, as before. She'd been thinking about us.

"Why aren't you afraid of me?" I asked.

"Why aren't you afraid of me?" she answered.

"Good question. I've been afraid of women before."

"Tell me why."

"I knew a girl in high school who wanted to make out in the back seat of my car."

"What kind of car?"

"Does it matter?"

"What kind?"

"An old Cadillac."

"Good. I like that. Go on."

"When I got really excited, I tried to get on top of her, even though we were fully clothed."

I paused, wondering why I should be telling her such things. But it seemed natural.

"Then what?"

"Then she kneed me in the crotch as hard as she could."

"Ouch!"

"More than ouch," I said.

"Did you leave her alone after that?"

"Are you kidding?"

"You learned your lesson?"

I nodded and stifled a laugh. "In answer to your question," she said, "let's just say I'm a good judge of character. Besides, if you were going to mistreat me, I doubt you'd have waited so long."

"But what if I'd simply made a pass?"

"A pass? To a naked woman? Maybe you are crazy."

"Or a demand?"

"You? No way. Give me some credit, will you?"

"Can I take that as a compliment?"

"Only if you've got one for me."

"I like talking to you. You're interesting."

"One of the better compliments I've ever gotten. And I don't even question your sincerity, as I would from most every other asshole I've ever met."

"I'm not an asshole?"

"You're not sure?"

"I'm not an asshole."

"Glad to hear it."

"Isn't it interesting how nudity brings out honesty?"

"A woman's nudity?"

"I suppose either one, or both, would serve the same purpose."

"Thank you for that clarification."

For the next half-hour we chatted about totally inconsequential things. Not a word about our private lives. She knew everything about birds and flowers. We both loved novels, *Anna Karenina* in particular. We agreed that *Lolita*, as great as it was, had cringe-worthy passages. She loved Beethoven and I loved Stravinsky, and we both preferred sitting at home listening to the stereo to going to concerts. I couldn't get her even close to revealing anything about her personal life.

The oddest part is that I began to take her nakedness as normalcy. It wasn't that I got used to, let alone bored, with looking at her lovely breasts and thighs; instead, I began to feel that she was like home, like what home really means, a place of trust and comfort and happiness.

"So, what was it you had to do yesterday?" I asked her finally.

"I can't tell you. But I'll give you three guesses."

"You had to pee," I said, laughing.

To my surprise, she didn't laugh.

"Okay, sorry. You had to call someone. Someone close to you."

"Nope."

"Was it something sexual?"

"What, you think I have a lover back at my campsite waiting...?"

"No. I don't know what I meant."

"Well, you were partly right," she said dismissively.

Again, she was up and wrapped in her towel before I knew it.

"See you tomorrow?" she asked.

"I'll be here," I said.

This time she walked away first.

CONTEXT NO. 2

Let me get this out of the way. Halfway to the end of our "friendship," beginning the next day, the fourth of our seven days together, we indulged in a casual form of sexual engagement. She asked me if I'd like to take my pants off, and I said yes. She rubbed some suntan lotion on her hand and gently gripped my penis. Then she paused for a moment to pour some lotion on my fingers and pulled my hand between her legs, placing my forefinger on her clitoris. This mutual manipulation resulted in almost simultaneous orgasms. It was the last thing we did before saying goodbye for the day. It was the least important, however pleasurable, of our interactions. Physically, we never went further. And neither of us spoke one word about it afterwards.

DAY FOUR

She wasn't there when I arrived. I sat and waited, worried I might never see her again, even though she had said, "See you tomorrow?"

After half an hour she showed up in her towel as before. I realized for the first time that she didn't have any footwear. The meadow was pretty rough ground, but it didn't seem to matter at all.

"Turn away, please," she said, then, "Okay."

Again, she was on her right side, her skin still gleaming from suntan lotion.

"What's your name?" she asked.

"Jeremy. What's yours?"

"I can't tell you."

"Even your first name?"

"I notice you said only your first name."

"Just being casual. It's Jeremy Fane."

"That's nice. A little Hollywood, but I like it. I can't tell you mine because of the reason I'm here."

"Let me guess. You're hiding."

"Yes, I am, though I've given you enough hints to figure that out."

"Hiding from whom?"

"Not a living soul. I'm not hiding from anyone. I'm not even hiding from myself."

"I don't understand."

She again started plucking small flowers and tasting their stems.

"I'll tell you a story. Like most stories it's only partly true, but the true parts are the most important. There was a young girl, only 18 years old, who was very innocent, but very interested in men. A virgin. Her first real boyfriend was a jet pilot, almost ten years older than she was. He was very handsome and courageous and he made her weak in the knees. She kept him a total secret from her friends and family because of his age. One evening, he took her walking in the woods. Without any warning, or asking, without a single word, he threw her to the ground and started to molest her. She struggled and told him to stop. Then, to her great relief, another couple came along and the girl thought she was saved. Just the opposite. The couple sat down to watch, as if it was a movie. The jet pilot continued to molest the girl as the couple cheered them on. You see, they didn't really think they were watching a rape, but something more like a wrestling match. That was because the jet pilot never took off his pants and didn't take the girl's clothes off either. And because the couple were both drunk and stoned. Finally, the jet pilot gave up. He sat back and chatted with the couple, who even offered him a few tokes of a joint. The girl seized the opportunity, got up and ran away. Then things got really scary. They were in deep woods, and before long she was totally lost. She couldn't call out, afraid the pilot would find her again. So she just ran and ran. The next day the couple said they saw a girl run off into the woods, and she never came back. They didn't say a word about her boyfriend or the attack. She was found two days later, dehydrated and in shock. She had broken her ankle and spent two weeks in the hospital, then another month in a rest home meeting with a psychologist every day."

She paused and I said, softly, "You seem fine now."

"But it wasn't me. Most of the story is true. I had to fill in a few details I'm not sure about. It's essentially true, but it didn't happen to me."

"Your sister? A friend?"

"I can't say."

"What does that have to do with you being here?"

"If you think about it, you'll figure it out."

It was clear she didn't want to talk about it anymore. I would spend years in vain trying to figure out just why she was there and what she was running from.

"Your turn."

"I don't have any story like that."

"That's a relief," she said.

"But I know what you mean about mental cruelty. This isn't in any way on the level of what you just told me."

I paused, afraid I was about to trivialize her story.

"Go on. I want to hear, whatever it is." She smiled encouragingly.

"My entire pre-med experience was traumatizing. The teachers and doctors all made me feel I was too young, too stupid, too clumsy; in short, not cut out to be a doctor. And yet I got straight As, and they all congratulated me in the end. It was like Marine boot camp for four years. The next eight years will be even harder."

"You seem to have some steel in you," she said.

"Funny you use that word. That's precisely what one professor kept saying I *didn't* have. He said I was made of soft copper. He called me Mr. Copperpot."

"He was an idiot."

"Maybe. Maybe he was right."

We chatted for another fifteen minutes or so, mostly about the meadow and the mountains around us. She pointed out a golden eagle flying just above us.

"You know he can see the color of your eyes?" she said.

"They're green like yours."

"You know, that's the first romantic thing you've said. No more, if you don't mind."

Embarrassed, I just laid back and watched the few clouds that seemed stuck in place above us.

"I want to prove to you that I'm not the girl I described, though I am suffering for her."

"Okay."

Then she said it.

"Would you like to take your pants off?"

Afterwards, when I'd put my pants back on, she said, "Nice. Nice. Nice."

"Yes, it was."

"Do you think I'm messed up now?"

"No. You're not like any woman I ever met before, but no."

"Thank you."

A moment later she was gone.

I yelled after her, "Tomorrow?"

She waved, running away, and shouted "Yes!"

DAY FIVE

When I woke at dawn that day, I made coffee and spent an hour thinking about her, wishing I knew her name. I wasn't emotionally involved, and I didn't think I would become so. If anything, she made me yearn even more for a real girlfriend, and not necessarily Jean back home. This woman sunbathed in the nude unashamedly in front of a man she didn't know; she didn't and wouldn't love me, which meant, in a strange way, that I wasn't worthy of loving her. I began to think of her as almost a superior kind of being, at least emotionally and probably intellectually. Yet she was also vulnerable. Not physically. Not that it would ever occur to me to do so, I thought she could break my neck if I tried to do anything against her will. But there was something in her afraid of being hurt or touched by emotion or, maybe, conflict. She had guts enough to live in the deep wilderness by herself; maybe not as much as those women who climbed El Capitan by themselves, but she had enough courage to lay naked in a meadow and talk to a total stranger without even a hint of apprehension. Yes, my appearance was a surprise, yet she'd determined in seconds that I represented no threat to her, or any reason why she should discontinue her sun worship. And the sex play? Why not? It seemed totally natural to her, and who was I to refuse such sweetness?

When I arrived in the meadow, she was leaning back slightly, her knees up, face tilted toward the sun. Her breasts were firm, high, her nipples hard.

"The sun turns me on," was the first thing she said.

"Me too," I agreed, though I'd never thought of it that way.

As I settled into my normal cross-legged posture, she surprised me with a question.

"What we did yesterday?"

"Yes."

"Don't you think it was unfaithful?" she asked, without any accusation in her tone.

I thought about that for a few moments, as I had that morning.

"No. As I said, it's complicated. We aren't pledged to each other, if that's what you're driving it. We're not engaged, and we're free to see other people. I guess you could say we're in a holding pattern, while we figure things out."

"And am I hurting or helping you figure things out?"

"Maybe both."

"I don't entirely believe you, but let it go. I have another more important question."

She waited as if wondering if I was okay with moving on, her curiosity not entirely satisfied.

"I'm ready."

"Are you religious?"

"Well, that came out of the blue."

"For you maybe, but for me it's very important."

"My standard answer to that question is that I am not a believer. I'm a seeker."

"Someone more cynical than I am would say that's a marvelous way to dodge the question, but I'll accept it as sincere."

"And you?"

"You name it, I don't believe it. I don't believe in organized religion, though I was brought up Catholic. I don't believe in Zen, Hinduism, Buddhism, the Bible, the Koran, the Upanishads, the Bhagavad Gita. What I do believe in, though, is Jesus, Muhammad, Bodhisattva, Buddha, etc. I believe in the men. I even believe in Mary, mother of Jesus. People I can believe in, though their words and acts, happening so long ago, I have to take with a jigger of doubt. I read and take from them what makes sense to me and discard the rest. I also believe in Rumi, in Rilke, in Emerson, Blake and the other great poets. And, of course, I believe in Spinoza, who is probably the man most responsible for me lying her right now."

"I haven't read Spinoza, I'm ashamed to say."

"He believes that all this," she spread her arms wide, taking in the universe, "all this is God."

She looked at me and smiled.

"Pretty highfalutin', huh?"

"A bit," I admitted, but admiringly. "I've read a bit of a lot of the names on your list. But when I say I'm a seeker, don't picture the wanderer looking for eternal truth, like someone out of Hermann Hesse. I take it as it comes."

I turned and pointed at the mountain behind me.

"Right now I believe in that mountain more than anything in the world." Then I looked back at her and without hesitation, said, "I believe in you."

"But not as much as that mountain."

"Maybe as much. The difference doesn't matter."

"You're a Zennist, you fake!" she laughed.

"I find Zen amenable, nothing more," I said, more pompously than I meant to.

"Let's test this 'amenable.'"

"Yes?"

"Do I exist?"

"Yes and no."

"Sorry. Fail, Mr. Copperpot."

That hurt my feelings, and she could see it did.

"I'm sorry," she said, reaching again for my hand. "That was crude and stupid."

"It's okay," I said and smiled reassuringly.

"I think what you were trying to say," she said, moving quickly on, "is that all is real and all is illusion and it's not for us to know the difference."

"Something like that."

"I totally concur."

"Now let me ask you a question."

She waited, smiling again at the sun.

"What will you go back to when you leave here?"

"You know I'm not going to tell you about myself."

"I know. Be as vague as you want."

"I'm going back to myself, whatever that is."

"Then we're very alike, you and me."

She closed her eyes, and so did I, for maybe ten minutes. Then she stretched out her legs and turned toward me.

"I think I want your hand on me again, if that's okay?"

Twenty minutes later she said, "See you tomorrow," and left me buckling up my jeans.

DAY SIX

As I did the day before, I spent the morning thinking about her. I came to one conclusion….

I found her waiting for me, lying on her (now left) side. The sun was particularly bright that day, and she glowed like a golden idol. It left me almost breathless.

She was wearing a black bikini bottom. She saw that I looked at it more than once and said, "No reason. I just felt like wearing them for a while."

She lifted her bottom and took them off.

"Who am I to question what you wear?" I said and laughed.

"I can't stay very long today. I have some letters to write for posting when I get back home. My head is full of them and I want to get it all down."

"Sure. Understood. Will I be in any of them?"

She leaned forward and looked at my face, and not just my eyes, almost as if to make sure I wasn't making fun of her.

"In spirit, yes," she said finally.

"I'm glad."

"I have another question," she said, settling back onto her side. "One of those awkward ones."

"My favorite kind."

"How come you haven't tried to have sex with me?"

I didn't pause for a second.

"Because you mean too much to me." That was the conclusion I'd reached that morning. "And even if I never see you again after you leave, I will always feel that way about you."

"You mean you love me."

"No, I mean what I said. You're one of the most important things that's ever happened to me. You count in my life. Like a wife or a daughter or parents. Like blood almost."

"Wow."

"I've been thinking about this for two days, about you. And that's how I feel."

"But what if I wanted to sleep with you. Right here. Right now."

"Look, I know you're not asking me to sleep with you. You're being rhetorical, and I appreciate your delicacy. You're just plain curious. No one has probably ever treated you this way. And the fact that you're lying there gloriously naked makes it even more important to you, not to mention puzzling. But the answer to your question is that you could probably seduce me if you tried. I think we'd both regret it. When we touch each other, it feels like stacking gold coins one on top of the other, right between my hips. If we made love, I'm afraid it would be like knocking them all down."

"You mean a great deal to me too."

We laid back and closed our eyes. Just enjoying the sun. Finally, I said, "I don't mean to break the spell, but I feel that you won't be here forever, right?"

"I have to leave soon."

"Do you know when?"

"Not exactly. I don't want to think about it now."

She sat up, leaning on her left arm and reached for my belt buckle.

"It's gold coin time," she whispered and looked deeper into my eyes than she ever had before. She smiled, finding what she was look-ing for.

Later: "Tomorrow?"

"Yes."

DAY SEVEN

Yes, this would be our last day. When I arrived, she was lying on her stomach, her sweet buttocks more prominent than the time before, showing off all on their own.

I sat down as usual.

It took me a moment to realize she had been crying.

"Today's it, right?"

"Yes."

"I'm glad you told me. I had visions of you just disappearing and me coming down here day after day and never seeing you again. Will I ever see you again?"

"No. That's not possible."

"I wish I knew why."

"You wouldn't want to know."

"Can you at least tell me that you'll be alright? You'll be safe? Someone will love you?"

"Yes, to the first two. As to the third, it depends on what you mean by love. Let's leave it at that."

I almost said I loved her, but I knew it wasn't true, and I didn't think she loved me. Everything we'd said the day before was absolutely true, and though it offered no future together, it was somehow as important as love, if not more so.

"And that young girl who was lost in the woods, that wasn't you?"

"No. In fact that story is only half true, and only half the truth, if that makes sense. But it helped being able to tell it."

"So I don't have to worry about you."

"Please wonder about me, but don't worry. By wonder I mean try to imagine I'm fine. I'm happy. I'm living with people who love me. You can imagine that, can't you?"

"Yes, and I hope you'll do the same."

"I'm not worried about you at all. What are you going to do now that you've decided against medicine?"

"Who said I…."

Those eyes. There was no fooling those eyes.

"That was a trick question, right?"

"I'm sorry. I was pretty sure, but I wanted to know."

"Yes. I'm not a doctor. My dad was. I didn't tell you that."

"I guessed it though."

"But I didn't really go through pre-med because of him. At the beginning, I thought that was what I wanted. But it's a bit like the idealistic lawyer who ends up defending pushers and rapists. Surgery. That's what I wanted to do. Surgery might be about healing, but it's also about blood and death and for every ten lives you save you might lose one. That one. The idea that I might be the reason for that one because of something I did became intolerable. I guess I'm a coward at heart."

"That's the only stupid thing I've heard you say since we met."

"I suppose so. But living out here like this. Meeting you. Especially meeting you, I realize I've let myself get off course."

"A wise person once said to me 'you can't make others happy if you're not happy yourself.'"

"I like that."

"I want to touch you twice today. Can we do it once right now?"

"What do you think?" I said, managing a grateful laugh.

Afterwards, she said, "I want to see your body," and handed me the lotion. I stripped off and coated myself. She massaged it into my back.

"Can we hold each other?"

"Yes," I said and joined her on the blanket. In a few moments we were fast asleep in each other's arms.

I slept for less than an hour, rolled away and dressed. I watched her sleep for another 20 minutes. Her eyelids fluttered, and it was clear it wasn't a peaceful sleep. When she awoke, she was still on her side.

"That was lovely."

"Yes."

"Do you realize you've never said a word about how I look? I like that about you."

"It's not that I didn't notice."

"Funny thing about nudity," she said. "It can make other things recede behind the very fact there are no clothes. Isn't that funny. Nudity actually hides my...."

"Beauty."

"Now you went and spoiled it," she laughed.

As she struggled awake, she hummed a bit, the first time since we'd met.

"What is it with the humming?"

She thought for a moment.

"It's like people who talk to themselves. It's a way of answering my own questions."

"What questions?"

"Nice try."

"It doesn't have to be an important question—a give-things-away question."

"Okay, for example. One of the questions I ask myself all the time, often not even consciously, is what time are you?"

"What time *are* you?"

"I know, it should be what time am I, right? But I'm talking to myself, to this other, so it's 'you.'"

"And time?"

"That sounds strange, I know. What I mean is *when* am I in the scheme of things. I know *where* I am. But when am I. Early? Late? Right on time? I'm seldom the latter. But I want to be, so my humming helps me to get back on time."

"I'm still lost."

"Put it this way. If you're early, you're going to waste your energy trying to catch up. If you're late, you've already wasted your energy running ahead of yourself. When you're on time, then you're exactly when you should be."

"Now you sound like a Zen master."

"I am master of nothing."

"Now *that* I understand."

"You understand everything I just said. You can't hide it."

"Enough to understand your humming, at least."

"My turn."

She took my hand again.

"What are you going to do when you leave this place?"

"The first thing will be to tell my childhood sweetheart that there's a reason we never got together and that it's time to part."

"Crap! That's not my fault, is it?"

"Not at all. Though you did help me think things through, even though you weren't trying to."

"And you're not sad about it?"

"No."

"But she will be, won't she?"

"It will hurt her, but honestly, I can't say how much. That's one of the problems with us. We have no real idea about each other. We'll both just have to deal with it. But I don't think she'll feel badly for long."

"What else?"

"That's much harder to answer. I'm supposed to be here for thirty days, but I think I'll sign on for another thirty. I have a lot of thinking to do."

Then, and I still don't understand why, she started to cry, almost hysterically.

I tried to comfort her, to console her, to reason with her. I said all kinds of nonsense, but she cried and cried. I took her in my arms and she cried even harder. She clutched me to her and kissed me, the only time we kissed, but it was a long kiss and nearly broke me in two. That seemed to calm her down, and soon she let me go.

"I have to go soon," she said, and then briefly cried some more.

The only things I could think to say were endearments, like sweetheart, darling, etc. And I knew every one would have made her stop crying, because they were false words. We weren't lovers. We weren't in love. We were something altogether different.

"You know one thing we could do before I go?"

"What?"

I was so relieved that she'd stopped crying.

"What we've been doing, but with our tongues."

For a moment I thought, why not? It was a logical extension of our finger-play, but I knew she was just being generous. She wanted to make that final gift to me.

"I think we better not," I said, stroking her red curls, which the humid day had made even curlier.

"Are you sure?"

"One thing I want more than anything?"

"I know. Let's not mess it up?"

"Yes."

Again, she grabbed the lotion and reached for my belt buckle.

When it was over, we said only one more word. When she stood and wrapped the towel around herself, she did it slowly so I could see all of her for the last time.

Then she leaned down and kissed my forehead, touched my cheek and turned away.

"Tomorrow," I said, but it wasn't a question.

"Tomorrow," she said. It wasn't an answer.

CODA

I ended up going home after the thirty days. Being alone for another eighteen days was more than enough time to think, if not actually to make plans.

Breaking up with my "girlfriend" turned out to be unnecessary. She'd found someone while I was gone, which was a relief.

I got a Master's Degree in Art History and then a PhD. I wanted to work for an art museum, so I took a minor in arts management. Eventually, I became a curator of painting for a small, but respected university museum in the west. I've been there for nineteen years. I'm married and have two boys in their teens.

Yes, I did hear from her. She searched my name online and sent me a letter at the museum from a P.O. box in Seattle: "I am fine. I hope you are too," was all she said. I wrote back: "I'm fine too," and told her a little about my life. We've been sending such letters, once a year for eighteen years now, in midsummer, when our meadow is in full bloom.

JACKIE, THE BARMAID

WALLACE Mone sits alone at the horseshoe bar in the Maverick Lanes Lounge rolling quarters. The thunderclaps of the lanes have faded to an occasional rumbling, deadened by twin glass doors into the lobby. After every drink is served, by a tall, good-looking redhead with wrinkles around her eyes and dressed in a tight-fighting server's uniform, a flick of Wallace's forefinger sends a quarter rolling with a metallic hiss, a harmonic hum that rises in tone as it follows the lip of the bar top around to drop with a brittle splash into a recessed shot glass at the other end of the bar. Because of the nature of the achievement, that all this, the great sculpted and polished hardwood of the bar, the building, with its kitchens and pool tables and locker rooms and four-dozen pin setters, should lend itself to this perfect mechanism for the rolling of quarters, Wallace, as have many others before him, rolls far more quarters than tips deserved, to watch them follow their steady, gyroscopic path into the glass. He wonders if the room isn't tilted, just slightly, since the coin always seems to pick up speed near the end. He marvels how, bars being the home of rowdiness that they are, there isn't one nick in the wooden lip to cause the coin even the minutest flutter, disturbing the vibration in its soft rising ringing. Even when the bar is full, Wallace has noticed how people are careful to keep their glasses and cigarettes and change away from the lip so as not to impede the progress of others' quarters. It is, in fact, far less interesting now, with the bar empty, the quarter absolutely assured of its destination, when at other times it has a gauntlet to run, under the elbows of up to twenty drinkers, each one ostensibly intent on a conversation or a pull on the glass in his hand, never without some recognition, winking or smiling or nodding, of the coin's passage, literally, right under the nose. Or if, once in a while, but seldom, someone forgets himself, is either too drunk or too emotionally involved in some bitter conversation, and a shirtsleeve or a finger stops the coin, a loud groan rises from around the horseshoe like the transmigration of the coin itself, in general condemnation of the criminal's negligence, continuing unabated until the coin has been set back on course down the bar by the embarrassed and apologetic perpetrator. More than once, a fistfight has been the result of a stranger's lack of familiarity with this rite, and the ejection of a drunk beyond his quota of booze has often been determined by his incapacity to adhere to the rules of the game. The waitress, new to Wallace, is fascinated with this pastime. She stands with her hands in the misshapen pockets of her uniform, shifting her weight from foot to foot, a damp cloth tossed over her shoulder. She smiles at Wallace, less for the free entertainment than for the stack of quarters he is adding to her first day's take-home pay. Wallace taps his cocktail glass with the next quarter and she drops in two cubes of milky ice and pours it full of single-malt scotch. She lingers, head down, thoughtful, dabbing the spigot on the Scotch bottle with her towel, resolves to speak, as he sends another quarter on its way.

"Damned silly of me, wearing this uniform." Her voice is husky, cigarette scarred.

"What's wrong with it?"

Wallace looks her over appreciatively as she steps back and spreads her arms, displaying herself. She is thin-hipped and long-legged. Her white uniform binds her breasts tightly with a hint of cleavage. She is perhaps in her late twenties, once quite pretty in her teens, but hardly a blown rose—more a tiger lily that needs watering.

"They asked if I had a uniform, for Chrissake. This thing," she says, patting the pockets, slack as two awestruck mouths, "is from when I spooned out slop at St. Mary's, only then I wore a snood, too. I never wore a uniform tending bar in my life. I didn't realize until later that what the manager had in mind was one of those little cocktail dresses. The littler the better. This was not what he expected for my first night on the job."

Her cynicism, knowing but sympathetic, neatly divides the manager's obviousness from the impulse behind it, condemning the lie only.

"He's okay," she says, an afterthought, "We had a talk. He knows where I stand."

"I like the shoes," Wallace offers, knocking back half of his drink.

The woman laughs, turning a heel from the toe. "They're elegant, don't you think? Nurse's issue. Black satin high heels don't go well with linen," she adds, smoothing her hands from her belly to her thighs. It is a nice figure, thinks Wallace. She smiles, coloring, as if the compliment has been received.

Wallace looks around the lounge. A small pool table glows green, a plateau of mown grass under a rectangular sun. He asks, "Where is everybody?"

"It is one-thirty," says the bartender, looking at her watch.

"On a Friday night?"

The woman shrugs. "It was crowded enough two hours ago. We had a fight, no, two fights." She leans over the bar and looks out the double doors. "I wish they'd close the lanes down already. Send a few more tips in here."

"What were they about?"

"The fights?" she says, relaxing back, setting her elbows on the bar and looking at him. Her eyes are bright green and clear, long-lashed, without much mascara. Her hair is the dark side of red, but full of light, the color and weight of Irish setter fur. She smiles with small, imperfect teeth. "A lot of shouting and pushing, the first one.

People really get upset about this Bunyon running for office. They may be registered Republicans, but they want their preachers to stay in their pulpits. That's one thing I heard loud and clear. And the fight," she winks, remembering, "that started when I caught a kid—who I shouldn't have been serving but I was, kinda cute—he had his fingers in my shot glass down there. After somebody threw him out it occurred to me he was probably going to roll the coins back in for me anyway. He was just out of change, poor kid. You'd think I'd have figured that out sooner. Anyway, the whole rolling-the-coins thing bugs me. It's almost an insult."

"An insult?"

"Yeah, like they're trying to fill my panties or something. It's creepy the way some of them do it."

Wallace isn't too drunk to suspect that her conversation has edged beyond the professional intimacy of bartenders. What he can't be sure of—is this just her way, like some waitresses will call you "honey," as if you were hers, except she calls everyone "honey" the same way too?

"Hey, I'm sorry, I won't do it anymore."

"No, it's not you. You're okay."

"Um, thanks, but I'm just happy to lay the tip on the bar from now on, okay?"

"You always were polite," she says.

He leans back in surprise.

She dispels the mystery by tapping the back of his hand with her long, red-nailed forefinger.

"You don't remember me, do you?" she asks, the lines around her eyes crinkling with the fatalistic vulnerability of a heart over-used to hurt, a heart full of fear and courage and hunger and love. He doesn't remember a thing about her.

"I'm sorry," he whispers.

"Jackie?" she offers, holding back any other name. Her smile is broad and sweet, like the invitation of opening arms.

Wallace searches her face, disappointed with the state of his mind, muzzy and hot, when, for the moment, she wants it sharp and cold. He's about to blow it. The damned booze is blocking his memory like a mirage. She's no one he's ever really known, he's sure of that, but the face is not unfamiliar.

"You used to look at me. I'd be sitting on the couch, waiting to go, and I felt like my clothes were on a hanger in the closet and I'd only show you more if I got up to get them."

Wallace realizes that she's had a drink or two herself. She shakes her head, "No?"

"No," he admits.

"I almost married your little friend's brother,"—a snide tang on 'little friend's'—"but I was too stupid."

He still doesn't get it.

She shakes her head again, still patient, but marveling at his density. She takes a breath, leaning forward, her chest down to the bar, head up. She tries again.

"Chuck Brittain?"

"I remember Chuck Brittain!"

"I was dating him when you were dating his younger sister. What was her name? Danielle?" She was being a little snide.

"Danae," he corrects her, uncritically.

"Right. I remember, it was sillier than Danielle."

He lets this pass.

"Jackie, hunh? I still don't remember your last name." It is a lie. He still doesn't remember her.

Pursing her lips, "Witcomb," she whispers.

Her face, resting on the curled fingers of her two hands, eyeing him, critical and curious, zooms, at last, into focus.

He'd met her only once or twice, but he remembers now, the sweet, sexy face, hair longer then, the skirts short and tight, the sweaters, sizes too small. Of course, he had looked at her like that! She had made no other impression. He wasn't sure they'd ever said more than hello and nice to meet you. He remembered, vaguely, the older brother, stopped by a police car, admitting, yes, he'd "slapped the bitch," but he couldn't believe she'd called the police on him—she'd slapped him first!

Wallace, perfectly matter-of-fact, tells her everything, even about her clothes, as though describing some other person altogether.

"Yeah," she laughs, unapologetic, "I was pretty hot, then. Stupid, too. He was a nice guy, really. I could have done worse." She shook her head again. "But I was just too hot. It took getting almost raped once to teach me any better."

Wallace's look of alarm makes her explain.

"Almost," she reassures him. "A guy I'd been dating. Several years later. He could have had me, actually, if he hadn't tried to force me. In the back of his stupid bug, no less," she concludes, with a shiver of disgust.

Wallace, after searching his mind quickly, as though he hasn't heard: "Whatever happened to Chuck?"

"He came back from Vietnam and tried to find me, believe it or not," she says, still amazed by the fact. "Only he didn't like much what he found." She shook it away. "There was too much history, my history, by then anyway. So!" she adds, putting an end to the subject. Even now, she is not afraid to hold him with her eyes. "I can tell you a little about yourself, if you like?"

Wallace contemplates the empty glass in his fingers and decides not to interrupt. "Be my guest."

To his disappointment, she stands up straight and backs away from the bar. She looks at her wristwatch, which she wears on the inside of her wrist. "But it's closing time and it'll cost you a ride home."

"All right."

"I'll meet you out front in fifteen, after I close up," she says, tossing the towel into a metal sink as she steps toward a heavy swinging door behind the bar, "And I've got to tell my girlfriend I won't need a ride after all."

"Girlfriend," Wallace muses in the parking lot, fumbling with his keys, the cold wind chilling his booze-cold head. He hasn't heard a woman use that word since high school.

He sits behind the wheel of a huge new station wagon, gunning the engine. On both sides, stenciled in bold red letters: "VOTE FOR JOHN BUNYON" and underneath in smaller letters: "NO MORE HELL ON EARTH."

He looks across the parking lot at the covered entrance, his eyesight, steady, clear and deep. The bottom half of his body feels numb from the cold plastic bench. He shakes his head, slaps his cheeks. "I'm okay to drive." Jackie appears in a purple raincoat, the belt pulled very tight. He puts the car into gear and nudges the accelerator. She waves.

He leans to unlock the door. "Hi!" she says, slightly embarrassed. Her coat hisses on the seat as she slides over next to him. One leg, long and white stockinged, up on the hump, tilted across the other at the knee.

Wallace pulls away from the curb, feeling her shoulder settle against his own.

"Are we going steady?" he asks, without a hint of facetiousness.

"Oh, this," she says, turning just her head, "In bucket seats I'm okay. I can't sit off by myself on a big bench like this. Even my father and brother...."

"It's not that I mind."

She takes his arm in both of hers, hugging.

"Like this?"

"I have to tell you"—knowing this isn't news—"you're still hot."

She receives this as her due, acknowledged with a kiss on his cheek—the smell of peppermint schnapps like old perfume.

"Where was I? Oh, yes, all about Wallace Mone."

Hearing his name is a shock. She does remember! But her next statement deflates him.

"Famous lottery winner, Wallace Mone. One in ten million!"

"Everyone knows that," he says, unable to hide his disappointment.

She leans away, glaring at him. He looks askance at her once, quickly, then asks, "Where am I going?"

"Take 20 out of town. I live halfway to Rockford."

"Just tell me where to turn."

She hugs his arm again.

"I *do* know about you," she asserts, sadly, as if it is no longer worth trying to dispel his doubt. "I know all about you."

"About me or about Danae Brittain," says Wallace, making connections.

"Same thing. At least how to get there."

Wallace doesn't understand. Is it his booze or hers? The highway writhes, wet and black, feeding itself into the headlights, just barely under control, which he has no fear of losing. The darkest stretch of road he knows; over the years, in the newspaper: out of control, head-on collisions, leaving the road, witness reports, retaining wall, motorcycles through the fence.

Then her tongue warm and wet on his neck, grazing teeth. He's not too drunk to be aroused.

She whispers, "I may have been younger and beneath your notice, but I had my eyes open. I watched you in the halls, you and, oh, two or three other guys your age or older. You were all just right." A wistful sigh. "You were the insecure one and too smart to try to hide it, and you lived in a big house and that was sad because you didn't have any parents. You always looked like you'd just walked into a roomful of strangers." She kisses his ear. "For a long time, you were friends with John Bunyon. And then you weren't. I even know why. He was one of them. I remember all the gossip. You never seemed to know what was really going on around you.

"He's not gay, if that's what you're suggesting."

"Not anymore. I think they call it 'experimenting.'"

"Well, it damn well wasn't with me!"

"I know that. Chuck used to tell me everything because his sister told him everything. How you saved her when she tripped out. How she thanked you. I know everything. People tell me everything.

They always have. Only it's wasted on me, 'cause I never know how to use it. Turn left here."

"Until now," he whispers, his erection tightening against his loose trousers. That the person she has been describing is entirely unfamiliar doesn't dim his excitement at finding a version of himself alive in a stranger's memory.

"What?" she asks, as though she hasn't heard.

Wallace shakes his head, meaning "Forget it." The headlights declare a swiftly climbing, narrow strip of new asphalt. At the top of the hill a large white farmhouse hides among towering pine trees. They fly past, off the hill. On the left, bare trees and tall grasses slant toward the Kishwaukee riverbed, little more than a stony creek this far below the dam. On the right, a field of harvested corn lies ground up, broken stalks like a giant's stubble. At a subdivision of a dozen houses, she tells him to turn in. Her silence, since leaving the highway, has seemed deliberate, time and space in which to consider the accusation fused with welcome in his two-word statement, resolving, perhaps, that his comprehension is nothing to fear. Reaching a fork, she directs him, pointing to the right. "All the way to the end," she says, beginning to squirm away from him on the seat. The drive takes him into a cul-de-sac, like the bottom of a thermometer. "This one," she says, pointing at a small, pale-blue ranch house, a rectangular box with two picture windows and a squat chimney. He pulls into a spotless concrete driveway flanked by lawn still littered with the large, flat leaves from two spindly, immature oak trees.

She lets herself out and hurries around the car, taking his hand to lead him, walking backwards, up the sidewalk to a concrete slab of stoop.

"I rent this from my father, believe it or not," she offers, tugging him forward impatiently. Why should he care? Wallace wonders, the cold air clearing his boozy head. "He owns the whole damn street," she adds, letting him go, taking keys from the pocket of her raincoat. Wallace notices, without offering himself an interpretation, that she doesn't carry a purse. "Son of a bitch charges me the same as everyone else, too. Sweet old daddy baddy! Stuck!" A brass doorknocker knocks as she shoves the door open with her shoulder. She flicks on the light. "Here we are!" A spare living room, long, dark brown couch, tufted, cotton; fake brick fireplace with a black screen; small TV set on a card table; beyond the couch, a yellow Masonite table with matching chairs in front of another large window framing a vast shorn cornfield lit by some dim reflection off the clouds above.

She comes close and puts her hands on his shoulders.

"Ouch!" he cries.

She backs away in shock.

"Sorry, you busted my cherry!" he cries, not laughing.

"What?"

He pulls down his collar which is spotted red.

"What's that?"

"It's called cherry angioma," he says, laughing now. He touches the spot. "It's basically a blood blister. It's grown since this morning. You must have popped it."

She runs into the kitchen and comes back with a paper towel, and begins to dab at the sore.

"It's stopped bleeding. Does it hurt?"

"Not at all. Sorry to startle you. I get them now and then. They're totally harmless."

"Popped your cherry. That's rich," she says. "Let me get you a BandAid."

"Okay."

Within a few minutes he is bandaged and she's pulled his collar back into shape. He kisses her then, for the first time. Long and deep.

"You're a nice man," she whispers.

"You're a lovely woman."

"Can I get you a drink?" she chirps, hastily pulling off her raincoat, tossing it on the couch on her way into the kitchen.

"No!" he says loudly, "Come back here."

She stops and turns to him, smiling slyly, hands on hips, one hip sunk, meaning, "Now listen." She says, "No, I must have a sip of something. You haven't been standing behind a bar for eight hours watching other people drink." She spins on her heel and disappears through a doorway beside the dining table.

"Nothing for me," he shouts, not really caring why she has just unnecessarily lied to him.

Before he can get his own coat off, she is back with a tiny brandy snifter between her fingers.

"You sure?" she asks, toasting him, the glass held high.

"I've had enough," he says, laying his coat over the card table behind the TV.

"This is B and B. It can't be too bad for you. It's made by monks or something. Men of God." She giggles, holding the glass with her two forefingers as she drinks. She is girlishly shy now, he realizes, somewhat confused. She stands behind the couch, he in front, hands in his pockets.

"No, thanks," he says again.

"It used to be the thing to do, drive around in Chuck's old Buick and drink Bali Hai wine. Remember that old fat guy from the automobile plant who would buy it for everybody in the hopes they'd buy some of his dope as well?"—not waiting to learn if he did or not —"Did you ever buy any of his dope? We sure did. He had everything, even coke. Smack was about the only thing I didn't do. But it didn't last long. Not more than a month or so. Chuck and I woke up once in the middle of the night on that old fat bastard's floor with him in only his t-shirt pawing both of us! I won't tell you what he was saying," she concludes.

She drains the glass and sets it on the dining table, pushing it away from the edge.

"Why did I bring that awful subject up?" she asks herself, half turned away. "Oh, yes, driving around."

She comes to the couch and takes his hand again, pulling him to sit beside her. She continues, bending over to untie her shoes: "We used to follow you around, did you know that? When you and Danae were running around? Chuck wanted to follow you. He said he was just taking care of his baby sister," she adds with emphasis, leaning back and kicking off her shoes. "Remember how you used to go and park in your own driveway?" she asks, startling him. "We used to park across the street, a couple of houses down, and watch your car for hours. And the funny thing is we knew what you guys were doing, but we just sat there and drank. We drank while you fooled around. Or did you screw?" She pauses for an answer, then hurries on. "It used to drive me crazy. Chuck was too nervous to feel me up even, afraid he'd miss his little sister screaming or jumping around to get away from you," she says, mock-dramatic, waving her arms.

"Can you believe it? He didn't care what you two did as long as little sis was happy. I used to get the biggest kick out of that. And you two. Who ever heard of making out in your own driveway? And yet what better place, right? No cop is going to stop you there!"

She stretches, arms reaching up, fingers curled, then, leaning away from him, slides along the couch until her head comes down against the armrest, her arm up behind her head. She draws one leg up until her knee touches the back of the sofa, pulling her dress tight between her stockinged thighs.

"You both must have been real talkers, I remember thinking that. We knew when something was happening, and when it wasn't, because we could see your heads. Two silhouettes," she says, stretching out her arm and pointing at his. "Most of the time we could see your heads. Hours, it seemed like days later you disappeared, sinking down out of the windows. It used to make me so horny. All I'd want to do is tear at Chuck's zipper and gobble him up, buuut," she sighs, closing her eyes tightly for a moment, "it wasn't to be. He was on duty. Couldn't be distracted. At least not till later," she concludes.

Her eyes on Wallace's, reaching with both hands to grab the fabric of her dress from mid-thigh and, with her legs lifting up her body, she pulls the dress up, wriggling her hips, past pink cotton panties to just above her squint-shaped bellybutton. Then—the reverse motion nearly—her thumbs under the elastic, she effortlessly lifts her pelvis and draws the panties down her thighs to her knees.

"Can you help?" she whispers. Wallace, with his left hand, draws the panties off her legs, which she raises one by one, letting her knees fall away from each other, both heels now on the couch. She thinks a moment, breathing quickly, considering, her eyes searching his. Like the extension of a new idea, her right hand drops to the dark red fur between her thighs, finger pulling aside a fleshy glistening lip.

"How much farther do you want me to go with this, Wallace?" she asks, her voice soft and hoarse.

"I like to hear you talk," says Wallace, beginning to roll—left, then right—the stockings off her legs.

"I once made a lover of mine come by just talking, do you know that? Not Chuck, that took hours...."

"I don't care about Chuck," Wallace interrupts.

Her eyes click wider, quizzical. She corrects herself.

"This guy—I think 'lover' might be the wrong word—wanted to sit naked, cross-legged on the floor, and have me talk to him. Just talk. With all my clothes on, halfway across the room. He didn't even touch himself. It took about four minutes. He said I said absolutely the perfect words. But it didn't do a damn thing for me. Just left me out in the cold."

She measures the effect of this.

"Are you cold now?" Wallace asks her, holding her bare left foot, small, cool, pink-nailed, in his hands.

"No, just anxious," she reveals, "It's like being on trial."

"Maybe. In a way?"

"How did we get into this?"

"I think you started it."

"What, should I have let you make the first move?"

"I don't think that was it."

She raises her other foot, points it under his arm and sets it in his lap. "Well, what do you think?"

"Keep talking," Wallace says.

"Do you want me to masturbate?" she asks, doing it a little.

"Only if you want to."

"I don't mind it at all."

"Good." She draws her knees up again, wide open, delves.

"You don't want to help?"

"Not yet."

"Just talk, hunh?"

"For just a little longer."

She looks up at the ceiling, squinting.

"I remember another guy…."

"No, something different."

This has brought her eyes down to his quickly.

"You think I've lost it?"

"No, not at all. Tell me about things back then."

"How about the time Danae Brittain and I…."

"Don't make things up."

"It has Chuck in it?"

"Go ahead."

She shook off the idea.

"Well, he once told me about what brothers and sisters do when they are growing up together, exploring things."

"You believed him? I wouldn't have. Not about Danae."

She drops one of her feet gently into his lap.

"Let's try something else. Okay?" he asks, stroking her arch.

"That's better," she says, turning her toes into his crotch. He waits, holding her eyes, unsmiling.

"I have a confession to make."

"What is it?"

"I had a crush on Danae, though we never did anything."

"As I said."

"I just thought, you know—some guys are into women with each other."

"So are some women."

He drives his thumb hard into the ball of her foot. She stiffens.

"Wait," she whispers. Her hips rock beneath the fulcrum of two fingers driving her into the sofa. Her lips bare clenched teeth. She lets out a small, breathy groan. Her body relaxes. She leans forward, lifting the hand up to him.

"Is that what you wanted, Wallace?"

He touches her fingers.

"I've come just for you. I've never done that for anyone. Not like this. It's like I've given you a little gift. Now it's your turn."

Wallace kisses her fingers, takes them between his teeth. She draws them away. He lifts her feet off his lap and stands up. Staring down, he takes off his clothes. She sits up and unbuttons the front of her dress, pulls it over her head, undoes the clasp on her bra and sloughs it off her shoulders, then scootches down on the couch, bringing up her knees, her arms behind her head. Wallace bends down, his knee on the edge of the couch, eyes sliding across the small pools of her pink-nippled breasts, down her white, flat body, to her disheveled cunt. A brief searing panic in his belly forces him back, dropping him to his knees on the hardwood floor.

"Come down here," Wallace whispers.

"Oh, yes. I think I know," she whispers, "Well, I have a secret or two for you too, sweetie," slipping off onto hands and knees, then pushing him with her hand on his chest back onto a pale gray rug.

They face each other on their haunches. Wallace's fingers graze the small mound of her right breast. Jackie leans and kisses him, searches the back of his teeth with her tongue. Then, turning away on all fours, she says, "I'm afraid there's nothing I hate worse than getting my ass banged on a hard floor, Wallace." Tossing her head back like a pony, she raises her buttocks up to him, arching her back, setting her knees apart.

As he grips her waist, she says, looking back, "No, not there."

He doesn't understand. He persists, touching his penis to her cunt.

"No, please. Here, let me help." She wets her finger and reaches behind. "This is my little secret, Wallace. Everybody has a little secret like this."

She works more of what he takes to be an opening for him. Wallace pushes her hand away and grips her again, lower, where her thighs turn into her hips.

"No! Shit, Wallace!"

He's already there. The other idea frightens him.

"Dammit!" she shouts, surprised, confused. He can't believe this isn't what she wants, so wet and open. "Dammit, Wallace!" she cries angrily, but without fear, wriggling, clawing the rug.

"This is not what I wanted!" He grips her hips harder, holding himself into her, not thrusting. Just her effort to get away is all it takes.

"Just—only—a moment more," he grunts. He holds her, cinching her closer, a last moment longer, thrusting once. Then he lets her go. She is up and stomping out of the room, looking back once, down at his spill out of her onto the floor, curious, as if she has no idea what it could be.

He sits back on his heels, hears her in the bathroom. Water running in a sink. The toilet flushing. Wallace is dressing when she returns in a white terry cloth robe, her face scrubbed and flushed, hair in a white band.

She drops a bath towel on the wet spot on the floor.

"What are you doing?" she asks, plopping down on the sofa, tucking her legs under her. Without make-up, her face is more pale and less sensuous, but fresh, even younger and therefore more attractive.

"I guess I'm dressing to go," Wallace answers; it is half a question.

"What the hell for?"

He sees that she understands. She doesn't like it, but she understands. She slaps the brown couch.

"Come and sit down."

"Can we go into your bedroom? There's more room," he suggests, looking off in that direction, tossing his shirt on the rug.

"Sure. Why not," she says, standing up and—surprising him—taking his hand, leading him down a brief hallway into a corner bedroom: white paint, double bed with powder blue comforter, a second small TV on a battered wooden bureau. Latticed windows look north and west onto expanses of ravaged cornfield rimmed by bare trees that look like stiff fog. The moon has come out from behind the clouds.

Without turning on the light, Jackie slips out of her robe and crawls onto the bed. Wallace removes his pants and joins her. They hold each other, getting warm, kissing to make up, without trying to excite each other. After a time, Wallace lies back beneath her arm, nestles his cheek beneath her right breast, staring at the ceiling. Her body is resentful and unforgiving next to his, a hardness. Then Wallace realizes that this is not a true interpretation—hers is simply the body of a stranger. He decides to take a risk.

"That was the best fuck of my life," he says with satisfaction.

"Give me a break," Jackie says. "How do you know that besides spoiling my secret I might *not* be on the pill."

"I don't think that's likely."

"Well, I am," she says, slightly hurt, "even though I haven't had sex in ages."

"Anyway, it really was."

"Are you trying to make me feel sorry for you?" she asks, turning toward him, head propped on her elbow.

"You already do."

She answers this by putting her finger in his ear.

"I liked everything *except* that you made the decision," Jackie says gently, with little emphasis.

"Maybe that's what I'm talking about," says Wallace, without enough conviction for her to believe it easily. "Other than that, all I can say is that I didn't know you," he concludes, which is as close as he comes to an apology.

"Will you next time?"

"Can't promise."

It was better than saying he wouldn't. But he wouldn't.

"Can't we talk about something else? How about politics?"

"Are you kidding?"

"Talking about fucking *after* fucking is like touching yourself in a crowded room."

Her voice is even, matter of fact. Even though he doesn't understand what she means, he likes her even more for saying it.

Then he blinks wide awake. Until this moment, it hasn't occurred to him that this woman is anything more than—the words run—a cunt, piece of ass, babe, slut, siren, bimbo, tramp, bitch, whore, ball buster, fuck—all of them only partially correct. The words vanish with her next sentence.

"Tell me about John Bunyon for the U.S. House of Representatives."

"You're kidding!"

"I'm interested!"

"I can't tell you anything you don't already know if you watch TV," he says, speeding the words, uncomfortable with the subject.

"What's it like being his, what is it, campaign manager?" she persists, with suspect girlish awe.

"Not a subject for polite company."

"Very funny," she says, slipping her thumb beneath his soft penis. "Don't worry. I won't tell."

He pushes her hand away.

All of this has happened very quickly, confusing Wallace.

"If you really want to know," he says, patting her hand where it lies on her belly, "It's like being an altar boy."

"Then why do it?"

"I fetch and carry for him," he continues, ignoring her, "write his letters, speeches, make appointments, drive him around, tell him where the TV cameras are. Pretty boring stuff, actually."

"But what about all that strategy and political intrigue?"

"He makes it up as he goes along."

She laughs, rolling on her back.

"That sounds like him!" she says, laughing louder. "He makes it up as he goes along? Ha ha ha, that's right! That's absolutely right!"

Her laughter is sane and intelligent and bitter. Wallace understands.

"So you know him?" He cannot hide his distaste.

"Honey, I know him well enough. I told you I used to watch the both of you, but one of you was watching back. He took about eight years to make his move, but when he did it was like a freight train coming right in my front door. And that's what he did, came right up and knocked and said," lowering her voice, " 'Can I come in, Jackie?' like he just saw me yesterday in the front row of his congregation!"

Her voice is full of laughter.

"First he wanted to take me for a walk in the park. Then he bought me a cheeseburger. He talked about all sorts of stuff, his school and his rehabilitation center, the lonely life of the clergy, how he was going to change the face of this town. It took me three hours to get up the courage to ask how a Baptist minister could be doing this —trying to make me—because, you see, I was brought up Catholic, too, and he said," her voice lowered again, " 'It's not a problem.'

"That was all. And that night he kissed my hand and left me on the front stoop almost begging him to come inside, and then he was back fifteen minutes later asking to come inside, all sheepish and bashful. I nearly ripped his clothes off only to have him sit right there on my rug and beg me…."

"Stop," Wallace whispers, and he means to stop her completely, rolling over onto her, up on his arms, pressing his belly into hers. She has spread her legs beneath him and contact between their genitals has made him quickly hard again. He looks down, her eyes points of pale light in the darkness, her smile a smudge.

"You know you have the damnedest way of knowing entirely too much that concerns me?"

She touches his forearms, smoothing the hair.

"What are you talking about?"

"I don't think I need to say," he says, arching his back.

"You just don't care about me, do you?" she asks, but before he can begin to understand, a ball of light explodes in the room, momentarily blinding him, stamping his eyes with the latticework crosses from the window behind Jackie's head. Wallace springs from the bed, trips on a shoe and falls to his knees. Then he is running down the hallway. He throws open the front door and leaps into the darkness, off the front stoop, running in cold grass around the west end of the house. There is only a narrow strip of grass between the house and the furrows of the cornfield, where the plow has nipped off the edge of the lawn as if to reassert its territorial rights. The three-quarter moon glares, sparking light in the dew on the grass, on the clods of dirt. No one in sight. Wallace peers out across the cornfields, anticipating some distant movement lost in the background of bare trees. He runs around back. The lawn here is slightly broader, with two folding lawn chairs collapsed beside an iron table and an empty glass bird feeder mounted on five feet of pipe. He can't find any footprints. Swearing to himself, Wallace continues, jogging around the house, steps on a garden hose which is hard as metal in the cold. The grass hasn't grown well in this narrow lane between the two houses. The cold dirt sticks to his bare feet. He shuffles through the grass to clean them before reentering Jackie's home. Beginning to shiver, he locks and bolts the door and hurries back to the bedroom. It is odd that she hasn't gotten up or put on her robe, with the appearance of an intruder, a peeping tom at her own bedroom window; instead, she is buried, only her head and fingers visible above the blue comforter.

"What were you doing?" she asks with a mixture of awe and hilarity, as though his behavior is the nicest surprise she's had in years. "Are you some kind of polar bear?"

"Didn't you see it?" The tone of his voice saying, "You saw it!"

"What are you talking about? I've heard of the cold shower, but I've never had someone bolt into the winter night to get rid of a hard-on!"

"Don't be ridiculous," he says climbing under the covers. He sees that she didn't see. Her eyes might have been closed, he supposes, might have blinked in that instant. "Somebody took a picture of us. With a flash. You didn't see it?"

"Darling, all I saw was somebody about to fuck me charging out of the house in the raw!" She laughs loudly, but with sympathy. "It was kind of thrilling, actually."

She can't hold back her laughter.

"A bold pervert at my bedroom window?"

"Well, you may not give a damn," he says, beginning to see the humor himself, to question whether it had really been a flash. Couldn't a light like that go off in your own head? Drugs had done something like that to him—rapid-firing synapses supercharging his nervous system—more than once.

It was cozy, returned from an adventure of sorts, stretched out here with this warm woman. She assumed so much less than a stranger. She could endure a threat with him and laugh and judge him gently like an indulgent wife. He puts his arms around her and holds her to him, twining his legs with hers.

"Why would anyone want to take a picture of us?" she asks, only vaguely interested in the answer, as if the question has no real meaning.

Wallace considers the question, and with the nurtured paranoia that follows naturally upon the lifelong pursuit of drugs and women, not to mention politics, rephrases it accordingly: "Who, Jackie? Who?"

"Some creep," she answers casually, dismissing even this possibility.

"Creep, yes. I know lots of creeps."

"Don't be silly," she says, twisting away in his arms, then looking back as if she understands. With awe, not excitement: "I know what you're thinking! You're crazy! John Bunyon doesn't have a chance! Why would Tower's people risk everything to play a dirty trick on *you?*"

Wallace's forefinger touches her lips, following the path of her thoughts, then veering from them. There is something entirely too glib about this, but there is still too much booze in his head to think it through.

"You've been following his race pretty closely."

It isn't really a question. She is silent, her eyes wide in the diffuse moonlight. He is still with her, but this question will tell, "When was the last time you had sex?"

"I don't know. Months maybe."

"You're lying."

"Get the fuck out of my bed!" she screams, pushing him away, kicking out at his knees, "Get out! Get away from me," as though the violation had been physical.

Wallace is satisfied. He can permit himself distrust. Though he hasn't made up his mind, he is in jeopardy either way if he stays a moment longer.

"And the last time you fucked Bunyon?"

"You are the creep! Fucking creep!"—pitch rising like a sailor's pipe—"Get out!"

"Is that why you wanted it up your ass, only they couldn't see us on the floor like that?"

She screams incoherently, a fearful keening.

"They didn't tell you much, did they?" he says and grabs his clothes. From the doorway, he can't see but a pale sketch of her upper torso, flailing, apparitional as mist. It is useless, perhaps, he thinks, unwise, to speak.

She quiets at his passing from the doorway, though as he stands in her living room, putting on his clothes, he feels her rage, down the pipe of the hallway, like a boiler pressurized by the valve of his own silence.

As he leaves, he pushes the button on the doorknob and checks to make sure the door is locked before letting the screen door slam. The station wagon is cold but starts immediately with a brash cough and roar, the cold metal zinging. He backs down from the driveway without looking in the rearview mirror, throws it into forward with a lurch. The other houses in the subdivision are all dark, and he notices that all the streetlamps are off.

"They saw his car and thought I was Bunyon!" he shouts and laughs.

He drives home on asphalt roads the waning moon is turning a dark shade of blue. Singing to an old pop song on the radio, he's happier than he's been since he won the lottery.

STICK THIS!

IRST, let me apologize for the rude title. The "stick" is a conductor's baton, and its importance in this tale will come clear in time.

My name is Byron Shelley—not my real name, of course. The symphony world is small enough without using real names.

My title was General Manager. In orchestra parlance that means the number-two administrative post. The top position is Executive Director or President or CEO. My primary role was to manage the orchestra, not as musicians, but as a unionized work force.

A few words about orchestra musicians: they are a combination of thwarted dreams (I should have been a star!) and bored indifference, not to the act of making music but to much of the music itself, the best of which they're required to play so often they could play it blindfolded. They behave with a five-year-old child's petulance toward all conductors, whom they rate on a spectrum from inept to boring to irrelevant.

Me, they hated. But it came with the job.

With few exceptions, musicians in any given orchestra represent a group case history in arrested development. Having practiced relentlessly in lieu of a childhood, they remain children—unruly, disobedient, vengeful, petty, bullying, self-important, and resentful.

The great irony is that all this chaos, bad faith and worse behavior, questionable morals, and jockeying for status results in what?

Glorious and joyful and exalting music, little black squibs on paper brought to life by 80 or more musicians performing at the peak of their considerable talents, with perfectly synchronized physical exertion and absolute concentration. Few things in life make the nonsense that goes into its creation so worthwhile.

The orchestra I worked for during the last quarter of the 20th century is one of the top-20 orchestras in the country. That's a pretty diverse group, by numerous measurements, from population to budget size. The dynamics, though, as I came to understand after less than ten years in the business (which is when this story takes place), are similar from orchestra to orchestra. If you live in Philadelphia or San Francisco, I'm talking about *your* orchestra. It won't be pretty.

The organization chart would show me beneath the President and CEO, and reporting to me, the directors of marketing, fundraising, artistic administration, operations, and education. My orchestra had 34 full-time staff members. By any definition, considering the stresses of the job, we were a happy band (sorry, the occasional symphonic pun will be unavoidable).

On an early August Friday night, after Charlotte, the CEO, and I had been meeting in her office for two hours discussing a variety of topics, we stood up from our chairs and found ourselves in each other's arms. That memorable kiss lasted a full three minutes, before Charlotte broke off, buried her face in my neck and whispered, "Finally!" To which I assented, "Finally."

I'd like to tell you that Charlotte and I had been having a secret affair for months, or that I had been pursuing her for months and she finally succumbed, or vice versa, but the truth is that it happened almost by accident.

It was all the more surprising, as we both discovered in bed at her condo later that night, that both of us had often wondered whether or not the other was gay.

Charlotte Austen was five feet, ten inches tall and weighed 175 pounds. She cut her smooth chestnut hair short and wore very lit-tle lipstick, always dark apricot. Yes, she was slightly chubby, but so was I. She didn't seem masculine in the least, but I wouldn't call her particularly feminine, let alone sexy. But she was almost mag-ically attractive. Her facial features were well proportioned and fit together like a portrait of a proud and imperious woman, but that im-pression was undercut by a radiant smile and laughing purple eyes, an effect she could turn on and off at will. But when she wanted to be, she was the platinum-eyed, unquestioned and unquestionable boss.

I was six feet tall and 210 pounds, with thinning black hair and eyebrows, big ears, a flat nose and good teeth. I was still relatively fit from racket sports, but I wore 40-inch trousers.

Both in our mid-thirties, we had high and prominent cheekbones that gave us an added portion of handsomeness and, I won't shade the truth here, the ability to project power, leadership, and, most importantly, control. No one fucked with Charlotte. If you pissed her off, you could expect a voice at the trombone decibel level and a virtual bust in the chops. In contrast, I was soft spoken and rarely raised my voice, which was pitched high enough that people often thought I was a woman on the other end of the phone. I wasn't a prick, but petulant would be an accurate description of my demean-or when roused by screw-ups. The fact was I didn't come to anger easily, so I had to fake it more times than not, especially with musi-cians. But when I blew up, people stood back.

Our incorrect assessments of each other's sexual preference were based on superficialities. Neither was married. We both worked such long hours that we had little time for romantic entanglements. She never wore dresses, only pant suits; I had a penchant for bow ties and French shoes.

So what happened that night in her office? Why the romantic breakthrough? Virtual serendipity. We'd turned our chairs to face each other to discuss a delicate personnel issue which I'll get to later.

There was probably only a foot between our respective knees. When we stood up simultaneously, our knees bumped and we stumbled, clutching each other's arms, then, without a moment's hesitation, embraced.

As we recalled it later, at the first instant of contact both thought we'd fallen into dangerous territory. Charlotte could be accused of sexual harassment because of her superior status; me of making inappropriate advances. Why we didn't just push away from each other has a simple answer—what occurred was something we'd both imagined over and over, always regretting that it seemed unlikely ever to happen. Certainly, neither of us would have asked the other on a date, or, worse, made a pass. We were trapped in our professional roles. Only an awkward accident could break the impasse, and when it did the proverbial clarions sounded.

We thought of the couch, but board members and others were too used to pestering her after hours. In moments we were on the street and almost running hand in hand toward her condo.

It was, to be imprecise, more than satisfactory. We literally lay waste to her bedroom. As we lay afterward, on the floor in each other's arms, we didn't talk for almost 20 minutes, our lips only an inch apart, each of us almost alone with our own thoughts. I didn't ask her what were hers, but mine ran on two rails: "Wow! I love this woman," and "What next?"

She spoke first.

"I can't believe…." she began.

I interrupted her with a kiss.

"I didn't…."

She returned the kiss and we were silent for another moment.

"I love you," I said.

"I love you too," she said. "For at least a year now."

"Since the European tour."

"That's right."

The orchestra was heading to Paris for the first time in five years, the beginning of a five-city tour. On the flight over, we'd sat together and for the first and only time our conversation turned to the personal. We talked of our similar upbringings, our lost loves (one each), and our romantic aspirations, which we both felt to be impractical, but not impossible. (Yes, that night we managed to talk about even that without completely dispelling the suspicion, one of the other, that we were gay.) It was a warm and comforting hour that created a personal bond, and then we agreed to get some rest. I didn't sleep, and I suspected she wasn't sleeping either. During the rest of the tour, and we were often together, neither of us signaled anything to the other of this bond, but apparently it had sunk in, sunk so deep it was virtually buried until that stumbling moment in her office.

"We're in trouble. You know that, don't you?" she said, hugging me tighter.

Though I was wide awake, all I could say in response was "hmm-mm."

"Get me pregnant, won't you? Then I can quit and you can be the boss."

I laughed and drew one of her marvelous top-tipped nipples between my teeth.

She gently pushed me away.

"That was nice. I'll do it more often."

"You'd better."

But for the moment, she needed to talk. She turned on her side and I threw my leg over hers, pulling her close.

"Yes, we're in trouble," I agreed. "But what can we do about it?"

"You mean other than hide it?"

"*Hiding us* is a given. We get caught and all hell will descend from heaven, and we'll both be thrown out. At least one of us for certain, and that would be me."

"I'd quit first."

"Maybe I want to quit," I said.

"We can't both quit. What a waste that would be."

"But if you quit, there's no guarantee they'd move me up. It's a one-in-ten shot."

"I could convince them," she said defiantly.

"Maybe, darling. But it's just not done. They might make me interim, but they'd do a search and poach a CEO from Europe or Canada or someplace, and I sure don't want to play second fellow to some ego-bastard with half my experience." Then I added, "By the way, you will marry me, right?"

"You had to ask?"

"No, but it felt good to."

"Yes, I will."

She paused.

"That did feel good. Words I never thought I'd say my entire life."

"Me too. When?"

"Soon. In secret?"

"It's our only line of defense."

She grabbed my penis and I was immediately hard.

"We'll set a date," she said, "after you put this all the way up two more times."

"That sounds reasonable."

After setting a date for our nuptials, we spent all of Saturday making love and raiding her ample refrigerator and liquor cabinet. Sunday morning found us still in bed at 10 AM; it was August and the concert season didn't start for three more weeks.

We now had a long conversation—how would we manage being married? We talked through all the likely reactions to our just coming out with it. From no angle did it seem to promise anything but chaos. We were both liked and respected, as much as one can be by people you're always saying "no" to (the musicians, and often the Music Director); or by arrogant board members bloated with either money or selfish concern about "appearances"—verging on terror of losing donors or what "reputation" we (read: said board members) had in the community, which was considerable.

Of course, the players would make a rumor festival of it, spiced with nasty and cynical jokes. We could hear them now: "That's what I call giving someone a raise," or, "talk about sucking up to the boss," or, "he won't have to cover his ass anymore," and, inevitably, "guess who'll be wearing the pantsuits in that family?"

But the players would get tired of that game pretty quickly. Their likely collective assumption would be that we'd both be forced to treat the players in ways more to their liking, with our fearing complaints of nepotism.

Strictly speaking, there was no policy against staff members being married. There were several married couples in the orchestra, which was something management actually encouraged, because it was a guarantee against one of them moving on to a bigger orchestra. The head of IT was engaged to a marketing assistant, a fact known to all, and without complaint.

But to have the two senior executives married was another matter. Which leads me to the personnel issue we'd been discussing the night before.

Hermann Valle, the orchestra's Music Director (the fancy title for a permanent conductor), who lived in Austria and conducted only 18 weeks a year here, posed the greatest threat. Valle predated both of us in our respective positions, having been hired after an international search, which was seen by the entire community (or sold to as) an amazing achievement. Valle was a commanding figure—not a hair on his Yul Brynner head, staring, blank gray eyes, a humorless slit of a smile, and jughead ears that somehow made him more attractive and added to his air of authority. He was muscular, just shy of six feet, with powerful shoulders, thin waist, and a flat stomach. Like most conductors he looked ten years younger than he was, mostly because of the aerobic exertion of conducting itself. His feet were improbably tiny in black shoes he bought in London, along with the rest of his formal clothes. His German accent was almost impenetrable, and his English vocabulary had stagnated at the eight-year-old level, which Charlotte and I thought was deliberate. It scared the hell out of board members. It was said that he hadn't negotiated his salary and other compensation; he'd written down his demands on a piece of paper and simply shook his head "no" at any other suggestion. He laughed when he was asked to make our city his primary residence.

A brief aside on conductors: Deprived of their dictator status decades ago by the union, they continue to act out their frustrations while on the podium, every one thinking, "Why did that Toscanini have to be such an asshole?" Since they can no longer demand four-hour rehearsals or summarily fire a clarinetist because he or she cracked a note, they take their revenge through humiliation, accusation, exaggeration, and intimidation. Our Herman was no different.

To give him his due, he was a fine musician, not great across the board, but his Mozart and Sibelius were impeccable, and his greatest strength, the late Romantics, had attracted the orchestra's first recording contract with a major label. He was a showman, with a flare with the baton that the players made phallic jokes about, but the audience adored. And the bastard sold tickets.

Valle was a naughty boy. He'd been caught making 900 phone-sex calls and charging them to the orchestra (all three of us had credit cards issued for business purposes only), something only Charlotte and I, and our comptroller, knew about and quickly squelched. But that was the least of it.

So far, he hadn't been accused of harassment, either of women in the orchestra, or soloists, with the exception of one gorgeous and very famous violinist half his age who told me that he'd tried to kiss her in an elevator but had backed off immediately when rebuffed. She refused to make an issue about it, fearing she might never be invited back, but warned me to keep an eye on him.

The most recent incident, and the subject of Charlotte's and my concern, was that Hermann was apparently sleeping with a board member, a married board member, whose husband wrote a six-figure check to the orchestra every year, on top of a five-year, $3 million pledge to the endowment, which he'd just begun to pay off.

Our strategy, which was the result of numerous conversations, concluding the night of our first embrace, was to let Hermann know that we knew, but that we intended to do nothing or say anything about it; instead we would simply warn him of the peril he was in and hope he wouldn't make a fool of himself.

Not a perfect strategy. It made us complicit. But the alternative was far more worrisome. If we blew the whistle, however subtly, perhaps by whispering the fact to the board chair and letting him deal with it, we could still be scapegoated. Hermann could call us liars and demand proof. The only evidence we had was my having seen them kissing in a hotel cloak room at the end of a reception. No polite European brush on the cheek; she had her tongue down his throat.

If we were seen as attempting to betray him, with the intent of getting him fired, we could ourselves be fired. On the other hand, in the social milieu of the board, if they figured it out themselves, there would be a few whispered warnings and the whole thing forgotten (with a 44-member board you could count on at least a half-dozen affairs among such a sophisticated crowd, and we knew about most of them). That seemed the safest course.

Our secret marriage could, should he find out, embolden our kind Hermann in his secret trysts. Like a pair of modern Pandaruses, we could even be enlisted in helping to arrange, or at the least help hide his assignations for him.

And it wouldn't be any better if we dared make our marriage public. As with most orchestras, the battle of money vs. art is perpetual, which is why there's never any love lost between the Charlottes and the Hermanns. The latter would put 100 musicians on the stage for every concert if Charlotte didn't rein him in. That ongoing war had recently peaked when the board backed her in thwarting Hermann's desire to program Messiaen's great, but absurdly expensive

Turangalila-Symphonie. He'd told her soon after the board's actions that he would never forgive her. She'd never seen him so angry, and I had never seen Charlotte so upset.

Thus, Hermann could see our public marriage as a power move, our "partnership" a new phalanx of influence meant to undermine his every artistic wish. A threatened Hermann could prove a very, very dangerous Hermann.

At this point in our deliberations, someone buzzed Charlotte's front door.

"That's got to be a mistake," she said. "No one visits me here."

She put on a nightgown and robe and went out to see.

As if we had conjured her from the city-noise-filled air, Eileen Moore, the board member we suspected of sleeping with Hermann, was waiting in the lobby.

Charlotte put her off long enough to run into the bedroom to ensure my silence.

Still in her robe, she rang Eileen up and let her in.

"Char, I'm so sorry to bother you."

"It's fine. Fine," she said, backing away. She told me later that Eileen was white as chalk, but for a smear of bright red lipstick.

"Can we talk?"

"Of course," said Charlotte, showing her into her living room.

They settled at opposite ends of Charlotte's ice-blue satin couch.

"I need to tell you some things. Some surprising things. And I need an absolute promise of secrecy."

Then Eileen paused, her eyes riveted on something behind Charlotte, who turned and saw my shoes scattered between the couch and the fireplace.

"Is someone here, Char?"

Charlotte mumbled something incoherent, blushed, shrugged, then mumbled some more.

Eileen brightened and color came into her cheeks as she smiled.

"Let me guess."

"Really, Eileen, there's no...."

"Is Byron in your bedroom, Char?"

Charlotte gasped.

"It's about fucking time! Byron, come out here this minute!" she yelled.

As they waited for me to dress, Eileen said, "So how long has this been going on? You two haven't fooled me for a minute for, not for, oh, at least the last six months."

As I walked into the room, I said, "Since Friday night, believe it or not."

"How exciting!" Eileen cried out, "I've so wanted you both to be happy. Your God-forsaken jobs? How I do not envy you for one minute. But this," she hurried on, "there's some redemption in this! Oh, yes. And it makes what I have to tell you both even easier to say."

We said nothing. Charlotte, of course, looked like a block of melting ice, hard, but losing it. Quite lovely, actually. I'd noticed before how confrontation added to her attractiveness. I must have been one big blush, hairline to collar.

"Oh, don't worry," she said, waving the thought away. "I wouldn't tell a soul about you two. What a hypocrite that would make me!"

"Do others know?" asked Charlotte, not having quite absorbed Eileen's admission.

"Honey, I'm sure not. I've just got a sixth sense about these things. You haven't betrayed yourselves in any way that I know of, I can tell you that."

"That's a relief."

"So, my turn," she said and turned away as if deciding whether she really should tell us.

I almost forgot myself and said, "You and Hermann," but I held back. I might be wrong, which would be bad, or worse if she felt humiliated.

Charlotte and I looked at each other and she said, "Eileen, you can trust us. Utterly."

I took an armchair on the other side of the fireplace and tried to seem relaxed, though I was shocked and terrified. If she'd guessed about us, who else might have, no matter what she thought?

"Of course," said Charlotte.

Eileen took a deep breath and, about to speak, picked up her purse from the floor and asked, "Do you mind if I smoke?"

"Not at all," said Charlotte, who had a cigarette now and then, as did I. She pushed a small onyx ashtray on the coffee table closer.

Having inhaled deeply, reminding me of a teenager with a spliff, she exhaled and spilled out her heart. She was desperately in love with Hermann. After 15 years of childless marriage, the last five totally loveless, she and Hermann had found each other during the European tour a year ago.

Charlotte and I smiled at each other. Of course! There had been a small contingent of board members who accompanied the orchestra, mostly as a donor benefit, and Eileen had gone, leaving her husband at home. The opportunities for privacy during two weeks of hotel rooms were ample for igniting an affair. Now we understood Hermann's real reason for insisting on a room at a different hotel, so, as he said, he would not be running into his musicians in the hallways. "Such unseemly," he'd intoned, using a word that seemed beyond his vocabulary.

Another brief aside, this time on board members: there are typically between 25 and 50, even in the smallest towns. Over-generalizing, let's say they are made up of three types: the bored socialite crone, too old to take a lover, who sublimates by trying to tell everyone else how to run things; the mid- to upper-level manager of a medium-size company trying to make a name for him/herself; and the CEO of the town's largest company who therefore has the biggest dick in town; orchestra boards typically being the "biggest and best" boards in town, serving as its Board Chair is the ideal opportunity to swing it around.

Eileen was the epitome of the first category, except when it came to "lovers." Herman was not her first, but all we knew of them was the odd rumor.

I wouldn't be sure until later what Charlotte thought of all this, but none of it reassured me in any way. Eileen Moore was born rich, married even richer, and would leave millions to the orchestra. But I had always considered her, even in my most generous moments, a hag. She could be a demanding and manipulative board member, thoroughly unpredictable, though often one of the smartest people in the room, which made her dangerous. More than once Charlotte had to cover a hasty retreat and circle around the right board members to keep out of trouble. Eileen was also one of the homeliest women I've ever known, with thick features, a cap of blue hair, and a shapeless body—however expensively dressed—a hopeless puddle. And, I suspected, she knew it only too well.

No secret, though, what Hermann saw in her, and it was neither a lover nor an advocate. She'd been careful not to side with Hermann in his disputes with Charlotte over money. That would have made her a minority of one.

The idea of Hermann as a gold digger made me smile, which I hid with my hand.

Hermann aside, I had always sensed that she was straining to be on her best behavior, at board meetings and especially now, when she needed us, but I had also divined a vindictive bitch beneath, suppressing her true nature for the sake of her high-society status. God help us if we ever got on her bad side, and even though she was arming us with a means of destroying her reputation, I couldn't help being suspicious of her motives.

Having finished her revelatory preamble, adding a few rhapsodic codas, she paused to take out a second cigarette.

I stood up and lit it for her.

"Thanks, Byron. Ever the gentleman."

The overly-polite word seemed to bring her back to herself, her mission.

"Hermann is threatening to leave, and not just me. He hates this city, this country, and, as we both know, the honeymoon with the players ended years ago. He despises them, almost to a person, mostly because he believes they're all second rate and he deserves better. And what he complains most about is you, Charlotte."

Charlotte didn't react; this wasn't news.

"The way you two fight! He wants his Mahler and Bruckner and all the big works and he's tired of the board siding with you on everything. He says to me 'Charlotte runs this orchestra, not me.'" Before Charlotte could respond, she continued. "He has the Vienna Chamber, as you know, and he wants another European orchestra. Two English orchestras have been courting him."

Charlotte and I sat silently, waiting for the ask.

"I don't want him to go."

"Eileen, if he's that adamant, I can't imagine I can do anything to change his mind."

"Well, actually, you can. And so can I. We'll have to be very careful."

"Where does Carl fit into this."

"Oh, he knows everything," she said dismissing him with a flourish of her free hand. "Neither of us is interested in divorce. It would cost a fortune just to get our finances sorted out. Besides, I'm content with things as they are. I just need you to help me keep Hermann here."

"And programming is all it will take?"

Eileen blushed.

"It's one of three things. First, we have to let him play what he wants to play. Second, I'm going to set up a trust for him that will mean he won't have to work another day in his life if he feels like it. I don't know if he'll go for it, but I'm tripling his standard of living."

"And three?"

She hung her head and we both thought she might start crying.

"Damn, that I should have to tell you, but I do, because I need the most help dealing with it."

We were now into cigarette number five. God knows why I was

counting, except it was almost hypnotic the amount of concentration she put into sucking each one down to the cork. It occurred to me—I don't know why—that not a single instrument in an orchestra makes a sound by the drawing *in* of breath, and here she was sucking away like a crazed piccolo player.

"There's someone else," she said, looking away. I thought she was talking about Carl. "He has a mistress half his age. He's obsessed with her. Me, he takes care of my needs, let me leave it at that. He loves me after a fashion, though not how I love him, but he wouldn't marry me even if I did leave Carl.

She stood up and said, "I'll be right back."

"What a moment to need to pee," I whispered to Charlotte, who shushed me.

Eileen returned, having touched up her make-up and looking ready for the worst.

"He wants her taken care of, apartment, furnishings, clothes, cash, the works."

I guessed before she said it.

"Goddammit" she exploded. "She's in the orchestra!"

I looked at Charlotte and we both shrugged: "No surprise there."

"I'm not sure you should tell me who it is," said Charlotte.

"I'm not sure I want you to know, but you have to help me, so you have to know who she is."

"Okay."

"It's that skinny little second oboe."

"Marilyn Mains? You're joking!"

Eileen looked both hurt and humiliated.

Marilyn Mains was five foot three and 80 pounds of attitude and, unfortunately, talent. The thought of Hermann on top of her, crushing her as flat as one of his musical scores, was beyond conception. Behind her back, most of the players called her "Hautbois," the archaic word for "oboe," pronounced "o boy," because she was as thin as her instrument and not unlike a little boy in shape.

"They've been at it every Sunday night for months, always at her shithole efficiency by the river. They don't dare go to a hotel, let alone his place. Now she's bitching that she can't stand the embarrassment of entertaining him in such a place. She's not only threatened to break it off, but to leak everything."

"Including you."

I was guessing.

"Including me. Hermann can be such an asshole. I slapped him red in the face when he told me he'd told her about us; he laughed at me for being a prig."

"But what can we do about Marilyn? She's been in the orchestra four years. She's tenured!"

"I want you to go after Hermann, not her. He needs to know how inappropriate it is to bed a player in the orchestra. If she wanted to, she could claim sexual harassment, or worse. He needs to understand he's playing with fire."

"Surely," I suggested, impressed that she understood the situation so clearly, "You've told him that already."

"I'm ashamed to say it, but it's the most one-sided relationship imaginable. I want him and he wants my money and his little slut, and it's the latter two he talks about all the time. Doesn't listen to a word I say."

I must confess, I was enjoying the hell out of this, even though Eileen had never tried to hurt me personally. Now she was getting what she deserved. She didn't love Hermann. She loved his prick and loved being—let's call it what it is—a starfucker, just to satisfy her boundless ego after Carl had written her off as a woman.

My *Schadenfreude* aside, she was putting us in a dangerous position and she had our new relationship to threaten us with, as well.

Now that it was all out there, Charlotte and I lit up. As with most things, I deferred to her.

She tried to lay out the options.

"We could go to Hermann and warn him. Bigger conductors than him have ruined their careers for less than sleeping with a player.

The likelihood is that he would feel threatened, which wouldn't solve anything. He might even retaliate against you, Eileen."

"I hadn't thought of that," said Eileen.

"We could talk to Marilyn and explain that she too is in jeopardy. That would probably blow everything up. She could claim sexual harassment and blackmail, even rape. Even if she chose to stay quiet, she might feel her hold on all of you is even stronger now. She might dare Byron and me to do anything about it. She'd be sure to bring us down as well."

Eileen twisted away—we were the least of her worries. Seeing this, Charlotte struck back.

"The fact that she knows about you makes it triply dangerous. She could say you encouraged it, even hid it from the board. She might even reveal that you were willing to set her up financially."

Charlotte paused when Eileen flinched at this.

"That is the plan, right? That you'd pay for that too?"

"I haven't made up my mind about that yet. Hermann won't let me alone about it, but I haven't agreed."

"Okay. Good," Charlotte continued, "This is my last question. You've given Byron and me a lot to think about."

"Go ahead."

"How do you, Eileen, want this to end?"

"I want her out of the orchestra, or dead. Take your pick."

I swear she was only half-kidding. The thought of Hermann taking Marilyn in his mighty hands and snapping her in two flashed only slightly shamefully through my bursting brain.

"You know that's not possible, Eileen," said Charlotte, as if to a child. "The union will protect her job unless she gives us a reason to fire her for cause, and that's not likely. She's too smart for that."

"I'm not a child, Char. I know the rules," she said, swallowing her own bitterness.

"What do you *realistically* want to happen?"

"Right. Sorry. He says she's a real character. Doesn't care what happens. She says to him, 'The only person likely to lose his job is Hermann Valle.'"

"Yes, we've dealt with her," I interjected, looking at Charlotte. "She's high maintenance. She's filed three grievances in the last two months. Every time I have to meet with her and the union steward she says, 'Byron, dear,' she always calls me 'dear.'"

"I didn't know that," said a surprised Charlotte.

"Of course," I continued, "there's never any merit to her complaints, which the steward points out almost immediately. She does it just to prove a little 'O Boy' is not going to be pushed around."

Charlotte put out her cigarette and looked at me, then at Eileen for some response.

"We're not there yet, are we?"

"No, Eileen. Let's think about it and talk soon."

Eileen stood and snapped her purse shut and slung it over her shoulder with a flourish, as if it had all been settled and she could relax.

"One last thing," she said. "You can't tell him I came to you."

"Understood," Charlotte and I said simultaneously.

When Eileen was gone, we bolted for the bedroom to rub off each other the foul effluvium of what we had just been forced to endure.

The first concrete step we took was to get married in a simple civil ceremony with no friends or relatives. We'd decided on the weekend before Labor Day weekend, and to take a week's vacation in Maine where Charlotte had a timeshare she hadn't used for two years. Our reason for expediency was unavoidable. We couldn't trust Eileen, now that she knew. We were subject to less criticism, married, than we would be if discovered having an affair. We'd keep it a secret, but while it would be awkward and still might get one or both of us fired if we were found out, in the near term, secrecy would be less disruptive, especially given what we'd come to call "the situation."

Joyfully married, we spent a lovely quiet week in seclusion in Maine. Our relationship not being central to this story, I'll say only that spending sixteen hours a day in bed, and the rest of the time eating in great restaurants and walking for miles on the beach, didn't include one moment of awkwardness or hesitancy about our emotional, intellectual, professional, or sexual relationship or compatibility. You might ask, "She was your boss. Didn't that change anything?" Two answers: 1: We didn't talk about work the entire week. 2: She just happened to be a great boss and we'd always gotten along. Any disagreements between us had always been minor and quickly resolved. That hasn't changed to this day.

It seemed inevitable the Tuesday after Labor Day when Hermann called Charlotte and asked her to dinner. Before she could ask if she could bring me, he said, "Bring Byron too if he's available."

Convinced he knew nothing about us, we felt that he was being particularly cautious about appearances.

We knew something big was up because he took us to his haunt, the most expensive French restaurant in town. Because the management saw him as an adornment, he was their only customer to have an "account," and his own table. Since he dined after many concerts and rehearsals, he must have spent a fortune there. He could afford it.

Hoping to keep things polite until they wouldn't be, we ordered modestly, though he treated us to several bottles of $100 Bordeaux. He drank most of them and, as always, showed only a single sign of inebriation—his eyes went dewy, forcing him to daub them periodically with his napkin.

We talked through dinner about the upcoming season and withstood the usual onslaught about the lack of star power in our guest artists and all the Beethoven-sized programming when the city was yearning to be "blow up by Strauss Alpine Symphony."

Charlotte didn't bother to give him the usual "balanced budget" speech because we both sensed he had something else entirely on his mind.

When he'd poured himself the last glass from the second bottle, he said, "We should talk, yes?"

I'd seen Charlotte's poker face before, but hers now was a masterwork. I wanted to kiss her, she looked so sweet.

"Understand I am here under protest, or I should say with great reluctance."

I thought it might be the wine, or simply the facade slipping under stress, but his English had gotten significantly more fluid and his accent softened.

"Okay," he sighed, "I suppose it's up to me to begin this, this...."

"We Americans call it an 'intervention,'" said Charlotte, having figured it out.

"Yes, I see. Eileen told me that you would say something like that. Well, go ahead."

Charlotte and I were relieved Eileen had taken the initiative; neither of us had relished the prospect of the painful first steps of broaching the subject of Marilyn Mains.

Charlotte was magnificent. She began by saying that we were just looking out for his best interests. She had only to mention "the recent revelations of bad behavior" in other musical institutions, without naming names, to get her point across.

When he objected that he wasn't treating Marilyn badly in any way, Charlotte spoke softly, in an almost bland tone of voice.

"Relationships that involve one person with considerable power over the other are always dangerous."

"But she seduced me!" he said, shocking us into momentary silence.

Charlotte's voice became even softer, more solicitous, almost kind.

"Hermann, that unfortunately doesn't make any difference. What matters is that you are able to improve her position in the orchestra or do harm to it."

"That's ridiculous."

"Let me give you an example. And you'll have to forgive me, but you did say this. Last winter when we were talking about the Mozart Oboe Concerto, you suggested Marilyn might be a better choice as soloist than Molly."

Molly was our Principal Oboe, and, in fact, not quite as talented as Marilyn, but it would have caused a considerable stir if Marilyn had been chosen over Molly.

"Yes, and you talked me out of it, which, frankly, cost me a lot of screaming followed by two weeks of the silent treatment."

"Exactly my point. And what if Marilyn starts to slack off, or just has a bad night?"

"I can do nothing about it is what you're saying."

"Yes. Nothing."

She drained her glass and continued, getting to the crux of it.

"Everything we've just been discussing assumes the affair remains secret. If it somehow gets out…."

"But that won't happen," Hermann interrupted her.

"You can't know that. Marilyn is a handful, right? She walks around, excuse me for saying, as though she had a reed stuck in her teeth."

That was her way of lightening things a bit, but it didn't work.

"Don't belittle, Charlotte," he said, threateningly.

"I'm sorry, I was just trying to make a point. The young woman has a temper is what I'm trying to say. We know it," she said, pointing at me, "and you admitted as much a few moments ago. Who knows what she'll do if it gets out?"

He stared at us suspiciously over his glass, as if trying to decide, "friends or foes?"

"I need to ask you a question, Hermann, and you need to be honest with us if we're going to be able to help you."

He didn't move an inch, didn't blink, didn't speak, didn't drink.

"Eileen told us what Marilyn wants, but those are just physical comforts. What does she really want, Hermann? Marriage?"

The wine had him laughing louder than he should have. Heads turned.

"Marriage! That's the last thing! Now let me tell you what even Eileen doesn't know, and you must not tell her. You promise, agreed?"

We both nodded.

"Marilyn wants to be just like a 19th century courtesan, with all the 20th century possessions. But it's not just for her and me. She insists that our time can only be Sunday nights. That made sense at first, because of the orchestra's schedule." He paused to swear under his breath: *"Ach, scheiß drauf.* What does she want? Really want? She wants to sell herself to me, yes, but it's all so she can live in the grand style with Molly!"

Charlotte and I traded stunned glances.

"I didn't even know it myself until. They weren't, what do you call them, 'partners,' until this spring, long after any talk about the Mozart. She says she loves me and Molly the same. She says she always loves men and women. Now she wants to have *all* of her wishes."

We didn't know what to say.

"We stop for now, my friends," he said, getting up, clearly drunk. "Stay as long as you want. Order more wine. We'll talk soon."

Like a buffalo throwing its horns around to clear a way through high grasses, Hermann left us there.

"Well now," Charlotte said and leaned against me, "we're well and thoroughly screwed, aren't we?"

"Do you want more wine?"

"You bet I do. The same good stuff."

We necked while we waited for the bottle and fresh glasses and I slid my hand up her thigh, then I backed off, as horny as I was that moment. We had business to discuss.

The wine now poured, I clicked her glass and began, "I think we could, without understatement, call this a colossal cluster fuck."

"Remind me in the morning not to take seriously anything we're about to say, even though we need to say it."

"We tell on them all, right?"

"Right."

We didn't even chuckle.

"I'm not sure where to start. If my math is correct, we have a quartet to manage."

"Sextet, darling," she said and kissed my cheek.

"Yes, I stand corrected," returning the gesture.

"At least he doesn't seem to know about us."

"Yes, he didn't stop acting as though I wasn't in the room."

She kissed me again and said, "I think we need to take care of us, first. I have no idea how we deal, or not deal, with the rest of them, but I think we should get married."

"What?"

"A big wedding, or at least big enough. Not only *not* act secretive or afraid, but put it in their faces. Have it at Davis (the chamber concert hall at the university) and invite everyone."

"Charlotte," I said, in a tone that hadn't a hint of the underling's enthusiasm I used to have when I complimented her, "that's why you're the boss. It's brilliant. Let the other little dramas play out and deal with them once we're safe. Or fired."

"They wouldn't dare. We have too much on Hermann and Eileen. They'd be forced to defend us to the end."

She thought about that statement for a moment, as if to convince herself that she really believed it, then added, "We'll make sure they don't."

Then she turned to me with a gentle but serious expression in her big brown eyes.

"A favor?"

"Yes."

"Don't call me 'boss' anymore."

"Even…."

"In front of others, call me Charlotte."

"Not even 'lover'?"

She laughed at that; we toasted and began to make arrangements.

The ceremony was performed by a Unitarian minister less than a month later. Neither of us had parents, but we invited siblings, grandparents, and other friends and family. It cost us half a month's pay, but we did it up right, with all the flowers, champagne, and good food a couple earning multiple six figures could afford. Most of the board and orchestra came, as well as the staff. We paid the four string principals to play short quartet works, and a reduced version of the wedding march. We hired a rock and jazz standards band for the reception, for which we rented the conference hall in the same building.

Our first step was to tell Eileen our plans and ask her to help tamp down any complaints. It was a risk, but we had to believe her happiness with our happiness had not been feigned. We told her there was no reason for the board to object, and they could deal with it later if we ever let the marriage intrude on our work. Though she had a lot to lose by alienating us, her agreeing seemed sincere and was the first gracious thing I ever saw her do.

Who gave away the bride? A broadly smiling, strutting Hermann Valle, totally over-dressed in a morning coat. That was my idea.

The acceptance of our marriage wasn't hard to understand. The board didn't say a word, except "Congratulations" over and over. Charlotte and I were already popular with the staff and we worked hard to prove that nothing was going to change for them. Their benevolent managers were in love and why shouldn't they, the staff, take it in stride? Yes, the players, being a gallimaufry of social and anti-social types, made us the butt of countless jokes and insults because they couldn't help themselves. We could have received the keys to the city and they would have ridiculed us. Inevitably, some tested us, asking for raises, or special treatment, such as the ability to miss rehearsals in order to sub with a bigger orchestra. We said "no" to everything, no exceptions. The road to a cacophony of complaints and grievances would be to succumb to pressure applied with the assumption that the players now had it over us. The one time a player even hinted at it, my whispered response was, "fuck with me and I'll tell the union a lie that will get you fired overnight." I was bluffing, of course, but I knew that you can't change musicians. There will always be those, like this fellow, who hate management and forever will. That's what you expect from people who can't get up from work to pee when they want to.

As agreed with Eileen, we let the "situation" simmer for a couple of months until the organization had accommodated a married couple on the administrative podium. That didn't mean that Marilyn stopped complaining about her living conditions or that Hermann didn't stop pestering Eileen for more and more money for Marilyn and himself.

In December, we began programming for the following season. We met with Eileen and explained that the budget would be strained even without adding big works. Without hesitation, she wrote the orchestra a check for $200,000.

"See how much you can mollify him with that," she said, snappishly. "Tell him it came from an anonymous donor."

Charlotte and I had to keep from reacting to the unintended pun. Eileen had no sense of humor when it came to money or almost anything else.

In her most officious board member's voice, she added, "And I want to see that it's used 'incrementally,' understand?"

In other words, she didn't want a penny of it used to underwrite the budget.

Hermann went mad with ambition. He wanted the Messiaen and the Strauss, plus Mahler's *Symphony No. 2,* Stravinsky's *The Rite of Spring,* and Respighi's *Pines of Rome,* on top of what we would have been able to afford without Eileen's 'gift.' By any reasonable calculation this would increase the budget by $400,000; but, after we did the spread sheets for him (and Eileen) that would show what the extra $200k could pay for, he agreed (not all that graciously) to drop Stravinsky and Respighi.

Unrelated to the budget, but in fact a savings over bringing in another concert soloist, Hermann programmed Molly for the Mozart Oboe Concerto. We could only imagine how that came about.

Come January, when the board accepted the programming for

the next season, Hermann seemed like a happy man, but only for a week or two.

Over lunch, he confided that the situation with Marilyn was heating up. She'd guessed, rightly, what Hermann had only suspected, that Eileen put up the money for the programming. Now, Marilyn insisted, it was her turn.

This led to a meeting at Eileen's mansion, her husband being in London, doing "God knows what," said Eileen, as she invited us in.

She poured cocktails as we settled into couches in a massive living room, which apparently reflected her husband's tastes, not hers. There were four white walls—only one with a door—with a single huge minimalist canvas on the other three, each one a different geometric shape of black surrounding a white circle. The furniture was equally austere and uncomfortable, modernist sticks, black marble, and spotless muslin.

"I understand your husband is an audiophile," I said, guessing that the white circles might be speakers.

"Yes, he has a mountain of amplifiers, tape machines, and turntables, in the next room. It's all piped into here. He loves to play Mahler so loud the house trembles."

"Then those are acoustic panels and speakers?"

"Yes," Eileen replied dismissively.

"I thought they were art works," said Charlotte.

We looked at each other as though we'd entered a madhouse.

Eileen turned away and smiled. The vicious hag surfaced.

"You know what air guitar is?" she said, pointing at what I'd first thought was a lectern or dictionary stand.

We nodded.

"He plays air baton!"

She laughed loudly and long.

"My living room is a bit more comfortable," she said finally, composing herself, "but I like to sit in here and smoke when he's gone."

She looked at us both to make sure we got the point: pure spite. Then she got serious.

"You know the situation?" she asked, lighting up.

"Yes, Hermann told us."

"And now there's this Molly business," she spat out with disgust that made her even uglier, if that was possible.

Charlotte gasped; she couldn't help herself.

"Don't worry, Char. Secrets abound. I knew Hermann was holding back something and I finally dragged it out of him."

"He swore us to secrecy."

"I know. Look, I just don't care. I find out everything I need to know. I always do. I don't hold it against you."

She took a supremely satisfied drag to celebrate her own powers of restraint.

"At least we know now everything we're dealing with, unless you want to tell me Hermann is bisexual too and has a partner tucked away somewhere."

She frowned that she didn't get a laugh out of us.

"Yeah, that was tacky," she admitted.

Charlotte chugged half her drink and put down her glass, a sign she was about to get very serious and wouldn't need any stiffening of her spine thanks to 30-year-old scotch.

"The solution remains what it's always been," she began. "Hermann is in great danger. He says he understands but I don't think he does. And giving him the money to set the girls up like they want, even if you were never implicated, would only make matters worse. Now, I've—"

"Before you continue, Char, tell me about this Molly. What's she like?"

"Molly Stephens," said Charlotte, a little of her wind leaking away. "Fine musician. Maybe the best in the orchestra. She's also one of the best paid, which you can thank Hermann for, since he's been her advocate for years when it comes salary time."

"But Herman told me that Marilyn was better."

"You can guess why," said Charlotte.

"Yes, of course. And that was before the girls...."

Charlotte was growing quiet, not sure what to add, so I stepped in.

"Molly is one of the nicest people in the entire organization, or that's what she wants people to think. Extremely passive, gentle, friendly, and whip smart. As you know, she's very pretty and petite, and very feminine, which has kept her, uh, sexual nature hidden. Probably passive aggressive and I suspect the instigator of her affair with Marilyn. In other words, I think there are hidden depths there and that she might be more dangerous than she appears."

"Do you have any evidence?"

"Just one funny thing she did two years ago. Remember Caroline Cooper?"

"The Principal Horn player?"

"Yes. She was up for tenure. Someone, I believe it was Molly, started a whisper campaign that Caroline wasn't good enough and, even worse, played too loud. The audition committee turned on her, out-voted Hermann, and she wasn't given tenure."

"And that was the end of her," said Eileen. "I remember the board wondering what the hell that was all about. All Hermann could say was that the committee had the right to do it. Go complain to the union, he told us!"

"I agree with Byron. I think she's dangerous. We know how dangerous Marilyn is because she's the one...."

She trailed off.

"She's the one sleeping with Hermann," Eileen concluded her thought.

"Yes."

"But Molly shafted a fellow musician. Marilyn hasn't hurt anyone as far as we know."

"So, what are you saying, Byron, that it's Molly we have to go after?"

"No, at least not directly. When it comes to the two women, we don't have any leverage at all. There's nothing we can do to them, or, worse, threaten to do to them. They have the ability to retaliate in a number of ways, whether they want to go through the union or straight to the board."

"They'd be nuts to go to the board. What would they say?"

"Regardless of how they attack, their weapon is to blame Hermann for sexual harassment, and they might well make it stick."

"Hermann says he was seduced."

"Yes," said Charlotte, "he told us that too, but it doesn't matter, does it? Marilyn can simply deny it. His word against hers. The problem Hermann can't get around is that he's her superior and she can say that he used her subordinate position, by threat or intimidation, to force sexual favors from her. It's the classic scenario, and there's only one solution. It won't be pretty. Hermann needs to give up Marilyn. Drop her flat. He can use Molly as his excuse."

"Yes, I can see that's the best thing for him. Not me."

"You still have, if you'll excuse the expression, the power of the purse."

"Thanks for being so insulting, Char."

She stood up, apologizing with a flick of her wrist.

"Let me think about it."

"Of course."

"You may have to be the messengers."

"However we can help," Charlotte offered.

"We'll talk more about that. I have some ideas," Eileen said.

And with that enigmatic statement our meeting was over.

That was the last time Charlotte and I talked with anyone about "the situation" until the end.

Here's what I know. Carl's trip to England had a purpose that Eileen didn't know about. He had done his homework via his businessmen's network and discovered that the Liverpool orchestra was considering Hermann as their next music director. Carl went there to meet with the Chairman of the Board to offer $1 million if they would hire Hermann, and the sooner the better. Hermann's contract was up for renewal with my orchestra and it was possible Hermann could be gone within a year.

It was all for nothing. Liverpool turned Carl down, taking British umbrage at his effrontery (though $5 million might have done the job), even threatening to contact the constabulary if he didn't go home immediately. Eileen found out from Hermann and raised hell with Carl, then promised Hermann everything he wanted, the programming, more money, and money for Marilyn. She had one condition. Not only would there be no deal that included Molly, but Marilyn had to agree to split up with Molly. Much later, when Hermann told us the story, Marilyn didn't shed a tear, didn't complain, didn't argue. He showed her a check for half a million dollars with her name on it, and that was all it took.

We never learned exactly how it went when Marilyn told Molly, but Charlotte and I made a point of attending the first rehearsal to take place after Molly learned the news. Ten minutes before the rehearsal ended, Molly put down her instrument and stood up, shocking the orchestra into silence. Hermann literally gasped and grew stiff as a mannikin, as Molly walked to the front of the stage and stepped up on the podium on his right side. She took his right hand, holding his baton, and bit his forefinger knuckle. She held his hand up and said, "Stick this in your ass, Maestro," then walked back to her chair and, before sitting down, leaned and whispered in Marilyn's ear.

Marilyn ran off the stage as I moved into the orchestra—whose members, most uncharacteristically, made way for me—and asked Molly to leave the stage. As I stood over her, she calmly gathered her things and followed me to the rear exit.

I said to her, "Please talk to the union steward and we'll arrange a meeting for tomorrow."

Then she was gone. Charlotte and I descended on Hermann and rushed him into his dressing room, which we locked. We didn't come out until everyone but the stagehands were gone.

Charlotte found a BandAid in the bottom of her purse for Hermann's knuckle. We probably didn't say ten words between the three
of us before we watched Hermann drive away. (He ended up the
next day getting a couple of stitches and a tetanus shot.)

"I can't remember the last time I had so much fun," said Charlotte, without laughing.

"I can," I said and took her in my arms.

"Yes," she agreed, "let's go have some more."

There would be no union involvement for a while. Molly informed
the personnel manager that she would not be available to perform
for a week or two. A week later, we were contacted by Molly's lawyer.
In Charlotte's office, with Molly beside her, the lawyer—a tall, thin,
and an angry black woman in a black business suit—explained to
Charlotte and me that Molly was claiming sexual harassment against
both Marilyn and Hermann.

Molly was prepared to be disciplined for her own behavior according to union rules, but she intended to argue that the knuckle
biting was a case for a court of law, and she was prepared to take the
consequences. Disrupting a rehearsal was not a particularly serious
matter, the lawyer concluded, and Molly had a good chance of keeping her job.

Charlotte, asked, "What does she really want?"

"Nothing," said the lawyer. "Not a thing, and I take offense at the
assertion that I am offering a bribe on her behalf."

"I apologize," Charlotte said, hotly, "I wasn't talking money."

"Apology accepted," said the lawyer serenely, after glancing at
Molly to make sure about something they must have previously discussed. "No, Molly just wants her complaints known to the board,
and to get back to work."

Molly did not say a word throughout the proceedings.

It all became a scandal, headline news that even made the New
York papers. The board asked Hermann to resign and kicked out
Eileen (who had cleverly post-dated her check to Marilyn, which

bounced). She and Carl remained married, and Carl was invited onto the board as a reward for trying to get rid of Hermann (and to keep the family's money flowing into the orchestra's budget).

Charlotte and I came out relatively unscathed. There was the obligatory inquisition. Eileen, again acting more graciously than I gave her credit for, claimed that we had been brought into her confidence not to hide anything, but to help resolve the situation, which resolved itself before we could take action. No one wanted to delve any deeper into it than that, especially since Hermann and Marilyn were gone.

Hermann had taken Marilyn back to Europe where he managed to maintain his position in Vienna; our city, with our "provincial morals" (Hermann said to me before he left), being too small for anyone over there to notice. There was no one to press charges against Molly for the biting.

Molly Stephens accepted a month's suspension for disrupting the rehearsal, even though there was no provision in the contract for her particular offense or its punishment. Firing her "for cause" would have only seemed like retribution, which would be actionable. And we would have lost an excellent musician.

Molly is still in the orchestra and she and the new second oboe are very good friends. Some people say they look like sisters. A year later, to celebrate getting tenure, the new "O Boy" married a young man in the second violin section.

JUDD ROY BEAN

JUDD Roy Bean was named by his father after the self-appointed western frontier hanging judge and saloon keeper Judge Roy Bean. David Allen Bean was a fan of the John Huston movie *The Life and Times of Judge Roy Bean,* starring Paul Newman. Like the fabled judge's lover and mother of his child, Judd Roy's mother died due to severe hemorrhaging after his birth.

The historical Judge Roy Bean (who tried to hang the attending doctor) was famous for his obsession with a great actress of the time, Lily Langtry. She was enshrined in his heart to the extent that any attempt to insult or even slight her name or image would result in immediate corporal punishment, or so the story goes.

Judd Roy was similarly obsessed with a movie actress of our time, Amber Heard. More of her later.

It wasn't until his freshman year in college that Judd Roy began to use his full name, in fact insisting that everyone use it. Even teachers were nagged to call him Judd Roy when they forgot.

The year Judd Roy Bean was elected student body president at Central Indiana University, his first act was to create a fundraising event called "Beans for ADD." A large pickle jar was filled with jelly beans. Students paid $2 to guess how many beans were in the jar; they could pay for as many guesses as they liked. The winner would receive a Starbucks gift certificate for $100 and the jar of jelly beans. Every day for a week, Judd Roy set up a table at the student union and gathered stacks and stacks of low-denomination bills. When the week was over, he announced in the school newspaper that $1,265 had been raised and the winner was sophomore coed Clair Codette, whose guess of 999 was only one off. Everyone congratulated Judd Roy, even the university chancellor, for his fundraising creativity.

After cutting a check for $1,165 to the campus counseling center, and the purchase, from the proceeds, of a $100 gift card, Judd Roy pocketed $844. He had already slept with Clair Codette—he was a handsome young man—thus ensuring her complicity, and her silence.

Not all of Judd Roy's schemes worked out so well—such as a wet t-shirt contest (nixed by the administration) and a dirty sonnet writing contest (similarly nixed).

Going underground due to these defeats, he created a "secret society" modeled on Yale's Skull and Bones, or what he thought it should be. Naming himself its first Grand Judge, he opened membership for only one night to all senior-class majors in Philosophy, Literature, Meteorology, and Anthropology. His four best friends were majors in these departments; they became known as his "Jury." The five of them interviewed seventy-five candidates who showed up based on a couple of nearly indecipherable ads in the school paper, and carefully planted rumor. The candidates were asked five questions; a "no" immediately produced rejection.

1: Do you masturbate?
2: Are you afraid of dying young?
3: Do you have a tattoo?
4: Are you stupid?
5: Do you love your mother?

As Judd Roy expected, the fourth question wasn't often seen as a trick question, but served to whittle the candidates down to a manageable number. He threw in question number five for no other reason than personal sentiment. The test was passed by 13 students, which left only the initiation and giving the society a name.

For the latter, Judd Roy settled on "Tits and Ass," which was quickly endorsed by his Jury (which agreed with him in all things because, well, it was that or immediate ejection). Judd Roy felt that saying "I belong to 'Tits and Ass' " or "I'm a 'T and A' " was sufficiently embarrassing that it would make revealing the true nature of the society that much more difficult. (He'd concluded that "Skull and Bones," and its like, was so braggadocios that members couldn't help revealing their membership.)

All members were obliged to submit to initiation, including Judd Roy and his Jury, which involved only this: each plebe would buy a fifth of Johnny Walker Black, drink the entire thing in less than five minutes, then ride a bicycle one mile over a country road and into a plowed cornfield. When asked, Judd Roy explained that it was the kind of thing his namesake would have done, except for the bicycle.

"The historical Judge Roy Bean," he explained, "would have required riding on the back of a bear or a steer, instead. Count yourselves lucky!"

All of this took place on a Saturday night. Judd Roy provided the bicycle. He also came armed with a pellet gun, powerful enough to sting but not pierce skin. He'd found a mile-long stretch of country road ending in corn fields not far from campus. Half the plebes stood at each end, waiting their turn as the bicycle went back and forth.

Judd Roy insisted on going first, as any strong leader would. Others asked to be first, and he said it would be cowardly for him not to go first. Two chemistry majors backed out, and Judd Roy pelted them with pellets as they ran toward their cars to jeers of "Pussies!"

Judd Roy made the usual effort unscrewing the bottle cap and chugged it in one go. He leaped on the bicycle and went the first mile and tumbled into the field. Then he stood up, brushed himself off, and brought the bike—a stout road bike with fat tires—back onto the road. The Jury went next. When the first one took out his bottle, Judd Roy took it from him and said, "No cheating now. I get to open the bottle to make sure it's not watered down. Anyone caught with an open bottle gets a few of these in his ass," he said, brandishing his pistol, "and the scum's brush."

He opened the bottle with a satisfying crunch, and handed it over. His deputy, Tom Nix (christened so by Judd Roy), also armed with a pellet gun, stood at the opposite end of the mile to keep the other half honest.

Out of sheer timidity in the face of Judd Roy's intimidating presence, no one was dumb enough to try this cheat. Judd Roy had earlier poured out half of his bottle, of course, and topped it off with water.

In all, two young men passed out before they could get their feet on the bike's pedals, two ran off the road never reaching the end, and the rest managed the trial, grateful that puking wasn't held against them.

No one was seriously hurt, though no one, even Judd Roy, escaped scrapes and bruises when their bikes inevitably crashed.

That left a dozen original members of Tits and Ass.

A week later, Judd Roy's presence was required at the chancellor's office. Chancellor Gregory Samuels was a sad specimen of exhausted administrative leadership. At 74, he should have retired five years before, but the trustees liked things just the way they were, because their chancellor liked things just the way they were.

In truth, there was little to separate the Tits and Ass society from the Board of Trustees of CIU. The Chairman of the Board, John Smith, like Judd Roy Bean, ruled. Period. Instead of a pellet gun, he had his tongue, backed by the stout bellows of his lungs. He seldom needed to prove it. Sitting on the board was too prestigious for the doctors, lawyers, businessmen, rich widows and token alums to even think of questioning his pronouncements (edicts, really). And the chancellor was his lapdog.

Judd Roy was ushered into the chancellor's office by a ginger-haired, blue-eyed, buxom woman in a purple dress and white blouse. Judd Roy estimated her age as late-twenties and noted the lack of rings on her left hand.

The chancellor's office was empty. Before the young woman, Janette Mallenbee, could close the door on him, he retraced his steps and whispered,

"Can I take you to dinner tonight?"

"I know about you," she said, pushing him away, "you rascal. I know all about you."

"Well?"

"It's not allowed."

"You're not a teacher, are you? And not *my* teacher."

She thought about that.

"That's true."

"No *in loco parentis*, miss."

"I suppose not."

"Meet me at Antonio's at seven."

"We'll see," she said and winked as she shut the door.

After Judd Roy had settled into the chair in front of a large oak desk with only one object on it—a Mount Blanc pen stuck in a marble holder—the chancellor entered through a door to a room with a huge table and multiple leather-bound chairs. Samuels was dressed like the stereotypical professor of the sixties and seventies—wire-rimmed glasses made him look bug-eyed. His pink, razor-worried face was scored with two short lines of blood on his right cheek. He was dressed entirely in brown corduroy and Hushpuppies, all of it rumpled and rubbed to nice shiny patches.

Judd Roy Bean was dressed in new blue jeans with perfect creases, a new work shirt, a western belt and black cowboy boots. (He'd dressed up for this encounter, his normal attire being the same, only well-worn and unwashed.) His broad white smile and twinkling gray eyes immediately put the chancellor on his guard. Who the hell was this extremely handsome young man, he wondered, not without a slight pang of emotion and regret.

Judd Roy sat, quietly waiting, thinking it an interesting test of wills. The stare-down ended when the chancellor stood up and extended his hand. Judd Roy reciprocated.

"Judd Roy Bean. Nice to meet you chancellor. I've heard…."

Taking Judd Roy's hand, the chancellor said, "Sit down, young man, and please don't speak until I ask you to."

"Certainly, sir," Judd Roy responded with mild defiance.

"What's all this about tea and…."

Judd Roy waited.

"Tea and…."

"Tits and Ass, chancellor?"

"Yes. Please be quiet, as I requested. And let's just leave it to the capital letters, T and A, shall we?"

"Yes, chancellor."

Judd Roy deliberately accented the first syllable of the man's title.

"My understanding is that you have created a secret society without the approval of this administration. It's not allowed, young man. It's not. Fraternities, which this tea, etc. resembles, have to be authorized and monitored. For the sake of everyone involved."

The chancellor paused, gaging the effect he was having, which was nominal.

"Do you want me to explain now?" asked Judd Roy.

"Did I ask you to?" the chancellor snapped with feigned umbrage. "Now, I have two students—who shall remain unnamed—that complain they were humiliated and shot at with a dangerous pistol because they refused to get drunk and ride a bicycle. Is this true?"

"No, sir," said Judd Roy after a lengthy delay, exaggerating his obedience to silence. "They were willing participants…."

"They maintain…."

"Until they weren't. They chickened out."

"So you shot them."

"Are they hurt?"

"No. Tiny welts, that's all."

"Not 'dangerous,' then."

"That's hardly the point, Mr. Bean. What was it?"

"I refuse to say, sir. I'm not prepared to convict myself of anything more than a bit of horseplay."

Judd Roy loved that word, "horseplay."

"Call it hazing, and mild hazing at that, compared to what I've heard some of your campus fraternities perpetrate."

"You may well face expulsion."

"On what grounds?" he replied calmly.

"I haven't been able to consult counsel on the matter, as yet."

"Then why am I here?"

"To find out if there's any truth to the two young men's accusations."

"Well, you have your answer then, chancellor. Can I go now?"

Judd Roy leaned forward to stand.

"I didn't give you…."

Judd Roy stood and, putting his hands on the chancellor's desk, stared into his weepy eyes and said, "Look, you ancient block of petrified stool. I haven't done anything, and you'll never get more than those two pussies who chickened out to say a word. I happen to know quite a bit about the law (a lie) and my rights (another lie) and I'll sue you and your trustees…."

Then Judd Roy noticed that the poor old fool was smiling pitiably and almost in tears. And, revealing all, he now put his hands on Judd Roy's. Judd Roy drew back and stepped around the desk and hauled the old man to his feet, threw his arms around him and kissed him full on the lips, inserting his tongue into a willing aperture and held it for as long as he could without gagging. Finally, he released the old man, giving him a last hug and a kiss on the neck. The shattered wreck fell back into his chair.

As he walked out of the room, Judd Roy, said, "Gregory, it's been a pleasure. All I ask is to be left alone, okay?"

Hearing no reply, he repeated his request.

"Yes, of course," said the chancellor as he put his head down on his desk.

Smiling as he passed the secretary's desk, Judd Roy returned her wink and said, "See you at seven, sweetheart."

Late that night, after receiving the best blowjob from a virgin he'd enjoyed since he was fifteen years old (she did accept what he liked to call a didgeridoo through her satin panties), Judd Roy was walking Janette home.

He had his arm around her shoulders and, having over dinner told her much of the story of his life so far, asked her what she knew about his secret society.

"You mean besides what I heard through Gregory's door?"

"You little marmoset! You eavesdropped!"

"What was that long silence at the end? When I went in a while later, he'd left through the board room."

"Let's just say we kissed and made up. How much trouble do you think I was in for?"

"I'm not sure. We'll find out, I suppose."

"Oh, no, that was it. Game over," he reassured her. "He hasn't told Chairman Smith, has he?"

"I don't think so. You really don't want that," she added and took his hand from her shoulder and kissed his fingers.

Laying in his own bed the next morning, Judd Roy decided it was entirely unfair of him to continue his pursuit of the chancellor's lovely secretary. She wanted marriage. If not with him then someone else. He decided he'd just stay in touch now and then. Keep her from cooling off altogether. She might become useful someday.

No, Judd Roy was not a complete asshole. He wasn't any more treacherous, predatory, or insincere than any other man his age. And he certainly wasn't an avid deflowerer of virgins just for the fun of it, as some of his friends were (or said they were).

The reality of his affections was, as mentioned earlier, his love for Miss Amber Heard. He was tenderly, totally, give-his-life-for-her in love. She possessed his thoughts for much of every day, even to the extent that he imagined he was sleeping with Miss Heard when he was actually with another.

Unlike men who think of a different woman while fucking often tend to seem distant, or detached, his Amber vision only increased his passion, attentiveness, and unvarying sexual success. He had a powerful imagination.

Miss Heard, always "Miss Heard" even though she'd been married, was to Judd Roy Bean what Lily Langtry was to Judd Roy's namesake. She was the most beautiful, the sexiest, the shapeliest, the sassiest, and the most charismatic woman in the world. To date, she had appeared in more than 30 films, often in a leading role. Horror, action, and thriller movies like *Zombieland, The Stepfather, Never Back Down,* and *Machete Kills* had largely played on her sexuality, but Judd Roy saw only a consummate actress. He'd searched out every movie she'd ever appeared in, even driving to Chicago to see her films not destined to play at the university. Her role as Mera in *Aquaman* was so far the pinnacle of her career.

For Judd Roy, her divorce from Johnny Depp, during which she accused him of serious physical abuse, was simultaneously a cause for jubilation at her being free of "that bastard," and the beginning of an obsession for revenge against "that bastard"—a word he reserved for Depp and Depp alone.

There were actually two movies about Judge Roy Bean that Judd Roy knew about. In *The Westerner,* played by Walter Brennan, Judge Roy Bean dies, shot by Gary Cooper, but not before he has the chance to meet Lily Langtry in her dressing room. She is the last thing he sees. Judd Roy liked this version the best, even though the John Huston movie was his father's favorite. In the latter, the Judge never gets to meet Lily Langtry, which was Judd Roy's objection. Long after the judge's death, she visits his saloon, which has been turned into a Lily Langtry museum.

Since he was sixteen, Judd Roy had sent love letters to Miss Heard, most of them just barely on the inoffensive side of erotic. He sent them to the various studios where she worked. None answered. Finally, one of them, which he'd written to several times, replied with the address of her agent. This also proved a dead end; the agent replied that Miss Heard didn't have time to respond to letters and therefore never read them. Judd Roy's letter came back unopened, folded inside another envelope.

His most brazen attempt to meet her came the summer after he was a college freshman. He'd learned that she was in New York City appearing in a small independent film called *Her Smell.* Not surprisingly, Judd Roy's father, who sympathized with Judd Roy's obsession, allowed him to travel by train to the big city. The movie was about a punk rock band. After scouring the newspapers and wandering various neighborhoods, Judd Roy saw that the likelihood of learning the location of the studio, let alone being able to catch Miss Heard as she entered or left, was slight indeed.

His only chance seemed to be the punk rock scene. He spent three nights hopping from punk rock bar to punk rock bar, asking if anyone knew about the filming of *Her Smell.* Finally, on his last night, a bartender told him the film was in production at a bar called CBGB in the East Village. Judd Roy rushed there by cab only to discover that the place had been closed for more than a decade. What a joke!

His train was to leave the next afternoon, and that morning he remembered that her agent's office was in New York; he still had the address in his wallet. When he arrived, he found only two small rooms. A secretary told him the agent wasn't in town and that the filming of *Her Smell* had wrapped two days ago. Amber Heard had left the country for England just the day before to star in a movie called *London Fields.* Judd Roy frequently wept on the train ride home. Not entirely without hope, he dreamed of someday meeting Miss Heard.

Seeing the wisdom suggested by his Jury that Tits and Ass should perhaps lay low for a few months, Judd Roy continued to think of ways to make a buck. One night, thoroughly high on hashish, he hit upon an idea that might accomplish two goals—make money and perhaps catch his idol's attention: an Amber Heard lookalike contest.

Not surprisingly, with a cash prize of $5,000, the competition generated a great deal of interest. Judd Roy rented the local indie movie house for a day and put up posters all over the campus, featuring Miss Heard at her most alluring. He filled the 500-seat theatre at $20 per ticket and collected $20,000 in entry fees (200 at $100 each), with which he planned to hold an Amber Heard film festival (yet another chance to catch Miss Heard's attention).

But it was a sad substitute for Judd Roy's dreams. Naming himself sole judge, he trotted out and interviewed 200 young women, in bikinis of course. The hooting and leering went on for twelve hours and ended when, the last contestant having left the stage, Judd Roy rose and addressed the audience.

"None deemed worthy," he shouted and left the theater in a state of pandemonium.

He didn't even select first or second runners-up. He returned all of the entry money, but refused to return the ticket fees, maintaining that everyone got more than their money's worth of oogling and jiggling. There were threats of retaliation for this on the web, but nothing came of it.

Not surprisingly, Clair Codette (with whom he'd struck up an exclusive love affair), with her honey-wet hair and tall, voluptuous body, achieved the closest resemblance, yet her having earlier won the bean contest was not what prevented him from giving her the prize. Perhaps the prettiest blonde on campus, she was for Judd Roy but a wraith compared to the real Amber Heard. The upshot was 199 sulking, humiliated young women, and a lost lover. In defiance, more than 100 women donated their $100 entrance fee to the campus Women's Center.

Judd Roy understood, of course, that awarding the prize would have placated most of the entrants, but he had his standards and he stood by them.

After being tied up in litigation (including Miss Heard's lawsuit that a body double had been used to suggest she actually appeared in the nude, which she emphatically did not), *London Fields* appeared to universally terrible reviews. Totally bewildered, Judd Roy saw the movie five times and concluded that his Miss Heard had performed her masterpiece.

Soon after, to salve his dejection over Miss Heard's blasphemous reception, he convened the members of Tits and Ass. It was a few weeks before the end of his junior year, and the spring being in full bloom, he chose an abandoned railroad bridge in the country some five miles away. As before, he injected drunken peril into the proceedings. Instead of scotch he required each member to bring a fifth of Wild Turkey. He directed them to sit on the two rails, six each facing each other. Behind them there was nothing to keep them from falling backwards off the bridge onto a gravel road.

Before he could even call the meeting to order, one of the Jury members spoke up. He was a meteorology major named Dan Drow, over six feet tall, and thin as a scarecrow.

"The others have asked me to speak on behalf of the membership."

"You may speak," said Judd Roy, taking a big swig. His bottle, this time, was not watered.

"Your little stunt with…."

"Hold it right there," Judd Roy interrupted him. "You will keep a civil tongue in your skull, understand?"

Slightly cowed, Dan continued, "Sorry. But do you realize what has happened to all of us since your stu…your lookalike contest?"

"Feel free to inform me."

"Every single one of us has been tossed—and that's a nice word for it—from our girlfriends' beds."

"So? I lost a damn fine lay as well."

"You don't understand."

Judd Roy stood up, flourishing his bottle over the gathering.

"You think I'm a dope? I know they're all pissed. The whole damn campus is pissed at me, and not just the girls who entered."

"We know. It's not just us," he said, gesturing at the assembled, "this gang. It's just about everyone. It's like that stupid Greek play, Liars, Lizars…."

"You mean *Lysistrata*," said Judd Roy impatiently.

"Right. When all the chicks refuse to fuck."

"They'll get over it."

"That's not what they say. Haven't you heard?"

"Heard what?"

"The freeze-out doesn't end until someone wins the contest."

"The contest is over."

"For you, maybe."

Judd Roy looked at the rest of the group, all of whom where cowering in the near darkness, afraid to speak.

Dan took a drink and said, "If you won't choose a winner, we will."

Judd Roy stepped up and, being considerably shorter, said to Dan's breast-bone, "You dishonor Miss Heard and I'll...."

"You and your Miss Heard," Dan said, now visibly drunk. "You're asshole obsess...."

Judd Roy slugged him in the gut. Dan doubled over and puked.

"Anyone else want to insult me about Miss Heard?"

A heavy, brawny anthropology major named James George stood up and, also drunk, began to swear incoherently, but the noise was surely directly at Miss Heard.

When he heard the words "Fuck Amber Heard," Judd Roy stepped up and pushed him. James stumbled backward, tripped on the rail, and fell off the bridge. They all ran to surround Judd Roy and without a single word of conspiratorial agreement picked him up and threw him off the bridge too.

That was the end of Tits and Ass. And also the end of young Judd Roy Bean. James George recovered from the fall, his large body having cushioned the blow, though he broke both of his arms trying to break his fall.

Judd Roy wasn't so lucky. He was found with his arms folded on his chest and his neck thoroughly broken. He had died instantly.

The police were summoned and things took their usual course. A flashlight revealed a smile on Judd Roy's face.

The members of Judd Roy's secret society were careful to get their stories straight—not that what they said was far from the truth. They explained that a fight had broken out over the Amber Heard lookalike contest and both James and George, while grappling, fell.

The coroner pronounced Judd Roy's a "death by misadventure," though the public prosecutor pushed for manslaughter. Eventually no one was arrested, though all the members of Tits and Ass were expelled.

Not surprisingly, when word got out, it all blew up on the web, particularly when Judd Roy's fixation with Amber Heard became a central component of the story. With Judd Roy's death, the "Lysistrata Scenario," as it was called, evaporated and sexual relations on campus returned to normal—returned, in fact, with renewed fervor, as attested to by the campus health clinic, with marked increases in pregnancies and STDs.

Judd Roy Bean's father had a heart attack the day after his son's death, and with Judd Roy having no other family the campus could turn to, the administration arranged to have Judd Roy buried in a small cemetery on the edge of the campus. His grave was soon graced with a hastily-made granite marker bearing Judd Roy's full name and date of death.

In the next few weeks two odd things happened to the marker. First, someone took a chisel to the second D in his name and made it (rather artistically) into a G. The artist never declared himself.

Later someone wrote on the stone with what appeared to be lipstick: "I wish we had met."

Rumors of the identity of the writer proliferated, some insisting they had seen a blonde woman in a black dress standing by the grave early one evening. On Twitter, Miss Amber Heard denied that she had ever visited Judd Roy Bean's grave, though she wouldn't rule out the possibility that she would someday.

GENIUS

*A*LEX Cluse had a hard time explaining why he chose to major in philosophy at the University of Indiana. It certainly didn't please his father when he found out.

"What the hell!" his father shouted over the phone. "That's what I'm paying for? How do you expect to make a living? You're no scholar, son. You don't have the makings of a teacher, either!"

"I want to learn how to think," Alex responded, not knowing just how lame that sounded until he said it.

"That's the stupidest thing you've ever said, and that's saying something!" his father shouted again and hung up.

His father was finally placated when Alex's brother—one of the most successful municipal bond managers in California—reminded their parent that he'd been a philosophy major too.

Alex wasn't dumb. His grades proved that. But it was a combination of snobbery and intellectual ambition that brought him to the decision. Yes, he'd read Nietzsche in high school, but it was the three-volume autobiography of Bertrand Russell he read the summer after his freshman year that convinced him. Bottom line? Philosophy was cool.

That first semester of his sophomore year exposed him to Plato and Aristotle, plus the fiction and some of the philosophical writings of Camus and Sartre. He felt confident that he understood most of it and wasn't shy of participating in class.

The second semester, though, found him totally mystified by the works of Hegel and Kant. During a class devoted to the first few chapters of Kant's *Critique of Pure Reason,* he thought to himself, "Not only do I *not* understand a single word he [his professor] is saying, I couldn't even formulate a question that wouldn't totally embarrass me."

Shelly Cord was the reason he didn't change his major that day. (Eventually he would change to English Literature, where he finally found safe haven, and a career.) Shelly was one of the prettiest girls he'd ever seen. Six feet tall and rail-thin, he towered over the five-three Shelly, with her numerous curves, blonde page-boy haircut and black eyebrows. For a young woman of considerable intellect, she was meticulous about her appearance, wore carefully painted makeup, and, for some reason he couldn't fathom, she enjoyed his company. She could speak Kantian gibberish as well as the professor, so Alex had to be very careful not to reveal his ignorance.

It wasn't quite dating when they began to spend time outside of the classroom. They both liked long walks and, happily, she didn't mind his near silence in the face of her long discourses on philosophical matters. An occasional "yes, I see" or "that makes sense" were sufficient.

He finally summoned the courage to ask her on a proper date (though he was careful not to call it that)—dinner, then a concert by the Indianapolis Symphony Orchestra at the Auditorium. The program included two works of Beethoven, a piano concerto and a symphony. As they were waiting for the concert to begin, flipping through their programs, Alex asked a question he thought was mildly provocative but innocent enough.

"Do you think the Beatles will still be listened to a hundred years from now, just like Beethoven?"

She flushed crimson and snapped, "Don't be ridiculous!" She hardly spoke to him the rest of the evening.

At the entrance to her dormitory, he apologized.

"Oh, forget it." She was still mildly disgusted.

"It's just that I'm so embarrassed, when what I want is for you to like me."

She looked over his shoulder as though a policeman were descending upon them.

"Is that what's going on?" she said, finally, and touched his cheek. "Listen, you're very sweet and a gentleman, Alex, but I have a boyfriend. He's at Tulane, which is where I'm going this fall. We're engaged."

Poor Alex. He muttered some fragment of an apology and turned away. She called him back.

"Alex, I know someone you need to meet."

"Really, it's not necessary."

"It is to me. It's my sister, Penelope. She's a freshman, but she's a philosophy major too."

Alex couldn't say anything but yes, he'd like to meet Penelope.

"Wonderful. I'll talk to her."

"Thank you," he said, and refrained from saying something even more vacuous, like "I'd really appreciate it."

As he was walking away, Shelly called to him.

"One word of caution?" she said.

"What's that?"

"Penelope's a genius."

In his disappointment over Shelly, the word "genius" didn't even register until a few days after he'd met Penelope Cord.

After the next Kant class, Shelly handed Alex a slip of paper with an email address on it.

"She's expecting to hear from you. I thought email was the best way to start. She's not much of a phone person."

Normally, she would walk out of the building with him, but today she simply said "Bye" and walked away. Yes, she was done with him.

Knowing nothing about Penelope, but unable to imagine she was any less attractive and interesting than her older sister, Alex emailed her the following:

To: P.Cord@indianauniversity.edu
Subject: Greetings from a friend of your sister
Hi, Penelope,
I understand that Shelly has told you about me and suggested we meet. I've really enjoyed getting to know your sister. If you'd like to have coffee sometime, please let me know.
Sincerely,
Alex Clouse

To: A.Clouse@indianauniversity.edu
Subject: Greetings from a friend of your sister
Alex,
I'm confused. It sounds like you want some help from me relative to Shelly. I assume she told you she was engaged. What she told me is that we should meet, that's all, but now I'm not sure to what purpose. Sorry.
Penelope Cord

To: P.Cord@indianauniversity.edu
Subject: Greetings from a friend of your sister
Hi, Penelope,
I apologize for the way I worded my first email. I can see now how you might have thought I was contacting you about Shelly. I think. But, no. I was just following up on Shelly's suggestion that we meet. If you'd rather not, that's fine.
Alex

To: A.Clouse@indianauniversity.edu
Subject: Greetings from a friend of your sister
Please don't put this off on me with your "I think." If you want to have coffee it will have to be next week. I have a major paper due Monday on phenomenology and I need every moment. If you can wait, I'll meet you at the Union awning on Tuesday at 8:30 AM. I'll have a half hour before class.

Alex read this exchange perhaps a dozen times, trying to sort it out, then responded, "See you then." What a bitch! he concluded. Eight-thirty in the morning? Half an hour before class? That Monday night he almost decided to forget it, then he thought of Shelly. It would be rude not to show up, and Penelope would tell her. Not that he was concerned about burning bridges with Shelly, he just didn't think she deserved it after her looking out for him. So, he went.

Penelope (with her close likeness to Shelly) stood beneath the awning with her arms full of small, thick paperbacks. Unlike every student in sight, she didn't have a backpack. She was a pony-tailed brunette with large dark brown eyes and flushed, clear skin. She wasn't as pretty as Shelly, but she was certainly cute. Her smile was invisible, but she had a curiously amused twist of her full lips that was skeptical, but not unfriendly. She was taller and more slender than Shelly, and she wore no makeup at all. With her natural high color, she didn't need it. Alex couldn't avoid the thought, what's she hiding behind those books?

"Hi, Penny?" he said without thinking. "I'm Alex."

"I'm Penelope," she said dismissively and took his proffered hand.

"I like that name. I could insist on Alexander, but it's so pretentious."

"You think I'm pretentious!"

"Why would you say that?"

He was genuinely embarrassed.

"Oh, forget it," she said drawing a strand of hair from her right eyebrow. "It's just me being stupid."

He tried a friendly laugh, but receiving no response, he suggested they go in for coffee.

She looked at her watch and frowned.

"I really don't have time. It was stupid of me to suggest such an hour to meet, even if just for coffee," she added pointedly. "Let's just stay here and talk, if you don't mind."

"Fine."

"You're probably wondering why two philosophy majors have never met."

"It had occurred to me as a little odd."

"I don't know what Shelly told you about me, but I'm already work-ing on my PhD."

"Aren't you a freshman?"

"Freshman in name only. All through high school I was taking the lower level courses at Northwestern. I finished my BA last semester and they're letting me combine my master's with my doctorate. I've done 90 percent of the coursework for my master's already. I have my first meeting with my thesis advisor this Friday."

Alex just nodded and nodded, trying to hide his astonishment. They had been leaning side by side against a railing. Now she turned and looked at him directly.

"Guess what my favorite word is."

"Sorry," he said, holding up his hands.

"No, it's not 'sorry,' smart aleck," she laughed. "But maybe it should be."

"No, I meant…"

"I know what you meant. I was just fooling."

"What's your favorite word?"

"Stupid. For example, here I am mouthing off as if you weren't here."

"I was impressed, anyway. If that's okay?"

"Not really. I'm impressed with myself enough for both of us."

"Well, you don't need…"

"I know I don't. At least I think not with you," she said and, for the first time, smiled. "How are your studies going? You're a soph-omore, right?"

"Yes, and this is only my second semester since I declared for Phi-losophy. Boy, was my dad pissed."

It was the best thing he could have said.

"God, how I envy you. Don't get me wrong. I love philosophy, but you'd think both Shelly and I were *enslaved* by our parents. They're both philosophy professors at Northwestern, so there was never a question we'd follow on. I think it's awesome you made the choice on your own."

Before he could say anything else, she looked at her watch.

"I have to go. Sorry."

"Can I walk you to class?"

"I wish you wouldn't. I have to think about what I read last night."

"I understand."

"That's generous of you to say," she said, laughing more awkwardly now. "I have been just plain rude to you, haven't I? And I need to make amends. Please email me tonight and we'll set up a proper date."

Then, astonishingly, she kissed him on the cheek and walked away.

The date turned out to be one of the most memorable nights of Alex's life, and only partly because of Penelope. The Indianapolis Ballet was performing "Swan Lake" two hours away in Indy and Penelope wanted to go. Alex's car was a wreck of a Mustang so rusted out you could see the road through the floor. Penelope agreed to drive her much newer Impala, which ruined the chemistry between them from the moment he got into her car. As a passenger, he felt marginalized, almost unmanned. He'd driven every date he'd ever had. For the first hour, they hardly spoke. Alex was paralyzed with embarrassment, fearful of saying something that would reveal his inferior intellect—like that Beatles boner with Shelly—and Penelope seemed to be extremely nervous herself.

"Don't mind me," she said finally. "I'm not the most comfortable driver in the world. Cars are a complete logical contradiction. They move, but you don't. I barely have to twitch my hands or feet and yet we're moving at 55 miles an hour. Leibniz would have loved this, but I just find it weird."

Alex had no idea what to say, having not read a word of Leibniz.

"Sorry, I'm not really showing off," she added. "My thesis will be on Leibniz, though I haven't completely nailed down my approach.

Did you know he wrote more than a million pages and most of it is still unpublished? Incredible. I was thinking...."

She was interrupted when the windshield exploded, showering them both with tiny cubes of safety glass. Penelope slammed on the brakes and the car shimmied.

"Oh, my Christ!" she shouted and pulled over as Alex flailed both of his arms, not to ward off the glass, which it was too late to do, but as if a terrible force was driving him backwards.

Penelope stopped the car halfway on the apron.

"More," Alex cried. "Off the road! Get off the road!"

Without a word, she yanked the car to the right and stopped just shy of a grassy ditch. Another two feet and they would have slid into it.

Then they realized what had happened. A flatbed semi in front of them—which was speeding away, the driver apparently unaware of what had happened—had hit a bump and a piece of wood four by four inches and three feet long, had bounced into the air and came down through the passenger side windshield and landed perfectly vertically on the floor between Alex's legs.

"Are you okay?" Penelope cried.

Alex gripped the wood in both hands and started to laugh, hysterically. Then he hugged it, rocking back and forth.

"Alex, it's okay. Stop! You're in shock! Take a deep breath and stop laughing."

When he'd finally calmed down, he continued to laugh, but in a normal fashion.

"'Lysistrata'!" he whispered, leaning his head against the wood.

"What?"

"'Lysistrata.' Have you ever seen it?"

"I've read it, of course," she said, then it occurred to her. "Those huge penises!"

Then she started laughing with him, and said one of the funniest and most adorable things he'd ever heard.

"You'll never have a woodie like that again, Alex!"

They sat there laughing until the police showed up.

While the Impala was drivable, they were both too shaken up to drive, so one squad car took them back to the campus, another policeman drove the car to the shop.

Ten o'clock found them sitting in her dormitory room listening to Wagner.

"You need something to take your mind off that near-death experience, and I have just the thing."

She put on the overture to *Tannhauser*. Now, Alex happened to be a fan of Wagner's orchestral music, if not very familiar with the operas themselves. He knew this work as much as a dozen listenings allowed, or so he thought. As she put on the CD, he envisioned them lying side by side on her bed silently absorbed as the melodies washed over them, thick as heavy surf. Instead, she put a pillow under his head, stood back, and proceeded to explain every nuance of the music. Moving almost like a dancer, she said, "The beginning is of course the pilgrim's hymn, hear that? The soft sacred music in the winds and horns. Now there's a louder, more insistent repeat by the trombones."

She closed her eyes and swayed to the sounds, until the music sped up.

"Now we're hearing the Venusburg music, which conveys the profane, sensual pleasures of Venus. So now you have the full picture, the holy versus the pagan. I'm not religious in the least, so I think of it in Nietzschian terms of the Apollonian and the Dionysian—reason versus passion, the calm concentration of the intellectual versus the constant motion of the lewd drunkard."

Alex almost asked her which she preferred, but wisely decided not to interrupt.

Then the music returned to the beginning theme, with strings in the background, followed by blazing horns, bringing the overture to an end.

"So, for now, the Dionysian loses out to the Apollonian," she said and stopped the player, then sat down next to him.

Alex felt it was time to gamble, or lose everything.

"And yet Nietzsche eventually turned on Wagner."

She looked at him, genuinely surprised.

"Yes, he did. But what's your point?"

"Just an observation, really. I loved your using Nietzsche's ideas to gloss Wagner's."

"And?"

Now he was really in trouble. He forged ahead.

"Well, although the Apollonian wins in the overture, Nietzsche fell out with Wagner, preferring Bizet, who was nothing if not a sensualist. I just like the irony of it."

Penelope smiled at him, evidently pleased, and stood up and held out her hand. He took it and she pulled him to his feet.

"I like that, Alex," she said, then, over-generously added, "I won't hear that overture quite the same way ever again."

He knew that now, more than ever, it was time to keep quiet.

"Come on, I'll walk you down. I have to reread the *Prolegomena* tonight and it's already after eleven."

She held his hand as they walked down the stairs. She certainly was full of surprises. He looked at her more than once, and though she didn't say anything, he could tell she was thinking hard.

Outside, she said, "It's been quite an evening," and they both laughed.

She reached up and kissed him on the lips with just enough pressure to show she meant it.

"Do you like movies?" he asked.

"Sure."

"Have you ever seen the Steve McQueen movie called *Soldier in the Rain?*"

"You found my weak spot, Alex! I love old movies. I'd go insane without them. And I particularly love that movie."

"And what does Jackie Gleason say?"

They said it in unison, "Until that time, Eustis, until that time."

"Email me tomorrow," she said and quickly stepped back inside.

As he returned to his dorm, he remembered the other famous line in that movie, with Gleason pointing both forefingers up, saying, of girls in the tropics: "breasts that tip *up*."

Their next meeting was in the campus library. Once again, it was Penelope's choosing. She wanted to look up something Alex might find interesting.

He arrived a bit late, and she'd already found a table and was reading a book. She'd let her hair free and there was a hint of rouge and lipstick. Just for him? Alex wondered. He took a seat across from her and said, "What's up?"

She only briefly looked up with a slight smile, then continued leafing through the book. He couldn't be sure, but it seemed like she was reading all of each page in mere seconds. Then she stopped.

"Here it is!" she exulted, with more enthusiasm than seemed warranted.

"Yes?"

Looking at him, now with a wide smile, she said, "It's been driving me crazy. Listen to this. It's by William James."

She read the following out loud:

"'The stronghold of the deterministic sentiment is the antipathy to the idea of chance. As soon as we begin to talk indeterminism to our friends, we find a number of them shaking their heads. This notion of alternative possibilities, they say, this admission that any one of several things may come to pass, is, after all, only a round-about name for chance; and chance is something the notion of which no sane mind can for an instant tolerate in the world. What is it, they ask, but barefaced crazy unreason, the negation of intelligibility and law? And if the slightest particle of it exists anywhere, what is to prevent the whole fabric from falling together, the stars from going out, and chaos from recommencing her topsy-turvy reign?'"

She paused.

"Bullshit," he said.

"God, I love you for saying that! Can you explain? I mean you know what determinism is, of course."

"Sure, I once had a set-to with a priest at Sunday school suggesting that 'mortal sin' is impossible because everything we say and do is determined by all pre-existing circumstances. He was not pleased."

"Exactly. So why 'bullshit'?"

"I assume this is all about the other night, right?"

"Of course."

"What were the odds of that block of wood coming through the windshield at precisely the angle it did, landing between my legs and not even touching me?"

"Exactly. Go on."

"Strictly speaking, you could say it was all predetermined, but it's like flipping a coin a thousand times and coming up heads every time. It's possible, of course, but it would be a miracle."

"You believe in miracles?" she asked, with slight disappointment.

"Not at all. And I don't believe in the supernatural or the intervention of a sentient being."

"Then how do you explain it?"

"I can't. But William James doesn't explain it either. Maybe no one has."

"Bravo!" She was genuinely impressed, which scared Alex to death.

"One of my professors at Northwestern once said, 'Chance is the barefaced mistaking of determinism for uncertainty.' I said 'bullshit' to him too, in so many words."

"So you don't believe it either."

"I'm not sure either way. Some things are inexplicable. It's like solipsism. It can't be proved or disproved."

"The existence of God, same thing," he added, gamely.

She frowned.

"Not quite. You should know that I'm an atheist, though I'd prefer to call myself a 'seeker.' But we both experienced that wooden block. Now, if you look at all the arguments for God's existence, like the argument from design...."

Beginning to panic, Alex looked at his watch and slowly stood up.

"I'm sorry, Penelope, I have to go. I have a class in an hour and I have some notes to write up."

"Sure, Alex."

"Until that time?" he said.

"Sure," she said, her head buried in her William James.

"I'll email you, okay?"

"Sure. Bye."

He hadn't been dismissed or ignored; rather it was like he'd disappeared and she hadn't bothered to look for him.

As Alex walking into the spring sunshine, he thought, I'm fucked. He really liked this girl. He remembered Shelly's caution about her sister, "the genius." He'd been incredibly lucky, he realized. Somehow he'd gotten through a couple of reasonably sophisticated discussions without making a fool of himself. A little Skinner, Nietzsche, and Wagner. And he'd just lucked into that "Bullshit" comment working so well. But that was the limit of his repertoire. He could always bring up Plato's *Republic,* and a smattering of existentialism, but if she prodded him, as she nearly did a moment ago, she'd know he was the near-empty vessel he really was.

Dammit! Why'd he have to be a philosophy major at all? If he was studying some other discipline, she wouldn't be likely to persist in talking about philosophers once she knew they were foreign to him; or, instead, she'd talk but she wouldn't expect an actual conversation. Let her talk. He'd be happy to be her student.

Then the futility of even that hit him. Genius! What did a genius really know, Alex, he asked himself. The answer is...everything! She knew Wagner, she knew ballet. Likely knew everything about politics, art, psychology, sociology, the sciences, history—everything! She even knew an obscure movie from the early '60s well enough to quote from it! She's a polymath! How was he going to keep her interested for more than another date or two?

Their next meeting was a proper date—dinner, a movie (a Japanese samurai movie, being a genre they both loved), and a walk through the campus. Alex managed to steer the conversation almost entirely toward their mutual growing-up. Her constant questions kept most of the discussion on his life in South Bend as the son of a head of a charitable foundation. Beyond her parents being philosophers, she'd had three siblings to cope with. She and the formidable Shelly had been forced to create a front against two older jocks, who ignored their parents' wishes on just about everything and were often in mild trouble—drinking, marijuana, girls—if their parents found out. College dropouts, but brilliant with computers, they started a company that designed graphics for Internet start-ups. Alex asked her why she and her sister had ended up at IU, instead of Northwestern or Stanford, or some other high-tone private college.

"It was our way of saying to our parents, 'you can't make all of our decisions,'" she explained. "But that was just what we told them. As you've discovered, the faculty here is first rate. We did our homework, and this is as good as it gets, except for maybe Tulane."

When they got back to her dorm, she invited him up. To his amusement, she put on the Beatles *Revolver,* though at a rather low volume.

She winked when she sat next to him on the bed.

"I know all about what you asked Shelly. She really can be a bitch sometimes."

"I was just making conversation."

"Right," she said and leaned to kiss him, as before, firmly, but prim, "Now let's stop talking for a minute and kiss some more."

She didn't touch him and he kept his hands to himself. After a few minutes she pulled away and said, "I want to see you naked." She paused to let this sink in. "I want you to see me naked."

"You're kidding. That's not...."

"No. I'm not either," she insisted. "Here's how it will happen, if you're willing. I'm going to turn off the lights. There's just enough light from that streetlamp out the window to allow us to see each other. We're going to stand five feet apart and simultaneously take off all of our clothes, except our underwear. Then, if we get comfortable with that, we'll take that off too. Here's the thing. You can't take even one step closer. Nor will I."

"You've done this before."

"I have actually, but only once, and it was a mistake, because I was just a kid. Not that anything bad happened."

"What if this is a mistake?"

"We'll just have to see. But I doubt it is. I'm sure you're curious what I look like and I'm aching to see what you look like. Think of it as ultimate empiricism."

They both laughed, but Penelope not so much.

"Then what happens?"

"Then we put our clothes back on and you go back to your dorm."

He paused, trying to decide not if, but how he should say it.

"I have to say this. You know I like you."

"Of course. I like you too. We wouldn't be doing this otherwise."

"It might be embarrassing."

"Not for me." Then she thought a moment. "Oh, yes. I understand. Don't worry about it either way. It has nothing to do with it."

"It will be out of my control," he said, already squirming to make room for his erection.

"Okay, stand up," she said, ignoring this last caveat.

She positioned him in the middle of the room then stepped back. They didn't speak. First came off his polo shirt and her blouse. As he already knew, she didn't have on a bra. Then they unbuckled their pants, his blue jeans and her brown slacks. She stooped and took off her shoes, as he did, then stepped out of her slacks. He mirrored her actions and they stood up straight and looked at each other.

Though skinny, Alex had strong legs and arms, though virtually no butt. Penelope, thought Alex, was perfectly proportioned, with a thin waist, small hips, and high breasts, not too large, with pale, small erect nipples like pencil erasers.

They stood perfectly still and both allowed themselves a smile.

"You ready?"

"I'm ready."

As she bent to pull down her white panties, she looked up to make sure he was doing the same, which he was, though slowly at the beginning. No, he could not believe this was happening. It was the kind of thing six-year-olds did, but Penelope was no child and was playing no naughty game.

She placed her hands on her hips and cocked a knee to the right. Alex did the same. Her pubic hair was abundant, but dark and trim. Alex's erection was proud, and neither impressive nor inadequate in any way.

"You okay?" she asked.

"Yes. You?"

"Yes. Just a few minutes more."

As the Beatles' "Tomorow Never Knows" finished, Shelly bent over and grabbed her panties and stepped into them. They played the entire pantomime in reverse until they were fully dressed.

A few minutes later, they were standing outside the dorm hugging.

"There's something you need to know about me."

"There's more?" he said, chuckling.

"No, this is serious."

"Yes?"

"I hope you don't mind my putting you through that."

"Are you kidding? You're lovely!"

"You are too."

They kissed again. For the first time she slipped her tongue between his teeth and hugged him even harder.

She broke away and kissed his neck, which he reciprocated.

"You were saying?"

"It's not an easy thing to say."

He waited.

"There are perhaps better words. Maybe not. But it's about 'passion.' I'm a very passionate person. You need to know that. Goodnight, Alex."

Then she broke away and was gone.

As he walked, very slowly, his left hand in pocket, his right hand acting out what was going through his mind: A genius and passionate. Brilliant beyond measure and horny, very horny. Isn't that it? Isn't that what you're getting yourself into, Alex?

He already knew the genius part would be a huge challenge, a barrier he'd have to get over, perhaps by divulging the truth about his own intellect and taking is chances. "Passionate" he thought he could handle. He had so far. Hadn't he passed some test tonight? He was convinced he had. And who knew? Maybe the one would make the other less of an issue. He knew enough about sex, he had to think, to satisfy her. At least until he discovered otherwise. Until he discovered otherwise. The thought both thrilled and terrified.

Spring break was the next week. In a cursory, too brief, hence confusing email, Penelope explained that she was heading back to Evanston to spend time with her parents. The dorms being closed, Alex went to Fort Wayne and spent most of his time playing pool and drinking with his high school friends, or reading and rereading and rereading that bastard Immanuel Kant.

He sent Penelope an email almost every day, most of which she didn't answer. Alex tried not to think much of it. An old girlfriend called him and he went to a movie with her, but he found himself bored and took her home early, even though he realized he was hurting her feelings. His thoughts were entirely of Penelope.

When break was over, Alex assumed that things would pick up where they left off, and he could hardly contain his excitement at what the next stage of their relationship might be. The word "passionate" boomed in his chest and elsewhere. To take his mind off it, he concentrated so much on Kant that he thought he might actually have begun to understand him on some rudimentary level.

The first thing he did on the day he returned to campus was go to Penelope's dorm without even emailing her first. He asked for her at the front desk. Someone called her room, and she said she'd be right down.

The Penelope Cord who walked into the lobby was almost unrecognizable. She was dressed in her pajamas. Her hair was in an untidy ponytail and she seemed to walk so slowly, Alex wondered if she hadn't hurt herself somehow.

"Let's sit over here," she said, directing him to one of the lobby couches. "I have something to tell you."

A terrible shiver of fear and disappointment ran down Alex's spine.

She sat more than a foot away and didn't look at him.

"Something's happened, and I can't go on."

He started to speak, but she held up her hand and said, "Please, let me finish."

"Okay."

"It's a man I met at Loyola three years ago. I was 16. He was 22 and a brilliant philosopher. He was a teaching assistant, and I took a class in the Stoics with him. Nothing happened until I turned 18, and then we became lovers. When it was time for me to go to college, we had already broken up. I don't really know why. He didn't want me to go, and I was stubborn about it. Then I caught him flirting with another student. And that was that.

"Last week, he called me, wanting to talk. We spent four days together and…." Her voice caught, but she didn't cry. "And now we're back together. At the end of the semester I'm going back for summer classes at Northwestern, and in the fall I'll begin my PhD with Edgar Bloom at U of C.

"I don't know if we'll get married, or if it will even work out. But I have to try."

"And that's it for me."

"Please don't be angry. I couldn't stand it."

"I'm not angry."

He knew that if he started talking, he wouldn't stop, so he didn't say anything.

"I'm so sorry, Alex."

"*You're* sorry."

"It's not like I deceived you. Two weeks ago I was absolutely free."

"It's because I'm not smart enough, isn't it?"

"No. But I must be honest. I think I would make you miserable. Face it, your heart isn't in philosophy, while it's what I live and breathe. I think we would never have made it. You'd have gotten totally bored with me."

"Or you with me."

"No!" she said emphatically.

"I'm changing my major to English."

She turned to him, genuinely surprised.

"Where did that come from?"

"I just decided, at this very moment, though I've been thinking about it for weeks. It's the subject I love the most."

"That's great," she said with real enthusiasm.

"And there's nothing I can say that will change...."

"Please, let's not prolong this. It's too hard for both of us," she said and stood up.

He stood and reached for her.

"No. Let's not. It will only hurt."

"Goodbye, then."

"Goodbye, Alex."

And, once again, she turned and was gone.

That week Alex officially changed his major to English Literature. He finished out the semester and got a C in Kant. He was three credit hours short of a minor degree in Philosophy, though he would never take those final three hours.

That summer he took an apartment near campus and worked in the college bookstore part time as he began his literary studies. Within a few days, he felt for the first time that he knew his own mind. He took nine hours in the 19th century novel, Transformational Grammar (required), and the first of two Shakespeare courses taught by one of the most popular teachers on campus.

Yes, Penelope had crushed him. Crushed him like the death of a best friend. He thought, this is exactly what that must feel like.

For a month or so he drank heavily and went to bed at eight every night. He began to feel that his constant hangovers were a kind of penance. She hadn't lied, so somehow it was his fault she could turn away from him so quickly. That wasn't rational, but to hell with reason, and sure as hell to hell with Philosophy. But he never once even thought the words, "To hell with her."

In early August he met a pretty, if somewhat flighty junior studying much the same authors as himself. They began to date and eventually she moved in with him and shared his rent. They were compatible, decent, loving, and loyal. Was Alex in love with her? He wouldn't have been able to say.

That fall, as he was walking through the Arboretum, he discovered Penelope reading under an oak tree. He stopped, unable to hide his astonishment.

They didn't speak. From the sadness in her eyes, it was clear she didn't want to speak, so he walked away.

That evening he sent her an email, saying it was nice to see her. He explained that his studies in English were going very well, that he was in love with a fellow English student, and he hoped she was happy and well. She wrote back, congratulating him, and said, "It didn't work out."

He considered writing back, or offering to meet for coffee. Perhaps she could use some consoling. He knew it would be a mistake and let it go. But, for a few minutes, remembering her sadness, he couldn't keep from crying.

A year later, they happened on each other again and talked over coffee. He had broken up with his girlfriend. Penelope was in a relationship with a History major.

"It's a good thing not to have to worry about, or even talk about our studies," she said, brightly, "He has his, I have mine."

This time he said "Goodbye" and was the first to leave. He turned to look back and she was still watching him. She waved goodbye. For the first time, it occurred to him that his mistake, all along his mistake had been not to fight for her. He should turn around this minute and confront her. Even ask her to sleep with him right that minute. After all, she hadn't said she loved the guy. It was just a relationship. But, of course, being a gentleman, at least according to Shelly, he just kept walking.

Six months later, near the end of his senior year, Penelope emailed him and asked him out for a beer. He suggested she come to his apartment and she agreed to bring the beer.

She was again footloose and was disappointed to find out that he was engaged.

"She's upstairs."

Penelope looked up at the ceiling and began to stand.

"Don't worry. She knows you're here. She won't come down. She can't hear us."

They sipped their beers looking at each other.

"You look wonderful," she said.

"You do too."

"Remember when…."

"I remember everything."

"Do you remember what my favorite word is?"

"Stupid."

"Still is."

"You're the least stupid person I've ever met."

"And your girl?"

"She's in theatre. Who knows if she'll ever make a living, but she really commands the stage."

"She must be very pretty."

"Yes, she's beautiful."

"I'm glad for you."

"And you?"

"Alex, the stars just won't align for you and me. I have no one. Sometimes I think I never will."

"You were hoping I was free again?"

"Of course."

"I'm sorry," he said, blushing. He took a deep breath and told her the truth. "Her name is Barbara and we're crazy for each other."

"That's what my second favorite word should be, 'sorry.' I'm sorry too."

"I wish we could be friends, at least."

"No. No way. Even the best two people in the world can't be friends. Not when there's a third."

"I suppose."

"Can I confess something to you before I leave?" she said as she drained her beer.

"Please."

"It's hard being a…." The word caught in her throat.

"A genius, Penelope. You're a genius. Shelly told me you were, and I tried to keep up, but you're a genius, and I'm not."

"Thanks for making that part easier. But here's the real problem."

She was close to tears, but controlling it.

"It's so hard. It's like being in an empty room, empty of people. Just books, and you've read every book in the room and remembered every word. What I mean to say is it's very lonely being what I am."

They stood up and he escorted her to the door.

"You'll find someone," Alex said with more enthusiasm than he felt. "You'll find another genius maybe."

Penelope laughed.

"God, no! That would make it ten times worse."

He didn't turn to look at her when he said, "You'll find someone. You will."

He opened the door for her, and she left.

Five years later, Alex received a letter from Shelly. He was teaching poetry in the MFA writing program at Northern Illinois University. He and Barbara had amicably divorced when she received several offers to act in London and moved there permanently.

Dear Alex,

I hope this finds you happy and well. I'm still teaching at Tulane. Penelope was on faculty here too until recently. I'm writing at Penelope's request and it's difficult to tell you. She attempted suicide several months ago. It was a half-hearted try with pills and she's recovered nicely. She's living with me until she gets her life back. The cause was a broken relationship. Poor Sis can't seem to make one work. She said to tell you that she thinks fondly of you and often. She cherishes the short time you had together, and she wishes you and Barbara all that is good.

She wanted me to write not wanting you to hear this from someone else. Please don't respond or try to contact her. She just wanted you to know.

Sincerely,

Shelly

The first word that came to Alex was totally beside the point, almost ridiculous, even crass, given the circumstances. Or maybe not. The word was "passionate."

The letter had a return address in New Orleans, which Alex took to mean that Shelly, at least, was not opposed to his responding. He flew to Louisiana a few days later.

His quandary was where and how to contact Penelope. He decided that finding Shelly first was best, so he located her office and camped out there for half a day until she arrived.

At first, she was not pleased to see him. She was if anything prettier than he remembered. There was no wedding ring. She reluctantly offered him a chair in her office.

"I asked you not to do this," she said. Her manner was stiff, but not angry.

"You mentioned Barbara in your letter. You didn't know I was divorced."

"You're right about that, but it doesn't change anything."

"I need to see her."

"That's a selfish thing to say."

"She needs to see me."

"You think you know her better than I do?"

"No. But what harm can it do?"

"Let me tell you what's been going on. She's had five boyfriends in the last seven years. She goes through them like cutting pages in an old book. She cuts, reads what's inside, falls in love, and then the pages magically stitch together again. The words disappear. No more lover. Did she tell you what happened with that asshole at Northwestern?"

"She said that it didn't work out."

"Did she tell you about U of C?"

"Only that she was going to do her thesis there."

"That asshole, her former teacher—his name was Robert Bale— realized by the end of the summer that she'd progressed far beyond him. He became jealous, couldn't stand to be in the same room with someone that much smarter than he was. And then you know what he did? He wrote a letter to the U of C Philosophy Chair and said that she was so overly 'involved with men,' that she would be a disruptive presence in the department. It was all very veiled, a lot of suggestive words like 'physically eager' and 'clinging' and 'emotionally opportunistic.' But it was all it took. The professor wrote to rescind his offer to oversee her thesis and she was denied admission to the program."

"But how could…?"

"The chair was his uncle."

"Son of a bitch."

"That's just the beginning. She told you about the history major?"

"That was the last one I knew about."

"He turned out to be an alcoholic *and* a pedophile. Besides high school history, he taught piano, and she caught him with an eight-year-old child on his lap. He was the only one that she dumped first."

"Jesus."

"Numbers three, four and five all followed the same pattern. Brilliant, handsome men with no more sense of self-worth than a turtle without its shell. They were all either philosophy students or teachers, bright but without even shadows of Penelope's intellect. Still, at least they could talk on some minimal level about what mattered to her most.

"You know she published three books, including her thesis? She's considered a leading authority on a number of topics I won't bore you with."

"Try me."

She laughed.

"Look, Alex. I don't mean to sound cruel or insulting, but I don't even understand half of what she writes without rereading it a dozen times."

"So, the other three?"

"They just couldn't deal with her. Not with her brain, and not with her…."

Alex let a few moments pass.

"Passion," he said finally.

Shelly took the classic double-take, eyes wide.

"You didn't know her long enough to find that out."

"Oh, not to the extent that all these others must have," he said, shaking his head, "but I won't tell you any more than that, except that it was her word for it."

"Okay. Then you have an inkling. Well, my Sis is a tsunami. None of them ever met anyone as brilliant and *more of a woman,* if I can use that euphemism. Every one almost drowned in her and when they came up for air, it was to whimper goodbye and paddle away, the little pollywogs!"

"You always had a way with words, Shelly," he said, laughing softly.

"It's not funny."

"I know it's not funny. Or weird. Or wrong. Or even sad, for me to come here. But she needs me. Even if it's just to talk for a few hours. I know I can help. I might be the only guy who's ever understood even a small part of her, but I do."

Shelly sighed and relented. "Okay. But I have to get her permission first."

"I understand."

"And if she says no?"

"I'll go home."

They exchanged cell numbers.

"It might take a day or too. She'll say no immediately. I'll give her a day or two to really decide."

"I appreciate that," said Alex, getting up from his chair. "Can I ask you a personal question?"

"I guess," she said, warily.

"You're not married?"

"No, that didn't work out either, but for other reasons. Us Cords just may not be the marrying kind. How's that for a way with words."

"Boyfriend?"

"Yes."

"I'm glad," he said, opening the door to leave. "I'll wait for your call. Give her my love, will you?"

To his surprise, she said, "I will, Alex."

Shelly called him six days later. He'd spent the time wandering around New Orleans, which he'd never seen before, and a few hours each day in the Tulane library seated at a carrell writing.

When he answered, Shelly said, "Where are you?"

"Here."

"You waited that long? I thought you'd have gone home days ago."

"Sorry. I'm still here. How is Penelope?"

"She thinks you're gone too. She kept putting me off."

"Call her right now and tell her I'll meet her anytime anywhere this afternoon."

"Okay," said Shelly, and hung up, not wanting to make a scene of it.

She called back ten minutes later.

"Where are you?"

"In the library."

"Good. She'll meet you in the large reading room there in thirty minutes."

"Perfect."

"Alex?"

"Yes."

"Don't get your hopes up."

"What hopes?"

She hung up and he waited in a low cushioned chair with another next to it, which he made sure remained untaken.

He saw her first, and she seemed fine. Her hair was a bit unkempt and she walked with a tentative step, as if she was testing the firmness of ice. She clutched two books to her chest. When she saw him, she waved and quickened her step. As she sat down, he could see she'd put on more makeup than usual, especially around the eyes. He guessed they were sleepless dark. She wore a tartan skirt, a white blouse and white knee socks—what a freshman in college might wear. Her dark brown eyes weren't completely lifeless or wary, which he took as encouraging.

"Alex, why are you here?"

"The same reason you are, Penelope. To talk."

"For six days?"

"I'd have waited sixteen days," he said without making a big deal of it.

"I'm fine, if that's what you're worried about. I did a stupid thing in a moment of, for me, rather uncharacteristic hysteria. I don't even know what triggered it. What's more to talk about?"

"And your career?"

"I'm not the first 'genius' to have a nervous breakdown," she said, spitting out the word. "If Tulane won't take me back, someone will. In the meantime, I've got several months to finish my next book."

"That's good…I mean that you're working."

She looked away and frowned, sighing repeatedly. Alex waited. She turned back and, avoiding his eyes, asked, "And you lost Barbara?"

"Lost is exactly the word, though it wasn't the first time conflicting careers destroyed a decent marriage."

She said nothing, listlessly staring at her fingers drumming the oak table between them.

"Am I boring you?" Alex ventured. He knew it was a bit cruel, but he needed to wake her up.

"Alex, no! How could you say that?" she said, fighting back tears, then, looking into his eyes for the first time, "I'm the bore. I'm the biggest fucking bore in the world!"

"You know," he ventured, in order to change the direction this was going. "This is the first time that we've both been free in the seven years we've known each other."

"Well, almost," she said and blushed.

"Yes, there were a couple of weeks there," he insisted.

"And then I…."

"Don't think about it. It means nothing. Nothing at all."

"Maybe to you."

"You might have meant to hurt me, saying that," he said, lowering his voice, hoping to provoke her further, "But you're going to have to try harder than that."

"Sorry."

She'd wiped the tears away. Between her wet eyelashes and her continued blushing, she was prettier than ever.

"Your second favorite word."

"My favorite word, now that I've exhausted 'stupid.'"

"Penelope, this isn't what I want to talk about and it sure isn't what you need to be talking about. I want to talk about you. The you you don't seem to understand. Or maybe I should say the you you think that nobody can live with."

"And what you is that?"

"Do I have to say the word? We've both said it before."

"Yes, you do."

"The genius," he said, then paused before adding, "the woman who once told me that she was a passionate person."

"I knew this would come up sooner or later," she said and pulled out one of the books. Before she opened it, she looked hard at him and asked, "How much did Shelly tell you?"

"Pretty much everything, but nothing that surprised me."

She nodded as though this was precisely what she needed to hear, then she opened to a bookmark and smoothed out the pages.

"Just listen. It's Hume: 'The sympathy betwixt the passions and imagination will perhaps appear remarkable; while we observe that the affections excited by an object pass easily to another connected with it, transfuse themselves, or not at all.'"

"Please read it again," he said, and she did so, then slammed the book shut and threw it on a cart behind her.

"Well?" she said when she'd relaxed.

"Believe it or not, Penelope, I understand. It's pretty much you, isn't it?"

"It's that 'Or not at all' that tears me up."

"Well, I've got one for you. It's Rilke," he said and recited from memory:

"Are not the nights fashioned from the sorrowful
  space of all the open arms a lover suddenly lost.
  Eternal lover, who desires to endure; exhaust
  Yourself like a spring...." Alex paused and interjected, "most springs being inexhaustible," and concluded, "enclose yourself like a laurel."

"Laurel, the symbol of victory," she whispered.

"That's how I read it."

She took another book, and showed him the spine—Spinoza's *Ethics*—and read aloud:

"'We endeavor, as far as possible, to conceive that which we conduce to pleasure; in other words, we shall endeavor to conceive it as far as possible as present or actually existing. But the endeavor of the mind, or the mind's power of thought, is equal to, and simultaneous with the endeavor of the body's power of action.'"

"That's you to a T, Penelope. Your stupid *boys* couldn't keep up with both, if even one."

"They hardly even tried," she said.

She was smiling now, her eyes bright. She reached out and briefly touched his cheek. He took her hand in both of his.

"I've one more by Rilke. It's the most comforting words I've ever read: 'Oh, why did I not, inconsolable sister, more bendingly kneel to receive you, more loosely surrender myself to your loosened hair. We wasters of sorrows! How we stare away into sad endurance beyond them, trying to foresee their end! Whereas they are nothing else than our winter foliage, our sombre evergreen, *one…*'"

"Only one of four," he added, then continued, "of the seasons of our interior year—not only season—they're also place, settlement, camp, soil, dwelling."

"It's okay to cry if it helps," he said, as she lifted her free arm and brushed her eyes.

"I'll stop. I promise."

"You okay?"

"Yes."

"I also wrote one over the last two days. It's called just 'Penelope.'

"The source of the erotic is mental,
  As dreams remind us with fleshly chaos.
  There can't be love and ideas without eros.

We decide love will be wild or gentle.
Only the lovers' minds can satisfy
Each other what is a real love, and why."

"Lovely," she whispered, bringing his hands to her lips.

They sat silently looking at each other for a full two minutes, un-smiling, unmoving.

"Are you ready?" she said, breaking the spell.

"Yes."

They stood up. She took his hand. They walked out of the library, lovers at last.

ABOUT THE AUTHOR

CHRISTOPHER GUERIN has two degrees in English Literature from Northern Illinois University. He worked in the symphony orchestra business for 26 years, 20 as the President of the Fort Wayne Philharmonic. His stories, poems, essays, and book reviews have appeared in numerous publications. His *The Story of My Universe and Other Stories* was published by Amika Press in 2020. His work of 600 sonnets, *My Human Disguise*, was completed in 2022, with the first 200 published by Voca Me Press in 2016. He has written a dozen children's stories, two novels, and six books of poetry. His poetry was anthologized in 2017 in *A Gathering of World Poets*. His one-act play, *Quartet*, received a staged reading with Equity Actors in 1998 by Open Door Theater. Combined with a second play, *Cat Murder*, it will be full staged in 2023.

www.ingramcontent.com/pod-product-compliance
Lightning Source LLC
Chambersburg PA
CBHW051230260626
47162CB00002B/345